INTRIGUE

Seek thrills. Solve crimes. Justice served.

K-9 Detection
Nichole Severn

The Perfect Witness
Katie Mettner

MILLS & BOON

K-9 DETECTION
© 2024 by Natascha Jaffa
Philippine Copyright 2024
Australian Copyright 2024
New Zealand Copyright 2024

First Published 2024
First Australian Paperback Edition 2024
ISBN 978 1 867 90262 7

THE PERFECT WITNESS
© 2024 by Katie Mettner
Philippine Copyright 2024
Australian Copyright 2024
New Zealand Copyright 2024

First Published 2024
First Australian Paperback Edition 2024
ISBN 978 1 867 90262 7

Published by
Harlequin Mills & Boon
An imprint of Harlequin Enterprises (Australia) Pty Limited
(ABN 47 001 180 918), a subsidiary of HarperCollins
Publishers Australia Pty Limited
(ABN 36 009 913 517)
Level 19, 201 Elizabeth Street
SYDNEY NSW 2000 AUSTRALIA

MIX
Paper | Supporting
responsible forestry
FSC® C001695
www.fsc.org

K-9 Detection
Nichole Severn

MILLS & BOON

Nichole Severn writes explosive romantic suspense with strong heroines, heroes who dare challenge them and a hell of a lot of guns. She resides with her very supportive and patient husband, as well as her demon spawn, in Utah. When she's not writing, she's constantly injuring herself running, rock climbing, practicing yoga and snowboarding. She loves hearing from readers through her website, www.nicholesevern.com, and on Facebook at nicholesevern.

DEDICATION

For you.

CAST OF CHARACTERS

Jocelyn Carville—Socorro logistics coordinator Jocelyn Carville has reason to believe a device planted by the vicious *Sangre por Sangre* cartel was meant to destroy evidence in a murder investigation—but convincing the grumpy chief of police becomes a mission in and of itself.

Baker Halsey—Chief of police Baker Halsey doesn't trust private military contractors. But as the investigation comes to a standstill, he'll have to turn to the enthusiastic operative intent on tearing down his guard...before the syndicate strikes again.

Socorro Security—The Pentagon's war on drugs has pulled the private military contractors of Socorro Security into the fray to dismantle the *Sangre por Sangre* cartel...forcing its operatives to risk their lives and their hearts in the process.

Marc De Leon—Suspected of hiring someone from within the cartel to plant the bomb that destroyed the police station, Marc is the only one who can give up *Sangre por Sangre*'s motives...if Jocelyn and Baker can find him.

Driscol Jones—Socorro's combat controller is all too familiar with explosive ordinance in the field, but as the cartel turns its sights on his team, Driscol finds himself back in the middle of a war zone.

Chapter One

She was making the world a better place one cookie at a time.

And there was nothing that said *I'm sorry that your deputy ended up being a traitorous bastard working for the cartel* than her cranberry-lemon cookies.

Jocelyn Carville parked her SUV outside of Alpine Valley's police station. If you could even call it that. In truth, it was nothing more than two double-wide trailers shoved together to look like one long building. The defining boundary between the two sections cut right down the middle with a set of stairs on each side. One half for the courts, and the other for Alpine Valley's finest.

A low groan registered from the back seat, and she glanced at her German shepherd, Maverick, in the rearview mirror. "Don't give me that pitiful look. I saw you steal four cookies off the counter before I wrapped them. You're not getting any more."

Collecting the plate of perfectly wrapped sweets, Jocelyn shouldered out of the vehicle. Maverick pawed at the side door. Anywhere these cookies went, he was sure to follow. Though sometimes she could convince him they were actually friends. He was prickly at best and standoffish at worst. Good thing she knew how to handle both. His nails ticked at the pavement as he jumped free of the SUV.

"Jocelyn Carville." The low register in that voice added an extra twist in her stomach. Chief of Police Baker Halsey had come out of nowhere. Speaking of *prickly*. The man pulled his keys from his uniform slacks, hugging the material tight to his thigh. And what a thigh it was. Never mind the rest of him with his dark hair, deep brown eyes or the slight dent at the bridge of his nose telling her he'd broken it in the past. Nope. She'd take just his thigh if he were offering. "Here I was thinking my day had started off pretty good. What's Socorro want this time?"

A tendril of resentment wormed through her, but she shut it down fast. There wasn't any room to let feelings like that through. Jocelyn readjusted her hold on the plastic-wrapped plate, keeping her head high. "I'm here for you."

Maverick pressed one side of his head against her calf and took a seat. His heat added to the sweat already breaking out beneath her bra. She was former military. It was her job to call on resources to aid in whatever situation had broken out and stay calm while doing it. To look at pain and suffering logically and offer the most beneficial solution possible. She was a damn good logistics coordinator. Most recently in the Pentagon's war on the Sangre por Sangre cartel. Delivering cookies shouldn't spike her adrenaline like this.

Baker pulled up short of the ancient wood stairs leading up to the front door of the station's trailer. "For *me*?"

"I brought you some cookies." Offering him the plate, she pasted on a smile—practically mastered over the years. Just like her cookies. "They're cranberry-lemon with a hint of drizzle. I remember you liked my lemon bread at the town Christmas bake sale last year. I thought you might like these, too."

"Cookies." He stared down at the plate. One second. Two. Her arms could only take the weight for so long. Lucky for her, she didn't have to wait more than a minute. Because the chief walked right up those stairs without another word.

Maybe *prickly* wasn't the right word. A couple more descriptors came to mind, but her mama would wash her mouth out with soap if she ever heard Jocelyn say them out loud. Well, if her mama made an effort to talk to her at all.

She didn't bother calling Maverick as she hiked up the three rickety steps to the station's glass door and ripped it open. Her K-9 partner was always in hot pursuit of any chance of cookies.

This place looked the same as always. Faux wood paneling on the walls, an entire bank of filing cabinets with files that had yet to be digitized, with the evidence room shoved into the back right corner. Though it looked like someone had gotten the blood out of the industrial carpet recently. Courteously put there by said deputy who'd turned out to be working for the cartel. Jocelyn tracked the chief around one of two desks and moved to set the plate on the end. "Have you had any luck finding a replacement deputy yet?"

Frustration tightened the fine lines etched around those incredibly dark eyes. "What do you want, Ms. Carville? Why are you really here?"

"I told you—I brought you cookies." She latched on to Maverick's collar as he tried to rush forward toward the treats.

"Nobody just brings cookies." Baker locked his sidearm in a drawer at the opposite end of the desk. "Not without wanting something in return, and certainly not when that someone is attached to one of the most dangerous and unrestricted security companies in the world."

And there it was. Him lumping her in with her employer. Seemed every time she managed to get a word in edgewise, Baker couldn't separate her from what she did for a living.

"I don't want anything in return." She motioned to the cookies she'd stayed up all night to bake. For him. Maverick was pawing at the carpet now, trying to get free. "I just thought you could use a little pick-me-up after everything that went down a couple weeks ago. I wanted to say—"

"A pick-me-up?" His dismissal hit harder than she'd expected. Baker faced her fully—a pure mountain of muscle built on secrets and defensiveness. He was a protector at heart, though. Someone who cared deeply about the people of this town. A man who believed in justice and righting wrongs. He had to be to do this kind of job day in and day out. "Let me make one thing clear, Ms. Carville. I'm not your friend. I don't want to pet your dog. I don't want you to bring me cookies or make arrangements for you to check on me to make sure I'm doing okay. You and I and that company you work for aren't allies. We won't be partnering on cases or braiding each other's hair. Police solve crimes. All you mercenaries do is make things worse in my town."

Mercenaries. Her heart threatened to shove straight up into her throat. That…that wasn't what she was at all. She helped people. She was the one who'd gotten Fire and Rescue in from surrounding towns when Sangre por Sangre had ambushed Alpine Valley and burned nearly a half dozen homes out of spite. She didn't hurt people for money, but no amount of explanation would change the chief's mind. He'd already created his own definition of her, and any fantasy she'd had that the two of them could work together or even become acquaintances instantly vanished.

Jocelyn's mouth dried as her courage to articulate any of that faltered. She almost reached for the cookies but thought better of it. "For your information, Maverick doesn't let anyone pet him. Not even me."

She dragged the K-9 with her and headed for the door, but Maverick ripped free of her hold. He sprinted toward the chief's desk. Embarrassment heated through her. Really? Of everything she could've left as her last words, it had to be about the fact her K-9 wasn't the cuddly type? And now Maverick was going to make her chase him. Great. No wonder she'd never won any argument about the importance of bonding as a team back at headquarters. She let herself be railroaded in the smallest conversations. No. She squared her shoulders. She wasn't going to let one tiff get the best of her. She was better than that, had overcome more than that.

But Maverick didn't go for the cookies.

Instead, he raced toward a door at the back and started sniffing at the carpet. The evidence room. Crap on a cracker. She didn't need this right now.

"You forgot your dog." The dismissiveness in Baker's tone told her he hadn't even bothered to look up to watch her leave.

"Thank you for your astute observation, Chief." Jocelyn dropped her hold on the front door. She'd almost made it out of there with her dignity in one piece. But it seemed that wasn't going to happen. At least not today. "You wouldn't happen to have any bomb tech in your evidence room, would you?"

Maverick's abilities to sniff out specific combinations of chemicals in explosives was unrivaled in his work as tactical-explosive-detection dog for the Department of Defense. And here in New Mexico. As cartels had battled over territory and attempted to upend law enforcement and local government, organizations like Sangre por Sangre had started planting devices where no one would find them—until it was too late. Soccer balls at parks, in a woman's purse at a restaurant in Albuquerque, a resident's home here in Alpine Valley. No one was safe. And so Socorro Security had recruited K-9s like Maverick onto the team in the name of strategy—find the threat before the threat found them. They were good at it, too. Protecting those who couldn't protect themselves. Ready to assist police and the DEA at a moment's notice. Founded by a former FBI investigator, Socorro had become the premier security company in the country by recruiting the best of the best. Former military operatives, strategists, combat specialists. They went above and beyond to take on this fight with the cartels. And they were winning.

Frustration and perhaps a hint of disbelief had Baker setting down his clipboard and pen on the desk. Closing the distance between them, the chief pulled his keys from his slacks once again. "Not that I know of. I can't account for every case, but most of what we keep here is from within the past five years. Unregistered arms, a few kilos. Maybe Fido smells the cheese I left in the rat trap last week."

Moving past her, Baker unlocked the door, shoving it open.

"He's a bomb-sniffing dog, Chief, and his name isn't Fido." She barely caught Maverick by the collar as he attempted to rush inside the small, overpacked room. The fluorescent tube light overhead flickered to life and highlighted rows and rows of labeled boxes in uniform shape and size.

A low beeping reached her ears.

Pivoting, Jocelyn set sights on the station's alarm panel near the front door—though it'd been disarmed when Baker had come inside a few minutes ago. "Do you hear that?"

Maverick pressed his face between two boxes on the lowest shelf and yipped. Her skin tightened in alarm.

"We have to get out of the building." Jocelyn unpocketed her cell from her cargo pants and whistled low for Maverick to follow her out. The K-9 growled low to argue, but he'd obey. He *always* obeyed when it counted. She hit Ivy Bardot's contact information and raised the phone to her ear. Someone had planted a device in the police station. She needed full response.

"What?" Baker asked. "I can't just leave, Carville. In case you weren't aware, I'm the only officer on shift today."

They didn't have time for bickering. She grabbed on to his uniform collar and rushed to the front of the station with the chief in tow. "We have to go!"

Fire and sharp debris exploded across her back.

Jocelyn slammed into the nearest wall.

The world went dark.

HE SHOULD'VE GOTTEN out of the damn trailer.

Baker tried to get his legs underneath him, but the blast had ripped some crucial muscle he hadn't known had existed. Oh, hell. The wood paneling he'd surrounded himself day in and day out warbled in his vision. That wasn't good.

The explosion... It'd been a bomb. She'd tried to warn him. *Jocelyn.* Jocelyn Carville.

He shoved onto all fours. "Talk to me, Carville."

No answer.

Heat licked at his right shoulder as he tried to get himself oriented, but there was nothing for his brain to latch on to. The trailer didn't look the same as it had a few minutes ago. Nothing was where it was supposed to be, and now daylight was prodding inside from the corner where the evidence room used to be. Flames climbed the walls, eating up all that faux wood paneling and industrial carpet inch by inch. A weak alarm rang low in his ears. Maybe from next door?

They had to get out of here. "Jocelyn."

A whine pierced through the crackle of flames. He could just make out a distant siren through the opening that hadn't been there before the explosion. Fire and Rescue was on the way. But that wasn't the sound he'd heard. No, it'd been something sullen and hurt.

"Come on." His personalized pep talk wasn't doing any good. Baker shoved to stand, though not as balanced as he'd hoped. His hand nearly went through the trailer wall as he grasped for support. Smoke collected at the back of his throat. He stumbled forward. "Where the hell are you?"

Another whine punctured through the ringing in his head, and he waved off a good amount of black smoke to make out the outline ahead. The dog. Baker couldn't remember his name. The German shepherd was circling something on the floor. "Damn it."

He lunged for Jocelyn. She wasn't responding. Possibly injured. Moving her might make matters worse, but the walls were literally closing in on them. He'd have to drag her out. The shepherd had bitten on to the shoulder of her Kevlar vest and was attempting to pull his handler to safety. Baker reached out.

The K-9 turned all that desperation onto Baker with a warning and bared teeth. His ears darted straight up, and suddenly he wasn't the bomb-sniffing dog who'd tried to warn them of danger. He was in protective mode. And he'd do anything to keep Baker from hurting Jocelyn.

"Knock it off, Cujo. I'm trying to help." Baker raised his hands, palms out, but no amount of deep breathing was going to bring his heart rate down. His mind went straight to the drawer where he'd locked away his gun. He didn't want to have to put the dog down, but if it came to getting Jocelyn out of here alive or fighting off her pet, he'd have no other choice. Though where the desk had gone, he couldn't even begin to guess in this mess.

He leaned forward, moving slower than he wanted. The fire was drawing closer. Every minute he wasted trying to appease some guard dog was another minute Jocelyn might not have. Baker latched on to her vest at both shoulders and pulled, waiting for the shepherd to strike. "I'm here to help. Okay?"

The K-9 seemed to realize Baker wasn't going to hurt its handler and softened around the mouth and eyes.

"Good boy. Now let's get the hell out of here." He hauled Jocelyn through a maze of debris and broken glass out what used to be the front door. His body ached to hell and back, but adrenaline was quickly drowning out the pain. Hugging her around the middle, he got her down the stairs with the German shepherd on her heels.

High-pitched sirens peeled through the empty park across the cul-de-sac and echoed off the surrounding cliffs protecting Alpine Valley. A lot of good they'd done these past few weeks. First a raid in which the cartel had burned down half a dozen homes. Now this.

Baker laid the woman in his arms across the old broken asphalt, shaded by her SUV. Ash darkened the distinct angles of her face, but it was the blood coming from her hairline that claimed the attention of every cell in his body. "Come on, Carville. Open your eyes."

Apparently she only took orders from her employer.

But she was breathing. That had to be enough for now—because there were still a whole lot of people in the trailer next door.

Baker set his sights on Fido. Bomb-sniffing dogs took commands, but he didn't have a clue how to order this one around. He pointed down at the K-9. "Uh, guard?"

Carville's sidekick licked his lips, cocking his head to one side.

"Stay." That had to be one. Baker swallowed the charred taste in his throat as he took in the remains of the station. Loss threatened to consume him as the past rushed to meet the present. No. He had to stay focused, get everyone out.

Fire and Rescue rounded the engine in front of what used to be the station as court staff escaped into the parking lot. Baker rushed to the other half of the trailer. A woman doubled over, nearly coughing up a lung.

He ran straight for her. "Is anyone still in there?"

She turned in a wild search. "Jason, our clerk! I don't see him!"

Baker hauled himself up the stairs, feeling the impact of the explosion with every step. Smoke consumed him once inside. It tendriled in random patterns as he waved one hand in front of his face but refused to disperse. Damn it. He couldn't see anything in here. "Hello! Jason? Are you still in here?"

Movement registered from his left. He tried to navigate through the cloud, fighting for his next breath, and hit the corner of a desk. The smoke must've been feeding in through the HVAC system, and without a giant hole in the ceiling it had nowhere to go. Smoke drove into his lungs. Burned. Baker tried to cough it up, but every breath was like inhaling fire. "Jason, can you hear me?"

He dared another few steps and hit something soft. Not another desk—too low. Sweat beaded down the back of his neck as a tile dropped from the ceiling. It shattered on the corner of another desk a couple feet away.

This place wasn't going to hold much longer. It was falling apart at the seams.

Reaching down, Baker felt a suit jacket with an arm inside and clamped onto it. "Sorry about the rug burn, man, but we gotta go."

Morning sunlight streaming through the glass door at the front of the trailer was the only map he had, but as soon as his brain had homed in on that small glimpse of hope, it was gone. The smoke closed in, suffocating him with every gasp for oxygen. Pinpricks started in his fingers and toes. His body was starved for air. Soon he'd pass out altogether.

A flood of dizziness gripped tight, and he sidestepped to keep himself upright. "Not yet, damn it."

He wasn't going to pass out. Not now.

Baker forced himself forward. One step. Then another. His lungs spasmed for clean air, but there was no way to see if he was heading in the right direction. He just had to do the one thing that never ended well. He had to trust himself.

Seconds distorted into full minutes…into an hour…as he tried to navigate through the smoke. He was losing his grip on the court clerk. His legs finally gave into the percussion of the explosion. He dropped harder than a bag of rocks. The trailer floor shook beneath him. Black webs encroached on his vision. This was it. This was when the past finally claimed him.

Baker clawed toward where he thought the front door might be. Out of air. Out of fight. Hell, maybe he should've had one of those cranberry-lemon cookies as a last meal.

"Jocelyn."

He had no reason to settle on her name. They weren't friends. They weren't even acquaintances. If anything, they were on two separate sides of the war taking over this town. But over the past couple of months, caught in his darkest moments, she'd somehow provided a light when he'd needed it the most. With baked goods and smiles as bright as noon day sun.

The smoke cleared ahead.

A flood of sunlight cut through the blackness swallowing him whole.

"Chief Halsey!" Her voice cut through the haze eating up the cells in his brain, though it was more distorted than he was used to. Her outline solidified in front of him. Soft hands stretched an oxygen mask over his mouth and nose. "Don't worry. We're going to get you out of here."

A steady stream of fresh air fought back the sickness in his lungs, and he realized it wasn't Jocelyn's voice that time. It was deeper. Distinctly male. Another outline maneuvered past him and took to prying his grip from the court clerk. Baker let them. He clawed up the firefighter's frame and dragged himself outside with minimal help. It was amazing what oxygen could do to a starving body.

The sun pierced his vision and laid out a group of onlookers behind the century-old wood fence blocking off the station from the parking lot. A series of growls triggered his flight instinct, but Baker pushed away from the firefighter, keeping him on his feet. The dog. He'd ordered him to guard his handler.

Baker caught sight of the German shepherd from

the back of Alpine Valley's only Animal Control truck. Fido was trying to chew his way through the thin grate keeping him from his partner. Baker's instincts shot into high alert as he homed in on the unconscious woman on the ground, surrounded on either side by two EMS techs. He took a step forward. "Jocelyn?"

They'd stripped her free of her Kevlar vest to administer chest compressions—and exposed a bloodred stain spreading right in front of his eyes. He didn't understand. She'd been breathing when he'd left her.

Baker took a step forward. "What's happening? What's wrong with her?"

"Chief, we need you to keep your distance," one of the techs said. Though he couldn't be sure which one. "She's not responding. We need to get her in the bus. Now."

Strong hands forced him out of the way, but all he had attention for was Jocelyn, a mercenary he hadn't wanted anything to do with but who had insisted on sabotaging his life. Baker tried to follow, but the firefighter at his back was strong-arming him to stay at the scene. Helplessness surged as potent as that day he'd watched everything he'd built burn to the ground, and he wanted to fix it. To fix *this*. "Tell me what's happening."

But there was no time to answer.

The EMTs loaded Jocelyn onto a stretcher and raced for the ambulance. "Let's go! We're losing her!"

Chapter Two

Okay. Maybe cookies didn't make everything better.

Though she'd kill for one right now.

Jocelyn swallowed through the bitterness collecting at the back of her tongue, like she'd eaten something burned beyond recognition. And a grating rhythm wouldn't let up from one side. Ugh. She'd always hated that sound. As helpful as heart monitors were to let physicians and nurses know the patient was still alive, they could've set the damn sound on something far more pleasant.

That wasn't really what she was mad about, but it helped her focus. She curled her fingers into her palms. Her skin felt too tight. Dry. One look at the backs of her hands confirmed the blisters there. The monitor followed the spike in her heart rate, but the pain never came. That was the beauty of painkillers. They masked the hurt inside. But only temporarily. Sooner or later, she'd have to face it. Though, based on the slow drip into her IV, she still had some time.

"Here I thought a visit from Socorro would be the worst part of my day." Recognition flared hot and uncomfortable as Chief Baker Halsey leaned forward in the chair set beside her bed. A few scratches marred that otherwise flawless face she'd memorized over the past six months. It was easy, really. To catch herself watching him. To lose herself in that quiet intensity he exuded. "Sorry to tell you I couldn't save the cookies."

"Good thing I made extra." She tried to sit up in the bed, but the mattress was too soft. It threatened to swallow her whole if she wasn't careful. Glaring white tile and cream-washed walls closed in around her. Right back where she didn't want to be. Her attention shifted to the chart at the end of her bed. Her medical history would be in there. Clear for all physicians and nurses to see. What she could and couldn't have in moments like this. A wave of self-consciousness flared behind her rib cage. Would the hospital keep it confidential during the investigation into the bombing? Or did Baker already know? "You got me out?"

"You wanted me to leave you there?" He was distracting himself again, looking anywhere but at her. "It was nothing. If it hadn't been for that small moose you order around, I would've gotten you out quicker. Maybe realized you'd taken a piece of shrapnel sooner."

Maverick. Her nerves went under attack. If he'd been hurt in the blast... Fractured memories of the seconds leading up to the explosion frayed the harder she tried to latch on to them. The monitor on the other side of the bed went wild. "Where is he?"

"Animal Control got hold of him at the scene. He was trying to fight off the EMTs, but that might've been my fault." Baker spread his hands in a wide gesture, highlighting the scraps and bruising along his forearms. "I told him to guard you before I nearly died trying to get a clerk out of the other side of the trailer. Apparently Fido took me seriously."

She didn't have the energy to fight back about Maverick's name. "But he's okay? He's not hurt?"

"Yeah. He's fine." Confusion, tainted with a hint of concern, etched deep into Baker's expression. "Gotta tell you, Carville. I figured you'd be more worried about the chunk of metal they had to take out of you than your sidekick."

"Maverick saved our lives." It was all she was willing to offer right then. "If it wasn't for him picking up that bomb, neither of us would've made it out of that trailer."

"You're right. I'm sorry." Baker scrubbed one busted up hand down his face, and suddenly it was as though he'd aged at least three years. He looked heavy and exhausted and beaten. Same as when he'd discovered one of his own deputies had secretly been working for the cartel.

Her chest constricted at witnessing the pain he carried, but she couldn't focus on that right now. They had more important things to contend with. Like the fact that Alpine Valley's police department was under attack. "Any leads?"

"Nothing yet. Albuquerque's bomb squad is en route. As of right now, all I've got is theories." Baker leaned back in his seat. "Alpine Valley hasn't seen any bombings like this before. Most of what we respond to is domestic calls and overdoses."

Until recently. He didn't have to say the words—the implication was already there. A fraction of residents in Alpine Valley had rallied against a military contractor setting up their headquarters so close to town. They'd believed having the federal government so close would aggravate relations between Sangre por Sangre and the towns at their mercy. So far, they'd been right.

"Socorro employs a combat controller," Jocelyn said. "Jones Driscoll has investigated IEDs overseas. I'm sure he'd be able to help until the bomb squad can get here."

"You want me to bring in a mercenary to investigate the bombing." It wasn't a question.

She wasn't sure if it was the pain medication, his determination to call her K-9 by the wrong name or his insistence that she was part of a group of people who killed targets for money. None of it was sitting very well with the explosive memories fighting for release and the blisters along the backs of her hands. Her determination to hang on to the silver lining was slipping, threatening to put her right back into the hole she'd spent months crawling out of. "Is that all you think of me when you see me in town? When I handed you that piece of lemon bread or brought you those cookies earlier today? Do you really look at me and see a killer?"

He didn't answer.

"Either you just don't get it or you don't want to—I don't know which, and frankly, I don't really care—but you and I are on the same team. We want the same thing. To keep Sangre por Sangre from claiming Alpine Valley and all those other towns just like it." She didn't like this. Being the one to tell the hard truths. Dipping her toes in that inky-black pool of who she used to be. "Socorro has federal resources you'll never be able to get your hands on, and shutting us out will be the worst thing you can do for the people you claim to be protecting. So use us. Use *me*."

Tension flexed the muscles running from his neck and along his shoulders as he straightened in the chair. Such a minor movement, but one that spoke volumes. The small fluctuations in that guarded expression released. "Does the dog have to come with the deal?"

The knot in her stomach relaxed a bit. Not entirely, but enough she could take a full breath. After months of pushing back, Baker was entertaining the thought of trusting someone outside of his small circle of officers. It was a step in the right direction. "Yeah. He does."

"All right, but I'm not going to blindly trust a bunch of mercs—*soldiers*—without getting the lay of the land first. I want to meet your team." A defensiveness she'd always wanted to work beyond encapsulated him back into chief mode, where no one could get through. "This is still my investigation. I make the calls. Everything pertaining to this case comes through me. I want background checks, service records, financials, right down to what you're all allergic to—the whole enchilada. Understand?"

Mmm. Enchiladas. Okay. Maybe a half a roll of cookie dough for breakfast wasn't the best idea she'd had today.

"I think that can be arranged." Jocelyn felt the inner warmth coming back, the darkness retreating. This was how it was supposed to be. Her and Baker working together for a common goal in the name of justice. Not on opposite sides of the table. Still, as hard as she might try to keep sunshine and unicorns throughout her days, she wasn't going to roll over to the chief's every whim. "But I have a condition of my own. You have to call Maverick by his real name."

A small break in that composure sent victory charging through the aching places in her body. "Why does that matter? It's not like he's going to take orders from me. I already tried that. Look how it turned out—he almost took my hand off."

"Maverick is very protective when he needs to be, but he deserves your respect after saving your life back at the station," she said.

"All right, then. Maverick. Easy to remember. He's not going to growl at me every time I'm around, is he?" Baker looked around the room as though expecting her K-9 partner to appear out of thin air.

"He just needs a couple minutes to get to know you. Maybe take in a good crotch sniffing." She tried to keep her smile under control, but the outright terror contorting Baker's face was too much. *This.* She'd missed this. The bickering, the smiles and private jokes. She hadn't gotten to experience it in a long time. Not since before her last tour. "I'm kidding."

Baker's exhale outclassed a category-one tornado. The tightness around his eyes smoothed after a few seconds. Wow. The man acted as though he'd never heard a joke before. This was going to be fun. "Oh. Good. In that case, I'm not really sure what we're supposed to do now."

"I think this is the part where you hike down to the cafeteria and get me one of those enchiladas you were just talking about. You know, seeing as how I'm injured and you're…" She motioned to the entire length of him. "Just sitting there with barely a scratch."

"You haven't seen the inside of my lungs."

A mere crack of his smile twisted her stomach into knots. Well, look at that. It did exist.

Baker pushed to stand, in all his glory. "I thought all you Socorro types ran on nuclear power. Never stopped or slowed down for anything when you took on an assignment. You're like that weird pink bunny with the drum."

"You're thinking of Cash Meyers, our forward scout, when he took on the cartel a few weeks ago." Made a hell of a mess in the process. Destroying Sangre por Sangre headquarters in an effort to recover a woman who'd become the obsession of a cartel lieutenant. His personal mission had been a success, too. Cash had brought the entire organization to its knees for the woman he loved.

A flare of pain bit into her heart at the memory

of what that felt like. Of not being able to save the people you cared about the most.

Nervous energy shot through her. She couldn't just sit here. That gave the bad feelings permission to claw out of the box she'd shoved them into at the back of her mind.

Jocelyn threw off the covers, only acutely aware of the open-backed gown she'd been forced into upon admittance. She grabbed for her singed pants and slid them on with as much dignity as she could muster. Which wasn't much given she was still attached to the damn monitors. "I happen to run on powdered sugar, a whole lot of butter and melted cheese."

Baker handed off her jacket as she pulled the nodes from her skin. Such a simple gesture. But one that wasn't coated in sarcasm or negativity. Progress. "Not sure anyone has ever told you this, but your idea of an enchilada sounds disgusting."

WHAT THE HELL had he been thinking agreeing to this?

Baker notched his head back to take in the height of the building as Jocelyn pulled into the underground parking garage. Sleek, modern angles, black reflective windows—the place was like something out of an old spy movie. Half-built into the canyon wall behind it, Socorro Security headquarters swallowed them whole. He was in the belly of the beast now. Who knew if he'd ever make it out.

Jocelyn navigated through the garage as though she'd done it a thousand times before. Which made sense. As far as he could tell, she, like the rest of her team lived, worked, ate and slept out of this building. No visitors as far as he'd been able to discern in his spurts of surveillance. If the operators employed here had personal lives, he hadn't seen a lick of it, and Baker couldn't help but wonder about the woman in the driver's seat as she shoved the SUV into Park.

She took out what looked like a black credit card. Heavy, too. Aluminum, if he had to guess. Maybe an access card. The bandages wrapping the blisters along the backs of her hands and wrists brightened under limited lighting coming through the windshield.

"I get one of those?" he asked.

She shook her head. "I didn't think accessing the elevators was high on your priority list of things to do today. Otherwise I would've had one made in your honor."

"What? No access to the secret vault?" He watched her pocket the card.

"Sorry. That's reserved for VIP members." Her laugh burned through him with surprising force as she climbed out of the vehicle. The flimsy fabric the hospital staff claimed was an actual piece of clothing was gone. She'd somehow managed to get herself dressed without much distress. Guess that was the upside of painkillers after getting stitched up.

While the EMTs had been forced to remove her Kevlar vest to get access to her wound, it seemed she carried an extra. As though she expected an ambush at any moment. In fact, Baker couldn't think of a time when she didn't have that added layer of protection. Even at the Christmas bake sale.

"You'll have to pay extra for that tour," she said.

He followed close on her heels, absorbing everything about the parking lot he could with barely visible lighting and cement walls. Most likely designed that way to confuse anyone stupid enough to try to breach this place. Though Jocelyn seemed to know exactly where she was going. Still, collecting as much information on these people as he could get would only prove his theory about military contractors' lack of interest in protecting towns like Alpine Valley.

"You been with Socorro long?"

She pressed the key card to a smooth section of wall off to her left and stepped back. "Six months. Signed on a little after my last tour."

Elevator doors parted to reveal a silver car.

Jocelyn stepped inside, holding the door open for him as he boarded.

His limited knowledge of gender representation in the military filtered through the catalogue he was building on her in his head. "Air Force?"

"Army." The small muscles in her jaw flexed under pressure. "Logistics coordinator. Same job I do for Socorro."

Baker filed that away for future reference. Logistics coordinators weren't just responsible for keeping track of military assets. They procured rare resources in times of panic, stayed on top of maintenance operations and covered transportation of any materials, facilities and personnel. People in her position were essential to strategy and planning in the middle of war zones and conflicts. Without operatives like her, the entire military would grind to a halt.

He noted which pocket she slid her key card into despite the admiration cutting through him. "Deployed overseas?"

"Afghanistan. Two tours. Then a third in Africa." There was something missing in that statement. It took him longer than it should have to recognize it, but no one else in his life had the ridiculous positivity Jocelyn seemed to emanate with every word out of her mouth. She didn't like talking about her service in the military. Interesting.

"Wow. Right in the middle of the action." He'd known a couple of deputies from surrounding towns who'd served in the Middle East over the past decade. None of them had held a candle to Jocelyn's level of optimism after what they'd seen. Question was: Was it just for show or a genuine part of her personality? Hard to tell.

The doors parted, dropping them off in the middle of the freaking Death Star. Gleaming black walls with matching tile. The artwork nearly blended in with the walls, only distinguished by outline of the frames. Blinding fluorescent lights reflected off the floors like a crazy hall of mirrors as Jocelyn led them through what he thought might be a hallway.

"Everybody's waiting for us in the conference room," she said.

He tried to map out a mental route through the maze, but there was just too much to index. Everything looked the same. How the hell did anyone navigate this place? "You have many visitors come through here?"

"No. Just you." She wrenched open a glass double door and held it open for him. Not an ounce of pain from her wound reflected in her expression. Hell, just thinking about his body slamming into the trailer wall made him want to cry. How did she do that? Jocelyn motioned him inside. "Welcome to the inner circle."

A wall-to-ceiling window—bulletproof, if he had to guess—stretched along the backside of the conference room. The oversized table led to two Socorro representatives waiting for their arrival. One he recognized. Driscoll. Jones Driscoll. He was the company's head of combat operations, according to Jocelyn. Someone who could help them with the investigation into the bombing. Made sense he'd be here. But the other... Baker didn't know her.

"Chief Halsey, thank you for joining us. I'm Ivy Bardot." The redhead stood from her seat at the head of the table, smoothing invisible wrinkles from her black slacks.

This was the founder of Socorro Security. Jocelyn's boss. Taller than he'd expected, thin and pale, with a few freckles dotted across the bridge of her nose. He hadn't been able to gather much intel on her other than a minuscule peek at her federal record. Former FBI. Highest number of cases closed in Bureau history, which meant she had to be damn good at her job. But clearly...unfulfilled. Why else would she have started Socorro and dragged a team out into the middle of the desert? Emerald-green eyes assessed him as easily as he'd assessed her, but Baker wasn't going to let her get into his head.

Ivy extended her hand. "I'm glad we finally have a chance to meet."

He took her hand out of social obligation as he tracked Jocelyn around the table before she took her seat down by Driscoll. "Yeah, well. Keep the enemy close and all that."

"Is that what we are?" Ivy withdrew her hand, careful not to let those perfectly manicured eyebrows move a millimeter. She was good. Maybe as good as he was at keeping other people in the dark. No, probably better.

In truth, he didn't know what they were at the moment. Not partners, that was for damn sure. Because the minute he trusted these people, they'd leave him and Alpine Valley for dead. They were a temporary solution. One at the mercy of the feds with no real attachment to his town.

"I've got a bombing investigation to get back to, so let's skip the small talk and get this over with," he said.

"A man after my own heart. Please, sit." Ivy headed back to her seat at the head of the table—a position of power she obviously cared about. "This is Jones Driscoll, head of our combat unit. He's our expert in all explosive ordinance and IEDs."

Baker nodded a greeting at the bearded, tattooed mountain man who looked like he belonged in the middle of a logging site rather than in a sleek conference room. Then took a seat beside Jocelyn. He interlocked his hands together over the surface of the table, right beside hers. "Albuquerque bomb squad got to the scene a couple hours ago. They're still trying to put the device back together, but from what little I saw of it before the explosion, we're most likely looking at homemade. Given your experience, I'm not sure why you'd want to attach yourself to a random bombing case."

"Because I don't believe this is random, Chief." Driscoll cut his attention to the company's founder, who nodded in turn. The combat head pried open a folder Baker hadn't noticed until then. "I took the liberty of getting in touch with Albuquerque's squad. They forwarded photos taken of what's left of the station."

"You went over my head." He barely had a second to give in to the annoyance clawing through him.

Driscoll templed his fingers over one of the photos from the stack and spun it around to share with the others. "The device that exploded in your station this morning? I've seen it before. In a car bombing outside of Ponderosa three months ago. The truck belonged to the chief of police there. Andrew Trevino."

Ponderosa. Baker sat a bit straighter under the weight of Jocelyn's gaze as he tried to come to terms with this new information. None of this made sense. He reached for the photos. "I haven't heard about any car bombing."

"You wouldn't have. Socorro was called to the

scene. Ponderosa PD kept as much as they could from the media out of respect for their chief," Ivy said.

"What the hell does that mean?" He locked his gaze on each of the operators in turn, but none of them were giving him an answer.

"It's not uncommon for the cartel to target law enforcement officers it believes might intercept their plans or to make an example out of them in front of the towns they want to move in on." Driscoll tapped his index finger onto the photo positioned between them. "It shows control. Power. Manipulation. Call it your friendly cartel calling card."

"You're saying this was a targeted attack." Baker sifted through the possible scenarios in a matter of seconds. He'd taken this job to keep what had happened to him from happening to anyone else, but most of the cases he'd tackled since being elected to chief hadn't invited this type of attack. Who the hell would want to kill him? "The bomb was left for me."

Chapter Three

She could be miserable before she had a cookie and
miserable after she had a cookie, but she could never
be miserable while she was eating one. Or the dough.

Jocelyn dug out another spoonful from the Tupperware container in which she'd saved the last bit of
cranberry-lemon dough. Whoever had said raw cookie
dough would make her sick was a liar. Some of the
best memories she had were between her and a bowl
of homemade dough. Though some kinds whisked
away the pain better than others. Gauging the mental
list of ingredients she'd need, she calculated how fast
she could whip up some chocolate chip dough while
Baker was floating every other theory past Jones other
than the most obvious.

Someone had planted a bomb in his station. Timed
it well enough to ensure Baker would be in the trailer.
And then detonated it with him inside. Well, they
couldn't actually be sure of that last theory until the
Albuquerque bomb squad recovered all the bits and
pieces of the device. But how many other options
were there?

Heavy footsteps registered, breaking her out of her thoughts. One of the most dangerous places to be. Cash Meyers—Socorro's forward observer—angled into the kitchen, dusted with red dirt. He'd been in town again, helping rebuild the homes Sangre por Sangre had destroyed in their last raid. She could see it in the bits of sawdust on his shoulder.

He nodded at her in the way most of the men on the team did, his chin hiking slightly upward. "Heard you saw some fireworks this morning."

"Quite the show, for sure." Her phone vibrated from the inside of her cargo pants, but she wasn't ready to leave the protective walls of the kitchen. To acknowledge there was an entire world out there. This was where she thrived. Where nothing existed past the buzz of her stand mixer, the radiant heat of the oven and timers beeping in her ears. Jocelyn stuck the end of her spoon through the softening combination of butter, flour, sugar and cranberries. "Got a souvenir, too. Unfortunately, they made me hand it over to the bomb squad. Otherwise I'd put it on my bookshelf."

"You're sick, Carville." Cash wrenched the refrigerator open and grabbed a bottle of water. In less than thirty seconds, he downed the entire thing. Then he tossed the bottle into the recycling bin—her initiative—and leveled that remarkably open gaze on her. It was the little changes like that Jocelyn had noted over the past couple of months. Ever since Cash had taken up with his client. Elena. She'd done something to him. Made him as soft as this cookie dough to the point that he wasn't entirely annoying to be around. "You good?"

"I'm good." What other answer could she possibly give? That the pain in her side was the only thing keeping her from running back into the numbness she'd relied on before she'd come to Socorro? That the mere notion of painkillers threatened to drop her back into a vicious cycle that absolutely terrified her? Cash Meyers wasn't the person nor the solution she needed right then. Nobody on her team fit the bill. After loading her spoon into the dishwasher, she topped off the Tupperware and set it back in the fridge. "Tell Elena I'll drop off a batch tomorrow. I know she and Daniel really like my peanut butter cookies."

She moved past Cash and into the hallway. Air pressurized in her chest. It was always like this. Like she was preparing for war. Only in her case, the metaphor fit better than anything else. The onslaught of pain and suffering and death outside these bulletproof walls had the ability to crush her. It was a constant fight not to retreat, to hide, to fail those she'd sworn she would help. Even a grumpy chief of police.

"Jocelyn." Cash's use of her first name stopped her cold. The men and women of Socorro worked together as a team. They relied on one another to get them through their assignments and to keep each other alive. They were acquaintances with the same goal: dismantling the cartel. While most military units bonded through down time, inside jokes and pranks, the people she worked beside always managed to keep a bit of physical and emotional distance. Especially when addressing one another. The fact that Cash had resorted to verbally using her name meant only one thing. Her cover was slipping. "You sure you're all right?"

She pasted on that smile—the one honed over months of practice—and turned to face him. In an instant, the heaviness of the day drained from her overly tense muscles, and she was right back where she needed to be. "Never better. Stop worrying so much. You'll get crow's feet."

Jocelyn navigated along the black-on-black halls and faced off with the conference room door. Baker was still there, immobile in front of the window stretching from floor to ceiling as the sun dipped behind the mountains to the west. One arm crossed over his chest, the other scrubbing along his jawline. She catalogued every movement as though the slightest shift in his demeanor actually mattered. It didn't, but convincing her brain otherwise was a lost cause.

Stretching one hand out, she wrapped her fingers around the door handle. She could still feel the heat flaring up her hands as she'd tried to take the brunt of the explosion for him. It'd been reactive. Part of her job. Nothing more. At least, that was what she kept telling herself. The bandages across the backs of her hands started itching as she shoved through the door. "You're still here. Figured you and Jones would already be meeting up with the bomb squad back in town."

Turning toward her, Baker dropped his hands to

his sides. Desert sunlight cut through the corner of the window at his back and cast him in blinding light. It highlighted the bruises along one side of his face. A small cut at his temple, too. "Guess he had something else to take care of. Said I could wait for you here."

"Right. Makes sense you would need a ride back into town." She tried not to take it personally. Of all the operators Socorro employed, her skill set didn't do much good in a bombing investigation.

"Well, yes. And no." Nervous energy replaced the mask Baker usually wore. "He told me you were the first one who responded to that car bombing in Ponderosa. Thought maybe you could walk me through it, see if anything lines up with what happened at the station."

"You mean other than the fact that the bomb that went off this morning wasn't attached to the undercarriage of your car?" she asked.

"Right." His low-key laugh did something funny to her insides.

As though she'd subconsciously been holding her breath just to hear it. Which was ridiculous. He didn't want to be here. Baker didn't want her help. He wanted to solve the case. She was only a means to an end. Tendrils of hollowness spread through her chest. Exhaustion was winning out after surviving the impact of the explosion. Her hand went to her side for Maverick but met nothing but empty air. Right. Animal Control.

"You know you won't be able to go back to your

place," she said. "At least not until we have a better idea behind the bomber's motive. Too risky."

"I've been crashing on the couch at the station for a while." Baker rounded the head of the conference table, closing the distance between them. A lungful of smoke burned the back of her throat. Still dressed in his uniform, he was walking around smelling as though he'd just stepped out of one of those joints that smoked their meat instead of barbecuing it. Her stomach rumbled at the sensory overload. "Does that make me homeless?"

"Well, it certainly doesn't make you stable." Her instinct to take on the problems of the people around her—a distraction she'd come to rely on through the hard times—flared hot, but Baker wasn't the kind to share. Let alone trust a mercenary with personal information. She could help, though. Maybe that would ease the tightness in her stomach.

Jocelyn headed for the conference room door. "Come on. I'm sure one of the guys has something you can wear. You can borrow my shower while I find us something to eat."

"Why are you doing this?" His voice barely carried to her position at the door, but every cell in her body amplified it as though he'd spoken into a megaphone. "Why are you helping me?"

"Because despite what you might think of Socorro, Chief, helping people is what we do." She didn't want to think about the ones she hadn't been able to save. The ones who took up so much space in her heart. "It's why we all enlisted. Whether it be military or law enforcement. It's what keeps us going. It might not seem like much, but even the slightest deviation from a recipe can alter the taste of a dessert. It makes a difference."

"Damn it. I was hoping you were going to say something like money or authority or to take credit for dismantling the cartel." His expression softened. "And now I'm hungry."

"Sorry to disappoint you." The bruising along one shoulder barked as she hauled the heavy glass door inward, but she'd live. Thanks to him. "We've got some prepackaged meals in the kitchen. I'll grab you one while you clean up."

"Baker," he said from behind.

She hadn't made it more than two steps before the significance of his name settled at the base of her spine. "What?"

"We survived a bombing together, and you and your employer are going out of their way to help me find who did it." He slipped busted knuckles into his uniform slack pockets, taking the intensity out of his body language. "You can call me Baker."

The chief was asking her to call him by his first name. Giving her permission to step beyond the professional boundaries he'd kept between them since the moment they'd met. It shouldn't have held so much weight, but in her line of work, the gravity hit as hard as that explosion.

"Baker." She could practically taste his name on her tongue. Mostly sour with a hint of sweetness. Like a lemon tart packed with sweet cream.

Or maybe she just needed to brush her teeth.

"THIS DOESN'T TASTE like an MRE." Baker stabbed his fork into another helping of turkey, mashed potatoes and green beans and took a bite. It was enough to thaw the past few hours of adrenaline loss and brought his blood sugar back in line.

"It's not." Sitting straight across the table from him, Jocelyn scooped up a forkful of what looked like chicken with some kind of green vegetable and brought it to her mouth. As she chewed, her hair slid over her one shoulder, brushing the surface of the table. Unremarkably mesmerizing. "I put together about six dozen meals every week to make sure we're not living off carbs and protein shakes."

He wasn't sure if it was the blast or finally getting something other than microwave noodles in his stomach, but Baker had only just noted the way the light reflected off the black waves of hair she usually kept in tight rein. A hint of sepia colored her skin from long days out in the desert, but there wasn't a single piece of evidence of sun damage. Jocelyn Carville fit the exact opposite of everything he'd expected of a soldier, yet there was no denying the part she played in helping him with this investigation. "You made this? Hell, maybe I need to come out here more often."

Jocelyn pressed the back of her hand to her mouth to keep her food in place. "I'd drop some off at the station, but as of this morning, I'm not really sure where I would take it. Have you heard anything from the Albuquerque bomb squad?"

Right. The station he'd taken to holing up in had become a crime scene. He'd almost forgotten about that, sitting here as though the world had stopped and nothing existed outside of this place. They'd taken their seats at an oversized dining table set just on the other side of the kitchen that didn't look as though it got much use. Though from what he knew of Socorro, the contractors had been here for over a year. Maybe they just didn't use the table due to the onslaught of assignments. "Not yet. It may be a few days, but once they have something solid, it's only a matter of time before we find the bomber."

All he needed was proof the bombing was tied to the cartel, and ATF would get involved. Then he could finally take down Sangre por Sangre. For good.

Baker forced himself to focus on his next bite and not the way Jocelyn's eyes practically lit up as she savored her meal. The woman liked food—that much he could tell. Lemon bread, cranberry cookies, full-sized meals packaged in to-go containers. Her physical training had to be hell to stay as lean as she did. Then again, he wasn't entirely sure what was under all that gear she insisted on carrying throughout the day. Even indoors. Then again, what the hell was he doing noticing anything about her when they had a case to work?

"Tell me what you remember of the bombing outside Ponderosa," he said.

"Sure." She hiked one knee into her chest. Playful. Relaxed. At home. The feeling almost bled across the table and seeped into his aching joints with its easiness. Almost. "Ponderosa PD called it in. They hadn't been able to get a hold of their chief that morning, even though he was scheduled for the first shift. The sergeant sent out two patrols. One of them came across the scene about a mile outside of town in one of the canyons nearby. Too far away for anyone to notice."

She took a sip of water. "It was a pickup truck matching the description of Chief Andrew Trevino's vehicle. They initially believed it'd been a fire. That maybe Trevino had forgotten to clean up some oil from under the hood or had a gas leak. He was a smoker. His deputies wanted to believe it'd been an accident."

"But you determined otherwise." Her combat teammate—Jones Driscoll—had said as much, and Baker couldn't help but wonder what an optimistic, high-spirited woman like Jocelyn had seen in her life to make that assessment.

Her gaze detached, as though she were seeing it all play out right in front of her. "The front half of the vehicle was missing. Not even a gasoline fire would instigate that kind of damage. I went through what was left behind, but the resulting fire had burned away most of the evidence. Except a police badge. The edges had melted slightly, but it was clear who was in the vehicle when the bomb discharged."

It was easy to picture. Her crouched in the dirt, studying a replica of the badge currently pinned to his chest. Would she have done the same thing had he been killed in today's bombing? Acid surged up his throat at the notion.

"Maverick recovered a piece of the device. It wasn't sophisticated in the least, but it got the job done. Jones was the one who determined nitroglycerin had been used as the explosive. He could smell it. Anyone with an internet connection can build a bomb, but there was one distinct piece of evidence we couldn't ignore that helped us determine it was planted by the cartel." Jocelyn twisted her fork into the center of her dish but didn't take another bite. "The pager used to trigger the device was registered to a shell company owned by one of Sangre por Sangre's lieutenants. Benito Ramon. Has a history of arson and a mass of other charges, growing up in the cartel."

Confirmation that his leads weren't dead after all sparked anticipation through his veins, but he ate another forkful of dinner to settle his nerves.

"I read about him." Baker wouldn't tell her why. "Sixteen bombings all over the state, each suspected of linking back to Sangre por Sangre, but there was never any evidence to prove he was the bomber. From what I understand the man is a ghost, a legend the cartel uses to keep towns like Alpine Valley in line. Like the boogie man."

Tingling pooled at the base of his spine. He'd never been able to find evidence Benito Ramon existed. All he'd uncovered was a trail of death and destruction when he'd assumed the mantle of chief of police. Crime scene photos, witness accounts, evidence logs—none of it had led to the man who'd taken everything Baker cared about. Until now.

"Ghosts—real or otherwise—can still do a lot of damage," she said.

He could almost read a hint of suspicion in her voice—as though he'd somehow become attuned to the slightest inflection since they'd survived the explosion together. "You think something else was going on. That's why Jones wants you involved in this investigation."

Her mouth parted. Jocelyn didn't answer for a series of seconds. Considering how much to tell him? Then again, he guessed that was the problem with military contractors. Always working their own agenda.

"You said it yourself," she said. "There was never any evidence Benito Ramon was responsible for those sixteen bombings. So why would he make the mistake of using a pager registered to one of his shell companies to trigger the bomb that killed Chief Trevino?"

Good question. Hell, one he should've had the sense to ask himself. "You think someone was trying to pin the chief's murder on Benito Ramon?"

"It's just a theory." Jocelyn collected her meal, snapped the storage lid on top and shoved to her feet. She set the food back in the refrigerator with far more grace than he'd expected out of a five-foot-five woman carrying at least thirty pounds of gear. There was a hidden strength in the way she moved. Practiced.

A theory. He could work with a theory. Baker gathered up his own dinner and set about disposing of what he couldn't finish. "This place is a lot quieter than I figured it'd be."

"Socorro is on call 24/7. It's hard to get everyone together when we're all working different shifts, but we try." An inner glow that hadn't been there a few minutes ago seeped into her expression. "Birthday parties, movie nights, Thanksgiving and Christmas. It's rare, but being together helps us bond better as a team, you know? Takes the harshness out of the work we do."

Baker watched the transformation right in front of him. Where a heaviness had tensed the muscles along her neck and shoulders, exhilaration took its place as she talked about her team. He'd never seen anything like it before. "You like this kind of stuff. Cooking, baking for people, movie nights…"

There was a hitch in Jocelyn's step that she tried to cover up as she moved from one side of the kitchen to the next. She'd taken a mixing bowl out of the refrigerator and peeled the plastic wrap free. Cookie dough, from the look of it. Did the woman ever just sit still? She dragged a cookie scoop out of one of the drawers and started rolling the dough into perfect golf ball–sized pieces onto a baking sheet. "Of course. Keeps me busy."

"Aren't you already busy responding to things like car bombings and coordinating resources from surrounding towns?" He couldn't help but watch her roll one section of dough before moving onto the next. It was a highly coordinated dance that seemed to have no end and drove his nervous system into a frenzy. He wanted to reach out, to force her hands to stop working, but Baker had the distinct impression she'd bite him if he interrupted. Like her dog almost had back at the station.

"Well, yeah, but this ends in cookies. And who doesn't like cookies?" Her smile split a small cut at one corner of her mouth. A sliver of blood peeked through.

His discipline failed him right then. Baker closed the short distance between them, swiping the blood from her mouth. One touch catapulted his heart rate into overdrive. A sizzle of heat burned across his skin faster than the flames created by the bomb this morning.

Instant paralysis seemed to flood through her. She stopped rolling dough into bite-sized balls, her hands buried deep in something that smelled a lot like peanut butter. Three seconds passed. Four. Her exhale brushed against the underside of his jaw.

Jocelyn took as big of a step back as she could with her palms full of dough. "What are you doing?"

"I'm sorry." He knew better than to touch her without permission. Cold infused his veins as he brushed his thumb against his slacks. They were already spotted with blood. A few more drops wouldn't hurt. "You just…had a bit of blood on you."

"Don't. Just…don't." Lean muscle running the length

of her arms flexed and receded as she peeled layers of dough off her hands and tossed it back into the bowl.

Right before she sprinted from the kitchen.

Chapter Four

No amount of cookie dough was going to fix this.

Jocelyn scrubbed her hands as hard as she could beneath the scalding water. She could still feel his touch at the corner of her mouth. Baker's touch. It'd been calloused and soft at the same time, depending on which feeling she wanted to focus on. Only problem was she didn't actually want to focus on any of it.

Her skin protested each swipe of the loofa. To the point it'd turned a bright red. The blisters she'd earned this morning were bleeding again, but it wasn't enough to make her stop. The dough just wouldn't come off. She could still feel it. Still feel Baker's thumb pressed against her skin.

"Jocelyn?" Movement registered in the mirror behind her. Baker centered himself over her shoulder though ensured to keep his distance. Dark circles embedded beneath his eyes, taking the defiance and intensity she was used to right out of him.

She ordered one hand to turn off the water, but she just kept scrubbing, trying to replace one feeling with another. It was working. Slowly. The tightness in her chest was letting go. "How did you get in here?"

"That guy Cash told me where your room was. I knocked, but there was no answer. I just wanted to make sure you were okay." His voice didn't hold the same authority it had while he'd been asking her about the bombing in Ponderosa.

"So you thought you would just let yourself in?" The conversation was helping, somehow easing her heart rate back into normal limits.

"I knocked for fifteen minutes," he said. "Listen… I'm sorry about before. I shouldn't have touched you. I was out of line, and it won't happen again. I give you my word."

Her hands were burning, and the last few pieces of agitation slipped free. She finally had enough control to turn off the water. All was right with the world. Jocelyn reached for the pretty hand towel to her left and took a solid full breath for the first time in minutes. "I'm not crazy."

Three distinguished lines between his eyebrows deepened as she caught his reflection in the mirror. "That didn't even cross my mind. A lot of soldiers have trouble differentiating the past trauma from the present. I've seen it in one of my deputies. There's no shame—"

"I'm not suffering from PTSD, Baker." She rearranged the hand towel back on its round metal hardware. No one understood. Because what she'd done—what she lived with every day—was hers alone. But what she wouldn't give to let someone else take the weight for a while.

Jocelyn turned to face him, the bathroom doorframe putting them on opposite sides of the divide. Here and outside these walls. "You want to know why I bake so many cookies and breads and cakes and pies? Why I feel safer with a glob of dough in my hands than with my sidearm? Because it makes me happy. It helps me forget."

"Forget what?" He moved toward her then, resurrecting that hint of smoke in his uniform.

Discomfort alienated the pleasure she'd found with her hands in that peanut butter dough. She'd already let her control slip once today. Did she really want to take a full dive into trusting a man who couldn't even stand to be in the same room as her? "My husband."

"Oh." His expression went smooth as he leaned against the doorjamb. "I didn't realize you're married."

"Was. I was married." She'd never said the words before, never wanted to admit there was this gaping hole inside of her where Miles used to be. Because that would be when the sadness got to be too much. When the world tore straight out from under her and past comforts reared their ugly little heads. "He passed away about a year ago."

"I'm sorry." Folding his arms over his chest, Baker looked as though he belonged. Not just here in headquarters but in this moment. "I didn't... I didn't know."

"Nobody knows. No one but you." She let her words fill the space between them, but the weight didn't get lighter. If anything, her legs threatened to collapse in the too-small bathroom attached to her room.

Eyes to the floor, Baker scrubbed a hand down his face. "So when I touched you—"

"It wasn't your fault." She crossed her feet in front of her, her weight leveraged against the vanity. Of all the places she'd imagined having this conversation, in a bathroom with the Alpine Valley's chief of police hadn't even made the list. "The most affection I get now days is from Maverick, and he's not as cuddly as he looks. You just…took me by surprise is all."

"As cuddly as he looks? Your dog nearly took my hand off when I was trying to get you out of the station."

His attempt to lighten the mood worked to a degree. But there was still a matter of this…wedge between them. One she wasn't sure she could fix with cookies and a positive attitude. "A spouse isn't usually someone you want to forget."

"It's not him I want to forget, really." She tried to put her smile back in place, feeling it fail. Her fingers bit into the underside of the vanity counter, needing something—anything—to keep her from slipping back into an empty headspace she didn't want to visit. "He died of cancer. While I was on my last tour. I tried to make it home—to be there for him, you know—but communications on assignment were spotty at best and arranging transport is hard when the enemy is shooting down anything they come across."

Tears broke through. The pain was cresting, sucking her under little by little, and she had nothing and no one to hold on to.

He took another step forward. "Jocelyn—"

"I know. Not exactly how you imagined your day would play out, right?" Years of practice had to be worth something. She swiped at her face, but getting rid of the physical evidence of her hurt wasn't enough. It'd never been enough. Turning to the mirror, she plastered that smile on her face. There. That was better. She could just make him out through the last layer of tears in her eyes. "First a bombing at your station, then a mercenary crying in front of you over her dead husband. Maybe next you'll get food poisoning from the dinner I put together. Wouldn't that be the icing on the cake?"

She had to get moving. Jocelyn grabbed for the first aid kit under the sink and started wrapping the blisters she'd broken open. Staying put gave the bad thoughts a chance to sneak in. They should've heard from Albuquerque's bomb squad by now. She had to finish those cookies for Elena and Cash, too. She should—

"Jocelyn, look at me." Baker's voice brought the downward cycle of to-do lists to a halt. He said her name as though it were the most beautiful word in his world, as though right then he saw who she really was. Not a mercenary. Not Carville. Just Jocelyn. Something behind her rib cage convinced her that he could fix everything with that single shift between them, but that wasn't how the world worked. How *grief* worked. No amount of pity was going to change the past.

But she still found herself locking her gaze on his.

Baker offered her his hand, palm up. Inviting. "I want to show you something."

He was giving her a choice to be touched, and appreciation nearly outpaced a rush of possibilities that crashed through her. She'd spent every day since getting the news that Miles hadn't survived his disease learning new languages, recipes, combat techniques and dozens of other experiences, but she couldn't imagine what a small-town police chief would want to show her.

She slipped her hand into his. His skin was bruised, cut, scabbing, harsher than she'd expected. But real. Baker dragged her free of the bathroom and toward the wall-to-ceiling window on the other side of her room. From here she could just make out Alpine Valley with the west end of the town peeking out from the canyon guarding it on both sides. An oasis in the middle of the New Mexican desert.

"You see that collection of buildings out there?" Radiant heat bled through the tinted panes of glass, but it was nothing compared to the warmth spreading through her hand. "Just outside of the canyon mouth?"

She focused everything she had on finding what he wanted her to see. Her heart pounded double-time in expectation of a full-blown breakdown as sadness worked through her, but the fear that usually rode on its coattails never came. As though their physical connection was holding her steady. "I see a barn, maybe a house. Though I'm not sure who lives there."

"I do." The window tint wasn't enough to block the sunset from highlighting all the small changes in his expression. "The barn, the house, the land. Three acres."

"So you're not as homeless as you led me to believe earlier?" She tried to make out the property lines to mentally gauge Baker's private kingdom, but there didn't seem to be anything but dirt and emptiness surrounding the structures. Dread pooled in her gut. "Why have you been crashing at the station for the past few months?"

"My sister and I had big plans to move out west and buy up land here in New Mexico. We were going to raise horses and start a bed and breakfast." He stared out at the land, not really here with her. "Took us a lot longer than it should have, but neither of us had built anything in our lives. We had to learn as we went. And buying up horses?" A scoff released the pressure of the moment. "Man, we were suckered into paying more than we should have, but we didn't care. We just wanted a place that was our own. Away from the chaos of the city. Somewhere we could hear ourselves think."

Why was he telling her this? "The two of you must be close."

"We were. Spent every second of our days together.

Well, almost. There were times we got on each other's nerves because we were overheated, sunburned and hungry from working the land all day, but we'd still sit down to dinner every night as though nothing had happened." His grip tightened around her hand. "The last time I saw her was during one of those stupid arguments. I don't even remember what I was so mad about. Guess it doesn't matter now, though."

Her mouth dried. "The last time you saw her?"

"About two weeks into getting the place off the ground, the cartel came calling. Talking some BS about how they owned the land we built on." Baker shifted his weight between both feet, his attention still out the window. She recognized the agitation for what it was: an attempt to distract himself. "Come to find out they'd set up one of their delivery routes straight through the property and weren't too keen on the idea someone had moved in on their territory. But we weren't just going to get up and leave."

"What happened?" In truth, she already knew the answer. Knew this story—like her own—didn't have a happy ending. How could it?

Baker locked that penetrating gaze on hers. "They burned everything we built to the ground. And took my sister right along with it."

HE HADN'T TOLD anyone about Linley before.

Not even his own deputies, but he didn't trust them anyway. Not after discovering one of his own had been working for the very people Baker despised. Of course, there'd been rumors. Questions as to why an outsider like him would want to suddenly apply for the position of chief of police. They hadn't trusted him. Still didn't. Not really. But he'd live up to his promise to protect the people of Alpine Valley. Especially from cartels like the one that had destroyed his life.

Baker memorized the rise and fall of the landscape as they shot across the desert inside Jocelyn's SUV. Surrounded by miles of desert, Alpine Valley had provided life to an entire nature preserve. Trees over a hundred feet tall crowded in around the borders and protected the natural hot springs and centuries-old pueblos tucked into the canyons. It was beautiful. Not in the same way he'd loved the leaves in the fall back east or watched snow pile up outside in his parents' backyard. There was honestly nothing but cracked earth, weeds and cacti as far as the eye could see.

But it was home now.

What had Linley called it? An oasis to forget their problems. If only that had been true.

"We need a plan." Baker turned his attention back to the file on his lap—the bombing outside of Ponderosa. Jocelyn had gone the extra mile to call in a favor from their department there, giving them full access to the case. They could dance around the present all they wanted with dark personal confessions and frank observations, but it wasn't going to change the fact that a bomb—most likely linked to the cartel—had been left in his station. Just as one had been left for the Ponderosa chief to find. "Albuquerque's bomb squad isn't going to like us just showing up on scene. There are protocols to follow so we don't disturb the evidence."

"It's all taken care of." Her hand—ringless, he couldn't help but notice—kept a light grip on the steering wheel as she maneuvered them along the familiar street lined with flat-roofed homes, rock landscaping and a few porch lights.

"What do you mean?" he asked.

Jocelyn didn't answer as she pulled into the parking lot that used to hold a much larger police station than what was left behind. Crime scene tape cut off access to approaching vehicles, but his cruiser was still parked outside the makeshift perimeter. She pulled the SUV beside it.

He'd reached out to his deputies to give them the rundown of what'd happened. It didn't matter that their station was sporting a sunroof nobody had wanted. Alpine Valley PD didn't get to take a vacation from answering calls. Though now his remaining two deputies would be answering and responding to calls for the foreseeable future from the town rec center. Good a place as any.

"Looks like the courts are barred from working out of their half of the building," he said.

"Standard procedure. Fire and Rescue doesn't want to run the risk of evidence contamination, even from people who know how important that evidence is in a case." Jocelyn put the vehicle into Park. "The fire marshal is waiting for us."

"You called Gary?" Baker shoved out of the SUV,

a little worse for wear. Hell, his whole body hurt from this morning's events. How did Jocelyn do it—moving as though she hadn't been impaled by a piece of debris as she pulled something from the back seat?

Gravel crunched under his boots as he followed the short path from the asphalt to the base of the station stairs. "I can't even get him to return my calls. Seems he doesn't agree with my choice in baseball teams. Though I'm not sure why he would take that so personally."

"You just have to know how to make him talk." She produced a plate of plastic-wrapped goods and grabbed her phone. With the swipe of her thumb, she raised the phone to her ear and rasped in a thick, Russian accent, "I have what you asked for."

She hung up. Waiting.

"Are we in the middle of delivering a ransom payment I don't know about?" Movement registered from the corner of the station to Baker's right. Instant alert had him reaching for his sidearm. Then recognition tendriled through him as Alpine Valley's fire marshal hauled his oversized frame closer. He relaxed a fraction. "Gary."

"Chief." Not Baker. Seemed grudges died hard with this one. Gary cut his gaze to Jocelyn, and the marshal's overall demeanor lost its bite. Yeah, she had the tendency to do that—ease into a person's subconscious and replace any darkness with rainbows and silver linings. "I believe you have something for me."

She handed off the plate as though embroiled in

an illegal trade. "Fresh batch of oatmeal. No raisins. They're all yours."

"You got ten minutes before Albuquerque wants me to check in." Gary had suddenly lost the ability to make eye contact, his entire focus honed in on the disposable plate in his hand.

"Thanks. We won't be long," Baker said.

The marshal didn't bother answering as he headed for his pickup across the street.

Baker motioned her ahead of him. "Seems you have your fingers in all the pies around here."

"Like I said, you just have to know how to get people to talk." Jocelyn took the lead up the stairs and produced a blade from one of her many cargo-pant pockets. The woman was better prepared than an Eagle Scout.

Cutting through the sticker warning trespassers of what waited for them if they were caught breaking into a crime scene, she braced her foot against one corner of the door to let him by. "With Gary, it's straight through his stomach. He kept coming back for my oatmeal cookies at the fundraiser last year. Later, I found a pile of discarded raisins in the parking lot."

"Here I thought the best way to a man's heart was through his third and fourth ribs." He unholstered his flashlight from his duty belt, then maneuvered past her, though he couldn't help but brush against her as he did. The physical contact eased the unsettled part of him that knew he was breaking a dozen different laws crossing into this crime scene, which he'd have to answer for, but the clock was ticking. The bomb squad's investigation could last days, maybe weeks. Possibly even months, if Chief Andrew Trevino's murder was anything to go by. They didn't have that kind of time—this was the first lead he'd had on Sangre por Sangre in months. He couldn't let it die.

Once inside, Baker punched the end of the flashlight, and a beam cut across the charred, debris-coated carpeting. "You always been able to read people like that?"

"I have a good sense for it." Jocelyn followed along the path through the building that the bomb squad had cleared for techs. She walked past what used to be the small kitchenette the former dispatcher had set up opposite the evidence room. "I see you more as a home-cooked-meal kind of guy."

"What gives you that impression?" The bitter scent of fire lodged in the back of his throat. Caustic. Suffocating. Baker felt his heart rate tick up a notch. He blinked to focus on the scene in front of him, but there were too many similarities. Sweat broke out across his forehead.

"You turned down my cranberry-lemon cookies this morning." Jocelyn's voice warbled there at the end. "And considering you've been crashing in a police station trailer armed with nothing but a microwave, I'd bet that dinner we had earlier hit the spot."

Baker couldn't move, couldn't speak. Every cell in his body put its energy into studying a half-destroyed coffee stirrer, and he lost any ability to get his lungs to work.

"Baker?" His name sounded distant. Out of reach.

Gravity held him hostage in that one spot despite the left side of his brain trying to catch up to the right. The flavor of smoke changed, contorting into something more acidic and nauseating. He took a step forward, though the layout of the station had vanished. He was walking toward the barn. What was left of it, at least. Intense heat still clung to the charred remains, flicking its tongue across his skin. "Linley?"

His shallow breathing triggered a wave of dizziness. She wasn't here. She couldn't be here. Because if the cartel had done this… No. He couldn't think like that. Baker took another step, his boots sinking deep into mud. The barn door nearly fell off its hinges as he wrenched it to one side. The entire building was about to crash down around him. All of this damage couldn't be from the result of a random fire. This was something far more explosive.

"Baker."

He knew that voice. Well enough to pull him up short. It whispered on the ash-tainted air around him. Like he could reach out and grab onto it. Jocelyn?

"Can you hear me?"

The fragment of memory jumped forward. To him standing in front of the body positioned in the center of the barn. Nothing about the remains resembled his sister, but he knew the cartel had done this. That they'd kept their word to burn his entire world to the ground if he didn't comply with their demands. And he'd let it happen. All because he'd gone into town for more hay.

Fury and shame and grief clawed through him as he sank to his knees. "I'll find them. Every single one of them. I give you my word… I'll make them pay."

"Baker!" Strong chocolate-brown eyes centered in his vision, replacing the horrors. Jocelyn fisted both hands into his uniform collar and crushed her mouth to his.

The past dissolved from right in front of him, replaced by physical connection tethered to reality. Her mouth was soft—hesitant—on his. The horrors clinging to the edges of his memory were displaced by the mint taste of her toothpaste and the slight aroma of oatmeal cookies. Baker lost himself in the feel of her mouth against his. On the slight catch of the split in her lip.

It was absolutely the most inappropriate thing to do in the middle of a crime scene, but his heart rate was coming back down. He had sensation back in his hands, and he latched on to Jocelyn as though he'd lose this grasp in the present if he didn't. The helplessness consuming him from the inside crawled back into the dark void he'd walled away. Until there was nothing left but her.

She settled back onto her heels, a direct mirror of his position on the floor. Her exhale brushed the underside of his jaw, and that simple rush to his senses was all it took. Jocelyn's eyes bounced between both of his, concern and fear and something like affection spiraling in the depths. "You with me?"

"Yeah." Baker tightened his hold on her vest. Because she was the only real thing he had. "I'm with you."

Chapter Five

Well, wasn't that just the milk to her cookies?

Jocelyn pried her grip from Baker's uniform collar and put a bit of distance between them. She'd kissed him, and in the moment, it'd been all she could think of to snap him out of whatever he'd been reliving. But now... Now there was a pressure in her chest reminding her that everything she touched died. House plants. Friendships. Her husband.

Shame burned through her as she tried to smooth the imprints of her hold from the fabric of his uniform. "I'm sorry. I...didn't know what else to do. You weren't answering, and I thought—"

"It's okay." Baker seemed to come back to himself then, but she couldn't help but wonder if his mind would pull him back into that terrifying void with the slightest reminder of what he'd been through.

She'd always known people who'd survived trauma—in war, in their own homes, as children or adults—could be caught in the suffocating spiral of PTSD, but the chief of police had never crossed her mind. And now his assumption that she suffered from post-traumatic stress made sense. It wasn't one of his deputies he'd been talking about who experienced nerve-wracking flashbacks. It was *him*. And she'd dragged him straight into a similar scene to what he'd witnessed.

"I shouldn't have brought you back here," she said.

He was still holding on to the shoulders of her vest. Gauging his surroundings, Baker finally let go. Yet he struggled to stay on his feet. Stable but weak. As though the past had taken everything he had left for itself. "I'm fine. It hasn't happened in a while. It just caught me off guard."

She reached out, resting her hand on his arm. She'd seen physical contact work in the field before. "If you need to wait in the car, I can go through—"

"I'm not leaving." There was a violence in his voice she hadn't heard until then. Just as she'd responded to him after he'd touched her mouth. It was reflected in his eyes as he seemed to memorize the scene around them. "I can do this."

Shame, guilt, helplessness—it all echoed through her just as it did him, and Jocelyn backed off. His response made sense. Fellow soldiers who'd lived through what could only be described as the worst days of their lives on tour kept going back, comforted by the very horrors that had scarred and disconnected them. Baker wouldn't admit defeat to the ambushing sights, sounds and smells in his head. No matter how unhealthy or unexpected. Because without them, he had nothing.

They were similar in that respect, and her heart

wanted to fix it. To make everything better. But she couldn't even help herself. How was she supposed to help him?

"Okay." Jocelyn swiped clammy hands down her pants. It'd been jarring and terrifying to see a man as confident and driven as Baker shut down right in front of her, but deep down she knew he wouldn't let it affect this investigation. The marshal had given them ten minutes inside the scene. She wasn't sure how much time they had left. They had to keep moving. "I'll see what I can find around the evidence closet."

She didn't wait for an answer. The hollow floor threatened to collapse from her added weight, but she kept to the path that the bomb squad had charted.

"Jocelyn, hold on." His hand encircled her arm, and she turned into him, though not out of some fight-or-flight instinct she didn't have control over. Because she wanted to. The flashlight beam cut across the floor from where he'd dropped it a few minutes ago, casting his expression in a white-washed glow. "I…"

Words seemed to fail him then. This man who fought for everyone in this town but himself. He didn't have to say the words. Despite the distance they'd kept lodged between themselves and the rest of the world, invisible connections were forged through survival. That was what they'd done today. Survived. And in that single act, she found herself more in line with Baker than she'd thought possible.

"I know. It's okay." She tried to put that smile

back in place. The one that could save the world, according to her husband. No matter what had been going on in their lives or how bad the pain had gotten from treatment, all he'd needed was that smile. And in the end, it was all he'd asked for, according to his nurses. But she hadn't been there.

The muscles around her mouth wavered. "We're all just trying to navigate the same road to healing," she said. "Every once in a while, we take a wrong turn or end up going in reverse. But that's why I'm glad you're here with me, in the passenger seat. Helping me navigate."

She slipped free of his hold, almost desperate to prove she could be his navigator in turn. That she could find something—anything—in this mess to give him some sense of peace. Squaring her shoulders, Jocelyn kept to the perimeter of where the blast had originated.

The bomb squad most assuredly had been through all of this. They would've spent hours trying to piece the device back together to identify its creator through a signature or fingerprint. But everything else would've had to wait. She took in the outline of the hole blasted through the far wall and low corner of what used to be a closet. The moments leading up to the blast played out as clearly as if they'd happened mere minutes ago, rather than hours.

Maverick had sniffed out the bomb's components in a box stacked at the back of a bottom shelf. It'd been a clever hiding place. But why there? "The evidence room."

"What did you say?" Baker kept his footsteps light as he carved a path through the makeshift kitchen-ette.

"Ponderosa's chief of police—Trevino—was killed with a bomb strapped to the underside of his pickup truck. There was no doubt that whoever set the de-vice had targeted him. His wife had her own vehicle, and their kids were raised and grown. Moved out of state to start their own families." Her mouth couldn't keep up with her theory—as it did sometimes when her mind raced ahead in a recipe she'd memorized but her hands didn't work that fast. "The device from this morning was planted here. In the station. Where anyone could walk in."

He closed the distance between them, his arm making contact with the back of her vest. Just the slightest pressure, but enough to elicit a response. "You and Jones were convinced the bombing was meant for me. Now you're saying it wasn't?"

"Did you see the device this morning?" she asked.

Baker stilled, his gaze narrowing as she practi-cally watched him replay the events of the day. There was still a hint of sweat at his temple. Evidence the tin man was all too human. "No. Maverick was in the way. He was sniffing around…an evidence box."

"It was on the bottom shelf. You remember?" She tried coming up with the case numbers marked on the outside, but there were still gaps in her mem-ory from when her head had been lodged at the far wall. "Albuquerque's bomb squad is working off our assumption the device was meant for you. They'll put everything into putting what they can find of the bomb back together, but what if it was actually planted to destroy whatever was in that box? To stop a case from moving forward?" Her voice hitched with excitement. "Think about it. There are countless other places they could've set that bomb to get to you. Why would they purposely choose a box stashed on the bottom shelf of the evidence room unless they wanted to make sure no one could put the pieces back together?"

"Makes sense." Baker stared at the space where the floor should've been. "Question is, which case would they have wanted to destroy?"

"Did you have any active cases running on the cartel? Maybe one of their soldiers or an incident that occurred within Alpine Valley town borders?"

"Son of a bitch." Baker took a step back, scrubbing a hand down his face. "I should've seen it before now."

"You had a case," she said. "What was it?"

"Cartel lieutenant. Guy named Marc De Leon. We arrested him about three months ago. He'd taken to strapping a bomb to a woman's chest after torturing her for a couple hours. Best we could get from him, she was a random target. Unfortunately, she didn't survive, and the extent of her injuries kept us from identifying her. We've searched missing persons reports and interrogated the bastard any chance we could, but it's gotten us nowhere. Everyone just calls her Jane Doe." Sorrow dipped his voice into a whisper. "We could prove he was at the scene. Dead to rights. Found his fingerprints on the weapon he left behind. I picked him up on foot just outside of town covered in blood within a couple hours. It was easy to connect him back to the cartel through his priors. The lawyers are going at it right now, trying to claim some insanity defense, but it's not working. He knew exactly what he was doing when he killed her."

She'd heard about the raid. Known the town had nearly burned to the ground the night that another lieutenant had ordered his men to bring Elena Navarro and her eight-year-old brother, Daniel, to him. They'd torn apart families, destroyed homes and shops and set Alpine Valley right back under their control. By fear and intimidation. But now Baker was adding murder to the list. Why hadn't she known about this before tonight?

"The case wasn't going away. What better way to get your man off the hook than to send in your resident bomber to destroy all the evidence?" she said.

"Yeah, well. They got what they wanted, didn't they? We had the knife. We had his fingerprints, witness statements, GPS from his phone that put him in that house at the time of the raid." Baker kicked at a half-cremated box that hadn't gotten caught in the blast. "All destroyed. The prosecutor won't be able to do a damn thing about it, and that woman's family gets nothing. No sense of closure. No justice."

Her heart hurt at the idea of the victim's family knowing what'd happened to her but never being able to move on. Because Baker was there, too. Haunted by what'd happened to his sister, never finding peace.

Never being able to move on from the past. Jocelyn wanted that for him. A chance to heal, to live his own life apart from the horrible trauma that'd taken away everything he'd loved.

And there was only one way to do it.

She stepped to his side, staring down at the singed hole where the evidence room used to be. It wasn't just Marc De Leon's case that'd been destroyed but all of them. Dozens of victims who'd never see the resolution they deserved. "Lieutenants like De Leon are indispensable. It takes years of loyalty and trust to rise up the ranks. It's what he knows about the cartel's operation that they'd go out on a limb to save, but that doesn't make men like him untouchable."

"You sure about that?" he asked.

"Yeah." Jocelyn breathed in smoke-heavy air, mentally preparing for the war they were about to start. "I am."

HE WAS BACK at square one.

The promise of a new lead in his sister's murder was wearing thin. Pain radiated up his side as the SUV's shocks failed to navigate the uneven landscape. He'd once believed Alpine Valley was where he belonged, that his future rested here in miles of desert, star-streaked skies and protective canyons. Somewhere he could build a future.

He didn't have a future anymore.

Not until Sangre por Sangre paid for what they'd done. To him, to the residents of his town. To the hundreds of future victims they would discard in a power struggle to gain control. It wasn't just about what'd happened to Linley or that lieutenant trying to squeeze himself out of a murder charge. It was *all* of it. The constant threat and the repercussions of a cartel's choices determined who would live at the end of the day and who wouldn't. And Baker couldn't accept that. These people deserved better, and he wasn't going to stop. Not until every last man and woman connected to the cartel was behind bars or six feet under.

The rush of adrenaline he'd suffered at the smallest inkling of a threat refused to let go. It was tensing his hands until he found it nearly impossible to release. His body had yet to get the signals there wasn't any actual danger right in front of him, and there was only one way to force it back into submission.

"I need you to do me a favor." His voice failed on the last word. Exhaustion had gotten the best of him long before now, but he was somehow still holding it together. They were coming up on the road that would either take them back to Socorro or to the edge of town. "Turn right up here at the T."

Jocelyn's mouth parted in the dim light given off by the SUV's controls behind the steering wheel. The slightest change in facial expression spoke volumes. She knew exactly what he was asking, and she was the only one who could help. "Are you sure?"

"I just need…" He didn't know what he needed. Something familiar? Baker didn't have the capacity to explain right then. The gnawing hollowness in his chest wouldn't let him. "I'm sure."

She navigated north.

He'd driven this way so many times, he could practically feel his breath coming easier as he anticipated every bump in the dirt road. But it wasn't enough. A war between getting relief and putting himself at risk raged as the rough outline of the structures separated from the surrounding darkness up ahead.

"You can stop here," he said.

Momentum kept his upper body moving forward as Jocelyn brought the SUV to a full stop outside the cattle gate, but the pain stayed at a low simmer. "I'll just be a few minutes."

"You don't have to go in there alone." Her hand shot out as he shouldered the passenger side door open, clamping on to the top of his thigh. The contact should've set him on high alert, but there was something about Jocelyn Carville that put him at ease. "I could come with you."

His automatic answer rushed to the front of his mind. He should shut her down, take the time he needed to get his head back in the game. But the logical part of him understood she'd already seen him at his worst, that walking into that house without support could break him.

Baker let his hand slip from the door. "Yeah. Okay."

The vehicle's headlights guided them to the gate. A chill ran through the air. A storm was on its way in, the first few drops collecting along the top of the gate. Baker grabbed for the padlock securing the gate to the frame and took out his key, twisting it in the lock. The chain hit the dirt, and he swung the gate open. "Welcome to my humble abode."

Gravel crunched under their feet as they hiked the empty driveway. The barn sat in the distance, more than half of the structure gone from the explosion. Its rugged outline stood stark against the backdrop of the last bit of blue behind the mountains. But the house was still intact. The single story was exactly as he'd left it. Tan stucco practically glowed in the beaming moonlight and highlighted the black window casings, two-car garage and front door. Mid-century metal floral details held up one corner of the porch, matching the color of the exterior of the house. It was a weird, old addition on a brand-new build, but Linley had insisted. Now he couldn't imagine taking it out.

Baker hauled himself up the front steps and gripped the front door handle with one hand. The oversized picture window stared back at him from his left, and he couldn't help but let his senses try to penetrate through the glass. As though his sister would be waiting for him to come home on the other side as she had so many times before.

Jocelyn followed his hesitant footsteps. "We can still turn back…"

No. As much as he wanted to pretend the past didn't affect the present, his body kept score.

Baker slid the key into the deadbolt. "Don't you know by now, Carville? There is no going back. Not for people like us."

Hinges protested as he pushed inside. A wall

of stale air drove down his throat. The breeze cut through the opening in the front door and ruffled the plastic coating the furniture, and an instant hit of warmth flooded through him. He tugged the key from the deadbolt and moved aside to let Jocelyn over the threshold, flipping on the entryway light.

"It's much bigger than it looks from the outside." She carved a path ahead of him. Her bootsteps echoed off the hardwood floors and tall ceilings. Taking in the stretch of the great room and the fireplace mantel he and his sister had crafted by hand, Jocelyn moved as though she'd been here before. "You built all this?"

Baker shut out the cold, letting the entire space seep into his bones. "Me and my sister. I did most of the heavy lifting. She picked out all the extras. The color of the floors, paint on the walls. A time or two I'd needed her help framing out the closet or installing the toilets. She really could do it all."

"What was her name?" Jocelyn carefully ran her hand the length of the mantel, as though she knew that was the final piece he'd installed in this house.

"Linley." It'd been so long since he'd let himself speak her name, it tasted foreign on his tongue. Though not as bitter as he'd expected. "She had a talent for stuff like this. I always told her she could be a designer, but she loved horses more."

Jocelyn intercepted the single framed photo and lifted it off the mantel. One taken of him and Linley, each holding hammers in a ridiculous power pose in front of their finished project. "Is this her?"

"Yeah." He maneuvered around the sectional, his thigh brushing over plastic, and took the frame from her. "This was the day we officially finished the house. We were trying to pose like those brothers on the renovation show, but we couldn't stop laughing because every time we set my phone up to take the picture on top of this bag of concrete, it fell off. I ended up cracking my screen, but we somehow managed to make it work."

Heat seared through him as Jocelyn's arm settled against his side. The need for something familiar didn't seem to have as great a hold on him. Not with her here. "She looks like you. Same eyes. Same smile. She's stunning."

"Does that mean you think I'm stunning, then, too?" Where the hell had that come from? And what did he care what she thought of him?

"I wouldn't call you ugly." Jocelyn backed off, hands on her hips, and he swore a flush rushed up her neck. "Unless you piss me off."

Baker pressed his thumb into the corner of the framed photo. "Well, I wouldn't want that. Who else is going to feed me something other than prepackaged ramen noodles?"

Her smile did more to light up the room than the light-fan combination above them. "Oh, is that all I'm good for? You got what you wanted out of me, and now I'm back to being the mercenary who bakes?"

"Nah. Once you survive a bombing together, you can never go back to being acquaintances." Baker set the photo back on the mantel. He liked this. The back and forth they'd shared since this morning. It came with a weird sensation of…lightness. Like he'd been cutting himself off from everything that made him happy as some kind of penance. "You heard from Animal Control?"

"Yeah. Socorro's vet picked Maverick up a little while ago," she said. "He's got a slight limp, but for the most part he's fine. Should be back to normal in a couple days. Just needs a bit of rest."

"He's not the only one." He prodded at the lump behind his left ear. It'd kept itself in check for most of the day, but after coming here, his nerves had reached their end. "If the hospital hadn't told me otherwise, I would've sworn I cracked my head open."

"Your head hurts?" She moved in close. Close enough he caught a hint of color in her eyes before she raised her hands to him. Angling the side of his head toward her, she framed his jaw with one hand while sliding her fingertips against his scalp. "I don't see any changes in the bruise patterns since we left the hospital. We've been running on fumes most of the day. I'm sure your body is just trying to get you to slow down. I can keep watch if you want to grab a couple hours of sleep."

His scalp tightened at the physical contact. At the way she kept her touch light. It shouldn't have meant anything, but for a man starved of the smallest comforts and pleasures since he'd lost everything, it hit harder than he'd expected. And he liked it—her touching him. "You noticed my bruise patterns?"

"Isn't that what partners are for?" Jocelyn moved to

retreat, only he wasn't ready for the withdrawal. "To notice each other's wounds and then poke and prod at them?"

Baker caught her wrist, tracing the edge of gauze across the back of her hand. Warning speared through him. Because just as he'd found himself reliving the worst seconds of his life back at the station, Jocelyn had her own regrets. Of not being there for her husband when he'd died. One touch was all it'd taken to send her running, and he didn't want that. For the first time in ages, he couldn't stand the thought of being alone. "I'm pretty sure if I prod your wound, you're going to bleed out."

Her breath hitched. "That's possibly the most romantic thing anyone has ever said to me."

A laugh took him by surprise, and he released her. A frenzy of feeling rushed into his hands, as though his body had been craving the feel of her skin.

"I'm glad you brought me here." She threaded an escaped strand of hair back behind her ear. Such a soft thing to do in light of all the weapons and armor she wore. A welcome contradiction to everything he thought he'd known about her. "I can tell how much you love this home."

"Home." The word tunneled through the driftlike haze clouding his overtired brain, but he forced himself to focus on the present. "Back at the station you said it takes years for lieutenants like Marc De Leon to rise up Sangre por Sangre's ranks, that the organization tends to protect them because of what they know. The cartel provides their lieutenants security, income, even compounds. But that they aren't untouchable."

"Yeah," she said. "There have been times when the lieutenants let the power and ego go to their heads. They take on their own agenda and use cartel resources as their own personal arsenal. I've seen it before. The soldiers—no matter how far they are up the ladder—are usually punished by upper management."

"You mean executed." He latched on to her arms as the burn of anticipation sparked beneath his skin. "If our theory about who planted that bomb at the station is right, that means the cartel ordered Benito Ramon to destroy evidence De Leon killed that woman. They know he stepped out of line, but they haven't put him down. Why?"

Jocelyn shifted her weight, the first real sign that the day was getting to her as much as it had to him. "I don't know. It makes sense they'd want to tie up that loose end before it unraveled their operation. Unless...he actually was ordered to kill her."

"We need De Leon to give us the name of the bomber." Releasing his hold on her, he tried to put everything he understood about the cartel into play. "And I think I just figured out a way to get Sangre por Sangre to stop protecting him."

Chapter Six

Life was starting to feel like a box of cookies.

Some she couldn't wait to bite into. Peanut butter. A really soft chocolate chip. Maybe a homemade Oreo. Others she'd always leave in the bottom of the tin. Peppermint. Orange. Even worse, orange peppermint. And this plan had an aftertaste that left a horrible bitterness in her mouth.

Jocelyn shoved the SUV into Park about a quarter mile from the house and cut the lights. It wasn't difficult to uncover Marc De Leon's home address, especially for Alpine Valley's chief of police. But being here—without backup—in the middle of the night pooled tightness at the base of her spine. She'd gone up against the cartel before. Using one of their lieutenants to flip on a bomber they believed to be the Ghost wasn't going to end the way Baker hoped.

"I don't see any movement or lights on in the compound," she said.

"Doesn't mean he's not there." A battle-ready tension she'd noted during the flashback that'd ambushed him at the station bled through his hands.

This was a bad idea. "Baker, I know you think you have to do this to find whoever blew up your station, but Socorro has ways of getting that information without—"

"Without what? Getting their hands dirty?" The muscles in his jaw ticked in the glow of the vehicle's control panel. "Not sure you know this, but most police work isn't done from a distance with unlimited resources and military equipment. Most of my job is climbing into the sandbox and uncovering the next lead myself. Marc De Leon is our best chance of confirming Benito Ramon is the Ghost, and I'm not leaving until he does."

Baker didn't wait for her response and ducked out of the SUV.

Damn it. He was going to charge in there with or without her. Maybe even get himself shot. Or worse. Jocelyn followed his silhouette to the front of the hood, then moved out of the vehicle. Taking on the cartel—no matter the angle—had only ever ended in blood. She wasn't going to let him walk in there unprepared. "Then you're going to need some of those resources."

Rounding to the cargo area, she punched the button to release the door. She flipped the heavy black tarp back to expose the full range of artillery at her disposal.

"You've been driving around with this back here the whole time?" His low whistle preceded Baker's hand reaching for the nearest weapon—an M4 automatic rifle. "I could have you arrested for some of these. You know how to use all this?"

Nothing like witnessing shock and awe when confronted with the fact the woman driving you around could do more than bake cookies. "It's all legal. Socorro operatives are licensed and trained with a variety of weapons. There isn't anything in this trunk I don't know how to handle." She gestured to the M4. "You'll want to be careful with that one. The trigger is sensitive. Extra magazines are closer to the back seat."

He collected what he could carry. "Why do I get the sense you've been holding out on me?"

"Funny coming from a man who's referred to me as a mercenary on more than one occasion." She armed herself with an extra magazine for the pistol holstered on her hip. More wasn't always better. Despite all of the resources and gear available, Jocelyn trusted herself over a gun in any situation. Because that was all she could count on at the end of the day.

"Yeah, well, I might have changed my mind over the past few hours." Baker threaded one arm through the gun's strap and centered the weapon over his sternum, barrel down like the good officer he was supposed to be.

She hauled the tailgate closed and locked the vehicle. Couldn't take the chances of someone else getting their hands on her gear. "You mean after I kissed you?"

"That helped." He seemed to be trying to steady himself with a few deep breaths. "You ready?"

"You really believe the only way to get to the Ghost is through De Leon?" Because the moment they crossed that property line, Sangre por Sangre would consider their visit an act of war. He had to know that.

He nodded. "Yeah. I do."

Her gut trusted his answer. It'd have to be good enough for her. She handed off a backup vest. "Then I'm ready."

They moved as one, keeping low and moving fast along the worn asphalt road. According to satellite imaging, the cartel lieutenant's property sat on the edge of a cliff looking down into Alpine Valley, though she could only see the front of the compound from here. Thin, modern cuts of rock, pristinely stacked on top of each other, created a seven-foot barrier between them and the main house. Hopping over the fence at one of the distant corners was the smartest strategy, but Jocelyn couldn't dislodge the warning in her gut. Like they'd be walking right into an ambush.

They each pulled back at the gate and scanned the interior of the compound. Heart in her throat, she stilled. No floodlights. Or any movement from a guard rotation. No signs of life as far as she could tell. Not inside the house, either. This didn't make sense. The cartel wouldn't leave their lieutenant unprotected. "There's no one here."

She set her palms against the gate and shoved. Metal hinges protested as the heavy structure swung inward. Something wasn't right. No security-conscious cartel operative would leave the gate unlocked. Jocelyn caught sight of a security camera mounted above her left shoulder, but the LED light wasn't working. Was the power out?

Baker paused before crossing over the threshold. "Guess that makes our job easy, then."

She didn't trust *easy*, but they didn't have a whole lot of choice here, either. She crossed beyond the gate. Every cell in her body ratcheted into high alert. Waiting for…something.

Thick fruit trees branched out from their line along the driveway and clawed at her exposed skin and hair as she headed for the front door. Pavers and old-world exposed beams created a feeling found nowhere else other than New Mexico. Drying chilis hung from beside columns built of the same stone as the wall they'd bypassed. Black sconces—unlit—stood as sentinels on either side of a wood double door. Marc De Leon was out on bail, but this place was a ghost town as far as she could tell.

"I don't like this," she said.

"I'm starting to understand what you mean." Baker nudged the toe of his shoe against the front door. It swung inward without much effort. "Ladies first?"

Once they stepped into the house, there was no going back. No reason she could give to Ivy and the rest of the team for explaining why she'd breached a cartel lieutenant's home without authorization.

Jocelyn centered the man at her side in her line of vision, but the shadows were too thick here. All she could see was that look on his face as he'd stood helpless in the middle of the station, caught up in the horrors his mind craved to process. It spoke of how little he'd let himself feel since losing his sister. His life had stopped moving forward that day the cartel had come calling. She could see it in the way he pushed everyone away, including her, in the way he committed himself to finding any angle, any strategy to catch Sangre por Sangre in the smallest infraction.

"You believe the Ghost is responsible for Linley's death." She wasn't sure where the thought had come from, but it explained a lot. Why he wanted to keep their little operation off the books, why he was so determined to get to De Leon.

Baker didn't answer, and he didn't need to. She already knew.

"Stay behind me." She unholstered her weapon and took that step over the threshold. For Baker. There was no end to the war raging in her head, but she could help him win the one in his. "Whatever happens, I want you to get yourself out alive. Socorro will help."

He didn't bother arguing. Of the two of them, she was by far the most trained, and they both knew it. Jocelyn tried to force her senses to catch up to the darkness, but all she could make out was a window detail cut into the entryway wall ahead of her. They were dead center in a long hallway, cut off from seeing the spaces straight ahead. This would be the perfect angle for an ambush—unprotected on either side. But nobody jumped out from the shadows.

Moonlight punctured through the windows to

her left, and she found herself stepping across dark-colored tiles in that direction for a better layout of the house. The entryway hall ended abruptly, revealing an oversized living room on the other side. This place was massive. Well over twenty thousand square feet. There was no way they'd be able to search it quickly. She memorized the configuration of individual sitting chairs and sofas. Untouched. Everything in its place.

"Where is everyone?" Jocelyn slowed her path through the living room to the kitchen visible through another window cut out at the end of the room. Her heart threatened to beat straight out of her chest as her reflection cast back at her from the large mirror angled over a stone fireplace spanning the entire wall.

A significant part of her work in the military and Socorro was based off being able to predict and anticipate the needs of those around her, and she'd jumped at the opportunity to take on Baker's personal demons instead of facing off with her own. But something wasn't right here. "We need to get out of here."

"Not yet." He made a move for the second entry into the living room, weapon raised. "He's here. He has to be here."

Baker was going off script. They were supposed to stick together. They didn't know what waited inside the house. They could be walking into a trap. Her brain grabbed for frantic imagines of her husband as Baker disappeared down the hall. Of Miles's head supported by that silky white pillow in the casket. Of the wrinkle she couldn't get out of his suit no matter how many times she'd tried. Of Baker's face replacing that of her husband's.

Jocelyn tried to suck in enough air to wash them out. It worked, but the pressure in her chest refused to let up. Holding her back. "Baker, wait."

The sound of shuffling cut through the darkness somewhere out of reach of her current position. She squeezed her sidearm between both hands. At the ready. Clearing the dining room, she moved into the kitchen. Another sitting room was attached to this space with a second set of furniture and a fireplace. She scanned every inch, but Baker wasn't here. "Damn it."

A breeze tickled the hairs on the back of her neck. She turned to face an open patio door.

And the silhouette waiting in the dark.

"Oh, good. You found the place."

A gunshot exploded.

Just before the pain took hold.

THERE WEREN'T ANY gunshots in his nightmares.

A groan worked through his chest. Baker eased onto his side. Cold floor bit into his skull and shoulders. Hell, his head hurt. A waft of smoke dove into his lungs and threatened to send him right back where he didn't want to be. Standing in the middle of his barn, taking in the aftermath of what the cartel had done.

He pressed one palm into the floor—no, this didn't feel like ceramic—trying to get his bearings. He rolled onto his back. And met nothing but a starry sky. Dirt infiltrated his clothing and worked under his fingernails. He was outside. The smoke was coming from his uniform. He blinked to try to get his brain rewired. The last thing he remembered was being inside the compound. How the hell...

"Jocelyn?"

"Is that her name?" an unfamiliar voice asked. "Sorry to say I didn't ask before I pulled the trigger."

Baker's instincts had him reaching for the weapon strapped against his chest. Only it wasn't there. He went for his service weapon. Empty. He rolled onto one shoulder, unable to get his hands under him. He'd been bound. Zip ties. The vest he'd borrowed from Jocelyn was suddenly much heavier than he'd estimated. His belt was gone, too.

Using his weight to his advantage, he got to his feet. Agony ripped through his head, and he doubled over before stumbling a couple feet and hitting what felt like a cactus with one hand. The sting spread faster than he was expecting.

"You're going to want to take it easy. Can't imagine two concussions in twenty-four hours will be a walk in the park." Movement registered from his right. Or was it his left? Hard to tell with his brain in a blender. An outline solidified as a vehicle's headlights cut through the night. "I'd apologize for the theatrics, but your showing up here left me with little choice."

Baker shielded his eyes against the onslaught, dead center in the headlight's path. His head pounded in rhythm to his heartbeat. The logical part of his brain attempted to catalogue distinguishable features of the man in front of him, but the added light only made it more difficult. "Who the hell are you?"

"That's not what you really want to ask me, Chief." The outline set himself against the front of the hood of what looked like a pickup truck. Similar to Baker's.

The headache was easing. Not entirely, but enough to recall he'd been ambushed the second he'd stepped into the hallway of Marc De Leon's compound. His fingers curled into the center of his palms to counter the heat flaring up his spine, but he couldn't keep the growl out of his voice. "Where is Jocelyn?"

"Inside." A slight shift of weight was all Baker managed to take in with the amount of space between them. "I'm not sure if she's still alive, but in all honesty, I needed her out of the way. To get to you."

Still alive? Panic and a heavy dose of rage combined into a vicious cocktail that had Baker closing the distance between them. "You better pray she's alive."

Something vibrated against his chest.

He froze, grabbing for whatever was lodged against his rib cage.

"That's close enough, Chief." The figure ahead took his own step forward. An LED light lit up the man's hand, and another vibration went through Baker. "You know what this is?"

Son of a bitch.

"I'm going to guess it's not a box of chocolates." Baker was forced to back off. He was still wearing the vest Jocelyn had lent him, but it'd been altered. Turned into a weapon rather than a protection, and he was instantly reminded of the woman Marc De Leon had tortured and killed. With a vest just like this. Packed with explosives. A touch of a button—that was all it would take for the bomber to finish what he'd started.

"Let me guess," he said. "You set the bomb in my station."

The man raised his hands in surrender, all the while pinching that little detonator between his thumb and palm. "To be fair, I didn't expect you to make it out of there. Otherwise I wouldn't have had to go to all these lengths."

"You're the Ghost. Sangre por Sangre's go-to bomber. Sixteen—well, now seventeen—incidents over the span of two years. All this time, we've been thinking a man named Benito Ramon was responsible, but that was just another alias, wasn't it? Marc De Leon." The bomber he'd been looking for. Who'd set the device that'd brought down his future and killed his sister. Undeniable grief and rage flashed through every fiber of his being. He dared another step forward. The vibrating intensified in warning. "You took everything from me."

"I never liked that name. The Ghost. Always gave too much credit where none had been earned." De Leon straightened, matching Baker in height. The lack of accent was telling. Baker had always found it out of place during their interrogations. Not born and bred from within Sangre por Sangre, but an outsider. A hired gun. A true mercenary who killed on orders and walked away with his pockets all the heavier. "But since we're getting to know each other, here's what's going to happen. You're going to get in the truck, and when I push this button, you're going to be blown to pieces and lefts for Albuquerque's bomb squad to put back together, and we can all live happily ever after."

Not a chance. "If this was your pitch to Ponderosa's chief of police, I gotta tell you, it needs some work."

"Let me ask you something, Chief." De Leon inched closer, within reach, though the headlights made it impossible to decipher the bomber's features out here in the pitch black. "When you found your sister's body, what was the first thing you did? Scream? Cry? Or did you just stand there staring at her, trying to find some semblance of the woman she'd been beneath all that burnt skin?"

A tightness in his throat threatened to wrench away his control. Baker pressed his wrists against the zip ties until the edges cut into his skin. "Shut your damn mouth."

"You think you're the only one who's lost someone to Sangre por Sangre?" De Leon lost a bit of aggression in his voice. "My friend, you don't know what pain is. They might've taken your sister, but you didn't have to watch her suffer. You didn't have to hear her screams while they held you down and made you watch as she begged for you to help her. You got off lucky."

"Lucky. Right. You know what? I do feel lucky." The fire that'd been driving him since finding Linley bound with a flaming tire around her neck threatened to extinguish itself. No. The man in front of him was not an ally, and Baker sure as hell didn't trust a single word out of his mouth. "You've obviously been keeping tabs on me. Knew I'd be here, looking for the man who could give up the Ghost. You might have even connected the dots. My sister was killed by the cartel with a device just like the one the bomb squad recovered. Stood to reason this incident might be connected to hers. Hell, you even called me by my first name. Like we're friends."

De Leon didn't answer, as though sensing the rising flood churning inside of Baker.

Baker took a step forward, ignoring the vibration from the device pressed against his midsection. "You probably think you know me pretty well. My habits, my motives. Who I've talked to, how I spend my free time. But do you know why I took the job as Alpine Valley's chief of police?"

"Wasn't hard to fill in the blanks," Deo Leon said. "Anyone with half a brain can see you'd want to use your authority to get to the cartel."

"See, now that's where you're wrong." Baker strained against the zip ties. "I took the job because I was afraid of what I'd do to the man who killed my sister and burned down my barn with her horses inside when I found him."

He took another step forward. "So you're right. I am lucky. I didn't have to wait my entire life hunting for you." Baker pressed his knuckles together and snapped the zip ties in one clean break. "You were stupid enough to come after me yourself."

De Leon's laugh penetrated through the low ringing in Baker's ears. "That's quite the speech, Chief. I like the theater with snapping the zip ties, too, but you're forgetting one thing." He raised the detonator between them.

"You think that little black box scares me?" Adrenaline dumped into Baker's veins. Out here in cartel territory there were no rules, but time didn't bow down to anyone. Jocelyn was injured, possibly bleeding out, and the longer he faced off with the ghosts of his past, the higher the chance she didn't make it out of this alive. He grabbed on to the bastard's collar and dragged him close. "As long as you and I are together, you won't pull that trigger. You'll just end up killing yourself in the process."

Baker cocked his arm back and rocketed his fist forward.

De Leon dodged the attempt, then again as he threw a left. "You don't want to do this, Chief. It's not going to end the way you think."

The momentum thrust Baker into the hood of the truck.

"You know what? I think I really do." He spun back, ready for an attack, but it never came. Frustration and an overwhelming sense of desperation to make this right burned through him faster than the flames had singed his skin at the station. Shoving off the truck, he aimed his shoulder into De Leon's midsection and hauled the son of a bitch off his feet.

They hit the dirt as one.

And an explosion lit up the desert.

The compound was engulfed in a dome of bright flames, black smoke and hurling debris less than a quarter mile away.

"No." De Leon pried himself out from Baker's grip and shot to his feet. "I was talking about your partner."

A fist slammed into Baker's face. Once. Twice.

Lightning struck behind his eyes as a burst of heat expanded out from the blast site, paralyzing him at the realization that someone he cared about had been lost to the cartel all over again.

Chapter Seven

Raisin cookies that looked like chocolate chips was one of the main reasons she had trust issues.

Jocelyn hurled herself through the open patio door.

Barely conscious, she let herself get sucked beneath the surface of the outdoor pool as a wave of flames splintered out from the house.

The explosion punctured deep under the water and pressurized the air in her lungs and ears. Bubbles raced upward from all the nooks and crannies of her gear and tickled her skin along the way. Chlorinated water drove up her nose and into the back of her throat, but she wouldn't inhale. No matter how much her body wanted to.

A submersive shift reverberated through her as debris rained down from above. Covering her head as best she could, Jocelyn tried to wait it out, but she hadn't caught a full breath before going in.

Something heavy hit the water.

She forced her head up just before a section of the compound's protective wall sank directly over her.

She kicked as hard as she could against the pool's bottom to get out of the way, but her gear held her down. The wall landed on her right ankle. Her muted scream echoed in her own ears as the wall's weight crushed down on the bones between her foot and calf.

Wrapping both hands around her thigh, she pulled as hard as the bullet wound in her shoulder allowed. Flames lit up the surface of the water and highlighted strings of blood floating out of the wound. She'd been hit. Now she was pinned beneath the pool's surface and running out of air. An entire pool of water battled for domination as she pulled at her leg again. The pain spiraled down into her toes and suctioned a larger percentage of air.

The harder she fought, the sooner she'd drown. Debris settled in the bottom of the pool, and she grabbed for something—anything—she could use to wedge beneath the stone wall. Dirt and rock dodged her attempts to placate her survival instincts. Fire flickered above her as the remnants of the house settled.

Her heart thudded too hard at the base of her neck. Each pulse beat stronger than the one before it until she was sure her chest might explode from the effort. Jocelyn pressed her hands to her vest, searching her own gear. The pain in her chest was spreading. Panic sucked up oxygen in the process. Black tendrils encroached on her vision as her fingers hit something heavy in her belt. Her baton. It was all she could think of.

Frantic to make the agony stop, she ripped the tactical baton free. With too much force. The steel slipped from her grip and disappeared into the inky darkness beneath her. Pinching her eyes closed, she tried to feel for it but met nothing but the coarse coating used to protect pools from cracking. It scraped against her knuckles and lit up her dying nerves.

Her toes had lost feeling. The sensation was spreading up into her ankle and taking hold, but she couldn't let herself pass out. The moment she gave up, her body's automatic functions would kick her lungs to inhale. She'd drown within seconds. No. She had to find that baton.

Seconds slipped through her fingers as she stretched her wounded arm. Her fingertips hit something cylindrical and heavy in the initial pass, but it slipped out of reach. The bullet had torn straight through her shoulder. If she could just extend a bit more—

Unimaginable pain ricocheted through her arm and into her neck. She lost the last reserves of air in a silent scream, sinking deeper. She tried to leverage her free foot beneath her, but the angle was all wrong. She had no strength here. Groping for the baton a second time, she couldn't ignore the crushing weight pressing against her chest.

She was out of time. Out of options.

Jocelyn fought against the drugging pull of heaviness and kicked at the section of wall on her foot. It wouldn't budge. This couldn't be it. This couldn't be how she was going to die. Because she hadn't really given herself a chance to live.

The days, weeks and months after Miles's death had been spent in pure survival. She'd shut down the part of herself that could connect with others on a cellular level while outwardly portraying a woman who was trying to pull her team together. Truth was she'd gone numb inside a long time ago. But the past twenty-four hours had given her a purpose. Something—no, someone—to focus on. A puzzle to solve. One she wasn't ready to give up on yet.

Jocelyn leveraged her free foot into the bottom of the pool and shoved off with everything she had left. It would have to be enough. The last few air bubbles shook free of her clothing and escaped to the surface as she forced her arm against the torn muscles.

Her fingers brushed over the top of the baton.

She wrapped her grip around the solid metal and extended it to its full length. There was a chance the steel would crumple under the weight of the wall, but she had to try. She wedged the tip alongside her trapped ankle and, using both hands, forced her upper body to do something impossible.

The wall shifted upward.

Feeling rushed back into her foot, and Jocelyn dragged her leg free. Relief didn't have a hold on her as the weight of her vest and weapons countered her one-handed strokes. Her insides were eating at themselves, the lack of oxygen shutting down organ after organ in an attempt to save energy for her heart, brain and lungs.

The very same armor she'd donned to protect herself would be what killed her in the end. Jocelyn tore at the shoulder of her Kevlar vest and loosened its hold. Its familiar weight was lost to the darkness creeping along the bottom of the pool. She couldn't think, couldn't remember what she had to do next. Her boots felt too tight. They had to go. She let go of the baton and pulled her backup magazines and weapons from her pockets.

In a last attempt at survival, she kicked at the bottom of the pool. The momentum carried her upward with the help of one hand grabbing onto what felt like a thin ladder.

She broke through the surface. And gasped.

Her chest ached under the influx in oxygen. Jocelyn clung to the side of the pool. Exposed skin was instantly assaulted by heat from all sides, but she couldn't convince her body to move. Someone had shot her and left her for dead. It was only when she'd regained consciousness on the floor of the kitchen that she'd noted the thin wires strung throughout the exposed rafters of the house. The ones connected to a similar device Albuquerque's bomb squad was currently trying to piece back together.

Only much larger and a whole lot more complicated.

If she hadn't woken when she had…

Jocelyn clawed her upper body over the edge of the pool and collapsed—face down—onto debris-ridden cement. Chunks of stone and what used to make up Marc De Leon's compound bit into her face. Hell, she hurt, but she couldn't stop now. "Baker."

He'd been in the house with her. But had he made it out alive?

Dragging one knee beneath her, she pressed herself up. The compound was burning right in front of her eyes. Embers raced toward the sky with thick clouds of smoke.

A rumble vibrated underneath her, and thin cracks split the cement beneath her hands. "Oh, no." The compound sat on the edge of a cliffside looking over Alpine Valley. If the explosion had been strong enough...

Jocelyn shoved to her feet. Her balance failed, and she stumbled into a low wall that'd somehow managed to survive the blast.

This whole area was on the verge of collapse.

They had to get out of here.

"Baker!" She forced one busted foot in front of the other. Making out the remnants of what was left of the kitchen, she maneuvered around a turned-over hood vent and crossed into a house on its last legs. An exposed beam crashed off to her left and decimated the fireplace from the sitting room off the kitchen. Old tile flooring threatened to trip her up as she tried to re-create the layout of the house in her head. She'd lost Baker somewhere between the main living space and the bedrooms on the other side of the house.

"Baker...can you hear me?"

No answer.

Her heart stuttered at the thought of finding him in

this mess. The house groaned under its attempt to stay standing, but another rumble threw her into a half-failing wall between the kitchen and dining room.

"Baker, we have to get out of here!"

Smoke chased down her throat and silenced her voice. No amount of coughing dislodged the strangling feeling of nearly drowning in a cartel lieutenant's pool. Glass and rock cut into the bottoms of her bare feet as she launched herself down what used to be the hallway.

He had to be here.

"Where are you?" Covering her mouth and nose with her soaked T-shirt, she stumbled through the house's remains, but there was no sign of him.

Except… She pulled up short of the hallway leading to the bedrooms. He must've turned left out of the living room when she'd gone right. Because there, in the middle of a section of broken tile, flames were in the process of melting something shiny and gold. Something familiar.

Her breath left her all at once, as though she were back beneath the surface of the pool. Trapped. Deprived. In agony. She grabbed for a piece of charred wood and knocked the police badge out of the flames. But no amount of staring at it changed the dread pooled in her gut. Jocelyn searched the surrounding hallway as another groan escaped from the home's bones. "No. No, no, no."

There was no point in denying it.

The chief had been inside the compound when the bomb detonated.

A POINT WAS coming where his head wouldn't be able to take much more.

Baker pulled his chin away from his chest. Pain arced down his spine as he dragged his head back. His skull hit something soft. Cushioning. Prying his eyes open, he stared out over his truck's dashboard. A hint of gasoline added to the burn of smoke in his lungs from earlier. Must've spilled some the last time he'd gassed up.

Pins and needles pricked at his fingers and forearms, and he moved to adjust. But couldn't. Two sets of cuffs slid along the curve of the steering wheel. "What the hell?"

It took a few seconds to kick his senses into gear. This was his truck, but he hadn't driven out to the middle of the desert... Jocelyn had.

Fractures of fire, an explosion and the hole in his chest tearing wider jerked him into action. Baker wrenched against the cuffs, digging the metal into the skin along his wrists. He always carried a set of handcuff keys on him. He went for his slacks, but the chains linking the cuffs refused to give. Just short of reaching his pocket. Pressing his heels into the floor, he tried to lift his hips to his hands, but it was no use. The seat had been moved farther up than he'd set it at.

A warm glow flickered through the pickup's back window, and Baker centered himself in the rearview mirror. Flames breached outward from what used to be Marc De Leon's compound. The structure was caving in on itself, lit up by dying fires. "Jocelyn!"

She'd been in the house. She might be hurt, suffering. He wedged one hand against the other and tried to slide the opposite cuff free, but it wouldn't budge. The son of a bitch who'd knocked him out had known exactly what he'd been doing. Baker thrust his upper body forward and licked the skin around the cuff on his right hand. Anything to get the damn thing off.

The Kevlar vest he'd borrowed from Jocelyn hit the steering wheel.

A muted beep issued from somewhere inside the fabric.

Baker's heart threatened to stop.

He pinched his elbows together, trying to get a view down the front of the vest, but it was too dark inside the cabin of the truck. He was still wearing the device. He hadn't gone through a whole lot of bomb training, but he knew any movement on his part—any shift in his weight—could set it off. Giving the bastard who'd ambushed him exactly what he wanted—Baker dead.

A flare burst from the scene behind him, and a thousand tons of grief and rage and loss knotted in the spot where his heart used to reside. He hadn't been there for his sister when she'd needed him the most. He wasn't going to sit here and lose Jocelyn, too.

Baker knew every inch of this truck. The Ghost had most likely stripped out the weapons and obviously had gotten hold of his keys, but the bastard wouldn't have been able to search every hiding place. Baker just had to figure out a way to get to them.

He tried to bring one foot up to leverage against the dashboard, but there was no room between him and the seat. Tugging one hand toward the center console, he jerked his wrist as hard as he dared. But the cuff wouldn't break. There was only one way out of here, and it would come with a lot of pain.

"You can do this." He had to. For Jocelyn. He'd sworn that day in the barn that he would see this through to the end, but he couldn't do that without his partner. No matter how incredibly frustrating her positivity and enthusiasm and outlook on life was, Jocelyn had somehow buried beneath his armor and taken over. They'd survived together. That meant more to him than anything else he'd known with his own deputies. Baker threaded one hand into the smallest opening on the steering wheel, grabbed hold of it with the other and set his head against the faux leather. "You can do this."

Taking a bracing breath, he pulled his wrist against the steering wheel frame with everything he had. The crunch of bone drilled straight through him just before the pain struck. His scream filled the cabin and triggered a high-pitched ringing in his ears. Every muscle in his body tensed to take the pressure off, but it didn't do a bit of good. Baker threw his head back against the headrest. "Damn it!"

The cuff slipped over his hand. Lightning and tears struck behind his eyelids as he drove his broken hand between the driver's side door and seat. The panel came away easily, and he pulled a backup set of truck keys from the hidden space. Along with a handcuff key. Exhaustion and pain closed in fast, demanding he shut down, but Baker wasn't going to stop.

Not until he knew Jocelyn was safe.

He made quick work of the second cuff and shoved the truck key into the ignition. The speedometer wavered in his vision, and he felt himself lean forward as the metric dashboard lit up. He paused just before the engine caught. What were the chances De Leon hadn't rigged the vehicle to blow as a backup plan?

Baker released his hold on the keys and stumbled from the truck. He couldn't risk it. Cacti and several acres of dry, cracked earth were all that stood between him and his partner. He took that first step. The device packed into his vest registered a beep. Then again as he took another step. Every foot he added between him and the truck seemed to anger whatever was packed against his ribs.

He clawed at the Velcro securing him inside the heavy material, but the damn thing wouldn't release. Warning shot through him. His entire nervous system focused on getting out of the too-tight armor while valuable seconds ticked away.

The house was crumbling a mere eighth of a mile away, and he couldn't hear any kind of emergency response echoing through the canyon below. He was all Jocelyn had. His own life be damned.

Baker pumped his legs as fast as they'd allow. His wrist was swelling twice its normal size, but he couldn't think about that. "I'm coming, Joce. Just hang on."

The flames were the only source of light a thousand feet above Alpine Valley. It would be impossible to miss them. Backup was coming. He had to believe that. He shoved through the front gate barely hanging by its hinges and up the now rippled paved path to where the front door used to sit. Jocelyn had been right from the beginning. They'd walked straight into a trap at his insistence, and now she was going to pay the price.

Just as his sister had.

The beeping coming from his vest kept in rhythm with his racing heart rate. Any second now, it would stop, but he'd do whatever it took to find Jocelyn before then.

The floor shook beneath him as the house fought to stay in one piece. Smoke fled up through the new hole in the ceiling, leaving nothing but an emptiness Baker couldn't shake. "Jocelyn!"

He forced himself to slow enough to pick out a response through the crackling flames licking up walls still standing, but he got nothing. He shouldn't have left her. They'd agreed to stick together because they hadn't known what they were walking into, but uncovering the link between Marc De Leon and the Ghost was the first real lead he'd had in months. It'd consumed him and wouldn't let go.

Now he knew the truth. He'd had the man who'd killed Linley within reach all this time.

Baker lunged back as a beam swung free from the ceiling and crashed into its supporting wall two feet ahead. Embers exploded from the impact and sizzled against his skin.

This place was falling apart at the seams, and unless they got out of here right now, they were going down with it. He shook his head to keep himself in the present. "Come on, woman. Where *are* you? Jocelyn!"

Another tremor rolled through the house.

Only this time, it didn't feel like it was from the walls coming down on themselves. Baker backed up a step, staring at the floor. A myriad of cracks spidered across the tiles. Most likely from the impact of the bomb, but his gut said that last quake was from something else. Something far more dangerous.

His vest hadn't given up screaming at him to get back to the truck, but the incessant beeping had become background noise to everything else going on around him. He took another step backward toward where he'd come in, watching one crack spread wider at his feet. The compound sat at the edge of a cliff overlooking Alpine Valley. This place wasn't just coming down on itself...

It was about to slide right into the canyon.

Panic welded to each of his nerve endings. He searched the rubble within arm's reach, then shot forward to clear as many rooms as he could. The living room, dining room, kitchen, patio—

He caught sight of the pool outside, nearly falling in as desperation to find something—anything— that told him Jocelyn was still alive took hold. That he hadn't condemned her to the same fate as his sister. But it was too dark, and the device's beeping had reached an alarming rate. He couldn't do a damn thing for Jocelyn if he suddenly became spaghetti. "The water."

The devices used in the Chief Trevino's murder and at the station had been triggered by pagers. If he could disrupt the signal, he might have a chance. Baker took a deep breath and launched himself into the pool feet first. The Kevlar dragged him straight to the bottom, and it took everything he had to claw back to the surface.

The beeping had stopped. Relief flooded through him. Whatever receiver De Leon had utilized to trigger the device had failed. Latching on to the side of the pool, he hauled himself to the lip. A footprint gleamed from a few feet away. Bare. No more than a size seven or eight. Jocelyn's?

A crack splintered through the cement in front of him.

A resulting groan registered from the ground. The split shot beneath the water, and a frenzy of bubbles escaped to the surface. Every cell in his body ordered him to move. What'd started as a hairline fracture widened until Baker had to swim to keep from getting sucked down into the cyclone forming in the middle of the pool.

Water drained within seconds, and he stabbed his toes into the wall for leverage. Only he wasn't fast enough to get out. Pain splintered through his broken wrist as he tried holding on to the edge with both hands to avoid getting sucked into the black cavern nine feet below. "Jocelyn!"

His fingers weren't strong enough to hold his weight. And he slipped.

Chapter Eight

She could give up cookies, but she was no quitter.

Jocelyn pumped her legs as hard as she could. Cacti and scrub brush tore at her soaked pants and threatened to bring her down, but she had to get the SUV.

It was the only way to warn Socorro of what was about to happen.

Tremors radiated out from where Marc De Leon's compound used to stand. The entire cliffside was about to slide into the canyon and wipe out Alpine Valley with it. They had to evacuate. She clamped a hand over the wound in her shoulder to distract herself from the pain, but it was no use. The bullet had torn through muscle and tissue and left her with nothing but a craving to numb out. She couldn't. Not now. Not again.

The SUV came into sight as she charged full force along the dirt road that'd once lead to the compound. Her head pounded in rhythm with her shallow breathing. She was almost there. She was going to make it. Jocelyn might not have been able to save her husband from the suffering and agony, but she could save those people down there.

Hitting the lock release on her keys, she slowed as the headlights failed to light up. She'd gone into the water. The mechanism had most likely shorted out. She pushed herself harder. Every second it took to get word back to Socorro was another possible life lost when the cliff crumbled.

"Jocelyn!" Her name tendriled through the focused haze. That voice. She knew that voice. It was enough to stop her short of the SUV and turn back to the flaming remains of the house.

"Baker?" A war raged behind her breastbone. He was alive! Within reach if she retraced her steps, but that need to bury the pain of not being there for her husband at his last moments held her incapacitated. Seconds distorted into frozen minutes as the ground crumbled beneath her feet. The cliff was failing. And it would take Baker with it if she didn't do something. Jocelyn cut her gaze to her SUV. It was right there.

But she didn't have time to warn the people of Alpine Valley and get to Baker, too.

"I'll make the choice easy for you." A fist rocketed into the side of her face. "You don't get to save either."

She hit the ground. The wind was knocked out of her as rock and dirt infiltrated the hole in her shoulder. She tensed against the kick headed for her rib cage. Her attacker's boot ricocheted off her kneecap and sent her body into overdrive. Jocelyn shoved upright with one hand. Hugging her injured arm close, she swung with the other. But missed.

"You're a fighter, aren't you?" The back of the bastard's hand swiped across her face. "Can't even be put down by a bullet. I'm impressed but in a bit of a hurry."

Momentum spun her to one side. Blood bloomed inside her mouth where her teeth cut into the soft tissues of her cheek. It took longer than it should have to recover, but she'd already been running on fumes. Adrenaline would only take her so far.

"Who the hell are you?" She stuggled to keep her balance.

"I've gone by a lot of names. Your chief of police called me a ghost." The dark silhouette with his back to the flames advanced. "But to my friends, I'm simply a craftsman."

The Ghost. The same bomber who'd killed Baker's sister?

"Your friends." She'd trained her body not to shut down in the face of danger, but the numbness was already starting to kick in. It cascaded from her fingers into her chest and blocked her ability to stay in the moment. And without that, she was nothing. "Sangre por Sangre."

"I'm curious. What made you think you'd be enough to take on an organization who pays back any strike tenfold in blood, Jocelyn?" he asked.

He knew her name. Had most likely researched her and her team. Read about her past. "Is that what this is? Payback for a Socorro operative destroying the cartel's headquarters?"

"That's a little above your pay grade." He turned his back on her, heading toward the compound. To finish what he'd started with Baker? "For now, walk away while you still can."

"The cliffside is about to collapse. Hundreds of people are going to die if we don't warn them to evacuate." Piercing pain burned through her side. The stitches. She must've torn them sometime in the last few minutes. Something warm and wet battled with the chill of pool water in her waistband.

"Blood for blood, Jocelyn." The bomber barely angled his head over his shoulder as he strode away from her. "The warning is right there in the name. Go home. You're going to need your strength before I'm finished."

Jocelyn dug her thumb into the bullet wound. Her nerves took care of the rest, sending feeling and another shot of adrenaline through her. She couldn't let any more innocent lives pay for her mistakes. Couldn't let Baker die. The weight would crush her.

"No."

She lunged. Grabbing for the bomber's shoulder, she dropped to both knees as he swung to face her and slammed her good elbow into his gut. He took the impact better than she'd expected. Right before arcing his fist into her face.

The world turned upside down as she landed on her chest. Her ribs couldn't take much more before they snapped. Jocelyn stared up at figure standing above her, and the first real tendril of fear snaked into her brain. She was supposed to be stronger than this.

"You really should've quit while you were ahead."

He reached for her. "Oh, well. I guess I could use you to my advantage after all."

Jocelyn rocketed her bare foot into his ankle with everything she had. His legs swept out from under him, and she rolled to avoid getting pinned beneath his body. His rough exhale was the only evidence she'd delivered any kind of damage, but she didn't have time for victory to take hold. Spinning on her hip, she secured the bastard's head between both thighs, then locked her ankles together. And squeezed. "I think you've done enough damage for one day."

He dug his fingertips into the soft skin of her legs to get free, but it was no use. His strangled sounds barely reached her ears. She was no longer ashamed of the thunder thighs other girls had teased her about in high school. Soon, they would be what saved Alpine Valley.

"You...need me." The bomber tried to pry her knees apart. Then lost consciousness.

Jocelyn unlocked her ankles from around each other and shoved back. He lay motionless on the ground, but the rise and fall of his back said she hadn't killed him. She thrust herself to her feet and ran for the SUV. Stabbing the key into the door lock, she twisted and ripped the door back on its hinges to get to the radio inside. "Socorro, this is Carville. Do you read? Over."

Static infiltrated the sound of her heart thudding hard behind her ears. She pinched the push-to-talk button again. "Socorro, this is Carville. Please respond."

"Jocelyn, what the hell is going on out there?" Jones's voice ratcheted her blood pressure higher. "There was an explosion at the top of the cliff. We need you to run logistics. Fire and Rescue can't get there in time. Where are you?"

She pinched the radio. "I'm already here. Listen, I don't have time to explain. It was a bomb, and the cliff is going to give out any second. We need to get everybody out of Alpine Valley. Now!"

Jocelyn didn't wait for an answer. She'd done what she could to raise the alarm. But Baker was still inside the compound. Tossing the radio, she pulled a set of cuffs from the middle console. The bomber was still there, lying face down in the dirt.

She centered her knee in his lower back and hiked each hand into the cuffs. "You're not going anywhere."

A burst of flame shot up from one side of the compound.

She raced across dry desert as her body threatened to fail. Blood seeped down her leg from the wound in her side, but she wasn't going to stop. Not until she got Baker out of here. Intense heat licked at her exposed skin as she wound through the front gate and back into the collapsing structure.

It was harder to breathe in here. "Baker!"

"Jocelyn?" His voice grew more frantic. Louder. Stronger. "I'm here! In the pool!"

She tried to keep her clothes and hands from brushing against the walls—afraid she'd take down what was left of the structure from contact alone—and cut through what used to be the kitchen.

She froze at the destroyed patio door.

A wide chasm split through where the pool should've been. The water was gone. The chunk of wall that'd pinned her to the bottom of the pool balanced precariously over a mini canyon before falling straight into the darkness. Her mouth dried. Had she been too late? "Baker!"

"Over here!" His voice cut through the panic setting up residence inside her and led her to the edge of the gap splitting the earth in two.

"Just hold on. I'm coming!" The chasm had widened to at least three feet and was growing every second she stood there, but she could make it. She had to. Jocelyn shuffled backward a handful of steps, then launched herself over the unending blackness. Glass and rock cut into the bottoms of her feet as she landed on the other side, but it wasn't enough to slow her down. Reaching the edge of the pool, she thrust her hand down. "Grab onto me!"

Baker's calloused palm grated against hers before it slipped free. He was at the bottom of the pool. Nine feet below her. He had to jump to reach. "You're too high!"

But there was nowhere else for him to go. The shallower the pool, the closer he'd get to the chasm tearing away from the canyon wall. She got down onto her chest, wedging her injured shoulder against the cement. "Come on. You can do it! Try again."

He jumped, securing his hand around hers.

Just as the cliffside gave way.

THE GROUND DISAPPEARED out from under him.

Baker leveraged his toes into the side of the pool, but it was no use. The rough coating merely flecked beneath his weight. He dropped another inch, threatening to take Jocelyn down with him. The pool was gone. Nothing in its place as the earth split in two.

"Hang on!" Her voice barely registered over the ear-deafening sound of destruction as rock, metal and cement gave into gravity. She clamped another hand around his and tried to haul him higher. "I need your other hand!"

He swung his broken wrist toward her, and she latched on. Agonizing pain radiated through his hand and arm. But his scream didn't compare to the compound slipping into the protective canyon around Alpine Valley.

Jocelyn somehow managed to drag him upward, high enough for him to get one foot over the edge of the pool. "Almost there."

Gravel and glass pressed into his temple as he collapsed face-first. Dust drove into his lungs. He fought for breath, but it was useless against the overwhelming tide of grief swallowing him whole. Staring out at the new ridge overlooking the town he loved, he willed the people below to survive. Though didn't know how they would.

"We were too late," he said.

Another tremor rumbled beneath them, and Marc De Leon's compound sank another foot into the ground. The entire structure leaned at an impossible angle, hiking Baker's nervous system into overdrive.

"We have to get out of here." Jocelyn shoved back from the edge of the pool with her hands and feet. No trace of enthusiasm or lightness in her expression, and he needed that slice of inner light. Just a fraction to counter the ramifications of Alpine Valley being crushed by thousands of tons of rock.

Dust kicked up and threatened to choke them both as they launched over the half wall blocking off the backyard from the house itself. Quakes seemed to follow their every step as they maneuvered around the perimeter of the compound. A gut-wrenching tremor divided the front of the house away from the back. The ground lurched beneath them, and Jocelyn fell into him.

"I've got you." He kept her upright as best he could while trying to stay on his own two feet. The chasm that'd split the pool in half had grown. There was no way to jump it, but they still had a way out. "We have to go over the wall. I'll give you a boost."

She didn't wait for an explanation as he bent down to clasp her foot. Blood stained his hand as he hiked her against the wall. Jocelyn turned back for him from the top, offering one hand. "Watch out!"

The ground shifted, knocking him off his feet. The cavity cutting through the backyard was inching toward him.

They were out of time.

Baker fought against the weight of the Kevlar vest packed with explosive and lurched upward. He caught Jocelyn's forearm, and together, they hauled his weight over the wall. But they couldn't celebrate yet. The crack in the earth was spreading. Darting right toward them.

They rolled off the top of the wall as one. Only Jocelyn didn't land on her feet. The thud of her body registered harder than it should have.

"Come on, Carville. We've got to move. This place is coming apart at the seams."

"I think I broke something." Her voice tried to hide the pain she must've been feeling, but he didn't miss it. Something was seriously wrong. Hell, she'd already survived two explosions. How much more could he possibly ask of her?

"Hang on to me." Out of breath, Baker threaded his broken wrist beneath her knees and dragged her away from the barrier crumbling two feet away. Meant to be a protective guard between the compound and the outside world, every stone was swallowed as the cliff broke away from the canyon wall.

The last remnants of the compound slipped over the edge as Baker collapsed with Jocelyn in his arms. The bomb had destroyed more than a single home. There had to be hundreds buried under rubble and dirt below. His heart strained to rip out of his chest as he considered the loss of life of the very people he'd sworn to protect. "It's gone. All of it…is gone."

"I'm sorry. I tried to warn them." Jocelyn framed one hand against his face. Cold and rough. Nothing like when she'd kissed him. Her voice wavered. "I… radioed my team…"

Her hand fell away, and every muscle in her body went slack.

"Joce?" He scanned her face in the bright moonlight. Then realized she was no longer wearing her vest. And noticed the blood. Wet, glimmering against her clothing. Oh, hell. The echo of a gunshot in his head rendered him frozen for a series of breaths.

Baker laid her across the desert floor, ripping at her T-shirt. There was a hole in her shoulder. She'd taken a bullet but somehow still managed to get him out of the compound in one piece. How was that *possible*? And where the hell was Maverick when Baker needed him? "Talk to me, Goose."

He couldn't think about all those lives down there in Alpine Valley with Jocelyn needing him right now. Struggling to his feet, he hauled her against his chest and started walking toward the SUV. Her added weight wiped his strength from him, and Baker collapsed to one knee.

Two bombs. Losing a fight to a cartel bomber. A device strapped to his chest. And now an apocalyptic event that'd destroyed everything he had left. All within twenty-four hours. He wasn't sure he could take much more, but he wouldn't leave Jocelyn out here to fend for herself. She'd saved his life. The least he could do was return the favor.

Baker bit back a groan when pain singed through his nerve endings as he regained his footing. A hundred feet. That was all he had left before they reached the SUV. They were going to make it. They had to. Because they'd survived too damn much to give up now. "We've got this."

But every step seemed to put them farther away

from the vehicle. Or maybe his mind had finally started shutting down from all the explosions going on around them. His clothing suctioned to him with Jocelyn's body heat furnaced against him. "Just a little farther."

He stepped on something that didn't belong. Metallic and light. Too far from the blast area. Maneuvering his partner out of the way, Baker made out a pair of cuffs lying there in the dirt. Open. Warning triggered at the base of his spine, as though he were being watched. Marc De Leon had left Baker for dead inside his own truck, but even though the son of a bitch's plan failed, that didn't mean this was over.

He set sights on Jocelyn's SUV. He couldn't trust his own instincts right then, but something was telling him getting in that vehicle would be the end of them both. Emergency crews would have their hands tied trying to dig residents out of the landslide. The SUV was the only way to get Jocelyn help in time. Baker took another step toward the SUV.

The explosion lit up the sky.

Heat licked over his skin and knocked him back on his ass. His head snapped back and hit the ground harder than he expected. Blinding pain became his entire world right then, and Jocelyn slipped out of his hold. It took too long for his senses to get back in the game despite his desperation to keep moving.

The threat wasn't over. He had to get up. Had to keep fighting.

Baker risked prying his eyelids open. The crackle of flames was too bright, too loud. His brain was having a hard time processing each individual sound, mixing it up with the pop and crack of those that'd burned down his life.

Jocelyn's hand moved to touch his between them, a simple brush of skin-to-skin. The past threatened to consume him from the inside. He felt as though he were about to leave his body, but the grounding feel of her kept him in one place.

Light reflected off her dark pupils as she set sights on him. The smile he'd once resented tugged at her mouth. "I've…got you. Always."

Adrenaline drained from his veins and brought down his heart rate as black webs spidered in his peripheral vision. Baker secured his hand around hers, and the constant readiness and vibrations running through him quieted for the first time in years. Because of her. "I've got you, too, partner."

Bouncing bright lights registered from over Jocelyn's shoulder. Flashlights? Baker couldn't be sure as he tried to force his body to move, but none of his brain's commands were being carried out. He'd given his fight-or-flight response permission to take a break, and now it would take a miracle to come back online. He gripped Jocelyn's hand harder. Then again, he was starting to believe in miracles. "I want an entire tray of cookies after this."

"Done." Her smile weakened as she slipped back into unconsciousness.

Heavy footsteps pounded against the desert floor. Closing in fast. Baker rolled to one side, ready to protect the woman who'd nearly given her life for him.

It took every ounce of strength he possessed to get to his feet. Then he raised his fists. He'd take on the entire cartel if it meant getting Jocelyn out of this alive. The bouncing flashlights merged into one. His brain was playing tricks on him, but he wasn't going to back down.

"Chief, is that you?" Jones Driscoll slowed his approach, a flashlight in one hand and a weapon in the other. Utter disbelief contorted the man's expression. Hell, Baker must've looked a lot worse than he'd thought.

The combat controller holstered his weapon and pressed his hand between Jocelyn's shoulder blades. "She's still breathing. Damn. You two sure know how to throw a party. What happened out here?"

"You mean apart from the fact a Sangre por Sangre bomber just destroyed an entire town in a landslide?" Baker stumbled back as the fight left him in a rush. His knees bit into the ground beside Jocelyn. "She saved my life."

Chapter Nine

Today would be a cookie dough day.

Because the beeping was back. The sound she hated more than Maverick's howls in the middle of the night. She was back in a hospital. Jocelyn lifted one hand, though something kept her from extending her fingers completely. She fought the grogginess of whatever pain medication the staff had put her on. Her breathing came easier when she couldn't feel, but it wasn't permanent. It couldn't be.

A low growl vibrated through her leg. Then something familiar. A metallic ping of ID tags. She turned her hand upward, fisting a handful of fur. "Maverick."

He was here. And pinning her to the bed with his massive weight. The German shepherd licked at her wrist before laying his head back down, and Jocelyn summoned the courage to force her eyes open. Only this time there were no bright fluorescent lights or bleached white tile to blind her.

She wasn't in a hospital.

Instead, black flooring with matching black cabinets encircled the private room. Socorro's medical wing. The overhead lights had been dimmed, and the beeping, she just realized, was definitely not as loud as it could've been.

"Thought you could use some time together after what happened." Baker's voice pulled her attention from her K-9 partner to the man at her left. Dark bruising rorschached beneath one eye and across his temple. There were other markers too—cuts and scrapes that evidenced what they'd been through. Though the splint around his wrist was the most telling of them all.

Jocelyn didn't have the will or the energy to try to sit up. "How long have you been sitting there watching me sleep?"

"About six hours." Baker got up from his chair positioned a couple feet from the side of the bed. "Dr. Piel—is that her name?—patched me up nicely, and hey, no waiting to get looked at. I think I might switch providers. Do you know if she takes my insurance?"

"I'm afraid she only sees private patients." Her laugh lodged halfway up her throat, stuck in the dryness brought on by aerosolized dirt and debris and ash. But there wasn't any pain—which, now that she thought about it, shouldn't have been possible.

Not as long as she'd been given the right painkiller.

Jocelyn followed the IV line from the back of her hand to the clear baggy bulging with liquid above her. Morphine. Dr. Piel wouldn't have known. Nobody in this building knew. She moved to disconnect the line from the catheter, but the moment she pulled it free, the pain would come back.

Maverick lifted his head, watching her every move. Not unlike Baker. He was intelligent, focused and observational. No one in their right mind would choose to go through unending waves of pain after what they'd been through rather than numb out with painkiller. Weaning herself off the meds now would only raise suspicion. And she couldn't deal with that right now.

"You okay?" Concern etched deep into the corners of Baker's mouth. "Do you need me to get the doctor?"

"I'm…fine." She tried recalling the events leading up to her arrival back at headquarters, but there were too many missing fragments. "Tell me what happened."

"Well, your warning worked." He moved to the side of the bed, sliding one hand over her wrapped ankle. The thin gauze around the joint said she hadn't broken it as she believed. More likely a hard sprain. "Socorro was able to evacuate nearly everyone who might be impacted by the landslide. Though that didn't stop the canyon wall from caving in. You saved a lot of lives, Joce. Without you, Alpine Valley would be in rough shape. Well, rougher shape."

Joce. He hadn't called her that before. It made her want to believe they were more than two people thrust together in the aftermath of a bombing, but her heart hurt at the idea. Of tying herself to someone else. Because when that tie broke—as they inevitably did—she would be right back in the dark hole she'd spent so long trying to climb out of. Just like she'd done after Miles's death. Her stomach twisted into one overextended knot. "Were there any casualties?"

"Not a single one." He shook his head, a hint of wonder in his voice. "You and your team, as much as I hate to admit it, really saved our bacon. Thank you, Jocelyn. For everything. If I hadn't rushed to find Marc De Leon, maybe none of this would've happened, and I'm so sorry for that."

"He killed your sister, didn't he?" she asked.

"Yeah. He did." Baker scrubbed a hand down his face, a habit he'd picked up on whenever he wanted to avoid a tough topic. It was a defense mechanism. Avoid the question to avoid the feelings that came with it, but it didn't make the hard things go away. At least, not in her experience. "I thought we would find De Leon and get him to identify the Ghost, but the explosive he packed into my Kevlar vest turned out to be the same blueprint for those used to kill Jane Doe three months ago. I had him, Jocelyn. All this time. I just didn't connect the dots."

Jocelyn bit back the urge to remind him of her warning before they'd gone into that house. A Sangre por Sangre lieutenant's compound had been attacked. The cartel would only take the event as an act of war. Sooner or later, they'd learn Alpine Valley's chief of police and a Socorro operative had been there, and then… The crap would really hit the fan. It was only a matter of time. "But?"

"I was so sure of myself, going in there." He shook his head again, much more aggressively as though to dislodge the theory altogether. "But something is off. The man we fought… He told me I didn't have to watch my sister die right in front of me, that I was spared that horror as she burned. Made it seem like he'd gone through all that himself. That he'd lost someone, too."

"Cartels like Sangre por Sangre experience infighting all the time. Hostile takeovers, executions for not following orders. Dozens of people have died in their attempts to claw to the top of the ladder." Her heart hurt. Which didn't make sense because the morphine was supposed to numb her from her scalp to her toes.

Jocelyn fisted her hand back into Maverick's fur. She needed to get out of here. To not be forced to stay still. To get her hands in some dough. "Or maybe, after everything you've been through, you want what he said to be true. Maybe, after all this time, you've been looking for someone who's been through the same thing you have."

"You could be right. Maybe everything he said out there was just another way to mess with my head. Unfortunately, Marc De Leon is in the wind. Nobody, not even his attorney, has been able to get a hold of him. The prosecutor is trying to go through the cartel, but it's looking like we've hit a dead end." He blew out a frustrated breath. "So far, he's managed to detonate three bombs without leaving much of a trace. From what I can tell, he was planning on blowing me up just like he blew up Ponderosa's chief of police."

Baker took up position at the side of the bed, the

mattress dipping beneath his weight and triggering a low growl from Maverick. "Cool it, Cujo. I got you out of your crate."

She scratched behind Maverick's ear. As much as it'd annoyed her in the minutes leading up to the explosion at the station, she found Baker's nicknames for the German shepherd the exact kick to get her out of the spiral closing in. "One of these days, he's going to make you wish you'd called him by his real name."

"One of these days?" Surprise glimmered in Baker's dark eyes and tendriled through the numbness circulating through her body. Hard to imagine a man like Baker being surprised by anything, but she'd somehow managed. "Does that mean you're not tapping out of this investigation?"

Jocelyn pressed her shoulders into the pillow to distract herself from the unpleasant thoughts waiting for a clear path through her mind. She'd fought them off this long. She could do it a while longer. She just had to concentrate and paste another smile on her face. "Hey, that guy blew me up, too, remember? I have as much a personal stake in this as you do."

"How do you do it, Jocelyn?" His voice dipped into a near whisper. "How can you stay so positive after everything that's happened?"

It was his turn to walk straight past the barriers she housed herself inside. Pinching the hem of the thin white sheet beneath her thumbnail, she sifted through a thousand answers in search of the one that would change the subject as quickly as possible. But her threshold for pain, for loss, for defensiveness had been reached long before they'd walked into Marc De Leon's compound. "It takes a lot of effort. A lot of forcing myself to look for silver linings on stormy days."

"Then why do it?" he asked.

"Because if I don't, I'm afraid of who I'll become." She'd been on the morphine too long. It was inhibiting her internal filter. "I'll go back to who I used to be. Hollow. Terrified of feeling anything real. I'll shut down, and without the sarcasm and baked goods, movie nights, Christmas parties and trying to bring the team together, I'm afraid they're going to realize I don't have anything to offer. No reason to keep me around, and I want to stay, Baker. I need to be part of the team. Socorro's team. Otherwise, I'll go back to..."

No. She couldn't. She couldn't give up that piece of herself. Not to him. Not to any of them. Nothing good had come of it before.

"Back to what?" Yet even as he spoke the words, he seemed to accept she wasn't going to answer that question. Baker interlaced his fingers with hers. A vicious scrape had scabbed over between his thumb and forefinger, arousing the nerves in her hand. "You run logistics for your entire team. You made sure soldiers got what they needed overseas. You fight for towns like Alpine Valley to get the resources they need in a crisis. I've seen it. You're vital to this operation." He swallowed hard. "If it wasn't for you, I'd be dead right now and half the people of this town would be buried under a landslide. Whatever you're afraid of, you're stronger than you think you are."

She wanted to believe him, with every ounce of

her being, she wanted what he said to be true. But that alone didn't make it reality. Jocelyn watched as another drop of pain medication infiltrated her IV line. "That was before."

His thumb skimmed over the top of her hand. "Before what?"

Closing her eyes, she lost the battle raging inside and let her eyes slip closed. "Before all I cared about was being numb."

JOCELYN HAD BEEN cleared to recover in her room.

Mid-morning sunlight infiltrated through the floor-to-ceiling window at his back and cast his shadow across Socorro's dining room table. Baker wasn't sure how long he'd stared at his own outline, willing his brain to produce something—anything—that would give him a clue as to where Marc De Leon had gone. And his motive for wanting him dead.

He replayed the bastard's words in his head too many times to count, until he wasn't sure which thoughts had been his own and which had belonged to the bomber. Baker leafed through Albuquerque's scene report from the initial bombing at the station. Nitroglycerin packed into a pipe bomb. De Leon obviously didn't care about the impact of his chemicals on the environment, but Baker couldn't actually name a cartel soldier who did. Newspaper dated over the past two weeks had been used as filler, but pulling fingerprints had been impossible.

The bomber had been careful. Most likely worn gloves. A brand-new car battery had been used to spark the initial charge, and the device had been triggered by a pager. In line with the other sixteen incidents accredited to the Ghost, including the bombing on Baker's property. Though he was looking at another dead end there. The company who'd manufactured this one had gone out of business years ago. A relic. No way to trace the purchase, and the number of the damn thing was registered to an unending list of dummy corporations. "Why trust an old piece of technology when you could get your hands on something guaranteed to go off?"

Why take the risk? Baker had been asking himself the same question for over two hours in front of a dozen crime scene photos scattered all over the dining room table. He'd helped himself to one of the prepared meals Jocelyn was known for—this one lasagna and a heavy helping of garlic bread and a citrus salad he hadn't touched yet. But no matter how much food he packed into his stomach or how many minutes he sat there with his eyes closed, the answer refused to surface.

The trill of dog tags cut through the headache building at the base of his skull. He was running on fumes, and he knew it. Awake for more than twenty-four hours. Hell, he shouldn't have been able to walk, but this was important. Cutting his attention to the German shepherd perched to one side, Baker bit back his annoyance. Maverick had followed him from Jocelyn's room. Though he couldn't think of a reason other than Baker had access to her food. "Are you allowed to eat from the table?"

Maverick cocked his head to one side and licked his lips. The K-9 really was something now that Baker got a look at him. Lean, healthy, warm brown eyes. It was any wonder Jocelyn had fallen in love with him, but how they'd ended up together was as big a mystery as why Marc De Leon had blown up his own compound.

Jocelyn worked logistics for the military. No reason for her to come in contact with explosive ordinance on tour. Which made Baker think they'd met through some other means.

"You protect her, though. That's why you nearly bit my hand off at the station."

Maverick pawed at the floor.

"You want to bite my hand off right now, don't you?" Baker collected his fork and took a stab at a section of lasagna, then offered it to the dog.

The shepherd licked the entire fork clean. Overhead lighting caught on the mutt's ID tags, and Baker got his first real look at them. "Those aren't military tags."

Maneuvering his legs out from under the table, he stretched his hand out. A warning signaled in Maverick's chest, and Baker stilled. No show of teeth, though. That was something.

"I'm not going to hurt you. Just want to look at your tags," he said. "I promise to stop calling you Cujo if you promise not to bite me while I do that. Deal?"

He inched forward again, slower this time. His fingers brushed against course black and brown fur at Maverick's neck, and the shepherd closed his eyes in exhilaration. The dog's tongue made an appearance as Baker targeted the area he'd noticed Jocelyn scratching in the med unit. "There. See? We're friends. You like that?"

He kept up the scratching with one hand and brought the other to the tags to read the stamped lettering: "Maverick. Federal Protective Service. Miles Carville."

An invisible sucker punch emptied the air out of his chest. More effective than any bomb he'd survived thus far. "Your mama wasn't the only one who lost someone, was she?"

Maverick's whine almost convinced Baker the dog had understood him. It made sense now. Jocelyn's husband had worked for the Department of Homeland Security, and when he'd died, Maverick would've been forced to retire, too. The relationship between handler and K-9 took years to cultivate, from the time the German shepherd would've been a puppy. Maverick wouldn't have responded to anyone else and ultimately would've become useless for the team once Miles Carville had died. But Jocelyn had kept him, literally kept a piece of her husband that followed her into the field and slept in her room at night. That protected her when it counted. "Damn, dog. I think I might be jealous of you."

"That's possibly the weirdest sentence I've ever heard in my life." Jocelyn leaned against the wide entryway into the kitchen, and hell, she was a sight for sore eyes. A few visible cuts here and there, but nothing that could take away that inner brightness that'd gotten him through the past day and a half.

His gut clenched at how much pain she must've been in. "You're supposed to be resting."

"Girl's gotta eat, doesn't she?" She limped into the dining room and dragged the chair beside his out from beneath the table with her good arm, then took a seat. "Besides, it's hard to sleep when you know the bomber you arrested in the middle of the desert got away. You find anything in Albuquerque's report that might give us an idea of where De Leon might've gone?"

Maverick moved in to be at Jocelyn's side, marking his territory. Funny—Baker felt inclined to do the same. To erase all the times he'd been such an ass to her over the past few months and give her a reason to feel again.

"Not a single clue." They were back at square one. "Bomb was pretty simple. Nitroglycerin explosive, a fresh car battery to initiate the spark, but there's one thing that doesn't make sense."

She reached over the crime scene photos and grabbed for what was left of Baker's dinner. "What's that?"

"The receiver was an old pager," he said.

Three distinct lines deepened between her brows as she sat a bit straighter. Warm brown eyes, almost the same color as Maverick's caramel irises, scanned the photos he'd set across the table. Setting down the fork, she picked up one image in particular. A photo of a motherboard. No transmitter on the once leprechaun-green chip. Just a receiver.

"You're right, but it fits with the Ghost's preferences," she said. "Harder to trace, maybe? Was the bomb squad able to recover a registered number?"

"Not yet." It was easy to look at her and see the

wheels turning. To know she was taking that incredible amount of knowledge she'd gleaned throughout her life to try to figure out why De Leon wanted him dead. Why after all this time, the Ghost had come back to haunt him.

Baker couldn't help but smile as she silently read something to herself. Despite her claim to have as much at stake in this game as he did, that simply wasn't true. She was here for him, and thank heaven for that. Otherwise he'd be at the bottom of that landslide or burned to the driver's seat of his truck. "They're still working through—"

"Let me guess. Dozens of shell companies." Leaning back in her seat, she took a bite of lasagna. Hints of exhaustion still clung beneath her eyes and in her slowed movements. Every shift in her body seemed to aggravate the corners of her mouth, but she wouldn't admit it. She'd never want him to know she was in pain, but not just that. There was something else she wasn't telling him, something she'd held back in the medical suite. Because she still didn't trust him. "I'm starting to feel like I've been here before."

"Chief Trevino's murder." Baker lost the air in his lungs. "Yeah. I had the same thought. By the way, Maverick licked that fork."

Jocelyn let the silverware hit the table. The metallic ping put a dent where it'd landed on the pristine wood, and understanding hit. There were no other dings in the table because nobody used it. All this time, he'd assumed Jocelyn's efforts to bond the team over Christmas breakfasts, birthday parties and family dinners had succeeded.

But the table said otherwise. She'd said she needed to be part of the team. Socorro's team. That she was afraid they'd have no use for her. Because nobody cared as much as she did. No one else made the effort like she did. She needed her team. Needed friends. A physical connection to this world.

"In that case, enjoy the rest of your food." She pressed away from the table, her long, ebony hair sliding against her back. "I'm going to get something from the fridge."

He'd never seen her like this before. The sight was surreal, as though he was witnessing the real her. Not what she wanted everyone to see. Not the logistics coordinator or the former solider. Just Jocelyn. Or, hell, maybe he'd hit his head a lot harder than he'd thought.

Baker tracked her into the kitchen, keeping his feet moving to close the distance between them.

"Don't say anything about how a dog's mouth is cleaner than mine." She wrenched open the refrigerator door between them and pulled a large metal bowl covered in plastic wrap, identical to the one he noted earlier, from inside. Discarding the wrap, she set the bowl on the counter and threw open a drawer to her left. She drove a spoon straight into what looked like a giant bowl of cookie dough. "I don't lick my own butt or chew on my feet."

"Good to know," he said.

She shoved an entire spoonful into her mouth and

seemed to sink back against the counter, completely at ease and absolutely beautiful.

Baker shut the refrigerator door and took the spoon from her hand.

Just before he crushed his mouth to hers.

Chapter Ten

A balanced diet consisted of a cookie in each hand. Or in her case a spoonful of dough.

But having Baker pressed against her was pretty damn fulfilling, too.

Her chest felt like it might burst open, and Jocelyn did the only thing she could think to do. She gave up her hold on the spoon. Sugar, butter, flour and a hint of peppermint spread across her tongue, but this wasn't the gross kind of peppermint. It was Baker. Kissing her. Deep and hard.

And she kissed him back. With every ounce of herself she had left. Because she felt something. As though she could breathe easier, like there was a life outside of her trying to force friendships and combating danger, secrets and grief. Despite all his sharp edges and barbed words, Baker's mouth was soft and determined and capable of washing the violence and fear out of her, leaving her utterly and completely defenseless against the past.

His hand found her waist, just shy of the wound in her side. He was being careful with her, didn't want to cause her any pain, but life never guaranteed there wouldn't be pain. Just that it had to be worth living.

Baker eased his mouth from hers, rolling his lips between his teeth. "Is that the cranberry-lemon dough you've been trying to get me to try?"

"Yeah." Her breath shuddered out of her. Uncontrollable and freeing. She'd only kissed one other man in her life. She and Miles had been high school sweethearts, marrying straight out of basic training before he'd gone to work for the Department of Homeland Security. He had always been able to knock her for a loop, but this... This was something she hadn't expected. Easy. And she desperately wanted easy. Free of fear and grief and expectation.

"It's really good," Baker said.

Jocelyn worked to swallow the taste of him, to make him part of her. The effect cleansed her from the inside, burning through her and sweeping the last claws of the past from her heart. She'd loved her husband. Deeply. And she should've been there at his last moments. But punishing herself day after day didn't honor him. That wasn't the kind of legacy he deserved. "It's even better when it's baked."

"Not sure it could get much better." Baker pressed his mouth to hers a second time, resurrecting sensations she'd forgotten existed. His hands threaded into her hair as though they both might fall apart right there in the middle of the kitchen if he didn't.

A profound shift triggered inside of her, reminding her she was more than a grieving widow, more than an operator for the world's best military contractor. More than her mistakes and flaws. Baker Halsey reminded her she was a woman. One who still had a lot of living to do. Here. In Alpine Valley. "You have no idea what I'm capable of."

A laugh rumbled through his chest and set her squarely back in the present. They'd just made out in Socorro's kitchen, in plain view of anyone who might've walked by. Jocelyn pressed her fingertips to her mouth to keep the smile off her face, but the effort proved in vain.

"Are you going to run away again?" Baker added a few inches of distance between them. "You know, like after I touched you."

"What? No." Her brain scrambled for the words to describe what she'd felt when he'd kissed her, but she was still wrapped up in the heat sliding through her. "This… Things are different between us now than they were then. And that kiss…" Jocelyn scanned the hallway just outside the dual-entrance kitchen. "It was not unpleasant, sir."

"Oh, good. 'Cause I'm a little out of practice. Other than when you kissed me back at the station." The tension in his shoulders drained, and right then she couldn't help but think another invisible scale of his armor was shedding before her eyes. "I didn't hurt you, did I?"

The reminder shot awareness into the wounds and threatened to break whatever this spell was between them, but she didn't feel any pain. There was still a hint of morphine left in her body that would take a

few hours to burn off. Blissful numbness that only
Baker seemed to penetrate.

The thought pulled her up short. She'd lost her
ability to feel because of the loss of one man and had
sworn never to go back to that shell of a life. What
would happen if she lost another?

Jocelyn forced herself to step back to give her brain
a chance to catch up. It was the painkiller throwing
the promises she'd made herself out the window. It'd
stripped her of her internal fight, but she couldn't lose
herself now. Not with a bomber on the loose. "Has
Albuquerque PD recovered anything from the landslide?"

They'd been so caught up in trying to locate Marc
De Leon, she'd let her focus be pulled in a thousand
different directions. The cartel lieutenant had been
charged with murder by Alpine Valley PD. The bomb
planted in the station had destroyed any evidence
the prosecutor could leverage against him. Though
it was starting to look like De Leon was working his
own agenda, they couldn't overlook a direct tie to
Sangre por Sangre.

"Not yet. I've got my deputies trying to help when
they can, but that's hard when they're stuck working
out of the rec center. Seems those volleyball players
aren't as nice as they look when it comes to sharing
the building." Baker slid his hands into his jeans,
and it was only then she realized he'd changed out
of his uniform. So this was what he looked like outside of his job.

A laugh escaped. But this time it wasn't forced. It

took her a few seconds to comprehend that unremarkable detail. Everything about her had been forced over the past two years…everything but this. "I guess it's a good thing you're stuck here with me, then."

The humor drained from his expression. "I'm not stuck, Jocelyn. I'm choosing to be here. With you. Because you're a good partner, and you deserve to have a team that supports you. Not out of obligation, but because they want to."

"What makes you think I wouldn't get that from Socorro?" If she had a tell, it would be all over her face right then. Uncomfortable pressure lit up inside her chest to the point she wasn't sure if her next breath would come without physical orders.

"The dining table." Three words that didn't make sense on their own but drilled through her harder and faster than the pain she'd run from. Baker reached for her, and an engrained shift had her accepting that touch. Needing it more than she'd needed anything ever before. "You talk about brunches and birthday parties. Thanksgiving and dinners together. Movie nights and all those types of things. But there isn't a single scratch or ding in that table except the one you just put there a few minutes ago."

Her mind raced for memories of Cash, Jones, Scarlett, Granger, even Ivy, having her back. "We're military. We watch after each other. No matter what."

"But which one of them would talk to you about your husband, Jocelyn? Which one of them would jump into the fray with you if the bullets weren't flying?" he asked.

And she didn't have an answer.

"I know you're hurting more than you let on. I know what lengths you have to go to to find the silver lining in all of this, but did you ever consider all you're doing is constantly escaping?" His words punctuated with experience she didn't want to recognize. They weren't the same. They hadn't been through the same experiences, but there was a line of connectedness she felt with him. A shared loss that linked them more than she'd ever expected. "Sooner or later, your positivity isn't going to be enough. Your mind and your body are going to force you to process everything you're running from, and you're going to need someone to be there for you."

Truth hit her center mass. He was right. She knew it, and maybe her desperation to bring the team together had been out of some kind of preparation for what waited on the horizon, but it wouldn't be today. Today they had a bomber to find.

Jocelyn straightened a bump in his T-shirt collar with her uninjured hand. "And here I thought you were nothing but a grumpy cop who'd rather save the world alone rather than trust anyone again."

His smile cracked through the intensity of the moment. "Yeah. Well, I guess you surprised me, too."

"Thank you. For having my back out there." She slid her palm over his heart. "And in here."

"You got it, Goose." His gaze locked onto her, and it took her a few moments to remember what it felt like to be fully grounded in the moment. To feel Baker's pulse beneath her hand, his warmth and strength. It was almost enough to bury the shame of the past. Almost.

"Not sure if you know this," she said, "but most women don't like nicknames that relate to overly loud pests of the sky."

"You can't expect Maverick to fly without his wingman." He motioned to the shepherd currently serving himself the rest of Baker's lasagna on his hind legs.

She was going to regret letting him have cheese. "Isn't Goose the one who dies?"

"Yeah, well. Eventually." He was trying to backtrack, and Jocelyn was going to let him keep digging that hole just to watch him squirm. It was endearing and human. Like a reward for all of her hard work to break through that tough shell over the past few months. "But they had a good run."

"If you two are done feeling each other up, we've got a problem." Jones Driscoll rounded into the kitchen, a tablet clutched between both hands. The scar running through his left eyebrow dipped lower as he scanned the screen. "Albuquerque's bomb squad is in the middle of going through what they can dig out of the landslide and what's left of your SUV. So far, they're convinced all three bombs were designed and detonated by the same bomber."

And just like that, they were thrust back into reality. Jocelyn severed her physical connection from Baker. "I'm wondering if you know what *problem* means, Jones?"

"They found a body," the combat controller said.

Baker cut his attention to Jocelyn, and her entire body lit up at the hundreds of possibilities of who else had gotten caught up in this mess. "There wasn't anyone else at the scene. We searched the entire compound."

Jones handed off the tablet. "Then you missed someone."

Jocelyn scanned through the report, horrified as a positive ID matched the burnt remains photographed at the scene. "Marc De Leon. I don't understand. He was the bomber. Why would he go back into the house?"

"He didn't. The coroner is examining the remains as we speak." Jones swiped the screen to bring their attention to a close-up of the body. "According to her, Marc De Leon was dead at least four hours before the bomb detonated."

Baker slumped against the counter. "Then who the hell is trying to kill us?"

IT WASN'T POSSIBLE. He'd been face-to-face with De Leon. He'd talked with the son of a bitch.

But there was no arguing with forensics. Baker had scoured through sixteen bombing reports a dozen times. Didn't change a damn thing. The man he'd wanted for his sister's murder was already dead.

He swiped steam from the mirror. No amount of hot water and soap had cleaned the gritty feel of ash and dirt on his skin, but it'd somehow managed to calm him enough to start thinking clearly.

What the hell had he been thinking to sign up for this job? To believe he could make a difference in people's lives? That he could protect the very town that'd welcome him as one of their own? He didn't have any prior experience. He'd never been through the police academy or basic training. Hell, he'd had to teach himself how to hold and fire a weapon from the internet, a secret that would die with him. He'd taken the chief of police position mere weeks after Sangre por Sangre had burned everything he'd loved to the ground, and the world had been so black and white. All he'd had was a promise. To protect Alpine Valley when no one else was stepping up to the plate.

But now… He wasn't the man for this job. And revenge wasn't enough anymore. Cartel raids, two-faced deputies, dead bodies, bombs going off everywhere he stepped—it combined into an undeniable sense of failure. He hadn't been able to stop any of it. And now the only light he'd found at the end of the tunnel had been snuffed out. He'd stepped into the middle of a war that had no end. Day after day, Sangre por Sangre and organizations like it were gaining power all across New Mexico—this place he loved more than his childhood home.

Who was he to stand up against a monster like that?

Memories infiltrated the hollowness pressing in on him from every angle. Linley smiling over her shoulder as she took her first ride around the horse ring. He'd never seen her smile like that. Never seen her so damn happy. He'd known then they'd never be able to walk away from the dream they'd built together. That they'd each found what they'd been looking for. In each other, and here, in Alpine Valley.

But it wasn't enough. Not anymore.

Baker made quick work of drying off and changing into a fresh set of sweats one of Jocelyn's teammates had lent him. The T-shirt was a bit too big, though, to the point that he looked like a toddler dressing up in his daddy's clothes. So he tugged it off, mindful of the aches and pains in his torso as he reentered Jocelyn's bedroom.

The space wasn't much bigger than a hotel room, and the dim lighting within it failed to compete with a massive bay windows that looked straight over the tail end of Alpine Valley. The sun had crept into the western half of the sky. The landslide was hidden at this angle, saving him a small amount of torment, but sooner or later, he'd have to face his failure.

Fire and Rescue, the bomb squad and his deputies were going through the rubble. Part of him wanted to be there with them, getting his hands dirty, searching for anyone who hadn't been able to evacuate. But the other part understood the sooner they found the bomber, the sooner this nightmare would end.

"It's not your fault." Jocelyn's voice slipped from the shadows and surrounded him as though she'd physically secured him against her. Warm, soft, accepting. "What happened up on that cliff. Neither of us could've stopped it."

Baker let his gaze settle on the scrap of land that had once held his entire future. "You and I both know we can tell ourselves we aren't at fault. Doesn't make it true."

"That goes both ways, Baker." She took up position beside him, the backside of her hand brushing against his. "We lie to ourselves just as easily."

She had a point.

"I don't know where to go from here." The longer he stared through the window, the less his eyes picked up the small differences of his property. Until he lost sight of the house altogether. "I was so sure I could protect this town, that I could stop the cartel from doing to someone else what they did to me, but I'm just one man. I've got two deputies heading for retirement, one six feet under from collaborating with the cartel, no police station, no dispatcher and a quarter of Alpine Valley under mud, rock and metal."

His laugh wasn't meant to cut through the tension cresting along his shoulders. It was a manifestation of the ridiculousness of that statement. He was supposed to be running a bed and breakfast with his sister, corralling horses, leading tour groups and making the stack of recipes he'd grown up on. And now he'd actually partnered with the very people he blamed for adding fuel to the cartel flames.

Baker half turned toward her. "This is where you tell me to look at the positives and list them out. Because that's the only way I see a way out of this."

"I don't think I can do that." Her voice seemed to scratch up her throat. "Truth is, the longer I'm with you, the more I realize my positivity has been nothing but toxic. For my team, for the people down there relying on us, for Maverick, even. I told myself if I could just focus on the good things going on in my life, they would be enough to drown out the bad, but partnering

with you… I don't want to pretend anymore. But at
the same time, you're right. There isn't anybody here
who would talk to me about my husband, about what
it felt like to lose him."

"You haven't told any of them." He wasn't sure
where the thought had come from, but he knew it to
be truth the moment he voiced it.

"No," she said. "But I'm sure Ivy knows. She runs
extensive background checks on all the operatives. It's
her job to ensure the safety of the team. It makes sense
she would know about the threats each of us carry."

"Grief isn't a threat, Jocelyn." The irony of that
statement wasn't lost on him. Because he'd buried his,
too. He'd taken everything he remembered about his
sister and replaced it with a dark hole that vacuumed
up any unwanted emotion so they couldn't hurt him.

"Isn't it?" She faced him, and Baker suddenly
found himself missing that wide smile he caught
her with every time they'd come across each other
in town. "Losing our loved ones altered our entire
beings. There are studies that prove traumatic events
such as ours physically change our genes and can be
passed down through our prodigy. It lives within us,
clawing to get free at any chance our guard is down.
It waits for just the right moment to sabotage us, and
I can't afford for that to happen in the middle of an
assignment."

"So you keep it to yourself. Pretend it doesn't bother
you." Just as he'd done all this time. Though it was
becoming clearer every day he stayed away from the
barn that he and his sister had built with their own

hands that Linley deserved better. She deserved to be remembered. The good and the bad. No matter how much it hurt. Because living as an entirely different person obviously hadn't worked out the way either of them had hoped. "What if tonight, we don't pretend anymore?"

"What do you mean?" Her hesitation filtered into the inches between them, thick enough for him to reach out and touch.

"I read Maverick's dog tags." Baker skimmed his thumb along her jaw, picking up the slightest change across her skin through touch alone. It was all he needed for his brain to fill in the gaps. As though she'd become part of him. "I know he was your husband's bomb-sniffing dog up until he died. DHS most likely wanted to retire him after your husband's death, maybe even send him to a shelter, but you brought him back home."

Jocelyn didn't answer for a series of calculated breaths. "When Miles was admitted to the hospital for the last time, it was because he collapsed in the middle of an assignment. The cancer had gotten into his bones, and there was no treatment—nothing— that would reverse the damage. Maverick was the one who got him to safety, then lay by Miles's bed until his final moments." She swallowed hard. "He wouldn't obey the commands of any other operatives. It got to the point Maverick became aggressive if anyone came close to my husband's body. Even handlers he'd worked beside in the field, but most especially the nurses. He hated them."

Her laugh slipped free and settled the anxiety building in his chest. "The hospital wanted Animal Control brought in so they could remove the body without getting bitten, but Mile's superior asked them to hold off as long as possible. Looking back, I think Maverick was waiting. For me."

Her voice warbled, but the dim lighting kept Baker from seeing her tears. "He waited there without food, without water or sleep. Protecting the one person who loved him most in the world, and I will always be grateful for that. It's hard to imagine he has any of those same feelings for me, but after Miles died and we were learning to live without him in our lives, I got so sick. To the point I couldn't get out of bed most mornings. I wasn't eating or sleeping or able to live up to my duties. Maverick was the one who pulled me out of the darkness and gave me the courage to take an opportunity we could both benefit from."

"One that brought you to Socorro," Baker said.

"Yeah." She craned her head to one side, presumably watching the German shepherd sleep in his too-small dog bed set up in one corner of the room. "He helped me get back on my feet. Though we both knew we couldn't go back to the way things were. I'd never be able to leave him behind if I got called up, and he couldn't go back to DHS, even with a handler he knew. We both had to figure out a way to move on. Without Miles. And for all the trouble he gives me, I know he loves me, too."

Baker angled his hands onto her hips and dragged

her close as a feeling of empathy and desire and attachment burst through him. He notched Jocelyn's chin higher with the side of his index finger and pressed his mouth to hers. "Does this mean I'm competing for your affections with a German shepherd? Because I feel now is the time to tell you I'm not really a dog person."

Chapter Eleven

Today she would live in the moment. Unless it was unpleasant. In which case she'd eat a cookie. Jocelyn stretched her toes to the end of the bed, coming face-to-face with the man tucked beneath the sheets beside her.

Sensations she hadn't allowed herself to feel since her husband's death quaked through her as memories of her and Baker's night surfaced. It'd been perfect. He'd been perfect. Respectful, careful and passionate all at once. They'd held each other long past cresting pleasure and fallen asleep secure in the moment.

She'd done it. Taken that first step toward moving on. For the first time since receiving the news Miles had passed, she felt...liberated. The weight of guilt and shame and judgment had lost its hold sometime between when Baker had kissed her and now. She'd almost forgotten how to breathe without it.

Early morning sunlight streaked across the sky, and while she normally liked to lie in bed to take it in, she couldn't tear herself away from the harsh beauty of the man beside her. The bruising around his temple was starting to turn lighter shades of green and yellow. The tension had bled from his expression. No longer the high-strung chief of police, she was getting a full view of the man beneath the mantle. Just Baker.

Jocelyn traced her thumb along his lower lip, eager to feel his mouth on hers once more. But she'd let him sleep. That seemed to be the only place he felt safe after everything he'd survived. His skin warmed under her touch, as it had last night, and she couldn't help but lose herself in this moment. One where they had permission to be still—content, even. Where the world didn't demand or push or threaten. She couldn't remember the last time she'd just let herself…be. Always afraid the bad thoughts and feelings would find her if she slowed down enough to let them in.

It'd taken a while to figure out that keeping her hands busy and her mind engaged distracted her from the heaviness she carried. It'd been a lifeline for so long, she couldn't actually remember what it felt like to live in the moment. But this… This was different. This was easy. Comfortable. Watching Baker sleep somehow hijacked her brain into believing she was safe here. With him. Her chest incrementally released the defensiveness always taking the wheel, and for the first time in years, she let herself relax. Because of him. Because of his willingness to take on her grief, to share it with her, to lighten the load.

And she'd done the same for him. Listened to his stories about his sister, of the two of them growing up back east and all the trouble they'd gotten into being so close in age. Only eleven months apart. About how once their mother had passed, their father had remarried and started his life over with a new family. Forgetting what he'd already had.

Maverick's dog tags rang through the room.

"Oh, no. Maverick, stop!" Jocelyn tossed her covers and hit the floor to intercept the shepherd. Too late. The overly loud ping of Maverick's bell pierced through the silence. And she froze.

"I'm up!" Baker shot upright in the bed. Every delicious muscle rippled through his back and chest as he reached for the weapon stashed beneath his pillow, and he took aim. At her.

Jocelyn raised her hands in surrender, her heart in her throat. "We're not dying. It's just Maverick. He needs to go out."

"Maverick?" Seconds split between heavy breathing and the pound of her pulse at the base of her neck. His gun hand and weapon collapsed into his lap. "For crying out loud."

"Sorry. I tried to beat him to it." She twisted the bedroom door deadbolt and let Maverick into the hall. He'd find his way outside through one of the dog doors before heading to breakfast with the other K-9s. Closing the door behind her dog, she padded to Baker's side of the bed. "I wanted you to be able to sleep a bit longer."

He leaned back against the pillows, and she went with him. "Well, that's out of the question now."

She settled her ear over his chest as the sun brightened the sky on the other side of the window. Pulling the comforter over them, Baker tucked her into his side until they breathed as one. She felt her heart rate settle back into comfortable territory, as though every cell in her body had attuned to every cell in his. Funny what surviving two bombings and fighting for each other's lives did for a relationship.

A relationship.

She hadn't really considered the words until now. Was that what this was? When the investigation ended and they had this new bomber—whoever he was—in custody, would they still have this? Or had last night been a one-time moment of comfort?

Ever since she'd lost Miles, she'd been running from this exact encounter. But now, relearning how to be close to someone, relearning how to trust and love meant it could all be taken away. By illness, by betrayal and the kind of work she did. But her soul craved that connection, and denying it would only make things worse.

Jocelyn committed right then. To make this moment last as long as possible. To not let the past infiltrate the present. No matter how much it hurt to let go. "What happens now, Baker? After all of this is done. What do you see happening between us?"

"Guess I haven't given it much thought," he said. "But I want this to be honest. I like you. More than I thought I could like a mercenary." He took her elbow to his gut with ease, his laugh filling not just the room but the empty places inside of her. The ones she'd denied existed. "Truth is, I'm not sure I could go back to the way things were. You on one side of the divide. Me on the other. We're a team. And I want it to stay that way."

A light that had nothing to do with the sunrise flooded through her. Not forced or created out of a sense of survival. Genuine warmth that could only come from one source. Hope.

"Me, too." But he wanted this to be honest. Something she wasn't sure she could reciprocate. Because the moment she admitted her darkest shame to him, she'd have to face it herself. And she wasn't ready to lose what they had. Not yet.

She ran her fingertips up his forearm, to the measure of warped skin spanning from his elbow to his wrist. She sat up, angling across his lap to get a better look. "What's this?"

"A burn scar." His voice scraped along his throat, barely audible. "Got it the day I found Linley in the barn. Most of the structure was still standing by some miracle, but one of the beams failed when I was inside. I tried to protect myself with my arm. Ended up with this piece of art."

"Marc De Leon had scars like this—burn scars. I remember them from his arrest photo." She memorized the rise and fall of the pattern burned into his arm as pieces of the puzzle they'd taken on flirted at the edge of her mind. Her instincts pushed her out of the bed and had her reaching for her rob draped across the end. She cinched it as carpet caught on the laceration across the bottom of her heel and threatened to slow her down, but this was important.

"Yeah. I catalogued them after the arrest. Scars,

fingerprints and tattoos. It's standard protocol so we can register him with the National Crime Information Center, but what does that have to do with anything?" The bed creaked under his weight as he sat up.

Jocelyn shuffled through the file she'd put together on the cartel lieutenant. ATF believed Marc De Leon had been recruited as an adult and risen up Sangre por Sangre's ranks in large part due to his proclivity for brutality and following orders to the letter. But he'd made a mistake. He'd killed an Alpine Valley woman three months ago. Jane Doe. He'd stepped out of line. But what if it hadn't been a mistake? What if it'd been a pattern?

She pulled a photo of Jane Doe free from the file, noting charred skin, curled limbs and missing teeth. An entire legacy of violence and death. Marc De Leon hadn't just killed the woman. He'd made her unrecognizable. To everyone but who he'd wanted the message sent to. "When was Linley killed?"

"Two years ago." Baker slipped free of the bed and reached for the sweats piled on the floor. "Why?"

"Cartels like the misery they cause. They use fear and grief and pain to keep towns like Alpine Valley in line and unwilling to turn on them. That's why they came after your sister. The soldiers who burned down your barn and murdered Linley knew you weren't there that day. They wanted you to see what they'd done." She spread out the photos taken of the scene where Jane Doe had been recovered. A tire had been strung around the victim's neck—just like Linley's—

but only after a device packed into a Kevlar vest had destroyed her insides. "They wanted you scared and compliant."

Baker stepped into her, his chest pressed against her arm. The contact was enough to keep her grounded but didn't diminish the buzz of anticipation for him to see what she saw in the details. "I'm going to need you to get to your point a lot faster, Jocelyn."

"You thought Linley's and Jane Doe's murders were connected, that they were the work of the same bomber." She handed him the photo of Jane Doe. "With good reason. The Ghost used the same devices, same amount of explosive packed into Kevlar, same brand of tires strung around their necks after the victims were already dead. But I don't think Jane Doe was the intended target. I think the cartel used her to deliver a message."

"Linley was a message for me." He stared down at the photo so hard she thought he might tear through it with his mind. "And Jane Doe was left for Ponderosa's Chief Trevino to back off. Right before they killed him."

THE PATTERN WAS becoming clearer by the minute.

All this time he'd been hunting the Ghost—a bomber who'd killed not only his sister but an innocent woman—and the bastard had been right in front of him.

Tremors worked through his hands as Baker rushed to dress into his uniform. This wasn't how this was supposed to end. He'd wanted to confront the son of a bitch, to show him all the pain and destruction he'd caused. To punish him. But Marc De Leon was dead. "I had him. I should've seen it before now. If I hadn't been so focused on justice for Linley, I could've saved Ponderosa's chief from...this."

"Marc De Leon didn't want you to see it, Baker." Jocelyn moved to reach out to him but seemingly thought better of it halfway. Hell, she was pulling away from him. After everything they'd worked through last night, he had to go and ruin it. "He was good at what he did."

"Why would someone else blow up my station to destroy evidence against Marc De Leon and claim to be the Ghost?" The question left his mouth more forcibly than he'd meant, and Baker caught himself losing his tight control on his anger. Just as he had after Linley's death. It wasn't him. It was the vengeful demon inside of him, and right now, there was a very thin line holding it at bay as his failures came into account. "How does that make sense?"

She didn't answer for a series of breaths, to the point that Baker sensed she might turn around and walk right out that door. Pinpricks stabbed at the back of his neck. He was on the brink of falling off that edge of reason.

"Tell me how I'm supposed to stay in this investigation when I can't even send the man I've wanted to arrest for two years to jail. What kind of chief of police does that make me?" The tremors were coming less frequent the longer he focused on her. On the way her right shoulder rose slightly higher than her left when she inhaled. The fact that the hair framing her face had a soft streak of lighter color. Baker memorized everything he could about her to keep himself from losing his mind, but he wasn't strong enough to keep fighting. Maybe he never had been. "Tell me what to do next."

"We know someone else is using Marc De Leon's recipe for the bombs. Socorro is trying to track down the sales of the nitroglycerin, but it's going to take time. There are still a lot of construction and mining operations that use it by the bulk. It would be easy for a few measures to go missing from one of the sites." She paused for a moment. "And I've reached out to a few contacts in ATF. They'll follow up with any reports of missing ordnance. Though if they haven't heard of any to this point, it's likely the bomber covered his tracks." Jocelyn took a step closer to him, breaking into his personal space. "Which means he's far more dangerous than we estimated. If we can't figure out how much nitroglycerin is missing, then we can't predict the next attack."

A shiver raced along his spine at the thought. The Ghost—at least, the man he'd believed to be the cartel's resident bomber—had gone out of his way to ensure Baker had been present at both bombings. First at the station when the son of a bitch had destroyed the evidence linking Marc De Leon to the death of Jane Doe. Then ambushing them at the lieutenant's compound.

He took a full breath. If Marc De Leon was Sangre por Sangre's Ghost, why would another bomber blow up proof he was guilty of murder and then take De Leon out? Had the cartel wanted to tie up a loose end that might admit to sixteen other incidents connecting back to the cartel? "Has there been any response from Sangre por Sangre for what happened at the compound?"

"Now that you mention it, we haven't seen any movement on their part. Cash would've let us know." Jocelyn grabbed for her cell phone, lighting up the screen. "Kind of hard to miss an explosion that almost buried an entire town. It's all over the news. Surrounding towns are sending in aid and raising funds for the cleanup. Jones has been handling the influx in help so we can focus on finding the bomber, while Cash has been keeping an eye on the cartel. You think they're keeping their distance for a reason?"

"Cartel soldiers are arrested all the time. My deputies and I have put the cuffs on more than our fair share, but the response is always the same. No one talks. Because if you give up the cartel, you won't even make it to your cell." Baker was trying to make sense of the thoughts in his head as fast as he could, but there were still too many moving pieces. The man they'd encountered in the desert had described the pain of watching someone he loved tortured and killed in front of him. Had said Baker had been spared. "No. I'm starting to think this is about something else altogether."

"Like what?" she asked.

"Whoever set that device in the station placed it in the evidence room. I think we were right in figuring it was purposefully detonated to destroy evidence in Marc De Leon's murder case." Baker paced across the room, to the window and back. "But how could the bomber have known we'd go to De Leon's compound? How was he waiting for us unless he knew we'd be there?"

"Easy to draw that conclusion once we realized the first bomb had been a means to destroy evidence in the murder investigation." Jocelyn leaned back against the desk built into the main wall of her room. No family photos staring back from shelves. No personal touches added over the course of her tenure with Socorro. This wasn't a home for her and Maverick. It was just a temporary way station until something else came along. "Could be the bomber has studied your protocols, knew you'd want to take up a case this big yourself rather than assigning it to one of your deputies. Especially if he knows what happened in your past. He went out there to set things up and then waited for us."

Damn, he'd missed this. Someone to bounce ideas off of, to solve puzzles with and test his limits. The feeling of partnership. Like he'd had with Linley. Building and working for something greater than the both of them. Sure, his deputies had his back in any given situation. They were there to do their job, and they did it well, but that didn't make them friends. More like acquaintances who sometimes took turns to bring in doughnuts.

But Jocelyn… She was different. She was more than an acquaintance. More than a friend. She was

everything he'd needed over these past couple days—
and everything he wanted for his life. Who else was
capable of looking him right in the eye and telling
him he'd been chasing a ghost? Who else surprised
him on more occasion than he could count? She was
the kind of woman who genuinely put others' needs
before her own, just to give them a sense of peace,
and hell, if that wasn't one of the most beautiful
things he'd ever witnessed. Not to mention the explosive pleasure she'd ignited in him last night. Jocelyn
Carville had ambushed him when he'd least expected
it, and he never wanted to give her up.

Baker slowed his pacing. "Or the bomber wasn't
there for me at all."

"What do you mean? He strapped a device into
your Kevlar and handcuffed you to your steering
wheel. The only reason you're still standing here is
because you figured out how to disrupt the pager's
receiver used to trigger the bomb." Confusion was
etched above her eyebrows, and with good reason.
"He was going to kill you, Baker. He tried to kill
both of us, or have you forgotten there was a bullet
in my shoulder less than twenty-four hours ago?"

"Because I was in his way." It was the only thing
that made sense. "That's why he shot you. We were
nothing but obstacles to what he really wanted."

"The Ghost." Her bottom lip pulled away from
the top. "Marc De Leon."

"Everything that's happened since that first explosion at the station has been centered around him."
A flash of nervous excitement spiraled through him

until Baker couldn't stop the words from forming. This was it. This was how they found the son of a bitch. "Sangre por Sangre soldiers are protected on the inside. Alpine Valley PD had evidence Marc De Leon murdered that woman during the raid, but what if a handful of years in prison wasn't enough for our bomber? What if he wanted the Ghost to suffer a hell of a lot more, without protection and with no chance of some defense attorney giving him an easy way out?"

Because Baker had wanted the exact same thing. For the man who'd murdered his sister and burned his world to the ground to suffer. That drive for revenge had been in his head from the moment he woke every morning and was the very last thought on his mind as he ended the day. Everything he'd done had been to make the bastard feel what Baker had felt upon finding Linley in that barn.

Jocelyn shoved away from the desk with her uninjured hand. "He wanted to add you as a notch in the Ghost's belt to double down on the charges. But why destroy evidence in the murder investigation? Why take away a sure conviction and a chance for Jane Doe to get the justice she deserves?"

The truth hit harder than he was ready for.

"Because the death of a second chief of police by the cartel would bring in the big guns." His blood ran cold at the mere suggestion. "One woman killed by one of their soldiers doesn't get much attention except from the people in Alpine Valley. By now, everyone has forgotten about her and moved on with their lives, but if two officers are murdered at the hands of the cartel?"

Jocelyn's expression fell, and damn it, he couldn't deny how much he hated seeing her without a smile. Forced or otherwise. "The feds would have no other choice than to call in every agency on their payroll, including Socorro."

"We've been thinking this is has been a targeted effort. One man trying to kill another, but we were wrong." Baker scrubbed a hand down his face. "The bomber wants to start a war."

Chapter Twelve

She couldn't be a smart cookie with a crumbly attitude.

Jocelyn hauled herself from the passenger seat of the loaner SUV she'd borrowed from Jones. With her vehicle in a million pieces and her shoulder in a sling, she'd have to rely on the rest of team to get her around for a while. Not a comfortable feeling, but she had too many other things on her mind.

Finding a bomber before he launched a war with the Sangre por Sangre cartel, for one.

She let Maverick out of the back seat as she surveyed the scene.

The landslide had been worse than she'd thought. Rain pelted against her face and soaked into the ground. It made balance harder for the volunteer cleanup crew trying not to slide down the new hill and threatened to land her on her ass. Mud, rock, cement chunks and wood framing had flooded through an entire street of homes. Far too many homes had been lost, and now there was nothing left but their roofs peeking out from areas Fire and Rescue had dug out.

This was a disaster in every sense of the word.

It would take months to excavate, and what happened to those families in the meantime? Jones had reported they'd been evacuated before the slide, but where were they supposed to go now?

"You okay?" Baker rounded the hood of the SUV, setting his hand beneath her slung elbow as support.

"My arm is just a bit sore." An understatement of the highest degree. The wound in her shoulder wasn't just sore. It was on fire. The last of the pain medication she'd received in the medical suite had burned off—most likely with help of last night's heart-racing activities—leaving her in a world of pain she hadn't known physically existed. "I'll be fine."

"You sure? Because you look like you're about to fall over." No hint of humor in his voice, which meant she looked as good as she felt. "Why don't you wait in the car? I can check in with the bomb squad alone."

"I said I'll be fine." Frustration had seeped past her control, and an instant shot of shame and embarrassment knifed through her as Baker removed his hand from her elbow. Jocelyn forced that practiced smile back in place. Everything was fine as long as she was smiling. She could do this. Because waiting in the car while the rest of her team and Baker worked this case wasn't an option.

She navigated up a sharp incline to where the rest of the volunteers and the bomb squad had set up a command center under a canvas pavilion. "Let's just see what they've found."

"Sure." He followed on her heels. Not as close as she'd come to expect. He was keeping his distance, and her skin heated despite the drop in temperature down here in the canyon and shade.

She watched her step as she climbed, but every movement took something out of her she couldn't really afford to give up. Agony was tearing at the edges of the bullet wound. Not to mention the stab wound beneath her Kevlar, but she wouldn't let it get to her. She just had to get through to the other side.

Maverick pressed into her leg as though she was about to collapse. Seemed Baker wasn't the only one doubting her capabilities today.

Jones offered her a hand as she summited the last few feet to man-made flat ground and dragged her upward. "Wasn't expecting you to make it out here today. You good?"

"Fine. How's it going here?" she asked.

"The excavators you recruited from Deer Creek and Ponderosa should be here this afternoon." The combat controller pointed out over the ridge that hadn't been put there naturally. "Right now, the bomb squad is digging to recover any other pieces of the device."

Jocelyn angled her head back to take in the view above. She shaded her face against the onslaught of rain pecking at them. A massive chuck of rock had broken away from the canyon wall, leaving the outline of an oversized bite. Her foot sank deeper into the shifting earth. "How long are they estimating the cleanup will take?"

"A couple months at least," Jones said. "The rains make it more difficult, but we're moving as fast as we can. The Bureau of Land Management sent in a geologist. From what he can tell, the threat of more rock coming down on us has passed, but we've been instructed to keep on alert. Just in case."

Shouts echoed off the canyon wall that'd always stood as a protection to this town, and the pain inside of her intensified. Jocelyn clamped a hand on her shoulder.

Jones's gaze cut to Baker, then back to her.

"Joce, maybe you should take a break." Baker stepped into her line of vision. "The pain meds Dr. Piel gave you are in my pack in the car. I'll get you one."

"No." The muscles in her jaw ached under the pressure of her back teeth. She bit back a moan and squeezed her eyes tight, waiting for the pain to pass. It didn't, and she couldn't stop the tears from pricking at her eyes. One deep breath. Two. The burn receded slightly, and Jocelyn dared to remove the pressure of her hand. Straightening, she faced both men. "I don't…need it."

Maverick *gruffed* beside her. He'd always been able to tell when she was lying.

"All right, then. Captain Pennymeyer is waiting for us in the command tent." Jones took the lead, cutting across the makeshift camp.

The sound of shovels, wheelbarrows and heavy breathing cut through the patter of rain as residents, Fire and Rescue and two deputies Jocelyn recognized as Alpine Valley PD worked to dig out the affected houses.

The combat controller held the flap of the pavilion

open for them, revealing a grouping of cops inside. The Albuquerque bomb squad. The man hunched over the laptop in the center straightened at their approach. His once muscular frame had gone soft. Too large on top, not enough stability in his lower half. The effect said while the officer in charge ran his department well, he wasn't usually out in the field.

"Chief Halsey. I'm Captain Pennymeyer." The bomb squad's commanding officer extended his hand past Jocelyn to meet Baker's. "We've managed to uncover several materials used in the device detonated at your station to compare with those recovered here."

"Grateful to have you." Baker shook before withdrawing. There was an invisible bond between cops and military units. She'd had that once, on tour, but having a captain of the bomb squad blatantly disregard her presence only added to the pulse in her shoulder. "This is Jocelyn Carville from Socorro Security. She saw the device before it detonated inside the compound."

"Then by all means, Ms. Carville, tell me if we got this right." Pennymeyer maneuvered around the standing desk he'd created toward a long table covered in plastic. Pieces of wire, motherboard and mud-coated plastic had been separated and studiously labeled for study. "Your statement said you saw the device tucked up into the rafters of the home. That right?"

Her mouth dried as she took in all the fractured pieces that'd once made a whole. The intricacy and placement of every one of these materials had nearly destroyed an entire town. "Yes."

"Did you see anything specific?" the captain asked. "Were there any wires leading away from the device? A countdown clock, or maybe you caught the branding on the battery before it went off?"

Her mind went blank as pain clawed down her arm and into her chest. She clung to her sling with her free hand as the world tipped slightly. Scouring the table, she tried to make all these tiny pieces fit into a puzzle her brain was desperate to put together. Had she seen the branding on the battery? Heat flared into her face and neck. "I don't... I don't know. I only got a glimpse of it before I ran for the patio door."

The captain stepped off to one side, and it was only then that she realized a blueprint of Marc De Leon's compound had been tacked to the flexible wall above the table. "Your statement reports you saw the device tucked into the rafters of the kitchen. Is that correct?"

Her heart rate rocketed into overdrive. She'd already been through all of this. The last reserves of her control bled dry. "If you've read my statement, why are you asking me again?"

Silence enveloped the tent, all eyes on her.

She tried to breathe through the pain, but it wasn't working this time. It crescendoed until it was all she felt. Consuming her inch by inch.

Captain Pennymeyer directed his attention downward to his table of explosive goodies. "We're just trying to get the most accurate information, Ms. Carville. It's been known that victims caught in an event like this tend to remember more a couple days after they've had time to recover."

"I'm not a victim." A barb of annoyance poked at her insides.

"Of course. I didn't mean…" The captain's face flushed, and his oversized upper body seemed to deflate right in front of her. "I apologize. I didn't mean any insult. I understand you've been through something quite traumatic."

Baker inched closer. "Will you give us a minute, Captain?" He lowered his voice. "Let's get some air."

She wanted to argue, but being inside the too-small tent packed with cops was getting to her. Cold air worked into her lungs once outside, but she couldn't distract her body from focusing on the throbbing in her shoulder.

Baker set his hand against her lower back, guiding her roughly ten feet from the men waiting for her confirmation that they'd recovered every piece of the bomb that'd brought down the compound on top of Alpine Valley. He pulled out a bright orange, cylindrical container with a white top from his front pocket. "Here. I had Jones grab your pain meds from the car."

Twisting off the cap with his palm, he dragged one of the pills inside free and offered it to her.

Every nerve in her body went on the defense. She took a physical step back. "I told you I didn't want it."

"You'd rather be in debilitating pain while we're here?" He countered her escape, keeping his voice low enough so as not to be overheard by anyone else. "Not sure you noticed, but if you weren't talking to me right now, I'd think you were dead you're so pale. You're having trouble focusing, and you just bit off the head of the guy running this investigation."

She couldn't take her attention off the pill in his hand.

"Joce, everyone in that tent knows you were shot," he said. "None of them are going to think any less of you for taking the edge off."

She shook her head. She could hardly breathe. "I can't."

"What is this? Some kind of punishment for what happened?" Confusion and a heavy dose of frustration had Baker dropping the pain med back into the container. He screwed the top on. "For not being there when your husband died? Is that it? You've convinced yourself you deserve to suffer? You were shot and stabbed by a piece of debris, for crying out loud. I'd say that's enough penance to last a lifetime."

The pain burned through her, and no amount of distraction was taking it away. Jocelyn headed across the cleanup site, the sound of Maverick's dog tags in her ears. Her shepherd knew she was on the brink of going over the edge. "No. It's not like that."

"Then what is it like?" Baker followed. "Tell me."

She turned on him. There was no hiding it. Not anymore. "I'm a recovering addict."

AN ADDICT.

Baker didn't know what to say to that, what to *think*.

He tightened his grip on the medication bottle, his hand slick with sweat. "I don't…" Clearing his throat, he tried to get his head back into the game. "I don't understand. You were on morphine in the medical unit after what happened up there. You didn't say anything."

Jocelyn released her hold on her shoulder, trying to make it look as though nothing got to her. She had a habit of doing that. Pretending. "Dr. Piel doesn't know my medical history. The nurses at the clinic that first time we were caught in the bombing at the police station had my chart. They knew not to put me on anything stronger than ibuprofen."

"You're going to have to start from the beginning." Baker found himself backing up, adding more than a couple of feet between them. "Because what you're saying right now doesn't make sense."

"What more is there to explain?" Her expression fell into something that could only be categorized as hollowness. As though she'd told this story so many times, she'd disassociated from the emotional toll it took. Though from what she'd just said, not everybody knew. "I lost my husband, Baker. I blamed myself for not being there in his final moments. I was getting messages from his friends, his family, calls from his doctor—all asking me why I wasn't there. Because all he'd wanted in his final moments was for me to be by his side, and I let him down."

Baker tried to swallow past the swelling in his throat, but there was no point. "So when you said you got sick after his death, you meant…"

"The pain hurt so much. I tried everything I could think of to make it stop, but nothing worked. The grief was crushing me, and I didn't know what else to do." The heartache was still pressing in on her. He could see it in her eyes, in the way she practically crumpled in on herself. "One night it got so bad, I thought I might hurt myself, but I found Miles's old pain meds in the bathroom cabinet. I took one." Her voice evened out. "All it took was one."

"You started taking the pills more often." Baker studied the orange pill bottle in his hand right there in the middle of what was left of his town. He'd responded to overdoses of all kinds while working this job. Mothers who'd only wanted to be able to do it all with a touch of ecstasy. Teens who started sniffing coke in the back seat of the bus on the way to school to fit in with their peers. A middle schooler who'd binged two bottles of cough medicine to get drunk. Sangre por Sangre had made it all possible—easier—to drag an ordinary life through the mud. And it turned out, he'd been partnered with an addict all this time. Bringing his gaze back to hers, he pocketed the pills, just in case the sight of them was enough to trigger something compulsive in her. "How did you stop?"

"I didn't. At least not before it got worse." Sweat slipped from her hairline. One push. That was all it'd take, and she'd collapse from the pain. How the hell was she still standing there as though she could take on the world? "The pills ran out. I went to my doctor. He wouldn't help me. Neither would any of the others. The military discharged me under honorable conditions, but I couldn't face the truth—that I was alone. So I did what I thought I had to at the time."

His heart threatened to beat straight out of his chest. Baker licked at dry lips, but it didn't do a damn bit of good. Because he knew what was coming next. "You found something stronger to replace the pills."

"I convinced myself I could handle it." She dropped her chin to her chest, shutting him out. "It was supposed to be a temporary fix, but the longer I used, the more I realized I didn't want to stop. I didn't want to hurt every time I walked through the door or thought about my husband. I don't really remember a whole lot during that time, but it got bad enough no one—not even my friends, my unit or my family—could help."

Jocelyn seemed to let go of something heavy, as though the rain were washing away the weight she'd carried. She stepped toward him. "But I'm in recovery now. I got myself into NA. I have a sponsor I check in with. I've been clean for over a year. It's… hard. Especially when I'm injured in the field, but I don't want to go back to being numb, Baker. I don't. And with you, I finally feel like I can leave that part of me behind. That there's more to my life than my mistakes."

A thousand questions rushed to the surface, but all he focused on was the hollowness in his chest. There were a limited number of organizations where she could've gotten drugs like the ones she'd talked about, and the entire town of Alpine Valley had slowly been dying because of one of them. "Where did you get the drugs?"

That shadow of enthusiasm and hope—nothing like when he'd first met her—drained from her expression. "Why does that matter?"

"I think you know why it matters, Jocelyn," he said.

Understanding cemented her expression in place. "Seems like you already know the answer you're looking for."

"From a cartel." He couldn't believe this. All this time, he'd trusted her to be on his side of the fight, but she'd kept a major part of her life out of the equation. Lied to him. "I can't tell you how many times I've walked into one of these houses and found a kid barely breathing because of the crap he put in his arm or describe how many babies will have serious complications throughout their lives because their mothers won't look at the people they really are in the mirror. And now you're telling me you're one of them."

Her face ticked at one side, as though he thrown a physical punch. "It's…it's not the same. You know it's not. I changed. I got help so I could start my life over —"

"Has it worked?" he asked. "You paste on that smile and try to find an upside to everything so you don't have to feel your loss. You're so desperate to avoid reality, you've created your own. Christmas parties, cookie bake-offs, movie nights and forced team dinners. You might not be on the drugs anymore, but you're still looking for ways to numb yourself, Jocelyn."

He regretted the words the moment they left his

mouth, but Baker couldn't seem to pull back. The cartel had taken everything he'd ever cared about. The bed and breakfast he built with his own hands, his sister. And now Jocelyn.

"Is that why you started working for Socorro? The reason you came to Alpine Valley?" Baker couldn't stop the words. "To make yourself feel like you were actually fighting the cartel? So you could pretend to be the hero? You outright supported the very people you've been investigating with me. You see that, don't you? You made them stronger while everyone in this town is simply trying to survive."

Tears glittered in her eyes. "And what have you been doing since the cartel killed your sister, Baker? Because I can tell you what you haven't been doing. You haven't been confronting your pain. You might not be going about it the same way I did, but you're just as guilty as I am of trying to escape."

"You might be right," he said. "But I wasn't the one who kept that from my partner."

She didn't have an answer for him.

In truth, he didn't want one. He didn't want any excuses. He didn't want to see reason. Baker pointed an index finger at her. "You know, I thought you were different. I thought we really had something, that it would be worth it to make it work between us, but I can't spend the rest of my life wondering if you're going to relapse or if I'm going to find you dead from an overdose."

He unpocketed the pills and threw them at her feet. The container lid burst free, sprinkling her meds in a two-foot radius. It was childish and petty and didn't do a damn thing to release the tightness in his chest. "Do whatever you want with these. Consider our partnership terminated. I'm done."

"That's it?" Her voice wavered from behind. "After everything we've survived together, after everything we've shared, you're going to condemn me and what we have because of a mistake? I thought you of all people would understand."

He didn't. He didn't understand how someone he'd convinced himself would never betray her beliefs could undermine his trust so quickly. "You were wrong."

Jones Driscoll and Captain Pennymeyer stood at the door flap of the command center, unmoving. Seemed the entire site had turned its attention to him. Waiting for his answer. But he didn't owe them anything. And he didn't owe Jocelyn, either.

Baker kept on walking back toward the command tent. Part of him knew while he hadn't taken up numbing himself the way she had, he'd taken this job to get back at the bastards that'd destroyed his life. He'd lived off of revenge, but he hadn't given up his morals in the process.

"Fine." A low whistle cut through the site, and Maverick's dog tags clashing together reached Baker's senses over the soft tick of rain. "But the next time you're facing down a bomb, don't call me for help."

A car door slammed a moment before the SUV's engine caught.

He crossed back into the command tent, knowing all too well the officers and operatives inside had heard every word. Baker took up position in front of the table with the deconstructed pieces of the bomb that should've killed him—would have if it hadn't been for Jocelyn. His heart dropped in his chest as he caught the tail end of her vehicle through the open tent flap.

"Show's over. We have a bomber to find."

Chapter Thirteen

She would've given up her last cookie for him.

Tears clouded her vision as Jocelyn floored the accelerator. She'd never been so humiliated in her life. Not just by her darkest shame but by having it exposed in the middle of a crime scene, surrounded by her team and other officers she worked with. But that wasn't what hurt the most. A hook cut through her stomach as Baker's words echoed on repeat.

I can't spend the rest of my life wondering if you're going to relapse or if I'm going to find you dead from an overdose.

His concerns were valid. Every day she fought the same demons. Every day she went to bed knowing she'd done her best and tallied another day of survival. Because that was what she was doing. *Surviving*. Constantly on the defense of a threat. But she'd never expected it to come from Baker.

The pain in her shoulder was nothing compared to the agony closing in around her heart. Jocelyn swiped at her face as a pair of headlights inched into the rearview mirror. She'd escaped the town limits, halfway between Alpine Valley and Socorro. Not nearly enough distance to put between her and what'd just happened. Open desert expanded ahead. Ten minutes back to headquarters. Then she could pack and get the hell away from this place.

Maverick whined from the back cargo area. His face centered in the mirror. As much as he preferred to cuddle with a stick rather than her, he picked up on her emotions better than most humans. He was hurting, too.

"I know, but we can't go back." She tightened her grip on the steering wheel. While she hadn't envisioned anything past this investigation, she'd gotten attached to this place. To Baker. He'd unlocked something in her over the past few days. Hope. Trust. Joy. He'd taken her pain and internalized it for himself, leaving her lighter and freer than she'd felt in a long time. He'd listened to her. Convinced her that grief didn't always have to call the shots. That she could be more than an addict. And she loved him for gifting her that relief. Damn it, she loved him.

But he'd made his opinion on her history clear. His personal agenda against the cartel ensured there was nothing she could do or say to change his mind. "There's nothing left for us here."

The headlights behind her got closer. Recognition filled in the paint job along the sides of the vehicle. Alpine Valley PD. Every instinct she owned asked her to slow down and pull over, that she should at least give Baker the chance to apologize, but she'd made her point clear, too. The crossbar lights lit up with red-and-blue strobes. The piercing chirp of the siren triggered her nerves. She tried to make out the face in the driver's seat through the rearview mirror. "Keep trying, but I'm not pulling over."

Jocelyn focused on the road ahead. A couple more miles. As much as she hated the idea of hiding out at Socorro, it was the one place he couldn't get to her.

The growl of an engine penetrated through the cabin of the SUV a split second before the patrol car tapped her bumper. The jolt ricocheted through the entire vehicle and caused her front tires to skid slightly.

Warning lightninged through her. She hiked herself higher in the driver's seat to get a better view. She didn't pull over, so now he was going to run her off the road? She was going fifty miles an hour. "Are you out of your mind? What the hell are you doing?"

The rear vehicle surged again. The hood aimed for one corner of her SUV. And made contact. The back tires of the SUV fishtailed off to one side. Jocelyn jerked in her seat as she lost control of the steering wheel. Maverick's howl registered a split second before the tires caught on something off the side of the road.

Momentum flipped the SUV.

Her stomach shot into her throat as gravity took hold. The seat belt cut into her injured shoulder just before the crash slammed her head forward. Dirt, glass and metal protested, cutting off Maverick's pain-filled cry.

The SUV rolled again. Then settled upside down.

"Maverick." His name mixed with blood in her mouth. He didn't answer. Jocelyn pressed one hand into the ceiling of the vehicle. Glass cut into her palm, and the seat belt had her pinned. The rearview mirror was gone. She couldn't see him in the cargo area. Visceral helplessness cascaded through her as she clawed for the release. No. No. Maverick wasn't dead. Flashes of that phone call, of the moment when she'd learned she hadn't been there for Miles before his death, were superimposed onto the present. All her husband had wanted in his last moments had been to be with her. And she hadn't been there. But she would be there for Maverick. She couldn't lose him. She couldn't lose the last piece of her husband. "I'm coming, baby."

Her shoulder screamed against the pressure of the seat belt. She jabbed her thumb into the release.

Jocelyn hit the roof of the SUV harder than she expected. The bullet wound took the brunt of her weight as she tried to dig her legs out from under the steering wheel. Pure agony rippled pins and needles down into her hand. If she hadn't lost function of her arm before, she had now. Swallowing the scream working up her throat, Jocelyn rolled onto her back. "Come on, Mav."

A car door slammed, distorting the hard pound of her heart at the back of her head. Followed by footsteps.

Not Baker.

Alpine Valley's chief of police would never put someone's life in danger. Jocelyn reached for her sidearm but came up empty. The impact must've ripped it free of her holster. She reached overhead and patted her hand over the bottom of the driver's seat. It wasn't there. Her training kicked in. Tucking her arm into her chest, she wormed her way between the front two seats. She had an entire arsenal at her disposal in the back with Maverick. She just had to—

The back passenger side door ripped open. Sunlight blinded her a split second before rough hands wrapped around her ankles and pulled her from the SUV.

Her attacker threw her from the vehicle.

Head snapping back, Jocelyn tried to roll with the force. She landed face down, her arm pinned beneath her. Trying to suck in a full breath, she caught sight of a shadow casting above her.

"And here I thought you'd be happy to see me." The voice played at the edges of her mind—the same voice she'd heard right before she'd taken a bullet in Marc De Leon's compound. "I understand. I mean, it's not like we're friends, but I am doing you and that chief of yours a favor."

She blinked against the spider webs clinging to the sides of her vision. Dirt worked into her mouth, down her throat with every inhale, but all she had attention for was the SUV. And the pool of gasoline leaking down the side. Jocelyn stretched one hand out to pull herself forward. One spark. That was all it would take for her to lose everything. "Maverick."

A heavy boot crushed her fingers into the dry

earth. "Come on now, Carville. You and I both know this has been a long time coming."

The pool of gasoline was growing bigger beneath the vehicle, and there was no sign of Maverick. She had to go. Now. Jocelyn jerked her body to one side, dislodging his pin on her hand. She grabbed for a rock protruding out of the ground and swung at his shin as hard as she could.

The impact knocked the son of a bitch off his feet.

She ran for the SUV.

A bullet ripped past her ear and lodged into the hood of the vehicle ahead. Then another. The third shot missed her by mere centimeters as she skidded behind the hood. Pressing her back to the front tires, she tried to get her bearings.

"You have nowhere to go, Carville, and you're wasting my time." His footsteps registered again. This time slower. More careful. As though he was trying to hide his approach.

Jocelyn inched to the back of the vehicle, trying to get a line on the bastard's location through the bulletproof windows. Unfortunately, the coating only made things worse. She couldn't see through them from the outside. Her body demanded rest as she pulled as the back driver's side door.

"There you are." A gun barrel cut into her scalp from behind. "On your feet. Slow. You reach for anything, and the next bullet goes in your head."

How had he moved without her noticing? Jocelyn raised her hands in surrender. She cut her attention to the Alpine Valley patrol vehicle parked twenty feet away. A police officer? "Who are you?"

"Let's just say your chief isn't the only one who wants the cartel to pay for what they've done," he said. "What better way than to frame Sangre por Sangre for your murder?"

"Chief Halsey is smarter than that." Movement registered from the inside the SUV, and her heart shot into her throat. Maverick.

"He may be, but what do you think will happen once Socorro discovers you're dead?" the bomber asked. "Do you think your team will listen to him, or will they pull in every available resource at the government's disposal to put Sangre por Sangre down for good?"

Doubt crept through her.

"That's what this has been all about? Dismantling the cartel?" Baker had been right. This entire investigation had been a cloaked frame job from the beginning. Jocelyn followed the motion of the attacker's weapon, taking that initial step toward the patrol vehicle. All this time, they'd been working for the same end goal. "That's what Alpine Valley PD and Socorro have been trying to accomplish. We're on the same side."

"Yet the cartel somehow still operates without consequences. They raid and kill and take what they want without answering for what they've done." A hardness that sent a chill down her spine added pressure to the gun at her skull. "But with you, I can do what nobody else has been able to."

A low growl pierced her ears. Maverick lunged from the vehicle, fangs bared. He went straight for the bomber's gun hand and ripped the bastard's forearm down.

The attacker's scream was lost to the desert as he tried to regain control of the weapon.

Jocelyn spun. Her fist connected with tissue and bone.

A solid kick landed against Maverick's ribs, and the shepherd backed off with a whine so heart-wrenching it brought up the memory of walking into Miles's hospital room to find Maverick waiting for her.

Air was suctioned out of her chest. She cocked her elbow back for a second strike.

But the bomber was faster. He wrapped his hand around hers and twisted down. Then slammed his forehead into her face.

She hit the ground.

BAKER COULDN'T FORCE himself to focus on the puzzle pieces in front of him. No matter how long he'd stared at them, he couldn't find anything to identify their bomber. The son of a bitch had covered his tracks too well. But worse, he couldn't stop thinking about Jocelyn. About what he'd said to her in those final moments.

"Take a break, Halsey." Jones slammed a hand into Baker's back, and the movement nearly catapulted him forward. "You're going to give yourself an aneurysm. I'll go through everything again. In the meantime, why don't you grab something to eat and catch some sleep. You've been running on fumes for days."

"I'm fine." Baker pinched the bridge of his nose. Truth was, he wasn't fine. He hadn't been for a long time, but having Jocelyn around had helped. Her enthusiasm had been annoying as hell in the beginning. Now he found himself missing it. Her sarcasm had broken through that need to push everyone away. She'd brought out a playful side to him he'd convinced himself had died that day with his sister and given him a sense of adventure. They hadn't just been two people working a case together. They'd been partners. In and out of the field.

And now... Now he felt like he was floating in a thousand different directions without an anchor. Shit. He'd had no right to throw her past in her face like that. She'd lost her husband, the one person she'd counted on being there for her for years. She'd done what she could to survive. Just as he had by making the cartel his personal mission. Two different paths leading to the same place.

He owed her an apology. Hell, he owed her a dozen apologies a day over the next ten years for the way he'd acted. Because despite what he'd said and how he felt about the sickness clawing through Alpine Valley at the cartel's influence, Baker had fallen in love with a mercenary.

"Yeah. You look fine to me." Jones unpocketed a set of keys and tossed them to Baker. "Take my truck. It has a Socorro Security garage pass in the center console. But if anyone asks, you stole it off me. I got you covered."

"Thanks." He let the keys needle into his palm as

he headed for the tent's flap but slowed his escape. "What Jocelyn said earlier about her addiction... I don't want this to come back on her—"

"I already knew." Jones turned back to the blueprints, hands leveraged at his hips. A thick scar ran the length of the combat operator's skull and down beneath his T-shirt. "That's the thing about being part of and living with a team as highly trained as ours twenty-four-seven. You tend to pick up on things. There's nothing we can hide from each other. No matter how hard we try." He released a breath. "That's why I know she's been a lot happier since you started coming around. Her hands aren't permanently stuck in a bowl of dough. She's smiling more. Nothing seems forced like it usually does. I just figured she'd tell us when she was ready. Seems she trusts you, though."

"She did." Baker fisted his hands around the keys.

"She still does. You just have to give her a reason." Jones notched his chin higher, accentuating years of disciplined muscle along his neck and shoulders. "But, Chief, if I hear you throw her past in her face like that again, it won't just be some petty bomber coming for you. Understand? You attack one of us, you attack all of us."

Baker didn't have the voice to answer. He nodded instead and slipped out of the tent. Every nerve ending focused on putting one foot in front of the other. The case, the bomber, the impending war with the cartel—none of it mattered right then. There was only Jocelyn.

"Chief!" Heavy breathing preceded his second-in-command hiking up the slight incline to the plateau of mud, rock and cement. The deputy hiked a thumb over his shoulder. "We just got word of a car fire outside town limits. You can see the smoke from here."

Car fire? Dread pooled at the base of his spine as he caught sight of a thick plume of black smoke directly west. "How long ago?"

"No more than five minutes," the deputy said.

"Anyone injured?" Baker jogged down the slope and hit the unlock button on Jones's keys. Headlights flashed from an oversized black pickup at the end of the street. Ready in case of escape.

"West went to check it out, but his patrol car is missing." The deputy tried to keep up with him.

Disbelief surged high. "He lost his patrol car?"

"No, sir. We believe it was stolen." A hint of embarrassment pecked at the man's neck and face.

Baker's instincts honed in on that cloud of smoke. The base looked as though it was coming from the road cutting between Alpine Valley and Socorro. Which meant… His gut wrenched hard. "Jocelyn."

His entire being shot into battle-ready defense. He raced for Jones's truck. "Get West and round up the Socorro operatives to meet me out there! Now!"

He didn't wait for confirmation. Hauling himself behind the steering wheel, he hit the Engine Start button and threw the truck into gear. Frightened and shocked residents gathered together in groups of two and three as more and more noticed the desert fire. He raced through town as fast as he dared, but the need to get to her as fast as possible had him hugging the accelerator. "I'm coming, Joce. I'm coming."

Trees thinned, exposing the mile-high cliffs on either side of town. Once considered protection, Baker could only look at them now as a threat considering one of them had come crashing down and buried part of his town. But Alpine Valley was resilient. It had to be to survive this long. And though he'd taken up the mantle to protect the people here, he wasn't alone. "Just hang on."

The truck's back tires fishtailed as asphalt gave way to dirt at the border of town. He glanced in the direction of his property, taking in the jagged structure left behind by the bomb and resulting fire, but dragged his attention back to the road. The bed and breakfast, his sister's death, revenge—none of it was strong enough to distract him now. They were in the past. Long gone, and as much as he wanted to hold on to the pain—to get justice for Linley—he had a future to fight for.

Dirt kicked up alongside the truck and pinged off the doors as he picked up speed. The smoke plume had dispersed, and he got his first real look at the fire.

An SUV.

"No. No, no, no." Slamming on the brakes, Baker pulled the truck off the side of the road and threw it into Park. He climbed out of the vehicle, instantly assaulted by the caustic taste and smell of rubber and gasoline. He stuffed his nose and mouth beneath his uniform collar and shaded his eyes before trying to approach, but the heat was too intense. "Jocelyn!"

There wasn't any answer. And he hadn't expected any. If she'd been inside…

Baker lost feeling in his fingers then both arms and that sucking sensation in his chest intensified as the past threatened to pull him in.

The fire grew taller, consuming everything in its path. The entire roof of the barn was missing. Smoke lodged in his throat. He had to get in there. He had to see for himself. The barn door nearly tore off its hinges as the barest touch. He couldn't see, couldn't breathe. Hay burned beneath his shoes, leaving nothing but ash. The horses. Where were the horses?

A sick smell accosted him as he stumbled toward the stall to the right. His stomach emptied right then and there, unable to take the smell. Baker forced himself away from the paddock into the center of the barn.

And he saw her.

Seated against the barn's support beam. Her hands wedged behind her back. Tied. Baker lost his footing. He face-planted mere feet from her bare feet. The dirt crusted in her toenails said she'd been dragged out here. Most likely from the house. Tears and rage and helplessness had him clawing to touch her to make sure she was real. He reached out—

Course fur warmed in his hand.

Baker blinked against the onslaught of sun beating down on him. The fire's heat beaded sweat along his forehead and neck. Cracked earth bit into his knees as he tried to orient himself in the present. He focused on the K-9 leaning into his hand.

"Maverick." Something like relief flooded through

him. Baker scratched behind the shepherd's ears before he pulled the dog closer. "Where is she, buddy?"

A low whine grazed Baker's senses just as he felt a matted section of fur. Wet and warm. Blood.

"Oh, hell. You fought for her, didn't you? You tried to help." He hugged Maverick closer, as though he could somehow reach Jocelyn. "You did good, boy."

Baker shoved to his feet, fully lodged in the present thanks to Maverick, and hauled the shepherd into his chest. "Don't worry. I've got you. I'm going to get you help. All right? Come on. Let's get you in the truck."

He lifted Maverick into his arms, but a fierce bark racketed Baker's pulse into dangerous territory. The German shepherd tried to wiggle free, his claws digging into Baker's skin. Maverick released another protest—stronger—and Baker set him down. The K-9 ran around the SUV engulfed in flames.

"Maverick, wait!" Baker pumped his legs as hard as his muscles allowed. If something happened to that dog, Jones's warning would mean nothing compared to that of Maverick's handler. He cleared the car fire as the chirp of a patrol vehicle echoed from behind. Backup had arrived from Alpine Valley.

But then who did the vehicles cutting across the horizon belong to?

Baker reached out for Maverick, and the dog took a seat. Dust and heat blocked a clear view, but he made out at least a dozen armored, black vehicles a mile out.

Headed for Alpine Valley.

His heart threatened to beat straight out of his chest.

Sangre por Sangre.

"Halsey, what the hell is going on?" Heavy boot-steps pierced through the adrenaline haze. Jones's voice did nothing to ease the panic settling in. "What do you have?"

Air crushed from his chest. "I think we've got a war on our hands."

Chapter Fourteen

She was a tough cookie. She wouldn't crumble under pressure.

Something splattered into her face. It ran from one cheek down her neck. Jocelyn tried to breathe through the swelling around her nose. Broken. She could still taste the blood at the back of her throat. Listening for signs of movement, she tried to gauge the bomber's location. Another splatter jerked her head back slightly.

"You don't have to pretend to be unconscious anymore." Shuffling scraped across what sounded like a concrete floor. There was a slight echo to it, as though they were in a large room without windows. A piercing shriek hiked her blood pressure higher as the bomber dragged a metal chair closer. "There isn't anything that's going to stop Socorro from finding you dead."

She swallowed the last globs of blood and dirt and risked opening her eyes. To pitch darkness. Pulling at her hands cuffed at her lower back, she gauged her abductor had zip-tied her. Twice. Less chance of breaking through the plastic. Something wet and cold seeped through her cargo pants and spread down her shirt. "Well, that just makes me feel special."

His low laugh wasn't villainous enough to trigger her nervous system, but it didn't fit, either. "You always had a way of making me laugh."

A lantern lit up the entire enclosed space. Cement floor, cement walls, cement ceiling. Another ping of water slipped down her face from the leaking pipe overhead. This place... She'd been here before. There was a slight charred smell sticking in her lungs.

The bomber leaned forward, letting the small source of light catch one side of his face.

Recognition sucker punched her square in the chest. "You."

"Me." There wasn't any pride in that aged expression. No sense of victory in his voice. Just a statement of fact.

"I don't understand." Shaking her head, Jocelyn tried to make every piece of this investigation fit into place in mere seconds. "The reports... They all said you were dead. That there was no way you'd survived that car bomb."

Andrew Trevino. The Ponderosa chief of police—alive and well—settled back in his chair. He'd aged significantly, or the months since his so-called death had been far crueler than she could imagine. Scar tissue shadowed across the backs of his hands. The skin hadn't just aged but smoothed into rivers in some places and valleys in others. Chemical burns. Nitroglycerin?

"Reports can say a lot of things and leave out others depending on who's writing it," he said. "It's all a matter of perspective, don't you think?"

"How?" Jocelyn pressed one hand flat against the wall at her back. Looking for something—anything—that might help get through the zip ties. Though without the use of one arm she feared she was only drawing out the inevitable. Still, she wasn't going to let her body be used to spark a war between the cartel and her team and Alpine Valley PD. She rushed to resurrect the details of that incident, a bombing of a chief of police's vehicle. Authorities had attributed credit to the Ghost. "You built the bomb and blew up your vehicle, using Marc De Leon's recipe. You faked your own death."

"You military brats are a lot smarter than I expected, especially one assigned logistics." Trevino hauled himself out of the chair. For a man closing in on his late fifties, he was surprisingly agile. No hints of wear and tear. Then again, one needed to be in tip-top shape to take on an entire drug cartel.

"Am I supposed to take that as a compliment?" Jocelyn took advantage of whatever he was doing on the other side of the room. Raising her wrists as one toward what felt like a mass of cement at her lower back, she clenched her jaw against a scream. Her abductor had removed her sling and strong-armed her wounded arm behind her back while she'd been knocked out cold. And now the pain had immobilized her altogether.

"Take it however you want. Doesn't matter to me."

He stepped outside of the pool of white light given off by the electric lantern. "Not much does anymore."

He was stalling. To what end? Didn't matter. If she had any chance of avoiding a war, it was because she got herself out of this insane frame job.

Jocelyn rolled her lips between her teeth and bit down to pull her brain's attention away from her shoulder. Sweat combined with whatever was dripping from the leaking pipe above and soaked into her shirt's collar. "You wanted authorities to believe Sangre por Sangre had ordered Marc De Leon to kill you."

"That was my first mistake." Trevino came back into the weak circle of light, though her senses still weren't adjusting to make out what he'd brought back with him. "Believing one soldier's arrest could make a difference. Believing I could inflict any kind of damage against an organization like that, but it wasn't enough."

A thread of regret laced his words. Similar to the way Baker's voice had changed when he'd trusted her with the loss he'd suffered at the hands of the cartel. Her insides twisted to the point it was hard to take her next breath. "They took someone from you. The woman Alpine PD hasn't been able to identify."

"That's what the cartel does, doesn't it? They take and they take until there's nothing left and nobody willing to stand up and fight against them. They spread their misery and violence into whatever town isn't strong enough to fight back with claims they're offering protection against bastards just like them, but it's all a lie." Trevino dropped his chin to his chest, staring down into whatever item he had in his hands. Still impossible to make out. "My daughter was one of the first to speak out against them when they started selling their poison in the high school. All she wanted to was to make our town safe enough to raise my grandkids while keeping an eye on me. Always said I was no spring chicken."

Dread pooled at the base of Jocelyn's spine. "Marc De Leon was sent to kill her."

"No. He didn't just kill her." The grief and sorrow in his voice was gone, replaced with a hardness she expected of a serial bomber instead of a chief of police desperate to protect the people he cared about. "He tortured her. For hours, right in front of me. He'd beaten me senseless. I couldn't do anything to help her except hear her beg me to save her. And after De Leon had strapped an explosive device packed into a Kevlar vest to her and detonated it, he said he'd come for my grandkids next if I kept coming for them."

Jocelyn pressed her skull into the wall behind her to keep her senses engaged in the moment. Investigators would've known about his daughter's death at the time of the bombing that had supposedly killed the chief. Why hadn't it come up in the past few days? The answer solidified. Because both his and his daughter's deaths had been blamed on the cartel. "So you faked your death."

"Victims die every day at the hands of Sangre por Sangre. The prosecutor's office can't keep up, but the truth is they can't do a damn thing to get justice for my daughter or others like her." Trevino took his seat in front of her.

Baker's sister infiltrated her thoughts, and suddenly Jocelyn was seeing Alpine Valley's chief of police in front of her. Beaten by the years of injustice, desperate to do the right thing, to make the cartel pay. Her heart hurt at the idea, but there were too many similarities between the man in front of her and the one she'd lost her heart to.

The words bubbled up her throat. "But the death of a police chief would get their notice—only Fire and Rescue never recovered your body. So you set about framing the cartel for as many crimes as you could. First with destroying evidence in Marc De Leon's murder case. Then by trying to add Baker Halsey's name to their victim roster."

"I have to admit, I didn't expect Halsey to team up with you, though." The chief's silhouette shifted, losing its caved-in appearance in the limited light. "You've certainly made my job a lot more difficult than I expected. I mean, you two just refuse to die, but then I had another idea. All this time I've been exhausting energy and resources trying to take down Sangre por Sangre alone when there is a high-skilled, highly funded organization equal to the very cartel I want gone."

"Socorro." Her mouth dried despite the building humidity inside the windowless room. "And Marc De Leon? You killed him for what he did to your daughter."

"Son of a bitch got a promotion to lieutenant after

that night," he said. "Took me weeks to find him. Thousands of dollars paid in bribes. Nobody wanted to talk. They called him the Ghost. All I had to go off of was pieces of the explosive device in my daughter's chest cavity, but my patience paid off."

Jocelyn strained to angle her wrists against the protrusion from the wall, but her shoulder wouldn't budge. "You found him."

"The bastard didn't even know who I was. Though to be fair, I didn't give him a whole lot of time to recognize me seeing as I was there to kill him." A hint of giddiness contorted the man's voice. And right then she saw the difference between him and Baker. The man she'd fallen in love with wouldn't have let his revenge get this far. "I had everything set up perfectly. Then you and Chief Halsey had to spoil my fun."

Her shoulder ached at the memory of taking that bullet just before the bomb went off. "Right. Because bringing an entire cliffside crashing onto a small town is fun."

"I didn't mean for that to happen," he said. "But I wasn't going to let it distract me from what I was there to do."

"So this is the part where I come in? You leave my body for my team to find. They gather all their federal allies and exact revenge against the cartel on my behalf." The edge of the first zip tie caught on the lip protruding from the wall, and Jocelyn shoved her weight down on her wrists. "Which means you'd have to leave my body somewhere that implicates

Sangre por Sangre. Making this the cartel's abandoned headquarters."

Her brain wasn't playing tricks on her. She had been here before.

"I know what you're thinking." Trevino stood, his outline blocking the shape of whatever he held between his hands. Closing the distance between them, he kicked his chair backward to give himself room to crouch in front of her. "They'll never fall for it."

He raised the item in his hands. Forcing the Kevlar vest over her head, the Ponderosa chief effectively pinned her arms to her side and took away her chance of escape. Something vibrated against her chest, and a red light emitted from inside. "Let's just say I've thought of that."

THE CARTEL WAS on the move.

Baker secured Maverick in the back seat of the truck and hauled himself behind the wheel. The engine growled to life at the push of a button, and within seconds, he, Jones and two Alpine PD deputies were charging after the armored caravan.

There was only one place he could think of for them to go this far out in the middle of nowhere. Their failed half-constructed headquarters. It was the perfect epicenter for the oncoming fight. Jocelyn was there. He could *feel* it.

Jones planted one hand against the dashboard from the passenger seat. "Did anyone ever tell you you're a bit intense?"

"A few. Though most of them were under arrest

at the time." Baker wasn't in the mood for jokes, but it came easier now that he'd spent the past few days learning from Jocelyn.

"Jocelyn is a fighter. There's nothing she can't handle," Jones said. "You know that now, don't you?"

He did. Because it took a hell of a lot of strength to survive what she had. But being capable of fighting for so long didn't mean she should have to. And she sure as hell shouldn't have to fight alone.

The line of vehicles ahead disappeared off the horizon, and Baker sat straighter in his seat. "Where did they go?"

"The headquarters was built underground." Jones pulled a laptop from the back seat and brought it into his lap. "Last time we were there, the structure was burning at the bottom of a sub-level hole. The cartel planned on burying it to avoid satellite imagery."

"When was that?" Baker's mind raced with every other question, but no number of answers were going to ease the tension in his chest.

"Two weeks ago. Right after Sangre por Sangre's raid on Alpine Valley." Jones hit the keys a few more times. What was he doing? Writing his biography? "Our forward observer, Cash, tore the place apart looking for Elena and her eight-year-old brother. When Jocelyn found them, they barely made it out before the building collapsed."

"It's cartel territory." There was still a piece missing here. If he and Jocelyn were right, the bomber had set about an intricate plan to bring down the cartel by adding a second chief of police's body to the tally. But that hadn't worked. Apart from a few bumps and bruises, Baker was still breathing. Which meant... His skull connected with the headrest. "His plan didn't work. The bomber. He didn't get the response he wanted by coming after me, so he had to raise the stakes."

"The bomber wants to use Jocelyn to pit Socorro and Sangre por Sangre against each other." Jones's fingers hesitated across the keyboard. Dread settled between them in the silence. "In that case, he's going to get what he wants."

Jones turned the screen to show an expanded geographical map. The screen blinked, zooming in on a rough patch of land. Then again. A square lit up around what looked like a car. "A single vehicle parked outside the building twenty minutes ago. An Alpine Valley police cruiser." The combat controller did whatever combat operators did with satellite footage, and another image took over the screen. "This was five minutes ago."

A ring of dark SUVs surrounded the lighter vehicle. Eight of them.

"Well, at least I know where West's patrol car went." Baker checked the rearview mirror. Both deputies were in the car behind them. No sirens. No lights. He caught sight of Maverick raising that caramel-colored gaze to his and floored the accelerator. The uneven terrain threatened to knock them off course, but there wasn't anything that could prevent him from getting to that building.

A chain-link gate materialized not twenty feet

in front of them. Baker didn't bother stopping. The metal scratched and thudded over the hood of the car and threw it up into the air before crashing down to one side of the cruiser. The deputies at the back had to swerve to miss it.

"You're going to pay for that," Jones said.

"Submit an invoice to the city clerk's office." The words left as more growl than reason. Baker raced along what felt like the edge of a crater in the middle of the desert. There was a decline up ahead. He didn't bother trying to slow his approach. The cartel was already inside, had possibly already found Jocelyn. The truck's tires skidded down the incline and thrust the hood into the back of one of the black SUVs.

"Come on, man!" Jones's annoyance simply grazed off Baker.

"What? Chicks love scars." He threw the truck into Park, unholstering his side arm. Then he checked the magazine. Half-empty. But, knowing what he did about Socorro operatives, he bet Jones kept extra ammunition on hand. "I'm going to need to borrow some fresh magazines. Watch the dog."

"You realize you're not the one who gives me orders, right?" The combat operative unholstered his own weapon. "And you're an idiot if you think you're walking out of there alive without me."

"Fine. I'll get one of my guys to do it." He shoved free of the truck. "So touchy. Here I thought you might like a babysitting job." Baker handed off orders to his deputies—one to watch Maverick, the other to cover the exit.

Staying low and moving fast, they maneuvered as one through the collapsed parking garage to an entrance that hadn't been pummeled with rubble. Shadows clouded his vision the instant they stepped foot inside. It smelled of fire and death and mold the deeper they navigated through what felt like a cement corridor.

"You good?" Jones asked.

Baker waited for the flashbacks, for the paralysis. For the hollowness in his chest to consume him completely. But it never came. There was only this moment. Of getting to Jocelyn. "I'm good."

"Then pick up the pace." Jones took the lead, weapon aimed high. Low voices echoed through the hall, but there were too many directions to pinpoint their location. Pulling up short, the operator handed off a radio. "We're going to have to split up. You take the right. I got the left. Try not to get yourself killed."

"Yeah. Ditto." Baker pinched the radio to his waist and took the corridor to their right. The voices were growing louder, clearer. Slowing his approach, he angled his head around one corner. But there was no one there. He took the turn and followed the hall to the end. Dead end. He pivoted back the way he came. "Shit."

Then he heard her.

Low. The words mixed together and muted as though coming through a wall. But he knew that voice, had relied on it to keep the past in its place. Baker raised his attention to the ceiling, then brushed his palm over the wall. There. An air-conditioning vent. "Gotcha."

He felt his way around the corner and slid his hand over a door. Pressing his ear to the metal, he made a response on the other side. Baker tested the handle. Locked. Of course—couldn't make it too easy. He backed up a step. Then hauled his foot into the space beside the lock.

The door slammed into the wall behind it, and he charged inside. Weapon raised, he made out two figures in the light of an electric lantern on the floor.

"Baker!" Jocelyn tried to pull away from the wall but couldn't stand. Blood crusted around her mouth and beneath her nose. The son of a bitch had hit her.

"You are a hard one to get rid of, aren't you?" The bomber centered himself between Baker and Jocelyn. All too familiar.

"Trevino." The puzzle fit together now. The lack of a body. The motive to frame and kill Marc De Leon. Ponderosa's chief hadn't died in that car bomb as everyone believed. He'd been exacting his own revenge against the cartel. "It was you."

"Surprise." Trevino raised something in his hand. A small black box, just wide enough for a single button. A detonator. "I'd stick around for the party, but it sounds like my guests are here."

A quick assessment of Jocelyn's Kevlar vest, pulled down over her arms, told Baker exactly what that detonator triggered. She'd been strapped with an explosive—the impact of which could bring down the entire building on top of them. Not to mention kill the woman he loved. "Put it down."

"I don't think you understand, Halsey." Trevino couldn't contain the smile plastered all over his face. "I put it down, and your partner here has a much bigger hole in her chest. You see, if I take my thumb off this button, we all die. So you might want to put down the gun instead."

"You son of a bitch." Baker took a step forward. "I could've helped you."

"Helped me?" The bomber raised the detonator. "No, Chief Halsey. I'm the one who's going to help you. This is what you want, isn't it? To see Sangre por Sangre pay for what they've done? Well, this is how we get it."

"Not like this." Holstering his weapon, Baker charged forward. His shoulder connected with the Trevino's gut and slammed the bastard into the wall behind him. He grabbed for the device.

The chief threw the fist clutching the detonator. Bone, plastic and flesh knocked Baker back, but it wasn't enough to knock him down. Jocelyn struggled to get free of the Kevlar vest in his peripheral vision. One slip of that detonator and he'd lose everything all over again.

Not an option.

Baker elbowed the chief in the face. A sickening crunch filled his ears. The bomber moved to catch the blood spraying from his nose. This was his chance. Baker hooked his arm around the chief's middle and hauled the bastard off his feet. They hit

the ground as one. And Baker wrenched the detonator out of the man's grip.

Air eased into his chest as he got control of the explosive, but the adrenaline had yet to fade. Baker rocketed his fist in Trevino's face. The impact knocked
the man's head back against the cement. Throwing
him into unconsciousness. "That's for breaking her
nose."

Staggering to his feet, he faced off with Jocelyn.
"You okay?"

"Yeah. I'm okay." She stared up at him, a million
things written on her face, but she must've known they
didn't have time to hash it now. The cartel was in the
building. Their time was up. "I could use some help
getting this vest off, though."

Keeping his finger over the detonator's trigger, he
crouched in front of her. The vest was heavier than
he'd expected. Packed to the brim. But he managed to
pull it over her head and make quick work of the zip
ties around her wrists.

"I guess I was the one who needed help this time."
Jocelyn rubbed at the broken skin on her hands.

"Anytime, Carville." Baker offered her his hand,
and for a moment, he didn't think she was going to
take it, but she did. Her palm pressed against his as
she got to her feet, and that instant contact took the
edge off.

Footsteps and flashlights broke through the door.
Unfamiliar shouts ricocheted around the room as
Baker and Jocelyn raised their hands in surrender.

Sangre por Sangre. He blinked against the onslaught of light, fully aware of the device in his hand.

"I think this is the part we get on our knees and hope they don't shoot us," he said.

They both lowered themselves to the floor.

Chapter Fifteen

One of the best things in life was a warm chocolate chip cookie.

And Baker's hand in hers as they faced off with a half dozen armed cartel gunmen.

Trevino lay unconscious behind them. Water soaked into Jocelyn's pants as they waited for Sangre por Sangre to decide what to do next. What were they waiting for? One wrong move. That was all it would take to put her and Baker out of their misery. Seconds pressed in on her lungs. Everything that'd happened over the past few days had led to this. To this one moment. Was this really how it was going to end between them?

She licked dry lips, knowing what might happen if she broke her silence. "Baker—"

"I was wrong before." He squeezed her hand tighter. "About what I said to you back at the camp. I've been so angry since Linley died that I've pushed everyone away for the smallest infractions. Because I was scared. I didn't want to lose anyone else, so I shut down any possibility of letting someone influence the way I feel, including you. I've been so focused on finding a way to bring down the cartel for what they took from me that I blinded myself to the best thing that's ever happened to me. You." He released a ragged breath. "I'm sorry, Jocelyn. For everything. You deserved better from someone claiming to be your partner."

A flashlight beamed straight into her face. *"¡Silencio!"*

Her shoulder burned with the possibility of taking another bullet, but it didn't hurt as much as it had before. Jocelyn moved her opposite hand to block the sensory assault, but there was no amount of distraction that could convince her that the man beside her would be able to ignore her past. Baker was law enforcement. He witnessed the results of addictions like hers on a daily basis, and he had every reason to worry he might find her unconscious and over-dosed. Because it was a possibility. This thing she carried inside her wasn't ever going to go away. And as much as she hated it, there was always a chance she'd give up the fight one day. She couldn't do that to him. The warmth given off by his touch urged her to forgive him, to let him into her world, to tell him she wanted to spend the rest of her life proving she was good enough for him. But she couldn't.

Jocelyn pried her hand from his, and she felt more than saw the collapse in his expression. "Let's just get through this."

Movement divided the semicircle of cartel soldiers in half. A single figure materialized at the back.

Male, heavily armored from the outline of his Kevlar vest. The flashlights and dim lantern did nothing to highlight his features, but there was something there she recognized. In his walk, in the way he held himself. Former military. Not born or abducted into Sangre por Sangre as most of the others had been. This one had converted to a life of violence, bloodshed and dominance of his own free will.

"Socorro has a lot of nerve showing their face here after what went down on that cliffside," he said.

The voice penetrated through her minuscule amount of confidence. Recognition filled in the shadows of the man's face. "Rojas. It's been a long time. Believe me, I wouldn't be here if it'd been my choice. Don't suppose you'd look past the fact Chief Halsey is holding a detonator that could bring this entire building down on us with the slip of his finger?"

Nervous energy rolled through the grouping of soldiers. A couple backed toward the door, eyes on the ceiling.

"You know this guy?" Baker asked.

Better than anyone. They were going to walk out of here alive, if she played her cards right. "Dominic Rojas, let me introduce you to Chief Baker Halsey, Alpine Valley PD." She nodded at Baker. "Rojas is a high-ranking lieutenant in Sangre por Sangre and a fellow baker. Though I'm not sure I would call what he does baking, really. Cookies aren't supposed to snap like biscuits."

Baker cut his attention to her, as sharp as a blade. "You realize we might die right now, don't you?"

"I knew you were going to go there, Carville." Rojas charged forward, and the lantern caught on his features. Neither Hispanic nor Chinese American, but a combination of the two. It was clear in the shape of his eyes, in the lighter color of his skin. She'd been right before. Former military—the Marines. A damn good one, too. Dominic Rojas had once been a Socorro operative named Carson Lang. And he'd taught her everything she knew about baking.

He shoved his finger into her face, but she wouldn't give him the satisfaction of knocking her off balance. "That was one time!"

"Yet it was enough for second place compared to my chocolate chip," she said.

Rojas's low laugh that didn't even own a hint of humor vibrated through the room. The lieutenant straightened. "You always were out to prove you have the biggest *cajones*, but this time might be your undoing, Carville. You think you can walk in here, insult my baking and expect I would let you leave alive?"

"That's a valid question." Baker's nerves were getting the better of him.

"To be fair, I think I was dragged in here. By him." Jocelyn tipped her head back. A groan registered from Trevino as he came around. "Recognize him?"

"Isn't he supposed to be dead?" Rojas asked.

"Seems Ponderosa didn't really lose their chief in that car bombing a couple months ago," she said. "The bombings at the station and Marc De Leon's compound? Both devices were built and detonated by him."

"Don't forget the device in my hand." Baker waved

with a half smile, but the possibility of war was still very real at this point.

Jocelyn leaned forward slightly. "Oh, right. He strapped me into that vest over there and planned to set it off with this handheld detonator. It's a dead man's switch."

"Why go through all this trouble? Did you insult his baking, too?" Rojas snapped his fingers, and two soldiers lowered their weapons, peeled off from the group and maneuvered around their lieutenant to drag the Ponderosa chief forward. They laid him and the Kevlar vest at Rojas's feet. "Because I'm starting to think he had the right idea."

"Marc De Leon tortured and killed the chief's daughter. Under orders, is that right?" Her heart tried to absorb the heaviness overtaking Baker's body language, but there wasn't anything she could do for him in that respect. Humans were tribal creatures. They craved connections and support and love just like the rest of the animal kingdom. But when that love was gone, they had to grieve on their own. She understood that now.

Rojas didn't answer, which was answer enough in and of itself.

Jocelyn lowered her arm to her side in surrender. "The chief constructed and detonated the bomb that blew up his truck to make it look as though the Ghost had targeted him, too. It gave him time to plan out his revenge. First by killing De Leon. Then by trying to frame your cartel for Chief Halsey's and my deaths."

"Starting a war between us and your employer and

anyone else your government sent after us." Registering what she'd just divulged, Rojas backed off a few inches. Then he nudged Trevino's ribs with the toe of his dust-covered boots. "It was a good plan, *amigo*. My bosses have been looking for a reason to take Socorro out for good."

Jocelyn lost the oxygen in her chest. If that was true, Rojas and his men could just finish the job Ponderosa's chief started right here, right now. Effectively eliminating any competition Rojas went up against at the next bake-off and making his loyalties clear. What had started as an undercover assignment in Sangre por Sangre would end with a target on his back from the very people he claimed as his own. Had he been Dominic Rojas long enough that was an actual possibility? Would he even have a choice when faced with blowing his cover?

"Whether that happens or not is up to you," she said.

Her pulse counted off a series of beats. Quicker than a couple minutes ago when she'd been sure they were walking out of here alive. She suddenly found herself missing Baker's hand in hers, wished she hadn't shut down that point of connection in the final seconds they had left together.

Rojas's men waited for the order, each of them all too willing to add two high-priced deaths to their belts. She could feel it in the shift of energy bouncing off the cement walls, a frenzy of battle-ready tension ripping the enthusiasm she'd tried to keep as a shield around her free.

"I'll take that detonator now." Rojas positioned himself in front of Baker, hand extended.

Baker twisted his gaze to her. Waiting.

The device in that Kevlar vest was the only thing guaranteed to get them out of this mess, but she couldn't risk starting a war between Socorro and the cartel. They'd come here to stop it. She nodded, and after a long moment, he handed it off.

"Great. I'll have one of my men bring your police cruiser around. Though you should know tips are not included in today's pardon." Rojos clutched onto the detonator as though his life depended on it. Which it did. All of their lives depended on it. "Oh, and please tell your friend Jones not to shoot me on the way out. I'd hate for our friendly rivalry to turn bloody."

Jones was here? Jocelyn sucked in a breath with the realization Baker had turned to a Socorro operative to come for her. A private smile hitched at one side of her mouth. Seemed he was warming up to the idea of teaming up with mercenaries.

Jocelyn shoved to her feet. "We're not leaving without him." She nodded to Trevino.

"He's not part of the deal, Carville." Rojas folded his hands in front of him, looking for a reason to withdraw his pardon. "He killed one of us. You know as well as I do—we can't let that slide."

And the bomber deserved that fate for what he'd done, but no amount of torture or blood was going to change the past or the pain he'd caused. Ponderosa's chief would see the inside of a jail cell. Not the inside of a flaming tire. "What if I trade for something you want?"

"You don't have anything I want," Rojas said.

That wasn't true. "Not even my chocolate chip cookie dough recipe?"

There was a slight melting of Rojas's expression. Bingo. He shifted his weight between both feet before moving out of their path. "Take him and leave before I change my mind."

Dragging Trevino to his feet with Baker's help, she called into the corridor just beyond the door. "Jones, we're coming out. Hold your fire."

The group of soldiers parted down the middle again, letting her, the bomber and Baker through. Socorro's combat controller met them on the other side, his rifle pressed against his chest, as he took in the situation. Most likely counting how many gunmen he'd have to take out personally if things went sideways. "You good?"

"We're good." Her attention shifted to Baker. Though she wasn't entirely sure what she'd said was true. At least, not for them.

They moved as a unit to keep up with Rojas's men leading them through the building's remains.

Baker hauled the bomber's arm over his shoulders. "Someday, you're going to have to tell me how the hell we just walked out of there alive."

HEATED DESERT AND blinding sunlight worked to hijack his determination.

Baker pounded his fist against the front door of

Socorro's headquarters. The past few days had taken everything he had to stay upright. Witness statements, arresting Trevino under charges, running operations at the cleanup site. And there was still a possibility Sangre por Sangre would change their mind about striking back for the death of one of their lieutenants.

He'd run through those miserable minutes in that basement room a thousand times. There was no explanation for the cartel letting them go. Both he and Jocelyn shouldn't have made it out of there alive. His brain kicked up a new memory as he stood there in the heat. Of Jocelyn in the rearview mirror, pulling Maverick into her lap as they'd driven back to Alpine Valley. She'd set her head back against the headrest and stared out the window, not uttering a single word to him.

She'd disappeared after that. Wouldn't respond to his messages or calls.

The door swung inward, and Baker took a step forward before he lost his nerve. "I love you."

The words he hadn't spoken to anyone—not his father after his mom had passed, not his sister before she'd died, not even his favorite chocolate glazed doughnut—rushed out beyond his control.

Jones Driscoll stared back at him, one hand ready to slam the door in his face. "Oh, thanks, man, but I just figured our relationship could be more of a casual thing. Not really ready for anything serious."

Baker's confidence collapsed in on itself. Great. Now the first person he'd ever said those three little words to was a smart-ass operator who'd most likely hold it against him for the rest of his life. "Is she here?"

The combat controller leaned his weight into the doorjamb, folding his arms across his massive chest. A roadblock from Baker getting inside. The humor between them was gone. Big brother—whatever that meant for a team like Socorro—was on duty, and Jones wasn't the kind of guy who could be convinced of Baker's sincerity. "She's here, but unless she gives the word, you're not coming in. We protect our own, Halsey. No matter what. There is one thing she wanted me to give you in case you showed up, though."

Anticipation undermined the guilt and shame of what he'd thrown in her face before his whole world had blown up.

Jones dipped to one side and collected an oversized paper bag from near the door. "She said she wrote the heating instructions on each of the containers and that she'll have someone run out another batch next week."

He took the offering, staring down into the perfectly packaged homemade meals. The aroma of marinara and garlic drifted from inside one of the top containers. Lasagna and bread. She'd made what looked like a week's worth of dinners, breakfasts and lunches in the space of a couple days. And despite the way things had ended between them, Jocelyn had come through with making sure he didn't have to live off of microwaved ramen.

"I get it. I screwed up." Baker stared past Jones's

shoulder. Not at anything in particular, but he saw the future he'd never thought he deserved. One filled with love instead of revenge, of inside jokes and home-cooked meals, of late nights cuddled on the couch and beneath the bed sheets. He saw him and Jocelyn. Her teaching him how to bake the lemon-cranberry cookies, of them handing out gifts to the rest of the team at Christmas, of movie nights and responding to calls together. Waking to that smile in the morning and kissing her senseless at night.

Of course, it would've been hard. Him dealing with what'd happened to Linley. Her guilt and grief over her husband… But they would've gotten through it. They would've found a way to make it work. Together. As partners.

Baker slipped his hand into his uniform slacks and produced what he'd hoped to hand Jocelyn herself. "Can you give her something for me?"

"What am I? The post office?" Jones asked.

"You're a lot more reliable in my experience." He handed off the collar and new set of tags he'd had made for Maverick. He wasn't much of a dog person, but Jocelyn was worth trying for. "Thanks."

He stepped down off the wide stone steps and headed for his patrol car with the prepackaged meals in hand. There would be other chances to see her. When she was ready. Hell, he'd host an Alpine Valley bake-off if it got her to face him, but for now, he had to accept Jocelyn needed space. From him.

"Baker." His name on her lips paralyzed him from taking another step.

He turned to put her in his sights, and damn, his entire body went into a frenzy. Though this time, he wasn't scared of losing control. This time there was no disconnect. Just Jocelyn.

She stood there covered in patches of flour down her front with a bit of egg sticking to the ends of her hair. White frosting grazed one corner of her mouth. It was obvious she'd been hard at work since they'd walked out of the cartel's headquarters. Had most likely forgone sleep and taking care of herself to process everything they'd been through with hundreds of cookies, and hell, she could probably make a few hundred more and take on the entire cartel given the determination in her expression.

"Why did you do this?" She flipped the collar over her uninjured hand, running her thumb along the strands.

"Maverick's tags didn't have an updated address on them. I figured if he gets lost or separated from you like he did after…" The bag in his hand got heavier every second this distance stayed between them. That was what she did to him. Made everything feel lighter. At first, he'd resented her attempt to bring any kind of lightness into his life, even if it'd been in the shape of a cookie. But now, he couldn't go another minute with this impossible weight. "Anyway, I thought it'd be easier for someone to make sure he got home."

"That's sweet. Thank you." Her voice remained even, but there was no enthusiasm to go with it. Tucking the collar into her cargo pants, she ducked her chin to her chest. Pulling away.

And he couldn't take it anymore. Couldn't let what they had slip through his fingers like he had the past two years. Baker took a step forward. "I love you."

"What?" Her gaze snapped to his, lit up by the sunset striking her head-on. The brown of her eyes turned iridescent, otherworldly and compelling in a way he'd never seen in anyone else before. Because Jocelyn Carville wasn't like anyone else.

"I wanted to say it earlier, when we were coming back from the cartel headquarters, and then I accidentally said it to Jones a few minutes ago." He was getting off track, and his nerves were about to toss him behind the wheel and launch him back to Alpine Valley, but he wasn't going anywhere. Not without her. He was done running. Done not letting himself feel. Done with trying to burn the world and everyone in it. "My point is I love you, Joce."

Her mouth quirked to one side. "Does Jones feel the same way about you? Because I'm not sure how I feel having to compete against someone on my team."

"No. Not even a little bit." The pull they'd shared throughout the investigation took hold, and Baker dared that next step toward her. "Jocelyn, I was nothing but a ghost living in this body before you barged into my station with a plate full of cookies. I'd lost everything I thought I cared about to Sangre por Sangre, and all I wanted was to stop feeling. For people to leave me the hell alone so I could find the bomber responsible for my sister's murder. I took the chief of police job to protect the town I love from the cartel, but after everything that's happened, I realize I was just like him. Trevino. I let myself become consumed to the point I forgot what it felt like to be happy. Until you gave me a reason to look for silver linings."

Her smile was gone. Instead, a deep sadness had taken hold. Jocelyn swiped at her face, then stared into the setting sun cresting the mountains in the west.

It wasn't enough. What he'd said wasn't enough. The realization constricted his heart, and Baker tried to block the emotional response lodged in his throat, but there was no use. He was going to lose her. He understood that now. "I know I hurt you. The things I said… I wish I could take them back, but I can't. All I can say is I'm sorry, and if you give me the chance, I will spend every day of the rest of my life proving that I believe in you and that I truly love you."

She took a step down, then another. Jocelyn closed the distance between them, sliding her palm over his chest. His heart beat so hard, he swore the damn thing was trying to reach her. Problem was it already belonged to her. Every inch of him was hers. He wasn't sure when it'd happened, but there was no denying it now.

"I need a partner, Baker," she said. "Someone who knows me inside and out, who's willing to talk to me when this demon tries to take over. Because it will. I need someone who doesn't just love and accept the person I am now, but all the different versions of myself. Past and future. Who's willing to work on his own pain while doing the best he can for the people he cares about."

"I want to be that someone." Baker dropped the bag of food at his feet, threading his hands around her waist and pulling her against him. Right where she belonged. "Whatever it takes. Forever."

"Good. Because I love you, too. More than anything." The smile he'd come to love stretched her mouth wide as Jocelyn leaned in to kiss him.

A tritone sounded a split second before a frenzy of paws, fur and slobber slammed into him. Baker lost his hold on Jocelyn as Maverick tackled him to the ground. The German shepherd licked at his face and neck, settling all one hundred pounds on Baker's chest. Low playful groans accompanied Jocelyn's laugh.

She stood over him, unwilling to help as the dog wrestled him into the dirt. "I forgot to tell you. You'll have to fight Maverick for the other side of the bed."

* * * * *

INTRIGUE

Seek thrills. Solve crimes. Justice served.

Dont miss
K-9 Shield by Nichole Severn,
available in-store and online soon.

www.millsandboon.com.au.

People were—or they became—what they pretended to be.

And Maggie Caddel had been pretending for a very long time.

Plastic cut into the sensitive skin of her wrists. She wasn't sure how long she'd been here. Getting dripped on from a leaky pipe overhead, told when she could eat, when she could stand, when to speak. Her tongue felt too big for her mouth now. Thirst did that. She'd pulled against the zip ties too many times to count. It was no use. Even if she managed to break through, there was nowhere to go. Nowhere she could run they wouldn't find her.

A thick steel door kept the animals out but kept her in. Maggie shifted away from the cinder block wall. She'd somehow managed to fall asleep, even with the echoes of shouted orders and footsteps outside her door. Another drip from above ripped her out of sleep. It splattered against the side of her face and tendriled down her neck.

This place… It held an Aladdin's cave of secrets she'd worked the past year to uncover. But not like this.

Not at the expense of ten American soldiers dead. And not at the expense of her life. The war waging between the federal government and the New Mexico cartel Sangre por Sangre had already cost so much.

A metallic ping of keys twisted in the lock. Rusted hinges protested as the door swung inward. El Capitan framed himself in the doorway. His eyes seemed to sink deeper in their sockets every time they went through their little routine. His irises darker than should be possible for a human. If that was what he was. Judging by his willingness to interrogate, torture and starve a random war correspondent, Maggie wasn't sure there was any humanity left.

She set her forehead back against the wall. It was starting again. The questions. The pain. She wasn't sure her legs would even carry her out of this room. "I'm guessing you didn't bring me the ice cream sandwich I asked for."

It'd been the only thing she could think of that she wanted more than anything else in the world. Other than being released.

El Capitan—she didn't know his real name— closed in. Strong hands pulled her to her feet and tucked her into his side. The toes of her boots dragged behind her, and it took another cartel soldier's aid to get her into the corridor.

The walls blurred in her peripheral vision. She'd spent the first few days memorizing everything she could. The rights and lefts they took to the interrogation room. The stains on the soldiers' boots, the rings they wore, the tattoos climbing up their necks. El Capitan, for instance, wore the same cologne day-to-day. It was overly spicy and would ward off demons in a pinch, but the ski mask that usually hid his face took some of the bite out. Given the chance, all she would have to do was smell him to make a positive ID.

But he wasn't wearing the mask anymore.

Which meant he wasn't worried about her identifying him anymore.

Because they were going to kill her.

Both gunmen thrust her down into the chair she'd bled in for the past… She couldn't remember how many days had gone by. Three days? A week? They'd all started to stitch together without any windows in her cell to judge day or night by. Like she'd been kept in a basement. But this room had a small crack in the ceiling. Enough for her to know they'd dragged her here in the middle of the night.

Maggie let the sharp back of the chair press into the knots in her shoulder blades. The wood felt as though it was swelling as it absorbed her sweat, her tears. Her blood. Could crime labs pull DNA from wood? She hoped so. It would probably be all that was left of her given what she'd witnessed.

"I'm losing my patience with you." El Capitan rubbed one fist into the opposite palm. Like warming up his knuckles would make any difference against her face. "Where are the photos you took? Who did you give them to?"

Same old game. Same old results. That first day

had been the hardest, when she had no choice but to be mentally present every second, to experience every ounce of pain inflicted. But now… Now she'd learned how to step out of her body. To watch from above while the Maggie below suffered at the hands of a bloodthirsty cartel lieutenant trying to clean up the mess he'd made. "What photos?"

The strike twisted her head over one shoulder. Lightning burst behind her eyelids. The throbbing started in her jaw and exploded up into her temple. And that was all it took. To detach. Disassociate. She wasn't in the chair anymore. Some other woman was. A part of her that was strong enough to get through whatever came next. She could stand there and observe without ever feeling that man's hands on her again.

"We've been through your home. We've been through your car. Next, we'll question everyone you care about." El Capitan was in a mood today. More hostile than usual. Desperate.

Maggie couldn't help but like that idea. That he was feeling the pressure of getting results out of her. That she'd held him off this long. The Maggie in the chair was having a hard time keeping her head up. She dropped her chin to her chest. "If you get ahold of my sister, tell her I want my green sweater back."

"You have no idea who you're dealing with, do you, little girl?" The cartel lieutenant stuck his face close to hers. Even separate from her body, she could smell the cigarettes on his breath. "What we can do to you, to your family, your life. All you have to do is give me the photos you took that night and this ends. You'll be able to go home."

Home? She didn't have a home. Didn't he realize that? All she'd done over the past two years was disappoint her friends, her family, her coworkers. Investigating Sangre por Sangre's growing influence throughout the Southwest was all she had left. And she wasn't going to let them get away with what they'd done. No matter the cost.

Except no one knew she was here.

No one cared. Certainly not her ex-husband.

Not even her editor would know where to start.

No one was coming to save her.

And the photos she'd taken of that tragic night— when the cartel had slaughtered ten American soldiers and then disposed of their bodies in an ambush meant to capture the cartel founder's son—would rot where she'd hidden them. Maggie licked her broken lips, not really feeling the sting anymore. Her head fell back, exposing her throat, as she tried to meet El Capitan's eyes. Sweat pricked at the back of her neck. "It's hot. Can I have that ice cream sandwich, please?"

The lieutenant fisted a handful of her hair, trying to force her to look at him, but Maggie wasn't in that body. All he was looking at was a shell. A beaten and bloodied ghost of the woman she used to be. "Take her out in the middle of the desert and leave her for the coyotes to chew on. She's worthless."

He shoved her body backward.

Gravity pitted in her stomach a split second before the Maggie in the chair hit the floor. The back of her head hit the cement, and suddenly she didn't have the strength to stay detached from that shell she'd created. In an instant, she was right back in her body. Feeling the pain crunch through her skull, realizing the warmth spreading through her hair was blood. Her vision wavered as she tried to reach for that numbness that had gotten her through the past few days, but it wasn't there anymore. Shallow breathing filled her ears. "No. No. Don't do this. You can't do this."

"Clean that up. I want this entire room and her cell scrubbed down." El Capitan threw orders with a wave of his hand as he headed for the corridor. "Make it so no one will know she was ever here."

Two sets of hands dragged her upright. Every muscle in her body tensed in defense, but she'd lost her will to fight back days ago. It wasn't supposed to be like this. She was going to make something of herself. This story…this was supposed to change everything.

Maggie tried to dig her heels into the cement, but pieces of the floor crumbled away with her added weight. Her arms hurt. This was it. Everything she'd done to rewrite her life had been for nothing. Tears burned in her swollen eyes. "Please."

The men at her sides didn't respond, didn't lighten their grip. Didn't alter their course. They pulled her through a door she hadn't known existed in the shadows until right then. One leading directly outside.

She'd been so close to escaping without ever even knowing.

A thud registered from behind her. Then another. She tried to angle her head around, but it was pointless.

Pointless to hope El Capitan had charged back into the room with a change of mind. She was going to die.

A groan rumbled through her side a split second before the gunman at her left dropped to his knees. He fell forward. Unmoving. She didn't understand. The second soldier marching her to her death released his hold, and she hit the ground. Another groan infiltrated through the concentrated thud of her heart behind her ears.

Then…nothing.

For a moment, Maggie wondered if the head wound had caused damage to her hearing or her brain had short-circuited. Then she heard him.

"Don't try to move. You're badly injured, but I'm going to get you out of here." Something wet and rough licked along one of her ears. "Gotham, knock it off. Don't you think she's been through enough?"

A small whine—like a dog's—replaced the sensory input at her ear. A dark outline shifted in front of her. Masked. Like El Capitan, but that wasn't… That wasn't his voice.

Maggie cataloged what she could see of his eyes through the cutouts in the fabric. She'd never met this one before. She would've remembered. Her vision wavered as a set of muscled arms threaded beneath her knees and at her lower back. He hauled her to his chest, and there wasn't a single thing she could do to stop him as darkness closed in. "You're not one of them."

SHE'D LOST CONSCIOUSNESS.

Jones Driscoll brought her against his chest, back

against the wall, as he scouted for an ambush. Sangre por Sangre's half-destroyed headquarters were settled at the bottom of a damn fishbowl in the middle of the freaking desert. Any number of opportunities for the cartel to take advantage. He'd managed to take down a couple of the cartel lieutenant's direct reports back in the interrogation room, but the man of the hour had managed to escape down one of the corridors. Ivy Bardot—Socorro's founder— would give him hell for that. Months of research, of tracking Sosimo Toledano's movements, of trying to build a case for the federal government to make a move. And Jones had blown it the second he'd laid eyes on Maggie.

He moved as fast as he dared straight out into the open. Cracked New Mexico earth threatened his balance as he headed for the incline that would take him back to his SUV. His legs burned with the woman's added weight, but Gotham wasn't helping either. The husky kept cuing Jones with every hint of human remains buried in this evil place.

Low voices echoed through the disintegrating parking garage. The structure was on the brink of collapse, yet satellite imagery and recon reported an uptick in activity over the past three days. Most recently utilized as a hideout for Sosimo Toledano, identified as Sangre por Sangre's prodigal son. Heir to the entire organization if and when the feds managed to capture the big dog. Seemed Sonny Boy was trying to make a name of his own. Ever since Ponderosa's chief of police had come back from the dead for revenge against the cartel, there'd been an increase in attacks on the small towns fighting to stay out of cartel business. Homes ransacked, residents running from public parks as gunfire broke out, businesses broken into and burned to the ground—all of it leading back to a single shot caller. Sosimo Toledano. Local police couldn't keep up with the onslaught, so they'd turned to Socorro.

But what was it about this place Sangre por Sangre couldn't seem to let go of? An explosion had weakened the supports months ago, the foundation was failing, water was penetrating the walls and eroding the floors. Yet the cartel lieutenant had abducted, questioned and tortured the woman in Jones's arms. Caddel. He'd called her Ms. Caddel. No first name.

Jones backed them into the shadows at the sight of two gunmen taking a cigarette break under the overhang of the underground parking garage, staying invisible. That was his job. To get in and out of enemy territory without raising the alarm. To discern the cartel's next move and calculate their strategy before they had a chance to strike. He'd lived and thrived in combat zones for half his life, but this... He studied the outline of the woman's face highlighted by a single flare of a lighter a few feet away. This felt different. What the hell could Sangre por Sangre want with one woman?

Laughter ricocheted through the hollow cement darkness. One move. That was all it would take, and the soldiers would be on him. Which wasn't normally a problem. He lived for the fight, to be on the front lines of defense. Just him and his opponent. Protecting a woman who'd been beaten to within an inch of her life was a whole other story. It would be hard to engage while worrying about whether or not she was still breathing.

Gotham pawed at Jones's cargo pants. A low groan signaled he'd found the scent of human remains close by.

"Shh." Pressing into Gotham's paw with one leg, Jones hoped to quiet the husky's need for attention. They were probably standing on an entire cemetery, given Toledano's recent crimes against humanity. But there wasn't anything he could do about it right now.

"You hear that?" One of the gunmen faced off with Jones's position. Though his lack of response said he hadn't spotted them yet. Too dark.

Gotham jogged to meet the nearest gunman. A low warning vibrated through Jones's throat, but the husky didn't pay him any mind. Jones adjusted his hold on the unconscious woman against his chest in case he had to make a jump for his dog.

The nearest gunman swung his rifle free from his shoulder, taking a step forward as Gotham waltzed right up to him, and a tension unlike anything Jones had experienced laced every muscle in his body. A smile broke out across both soldiers' faces, and the second took a knee, hand extended. "Where'd you come from?"

Hot damn. Gotham had provided a distraction, giving Jones the chance to get out without raising suspicions. Jones sidestepped his position, keeping to the wall as the gunmen searched for something to give the dog.

Joke was on them. Gotham only ate a certain brand of dog food and jerked pig ears.

He tightened his hold around Ms. Caddel as one of the spotlights swept across her face. Matted blond hair streaked with dirt and something like liquid rust caught in his watch. Not rust. Blood. His gut clenched as he got his first real good look at her swollen eyes, the cuts along her mouth, the bruising darkening the contours of her face. This woman had been through hell. But he was going to get her out.

Jones hiked the incline he'd descended to get into the structure. Sand dissolved beneath his weight, but he put everything he had into keeping upright with an added hundred and thirty pounds. Just a little farther. He could almost see his SUV on the other side of the barbed fence in the distance. He cleared the incline and stepped onto flat ground.

A yip pierced his senses.

The sound fried his nerves as he recognized Gotham's cry for help.

He turned back. The husky was hanging upside down by one foot in the soldier's extended hand, arcing up to bite at the man's wrist. Another series of laughs drew out a full bark from his dog. Setting Ms. Caddel down as gently as possible on flat ground, he tried to breathe through the rage mixing into his blood. He might not like being weighed down by a K-9 sidekick who'd rather chase his own tail than pay attention to anything Jones had to say, but no one touched his partner.

He descended the incline, not bothering to keep

to the shadows this time around. Two armed gun-men didn't stand a chance against a combat controller employed by the most-resourced security company in the world.

Surprise etched onto one gunman's face as he locked on Jones's approach. The guy unholstered a pistol at his hip and took aim.

Jones dodged the barrel of the weapon, sliding up the soldier's arm. He rocketed his fist into the gun-man's throat. A bullet exploded mere inches from his ear and triggered a ringing through his skull. Grab-bing on to the cartel member's neck, Jones hauled the attacker to the ground. They fell as one. He pinned the gunman's hand back by the thumb until a scream filled the night. The gun fell into Jones's hand as the second soldier lunged.

The second bullet found home just beneath the bas-tard's Kevlar, and the soldier dropped Gotham as his knees met the earth. The K-9's yip and quick scram-ble to his feet let Jones know he hadn't been hurt.

Jones pressed one boot into the gunman's chest and rolled him onto his back.

"What did your boss want with her? The woman you were supposed to execute." He hiked the soldier's thumb back to increase the pressure on the tendon running up into the wrist and forearm. Once that tore, there'd be no squeezing saline solution into a contacts case or a trigger for the rest of his life. "Why take her?"

The resulting scream drowned out the ringing in his ears.

"She was there!" The cartel member shoved into

his heels, trying to break away from Jones's hold, but there was no point. The harder he tried to escape, the more damage was done.

"Where?" he asked.

"I know who you are." A wheeze slid through crooked, poorly maintained stained teeth. That was the thing about cartels. Every member worked for the good of the whole, but that relationship didn't go both ways. No dental coverage. No health coverage. Just a binding promise to die for the greater good. "I know who you work for."

"Then you know I won't stop until every last one of you are behind bars." Clutching the gun's grip harder, Jones pounded his fist into the soldier's face. Bone met dirt in a loud snap that knocked the son of a bitch unconscious.

Gotham raced to Jones's feet as he stood, coming up onto his hind legs.

"This is why you're not supposed to leave my side. How many times do we have to talk about this? There are mean people in the world. Guys like that don't care how nice you are." Jones wiped down the handle of the pistol with the hem of his T-shirt and dropped the weapon onto the gunman's chest. Scratching behind the husky's ears, he headed for the incline to get the hell out of here. "Though I've gotta say your distraction was on point."

Jones pressed his palm into his ringing ear. It wasn't so much the noise that bothered him. It was the percussion. He'd bounced back before when a gun had gone off next to his head. This time shouldn't be any different, but he'd check in with Dr. Piel when he got back to headquarters.

He hiked the incline to the spot where he'd left the woman he'd pulled from the interrogation room. Only, she wasn't there. Jones scanned the terrain, coming up empty. She couldn't have just walked out of here on her own. He'd known men overseas who wouldn't have been able to string together a sentence with the injuries she'd sustained. "I wasn't gone that long, right?"

Gotham yipped as though to answer.

A pair of headlights burst to life a hundred yards past the barbed fence. From his SUV. The beams cut across him a split second before they redirected around. Jones shaded his eyes with one hand and pulled his cell from his cargo pants pocket with the other. Seemed Ms. Caddel hadn't been unconscious, after all. Clever. Then again, it made sense. A woman in her position couldn't be sure of anything after going through what she had. Trusting the man who'd pulled her out of that torture chamber most assuredly came with suspicion.

Jones called into headquarters and lifted the phone to his good ear as the first ring trilled. Then started jogging-walking to catch up with the SUV. "That's what I get for leaving the keys in the ignition."

Don't miss the stories in this mini series!

NEW MEXICO GUARD DOGS

K-9 Detection
NICHOLE SEVERN
February 2024

K-9 Shield
NICHOLE SEVERN
March 2024

MILLS & BOON

The Perfect Witness
Katie Mettner

MILLS & BOON

Katie Mettner wears the title of "the only person to lose her leg after falling down the bunny hill" and loves decorating her prosthetic leg to fit the season. She lives in Northern Wisconsin with her own happily-ever-after and wishes for a dog now that her children are grown. Katie has an addiction to coffee and Twitter and a lessening aversion to Pinterest—now that she's quit trying to make the things she pins.

Visit the Author Profile page
at millsandboon.com.au.

DEDICATION

For Linda

Thank you for believing in me when I didn't believe in myself. The memories of your loving encouragement in every aspect of my life are the reason I had the courage to make *our* dream a reality. Wherever you are over the rainbow, I still love ya more.

CAST OF CHARACTERS

Cal Newfellow—As a security expert, he excels at keeping people safe. As a man, he has enough experience to know safety is an illusion.

Marlise—As the star witness against her ex-boss, she's in hiding until her trial. She has secrets she's told no one, and they're the reason she's being hunted.

The Miss—She's MIA, but she wants Marlise. The secrets she thought would die in Red Rye were about to be revealed, and she couldn't let that happen.

Charlotte—Defecting on a mission for The Miss was a death sentence, but it was a chance she had to take.

Mack Holbock—Cal's right-hand man at Secure One. He'd fought alongside Cal and Roman in the army, but now Secure One is the only country he serves. He just needs a chance to prove his worth, even if that means breaking orders.

Roman Jacobs—Married to the other key witness in The Madame's trial, he knew they had to find The Miss if they wanted to live happily-ever-after.

Mina Jacobs—Tortured by The Miss in Red Rye, would she go undercover to root her out and bring her to justice?

Chapter One

"Meanwhile, in Minneapolis, the trial for Cynthia Moore, aka The Madame, the famed head of a sex trafficking empire, is underway after a lengthy eighteen-month delay. The extensive evidence for the case was nearly insurmountable for both the prosecution and the defense. The trial is expected to last several weeks while the jury remains sequestered. Later today, the defense will put a woman on the stand who was in charge of the household at the Red Rye escort house before it burned. That witness, whom courts are only identifying as Marlise, is expected to testify against her former boss, Cynthia Moore, while revealing what she knew about other illegal activities under The Madame's eye. Former FBI agent Mina Jacobs, the undercover agent sent in to find evidence of prostitution, is expected to testify after Marlise. Jacobs's testimony is expected to take several days, considering her connection to her then boss, and Cynthia Moore's husband, David Moore."

Marlise's gaze flicked to the screen as her heart

rate crept up to near heart attack level. She was waiting for Cal to pick her up for the drive to the courthouse. Secure One was three hours away from the
city, so they'd all driven in last night and stayed at
a hotel. Cal didn't like it, but realistically, they had
no choice. With The Miss still on the run, everyone
was worried she'd pick today to tag them. Marlise
knew it was a real possibility, but if she made it to
the courthouse today and gave her testimony, The
Miss would have no reason to hunt her. Unless she
wanted revenge. If that were the case, Marlise would
never be safe or free.

"We've asked our law expert to break down the
case for us," the newscaster continued. "He is in no
way affiliated with the case but can offer insight into
both the defense and the prosecution's plan of attack.
Thanks for being here, Barry."

"It's my pleasure," a man in a tweed suit said.
He was sitting in an office on a blue couch, and the
windows behind him gave the audience a view of
the Minneapolis skyline lit with a thousand spar-
kling lights. It was early, and the sun wasn't up, but
that didn't mean the city was quiet. That was one
thing Marlise hated about the city. The dark. It hid
the worst side of humanity, and she'd experienced
the worst side of humanity enough times in her short
life to fear it. She preferred the quiet solitude of Secure One, where she worked keeping Cal's men fed
every day. Whenever she was scared or nervous, she
could walk out to the lake and watch the water ripple

while taking deep breaths. Cal's property lent itself to isolation and made you forget the outside world existed. Marlise had lived on the streets for years, and no one knew what a jungle they were more than her, so she appreciated being wrapped in a womb of safety and protection at Secure One.

"There is no perfect witness," the lawyer said when she tuned back in to the news program. "Both sides will find something to use against any witness. A small misstep, a social media post or even an image taken out of context can throw doubt into the minds of the jurors. You have to remember that the prosecution has to prove beyond a reasonable doubt that crimes were committed, but all the defense has to do is prove reasonable doubt that the defendant is innocent. Each side will look for any chink in the witness's armor before putting them on the stand."

A shiver ran down Marlise's spine. *There is no such thing as a perfect witness.* Was that true? She still had to try. She had to do her part to put The Madame and her husband behind bars. She refused to acknowledge the woman's real name. She would always be The Madame, a badge of shame for the damage she'd done to girls like her. Yes, The Miss was still out there, but Marlise had to start where she had a little bit of power and control. Her entire life had been about lack of control, and she was tired of it.

Living and working at Secure One had changed her. She was stronger, both physically and emotionally. When Mina was kidnapped by The Madame, she had hurt her foot beyond repair and, because of that, was now an amputee. Marlise watched her come back from that stronger and more determined to make a difference in the world. Mina's fighting spirit inspired Marlise's.

Absently, she rubbed the leathery skin on her arm. She had healed from the extensive burns she'd endured at the house in Red Rye, but the nerve damage and disfigurement were still hard to live with some days. Cal had insisted that his nurse, Selina, treat her skin with a gel to care for the disorder better, which was something she could never afford on her own. The skin felt better with each passing day, and she had hope that it might lessen the burning pain even more. When she'd first woken up in the hospital after the fire, she'd wished she'd died there rather than be alive inside her burning body. Her heart paused in her chest when memories of that day came rushing back to her.

"I heard them talking. They know you're an FBI agent. You're not getting out of here alive, Agent August."

The woman Marlise had come to see as her only friend in the house hesitated before a shaky smile lifted her lips. Marlise turned back to the mixer, the cookie dough swirling around inside the bowl while terror swirled through her gut. She worried about what would happen next if her friend actually was an undercover FBI agent. Would she be arrested? Marlise wanted to throw up at the thought. She was just the cook! She wasn't involved with the escort service. At least she wasn't anymore. They could still say she was or at least say she knew about it and should have reported it. She knew better, though. Red Rye was like fight club. That was the only rule.

At least she had Agent August. Maybe she'd tell the authorities that Marlise didn't go out on dates the way the other girls did. She swallowed over the nervous lump in her throat. Her life was about to change again, and she wasn't ready. She wasn't ready to go back to the streets.

"Thanks for this, Marlise," Agent August said as she snagged a cookie from the tray with a wave.

Marlise didn't react. She didn't look at her or do anything until she was gone. Then she calmly turned and pulled out another pan of cookies from the oven.

"What does your gut say about the agent who was undercover there?" the newscaster asked, bringing Marlise back to the present. "Wouldn't she be considered the perfect witness?"

"No," the lawyer insisted as Marlise's attention snapped back to the television. "Again, there is no perfect witness. The defense will try to discredit the agent. They'll say her boss at the FBI, former special agent David Moore, who is also The Madame's husband as you'll recall, put her there unknowingly, but she was there long enough to find a smoking gun. She was injured while undercover and again while arresting David Moore. The defense will try to convince the jury that she's got a vendetta against the Moores now."

"Could you blame her? I don't know anyone who wouldn't feel intense hatred toward the people responsible for their torture and attempted murder."

"On the human nature side of the case, that will play well for her, but it could harm her on the legal side of the case."

"The same can be said for Marlise?"

"Absolutely. Of course, Marlise is a victim of The Madame, and on the human nature side of the case, she will be a stellar witness, but they will find something to discredit her. It will be harder with her since her past was wiped away, but if they have to, they'll twist something perfectly reasonable into something ugly."

Marlise flicked the television off, disgusted with how the media had turned The Madame's trial into a sideshow. She knew firsthand that it wasn't a sideshow for the girls in those houses. The human nature side of those houses was a terrifying way to live while constantly worrying about dying. It tossed her right back to that day, and the swirling in her mind dropped her to the bed.

A thud. A muffled scream. Another thud. A moan of agony. Why didn't the FBI come and help her friend? Where were they? Marlise had noticed Agent August tap out a message on her phone before she left the kitchen.

Do you want to be here when they show up? that little voice asked. It's time to make like a tree and leave.

The voice was right, and she had to do it now. She scurried to her room, another thud from overhead bringing her shoulders up to her ears. Marlise waited for the scream from her friend to follow, but this time, the house stayed silent. She ran down the hallway now, her feet swift. It was only then that she realized the other girls weren't in the house. She swallowed around the truth that clogged her throat. They didn't care what happened to her. The other girls were cash cows for the organization, but she was disposable. She always had been.

Her gaze swept her tiny room for someone waiting for her, but it was empty. She reached for her backpack and hesitated. She should only take her money. No bag to slow her down or make it evident that she was running. She pulled out a wad of one-hundred-dollar bills from under her mattress with a grim smile. It wouldn't get her far, but it would get her out of Red Rye. She grabbed a jacket and threw it on, stashing the money in a secret pocket.

The Miss's words ran through her mind. "I'm taking the girls and getting out before the FBI breaks down our door. Only the moneymakers. Yes. No. She's dead weight to me now. I don't need her. I think she knew all along the FBI were involved."

Marlise didn't know her friend was an FBI agent, but she wasn't sticking around to get the same kind of treatment Agent August was suffering. Another *thud, another scream, and then something tickled her nose. She sniffed.*

Smoke.

The cookies were burning! Too bad. Marlise wasn't going back to the kitchen. They could be waiting for her there. She hoped the smoke would distract them and give Agent August a reprieve. Marlise had to get out before she couldn't. If they stopped her, they'd kill her. She had to get out of Red Rye, but she had one more thing to do. She hated to waste precious time on it, but if she didn't stop for her treasure, the proof would be gone for good.

Run, her brain told her feet, but she forced herself to enter the hallway at a normal pace. Smoke filled the space, and she realized nothing was normal. It wasn't her cookies burning. The house was on fire, and she had to get out! Choking on the acrid smoke, she got as low as possible and kept her hand on the wall. She was desperate for fresh air as the cloying thickness choked her, tempting her to open her lungs to it. It wanted to work its tentacles through her until she followed it down into the bowels of hell.

She wouldn't. She couldn't. She needed to get out of this house alive, or everything Agent August had worked for would be lost. If they ever caught The Madame, she'd have the evidence to help put her away for good.

There was a knock on the hotel room door, and she jumped. Her heart rate, already up from being trapped in the memories of Red Rye, kicked up another notch until she heard his voice.

"Mary."

Cal.

He'd started calling her Mary last summer when she'd moved back to Secure One to work for him. She hadn't used the name in a decade, but he insisted on using it when they were alone together. She wasn't sure why. She'd ask, but she was too afraid of the answer. Cal held power over her life, whether it was intended or not. He kept her employed, housed and fed while they awaited the trial, but there was more to it. He sheltered her—both physically and emotionally.

She checked to make sure it was him before she opened the door. He was inside the room with the door closed before she saw him move. He was that way. Even at six foot four inches tall, two hundred and fifty pounds of muscle and with tats covering both arms, he moved like a ghost. Cal was always intense, but this morning, he was laser focused on the details as he prepared her for the trip to the courthouse.

He slung a bag onto the bed and started pulling out items. "Mina and Roman are preparing the cars. It's time to get dressed for court."

Marlise glanced down at her pants and long-sleeve blouse. "I am dressed for court."

"Correction," he said, handing her a black jacket. "For the drive to court."

She took the jacket, but her eyes widened when he

pulled out a bulletproof vest. "Don't you think that's going a bit far, Cal?"

"If anything, it's not going far enough, but it's all we have, so put it on."

Marlise had learned when Cal issued an order, he expected you to follow it. He lowered it over her head and then tightened the side straps down.

"I should have gotten a child's size. You swim in this thing."

"If they make child-sized bulletproof vests, I don't want to be part of humanity," she muttered.

He cocked a brow at her, and she sighed. Of course, they made them. Cal held up a small walkie-talkie and attached it to her vest before he helped her cover the vest with her jacket. "The walkie-talkie will only contact the other people on our network." Marlise nodded, but she swallowed over the fear in her throat when he turned away. She could see in his dark brown eyes that he was scared too. If Cal was scared, there was a good chance she could die today.

When he turned back to her, he handed her a small handgun and showed her the full magazine before popping it back into the gun. "You can't take this into the courthouse, obviously, but until then, it stays within reach."

She grabbed his hand before he could tuck the gun into the front of her vest. "That doesn't look familiar."

"It's just like our training guns, but it shoots live ammunition. Remember, the safety is on the trigger.

Don't aim. Just point and shoot. And while you're shooting, run."

"Cal, this feels a bit overboard for a fifteen-minute drive to the courthouse."

"Maybe, maybe not," he said with a clenched jaw. "If The Miss is out there, and she's worried about what you'll say on the stand, she knows exactly where you will be and when."

"We don't even know if she's still in the country. It's been radio silence for years, Cal."

He grabbed her packed backpack off the bed and slung it over his shoulder. "That doesn't mean she's not in play. I've worked too hard to keep you alive the last year to take any chances on the one-yard line. Mina is dressed to look like you and will be riding with Roman. I'll be driving the other SUV with you in the back."

"It's not smart to put Mina at risk, Cal. She has to testify too."

"We're making it look like we're bringing you in one at a time. If my car is empty, they'll think on a passing glance that Mina is you. They're trained agents with more years under their belts combined than you've been alive, so don't worry about Mina and Roman. We'll get you to the courthouse safely, and once we do, you're one step closer to living your life free of The Madame."

Cal walked to the door and checked the peephole before radioing down to Roman and Mina in the underground garage. He was right. The media had broadcast loud and clear when she was testifying at the trial. It had been on the evening news a week ago, and she wouldn't forget that scene anytime soon. Cal had been so angry he'd thrown his coffee cup against the wall before he walked out of the control room and disappeared for an hour. Roman had assured her that his brother was just frustrated with the media turning the trial into a circus and putting people's lives at risk, but she still carried guilt about it. If Roman hadn't gone to Cal for help when he found Mina, Cal would never have met Marlise, and his life wouldn't be so complicated.

Mina told her she couldn't think that way because Cal didn't, but it was days like today that she wasn't so sure. As much as it pained her to think about leaving Secure One, and this man, she wouldn't have a choice if she made it through today. They both deserved to be free.

CAL BRAKED AT the exit to the parking garage. Roman had just pulled out with Mina in the passenger side dressed as Marlise. With a wig down over her face and a pair of sunglasses, Mina could pull it off. He didn't like putting his brother in the position of risking his wife, but she was a former FBI agent and could hold her own. Two years ago, his brother showed up on his doorstep with his compromised partner in tow. Mina had been on the run from a woman they called The Madame for a year, but she was desperate for protection and a chance to heal.

He was convinced Secure One could take care of her. He'd naively believed he had all the safeguards on his property to protect them, but he soon learned nothing was further from the truth. The Madame's men infiltrated his borders and took Mina right out from under their noses. They got her back, but he'd learned some hard lessons that day, and he wasn't giving anyone another chance to attack his home or his people.

One of those people was in his back seat dressed in bulletproof armor, and he hoped this ruse would work long enough to get her to the courthouse. Marlise used to live in the Red Rye house, an escort service and modern-day brothel, run by The Madame. She was also Mina's only friend on the inside. When that house burned to the ground, with Marlise still inside it, The Miss and The Madame thought they'd mitigated a threat. They were wrong. Marlise knew things no one else did, and that was why The Miss could be waiting to ambush them on their route. She was a dangerous, invisible woman, but the chances she'd become visible today were almost 100 percent.

Truthfully, he didn't know if she was even in business anymore, but the part of him that had done bad things in the name of helping good people told him she would soon turn up. The Miss was hunting for the last two people who could identify her. In the eyes of The Miss, Marlise was a nobody, but she also knew more about the operation than even Mina did. The Miss didn't want either woman spilling the beans about what went on in Red Rye, but she would see Marlise as an easy snatch and grab. Worst-case scenario, she was willing to shut her up any way she could, including with a bullet from a distance. He wouldn't let that happen.

"Are you okay back there?" he asked, waiting for his turn to leave the parking garage.

"Snug as a bug," she replied sarcastically, and he snorted.

"I know it's uncomfortable, but it's better this way."

"If you say so."

Cal slid his sunglasses across his face and followed his brother down the street. Following his brother defined his life. The moment Roman joined the army, Cal never considered doing anything else. He signed up at seventeen. At eighteen, Cal followed his brother into special training for the military police. By nineteen, he was the youngest member of the Special Reaction Team at Fort McCoy. They'd called him "kid," but Cal didn't mind. He knew why he was there. To do the job. Protect his country. To stand next to his brother again. His team may have teased him about being a kid, but they knew he wasn't one. They had each other's back every time and all the time until that one time.

People always said blood was thicker than water, but not when it came to Cal Newfellow and Roman Jacobs. They may not share a last name, but they shared a bond that went deeper. They grew up together as best friends and foster brothers, but Roman never treated him like a kid. Over the last decade, Roman looked to his little brother for help more often than not. When Mina had gone missing, driven into hiding by The Madame after their undercover operation went south, Cal helped Roman find her. They complemented each other's strengths and weaknesses, and that made them an effective team.

That was the reason Roman and Mina left the FBI last year to be part of Secure One. Roman's extensive combat training had made his men sharper, stronger and more advanced in self-defense and combat fighting than half the guys in the military. Mina's skills at a computer kept his security business running smoothly. Over the last year, she had stopped two cyberattacks aimed at several of his VIP clients.

On days like today, he was glad to be working with his brother again. Cal had done enough bad things in his life. Now his goal was to do good things to better the world. He blew out a breath as he checked all the mirrors of the SUV. He had to stay sharp. He had a witness to protect.

Is she just a witness though?

That is all she can be, he reminded himself.

Marlise had arrived at Secure One broken, in pain and terrified. He'd made sure she healed better than anyone could have predicted. Once she had her strength back, he trained her in self-defense and gun safety. While she could bake a mean chocolate chip cookie, she also had deadly aim with a firearm. He got off on giving her back power over her life. He hoped that she could find newfound freedom once this trial was over. He wanted her to stay at Secure One, but he understood she'd been bought and paid for over the last decade. Hell, her name wasn't even Marlise. It was Mary.

Cal shook his head and readjusted his focus on the road. Fifteen miles separated them and the courthouse, and he had to get her there in one piece. He reminded himself to send a thank-you to the media and their useless mouths. Now was the time to attack if The Miss wanted to throw the entire trial into chaos and get away a free woman. If she tried hard enough, she could get a twofer with Mina without even knowing it. He could feel the evil coming. The hair on the back of his neck was electric and fear crackled in his chest.

"Do you think there's such a thing as a perfect witness?" Marlise asked from the back seat.

"Absolutely not. Humans are imperfect, so it's relatively easy to discredit a witness. Why do you ask?" Cal asked, waiting at a red light.

Roman was third in line, and he hoped his brother remembered they both had to clear the green light, so they didn't get separated. Cal hated driving through the concrete jungle with a witness as hot as Marlise, but he had no choice. If they hadn't stayed over last night, the drive would have been three hours long, and by the time they reached the city, they wouldn't be sharp or reactive. Unfortunately, the city made escape routes challenging to plan, and he always felt like a caged animal trapped by the street grids with no easy way out.

"I heard a lawyer on the news say no witness is perfect. The newscaster asked about Mina, and the lawyer said the defense would claim she stayed in Red Rye too long and should have had the evidence sooner."

Cal pressed down the accelerator to clear the yellow light. "I'm sure they'll throw anything at the wall and hope it sticks, but we know none of it is true. Mina never had the evidence because her boss was pulling the strings to keep her there."

"It made me think that I might be the perfect witness."

"I don't follow."

"Think about it, Cal," Marlise said. "Thanks to David Moore, my past before I moved into the Red Rye house is gone. There's nothing for the defense to dig up."

"That's true, but everyone is vulnerable," he reminded her. "They can twist simple things to make you look bad."

"It would be hard to discredit someone held against their will."

"They'll simply say you were free to leave at any time."

"I wasn't though!" Marlise hissed. "I wasn't. You know I couldn't leave. If I left, they'd have killed me." He heard the terror of those years in her whispered words. Cal wanted to pull the car over and gather

her in his arms to protect her. That was a reaction
he'd had a lot since she'd first stepped foot on his
plane, injured and scared. A reaction he didn't like.
He reminded himself his only job was to get her to
the courthouse to testify. Once that was over, they
could part ways and go on with their lives independently of each other.

That little voice inside his head laughed.

"Deep breaths, Mary," he encouraged, his focus
still on the back of Roman's SUV. They were ten
minutes out now. "We know you couldn't leave, but
the defense will try to throw doubt into the jurors'
minds any way they can. That's their job. It's widely
accepted that women who are sex trafficked into
those houses aren't there by choice. It's the prosecutor's job to explain that to the jury. You just have to
relax, okay? You're not going to be charged with a
crime. I won't allow it."

"I don't know if even your steely determination
can outpower The Miss," she whispered. "But, just
in case something happens, thank you for taking care
of me the last few years and getting me this far. You
didn't have to do it, but I would be dead already if
you hadn't let me stay at Secure One."

"I'm going to get you there safely, Mary. Don't
give up on me now," he begged.

"I'm not," she assured him. The sound of Velcro
being unstrapped reached his ears. "I've got my gun,
and I know how to use it, thanks to you."

His lips broke into a grin that made him glad that

neither she nor his team could see it. "Mary, it has been my greatest honor to be part of your life. You don't need to thank me for anything. Just get up on that stand and put these people away. I'm proud of you and your tenacity, so let's cross the finish line. We're in go time."

Marlise knew what that meant. He heard her take a deep breath before she went silent. He punched a button on the dash that connected him to Roman's car. "Five and in. What do you see?"

"Road construction up ahead. Slow traffic."

Cal hissed out a cuss word before he responded. "There was no planned construction anywhere on the route."

He heard Roman's laughter before he answered. "As if the city of Minneapolis cares?"

He was silent, and Cal waited for an update as they crawled forward. Since Roman was the lead car, he would have to be the one to assess the scene.

"Utility work. Looks like a city truck. We're fine. Just go slow around them."

"Six and in now," Cal said, updating them on the GPS arrival time.

He wasn't happy about the added minute. Extra seconds could mean lives, and the one he was carrying was a life he'd worked hard to save for reasons he refused to address. He might bury his head in the sand about how he felt for the tiny woman in the back seat, but he would never give up on keeping her safe.

Roman's SUV skirted the truck with ease, but

Cal's bigger vehicle would be a tight squeeze, so he slowed to pass the truck. "Almost there," he said to keep Marlise calm.

There was laughter from the back seat. "No, we aren't, but nice try, Newfellow."

As he approached the truck, his lips turned up in a grin, but his amusement quickly disappeared when the scene before him registered. The truck wasn't from the City of Minneapolis. The last time he checked, they didn't arm their city employees with automatic rifles.

"Stay down!" he yelled as the first bullet collided with the side of the SUV.

Marlise's scream filled his ears as he yanked the car to the right and slammed into the parked truck in an attempt to unbalance the shooters. He didn't wait to see if it worked before throwing the SUV into Reverse and slamming his foot down on the accelerator. He should have listened to that hair on the back of his neck. It had never let him down.

Chapter Two

"Cal!" Marlise yelled from the back seat, where she hid under a heavy black blanket. She no sooner got the word out than the SUV lurched and nearly threw her to the floor. She had a seat belt around her waist, and she threw her hand out to brace against Cal's seat. "I'll return fire!"

Before she could, his words chilled her to the bone. "Stay under that blanket, Mary! We're outnumbered, and they have way more firepower!"

Another bullet slammed against the SUV's window, and the bulletproof glass cracked. Marlise tossed the blanket off her head and noticed the front passenger-side window was also hit.

"Cal!" Roman's voice on the radio filled the car as the utility truck rammed them from behind. "Evade! Evade! There are more waiting ahead. We're going left! Do not go to the courthouse! They know you have Marlise!"

A barrage of bullets hit the car, and this time, Cal must have slammed the accelerator because the car jerked, the tires spun, and then they were flying across the city streets, barely avoiding oncoming traffic. All she could do was pray no innocent people got hurt because of her. Marlise wrapped one arm in the seat belt and held her gun in the other. She was ready to defend their lives if it came down to it. That was the least she could do for this man after everything he'd done for her.

"Scatter plan!" Cal yelled.

"Ten-four," Roman answered, and then the radio went silent.

Cal muttered a string of cuss words that would make any girl blush, but she noticed that he didn't slow down. A terrified pit had opened in her belly, and she wanted to cry, but she refused. She would not let The Miss win this time! A bullet slammed into the back window, and then another one tagged the rear door.

"Hold on! We don't stand a chance if I can't lose them!"

"I'm returning fire!" she yelled, but the window refused to budge when she hit the button.

"No!" He yelled the word in anger as he twisted the wheel hard to the left. "If you stick your head out, you're dead. Stay down!"

The words weren't out of his mouth when another bullet smacked the back of the SUV. They'd managed to damage the glass to the point if they got a clear shot, a few more rounds would shatter it. Marlise's arm burned from being twisted in the seat belt, but she didn't have time to worry about it. Sirens had filled the air, and she was worried more people would get hurt because of her.

"Hang on!" Cal yelled to her. "We're using the cops as cover and going off-road!"

"Cal, we're in the city!"

"No choice. Hang on!"

The SUV jumped and metal grated on the undercarriage before they fishtailed, landed hard and straightened out.

"What's your plan, Cal?"

"Once we're clear, we have to find a new vehicle and work our way back to the gathering point so Secure One can extract us."

He fell silent as the SUV hurtled down a bumpy surface while she was rocked back and forth like a boat. A boat!

"What about the river?" she asked, throwing the blanket off her face, securing her gun back in her vest and preparing to unbuckle her seat belt when he stopped. She had memorized the same plans Cal and Roman had and knew exactly what steps to follow.

The bullets had stopped coming for now, but that didn't mean more weren't waiting for them up ahead. "If we could find a boat, we could use the river to get out of the city and closer to Secure One."

"We'd still need a car," he muttered. "We can't take the river any further than St. Cloud."

"At least we wouldn't be here!" she exclaimed, her

voice holding all the fear bubbling up in her belly despite trying to remain calm.

"If the opportunity presents itself, I'm not against it," he said as they bounced over something that made a grinding sound under the car. "Get ready. I'm about to dump this in a grove of trees, and we're going to bail. Grab the go bags!"

She leaned over the back of the seat and grabbed the two black backpacks. Her arm burned, but she ignored it to focus on the plan. After hauling them onto the seat, she unbuckled her seat belt and braced her feet on the front seat until Cal slowed the car and threw it into Park. It had barely lurched to a stop before they were out and running for the trees along the river.

Engulfed by green branches, Cal weaved through them, and she knew he expected her to follow without question. She was grateful for the strength and stamina workouts Cal insisted she do, but the longer they ran, the heavier she breathed. Cal was pulling her along behind him now, and she went down to one knee, his arm pulling hers taut for a moment until he turned back.

"I need a break," she said, her chest aching from carrying the pack and the heavy vest.

He leaned toward her, scooped her up and started running again. "We need more distance between them and us," he huffed as she held on around his neck.

Marlise jumped in his arms. "I have to testify! You have to take me back!"

"That ship sailed, Mary," he said, his breath coming harder now that he was carrying her. "There's no way you're getting near that place. If we're lucky, the cops pick up some of The Miss's women, and they lead them to her."

"And if they don't?"

"Then this doesn't end until someone roots her out of her hole and kills her."

"Stop and put me down!" she ordered. She held her demand in her gaze when Cal glanced down at her. Eventually, his pace slowed, and then he stopped next to a large tree trunk and lowered her back to the ground. "Thank you." Marlise straightened her vest, stiffened her spine and lifted her chin high.

"We can't stop for long. We have no idea if anyone followed us, and the SUV isn't exactly hidden. I don't even trust the cops at this point."

"Understood, but you have to think smart, Cal. You told Roman to follow the scatter plan, which means we do too."

His hand went into his hair as his chest heaved. "I was prepared for an assault, but my heart is still pounding. I can't believe they tried to take us out that close to the courthouse."

"It was their only choice," Marlise said, her trained eye searching the shoreline past the trees. "They didn't know what direction we'd be coming from, but they knew once we funneled down into the hot zone, there would be only so many choices we could make."

Another cuss word fell from his lips, and she bit

back a smile. Men were so transparent, even when they thought they were big bad security agents. "We need to distance ourselves from that mess."

"They're going to be looking for us, Cal. I'm one of their star witnesses."

"You're not going near the courthouse right now. The FBI should have done their job and found The Miss before the trial!"

Marlise rested her hand on his giant forearm. "Cal, take a deep breath. I understand that I can't go there now. We have to get out of here since the prosecution will be on the hunt for their star witness. Besides, we were the ones who decided not to use the FBI for protection."

"Not true," he said with a shake of his head. "They were supposed to be part of the transport team for you. That was why we were in the hotel this morning."

"You never told me that," she said, planting her hand on her hip.

Cal took his hat off and wiped his brow before putting it back on. "It was need-to-know information, and I didn't want you to worry. Ultimately, it was still Secure One that was protecting you. The FBI just wanted a hand in getting their witness to the courthouse. They were in the air as well as waiting on the surrounding streets."

"Then where the hell were they when we needed them?" she demanded. It made her angry that even surrounded by the FBI she wasn't safe.

"I don't know," he admitted with a puff of air.

"That's what scares me about this. We need to get back to Secure One and get Roman and Mina on the official wire with them."

"How did the FBI miss this?"

"Maybe they didn't," he said, cocking a brow.

"No. There's no way the agency still has someone in play, Cal. It's been years since David Moore was arrested, and Mina said everyone in the field office went under a microscope before they were allowed to continue working."

"Sure, in Minneapolis. That doesn't mean every office worker and agent in the FBI was looked at under a lens. Remember, money talks."

"What are we going to do, Cal?" she asked, anxiety filling her.

He tipped her chin up to force eye contact. "We're going to stay alive. Are you ready to run again?"

"We could run, but we need to conserve our energy, Cal. The scatter plan says we find a way back any way we can. We can't use one vehicle longer than an hour before finding another. Gloves must be worn at all times, and the last five miles to the extraction zone has to be approached on foot." Marlise took pleasure in the way his mouth dropped open when she finished the instructions.

"You memorized the scatter plan."

She stepped up to him, chest to chest, and poked herself in the vest. "Of course, I did. It's my life on the line. I've been in life-or-death situations more times than I want to count, Cal. I know how to live and hide on the streets. You'd do well to remember that."

A smile tugged at his lips, and he wrapped his arms around her, giving her a brief hug. Marlise languished in it, glad to be in his arms again in a way that wasn't scary. She would never admit to his face that she was terrified, but she had been for days. There was never any doubt that if The Miss were still out there somewhere, she would look for her at the trial. At this moment, she just needed to feel safe, and his arms always did that for her.

When he released her, he straightened her vest and ensured her gun was secure. "I would never discount your experience, Mary. But this is an urban jungle, and we have few choices but to run."

Marlise motioned him closer to the edge of the tree line along the riverbank and then squatted down. Cal knelt next to her, and she made an arc with her arm as it swung out to the left. It stopped on a bobbing speck on the bank of the river. "That's our run target."

"How did you even see that?" he asked, pulling her up to standing again.

"The Jolly Green Giant was carrying me, and the light glinted off it and into my eye."

Marlise took great pleasure in his snicker as he shook his head. "I'll let you get away with that once." His brow furrowed, but she saw the smile tugging at his lips. "It looks like we're about three miles out from the boat. Let's move."

Cal grabbed her hand and headed deeper into the trees again. She knew he would wind his way there rather than attempt the path of least resistance. He was always looking for a secondary path if their first one was blocked. She matched her steps to his, hard as it was, so she didn't let him down. Marlise would follow him anywhere, but she'd also be ready to defend herself if she had to. He'd said it himself; they were in the concrete jungle now, but she knew that life like the back of her scarred hand.

Cal knelt, and Marlise slid down his back as she did the same. They'd reached the end of the trees near the back of a property on the Mississippi. There were multiple boats and kayaks tied up to a dock, but he had his eye on just one. A brown Jon boat. It was built for the waters of the Mississippi. He'd had enough experience with them in the service to know their capabilities.

"I need to do some recon before we make any decisions."

"We don't have time to use military strategy, Cal," she hissed from behind him.

He spun and took a knee, grabbing her shoulders so she didn't tip over. "We don't have time not to, Mary. For all we know, that house is full of people! There could be cameras anywhere on that property. We can't waltz in and take a boat if we don't know what we're waltzing into."

He felt her defiance wane as he held her. "Fine, but I'm going with you."

"You don't know the first thing about recon, Mary. While I'm gone, you have a job. Listen and look. You've got the bird call?" She nodded and dug it out of one of her pockets. "Good. You're my eyes from up here. If you see or hear anything, blow that call, then get hidden and stay hidden. Remember the sound of the drones at Secure One?" he asked, and she nodded again. "Listen for that sound. It's unlikely they'd send them this far down the river, but the police will be searching for us eventually. Understood?"

"Got it. I'm not helpless, Cal. Go."

A cuss word slipped out when he ran his sentence back through his head. "We can't go for the boat."

"Why?" she asked. Her question sounded frustrated, but Cal heard the fear and fatigue hiding under it.

"Drones. I can hide you from anyone on land in the center of that boat, but not from the air." Her face fell, and he swore a blue streak internally. "I'm still going to go check the place out. We may not have a choice." He double-checked his gun and turned to her. "Stay alert. Keep your head on a swivel. When I'm ready for you to join me, I'll blow the bird call."

He winked before he headed to the left of her and down a steep embankment. A quick flick of his wristwatch told him it had been two hours since the first bullets flew. He wouldn't hear from Roman again unless he could send out a text. No voice communication could be risked, so he had switched his walkie-talkie off when they'd stopped the first time. When he got back to Mary, he'd check the phone in her pack for a message. It was silent and untraceable, but, with any luck, Mack would have an extraction plan in place.

Cal knew Roman and Mina were fine. The Miss's gang saw right through their plan to keep Marlise hidden and went for his SUV. He kicked himself for not realizing that was a dead giveaway. He and Roman had hoped that the flak jacket and double car entourage to the courthouse would fool them, but they were only fooling themselves.

How could he have been so stupid? Mary could have died today! Cal's steps faltered, and he nearly fell down the slope headfirst. His breathing was ragged, so he took a second to slow his heart rate and calm his breathing. He prided himself on being a ghost, but he felt like a bumbling oaf right now. His focus was split between getting them to safety and how close they came to death today.

Focus. Slow. Steady. Look for signs of life. Are there dogs? Where are the cameras?

The questions forced him to concentrate, and he picked his way down the embankment, avoiding sticks and leaves that could alert a homeowner or a dog. Autumn had arrived in Minnesota, and the dry, fallen leaves weren't doing him any favors. He paused at the bottom of the hill, knelt and let his gaze travel the eaves of the house. They would have to avoid the area if the house had cameras. He saw none at the back of the building, which didn't make sense. They had nearly a quarter of a million dollars' worth of boats at the dock, and they weren't monitoring them?

Sliding along the side of the garage, Cal peeked inside a window. It was empty of cars, but that didn't mean no one was inside the house. Another few feet, and he could stick his head around the side of the garage. His trained eye took in the uncut lawn, the wilting summer flowers, and the front porch swing wrapped to protect it from the winter weather. He ducked back and let out a breath. It looked to be a weekend and summer cabin, but with no cameras on the property, that meant one thing—the boats themselves were protected from theft.

Even if he could break through one of the security devices with his limited tools, he had to face the truth. It wasn't safe on the water. It left them far too exposed, especially in the daylight. A boat battle was nasty business, and Marlise didn't have the experience to live through a gunfight on the water. Especially the Mississippi. They needed a new plan, and quick. Marlise wasn't going to like his decision, but it was his job to keep her safe. He'd already failed once, and the next time might be the last.

Think, Cal.

He scanned the property again, and then he saw it. Salvation. He put his bird call to his lips and blew.

Chapter Three

They hit a boulder and caught a little air before settling back onto the trail. Marlise gripped the door
handle on the old door as they tore across the tundra.
The Jeep turned off-road vehicle had been a lifesaver
when Cal found it hidden under a tarp at the back
of the property. It might be the only thing that kept
them out of sight long enough to find safety.

A shiver ran through her as she remembered the
gunfight a few hours ago. There was no question in
her mind that The Miss was doing business again.
The bullets told her The Miss was worried that what
Marlise knew would put her newborn business at
risk. Marlise did have a secret, but she was afraid
to tell Cal or Mina the truth. If they knew what she
was hiding, they might kick her back to the streets,
where she wouldn't last a day.

Did that make her a bad person? She was holding out on the people trying to help her, which was
wrong, but she didn't think it made her a bad person.
It made her a person with no good options. Telling

them the truth wouldn't help matters if she couldn't cough up the proof.

"How much further?" she asked, noticing the sun was starting to set. Her back was sore from riding in the bumpy Jeep for the last two hours, and she needed to stretch her legs.

"Not much since we're almost out of gas," he said, his jaw pulsing as he avoided another rock in the nick of time. "We don't dare stop for a fill either. We're too memorable in these vests, and we can't risk taking them off. Check for a message from Mack again, please."

Marlise fished the secure phone out of her pocket and flipped it open. The last message had come through about two hours ago from Roman that they were safe and awaiting further instructions.

"He sent a message fifty minutes ago. It says 'Trigger Lake. Mack. Seven. End.' What does that mean?"

"It means Mack will extract us if we get to Trigger Lake by seven tonight. Otherwise, we're on our own."

Marlise glanced at the clock on the phone. It was a little after five. "How far is Trigger Lake?"

"An hour."

"Then we have time," she said, buoyed by the idea of getting out of this alive, even if it was only a reprieve while they regrouped.

"An hour by vehicle. We maybe have fifteen minutes before we run out of gas."

"Then we find another car. We need the servers

at Secure One to find The Miss," she said, a tremor in her words. "She knows where I am, Cal."

"We don't know that," he said, glancing at her for a moment. "She knew where we were going to be. That doesn't mean she knows where we're going."

With a deep breath in and out, Marlise tried not to let the panic take hold. "If that's the case, we need to find her before she finds us."

"Now there's something we both agree on, Mary," he said with a smile.

"Why do you call me Mary?" she asked, her words soft against the grumbling of the Jeep's motor.

He gave her a shrug. She figured he was going for nonchalant, but it didn't look that way to her. The shrug told her the answer wasn't simple. "I like the name Mary."

"But I go by Marlise now, Cal."

"Is that by choice though?" he asked, steering around another boulder on the path.

The Jeep was silent other than the growling of the engine. It was the first time she'd thought about it. Was she using Marlise by choice now or by habit? It was easy to give up Mary to become Marlise when The Madame recruited her. It was a second chance for her—a new beginning. A season of change to be someone other than Mary Liberman—a homeless no-body. Then along came The Madame who made her Marlise—a woman people depended on every day.

"Do you know what the name Mary means?" Cal asked.

"No, Cal. I grew up in foster care, trying to avoid the abuse at the hands of older kids and foster dads. There was little time to look up the meaning of my name."

When she turned to look at him, his jaw was pulsing as though he were working hard not to say something to upset her. She got it. Foster life was miserable for her, but it had been fantastic for his family. Roman was his foster brother, and they'd grown up together and fought together in the service. There were two sides to every coin. She was just one of the unlucky ones who got tails instead of heads.

"The name means rebellious. I have never known a Mary who wasn't rebellious. You included."

"I'm not rebellious. I'm lost, Cal. Lost in this big world without an identity that I can relate to."

"We're all a little bit lost, Mary. You might as well accept that now. You have several identities, but only you can decide which one you connect to the most."

"What identity do you connect to?" she asked, watching as the gas gauge hit the last line on the dial.

"I'm a ghost, Mary."

Her amused snort could be heard over the engine's sputtering as it tried to keep going despite its lack of energy. "You might be a ghost when you're on missions, but people know that Cal Newfellow runs Secure One. No one outside of Secure One knows Marlise or Mary even exists."

"That's not true. The Miss knows, and as evidenced by this day, you mean something to her. You mean something to me, Roman, Mina, Selina and Mack. We will give you your identity back and a real second chance."

The Jeep sputtered and died, coasting down the path until the last of its forward momentum was spent. "I guess that's that," Marlise muttered, grabbing her backpack off the Jeep's floor. "We better hoof it if we're going to make Trigger Lake in under two hours."

Cal turned and touched her forearm before she could get out of the car. Her yelp was immediate, and he lifted his hand from her arm as though it had burned him. When he saw the blood covering his palm, a look crossed his face that she couldn't define.

"Are you hurt?"

"It's nothing," she insisted, bringing her left arm to her side to hide it.

"You're bleeding, so it's most definitely something." He gently pulled her arm back over where he could see it. He turned his headlamp on and grabbed scissors from his bag, slicing her coat open. "Why didn't you tell me you'd been cut?"

"I don't know what happened to it," she muttered, keeping her eyes off the wound. It had been burning for hours, but she refused to let it slow her down. "It started burning in the SUV while we were under fire. It doesn't matter. We can worry about it later. We have to get to the extraction point."

With a grunt, he dug in his pack and came out with gauze and tape. Cal wrapped the arm tightly to stem the oozing blood. At first, it burned worse, but then it slowly became numb.

"I can't believe you knew you were hurt and didn't say anything." He snatched the phone from her vest and flipped it open, typing something out in silence.

"When you're a girl like me, you learn what injuries need immediate care and what injuries can be ignored. You learn to separate yourself from the pain and keep moving. You learn that you're always in pain, and there's no sense fighting against it. Stop the bleeding, accept the pain and soldier onward. Isn't that what they teach in the military too?"

Cal tucked the phone back into her pocket and held her gaze with his steely one. "The difference is, you're not a soldier in the middle of a war."

"That's where you're wrong, Cal," she said, opening the door and stepping out of the Jeep. "I've been a soldier in one war or another for the last twenty-eight years and survived them all. Don't forget that."

HE HOVERED IN the med bay while Selina worked on Mary's arm. When he discovered her injury, he'd sent a text to Roman telling him she was hurt and they should wait at all costs for them. By the time Mack got them out of there and back to Secure One, her wound had soaked two bandage wraps. She was getting paler by the minute, so he'd taken her directly to Selina. He was supposed to meet Roman and Mina in an hour, but first, he had to be sure Mary would be okay.

"It's oozing because a piece of the seat plastic is

stuck in her arm," Selina explained from where she sat working. Rather than stand over her shoulder, he forced himself to take a step back, so he didn't crowd her.

"I think a bullet must have come through and hit the back of the seat, which sent the plastic shrapnel into my arm," Marlise said. "Look at it this way. At least it's not a bullet lodged in my arm."

"Can you get it out, or do I need to find a doctor?" Cal asked, his lack of faith making Selina roll her eyes. She had sass, that woman.

"It's fine," Marlise said from where she lay on the hospital bed with her arm stretched out. She was already getting IV fluids and antibiotics and was less pale, but he still worried about infection.

"It's not fine," he snapped, and she shrank back against the bed. Selina glanced over her shoulder at him with impatience and disgust. "I'm sorry," he said, running his hand through his hair. "She's injured and acting like it's no big deal because she's afraid to be a burden. It's not fine, and we will take care of you," he promised, walking to Mary and taking her other hand. "I didn't mean to snap."

"It's okay," she promised with a shy smile. "It was a long day, and we're all tired."

"Amen," Selina whispered as she kept working. "Can you feel this?" she asked Marlise as she poked her arm.

"No, it's numb."

"Excellent. Let's get that debris out of there, and then we'll stitch you up so you can rest."

Cal knelt in front of the bed to focus Mary's attention on him. "I need to meet with Roman and Mina. Once you're patched up, have Selina help you shower and then go to bed."

"But I have to cook—"

He put his finger to her lips to hush her. "You're not going near the kitchen until tomorrow. There are plenty of premade meals available. You need to rest, or I will have to find someone here with the same blood type to give you blood, considering how much you've lost."

Marlise glanced at Selina, who nodded and added a shrug at the end. He appreciated that she didn't undermine him even if the truth was something else. He didn't know if she needed a blood transfusion, but he knew she needed rest. They were in the calm before the storm. There was a tornado on the way, and the tingle at the back of his neck was intense. He wasn't listening this morning, but he was tonight.

"I do have a headache," she admitted with a sigh.

Cal stood and kissed her forehead, stroking the hair back off her face and running a thumb down her cheek. When her eyes widened, he yanked his hand back as though the heat of her skin had burned him.

What was he doing?

He stepped back and avoided their gazes as he backed up to the door. "I'll leave you to it. Radio if you need anything, Selina. Mary, rest. I'm serious."

She gave him a salute, and he turned on his heel sharply and strode to the control room while berating himself the whole way. He had to keep his hands and lips off that woman before things happened that he couldn't take back. Mary wouldn't be part of his life once they caught The Miss, and he planned to do that sooner rather than later. Relationships were a no-no for someone like him. They caused entanglements that dulled your senses and shifted your focus away from the job at hand.

He slammed his way into the control room like a bull in a china shop, and his trained gaze picked out the vital activity in the room. His security team was in place monitoring his clients' businesses and homes. The other two people in the room took him by surprise—his brother and Mina. "I thought I told you two to rest," he said as a greeting.

"Hello to you too, brother," Roman said, biting back a smile. "What crawled up your pants and bit you in the a—"

"How's Marlise?" Mina asked, interrupting her husband's tirade.

"She's in the med bay," Cal said, running his hand through his hair again. "She has a piece of plastic in her arm because I dropped the ball." His finger in his chest punctuated his words. "She's tired, scared and lost too much blood. That's my fault."

"No," Roman said, standing and walking over to him. "That's The Miss's fault. You got Marlise out of there alive. She has lived through much worse than plastic in her arm and a little bit of bleeding. She's tougher than both of us combined, Cal."

"But she shouldn't have to be," he said, his shoulders deflating. "We should have seen this coming."

"We did," said Mina from where she sat at the computer. "We all knew if The Miss was still in play, the trial was where she would try to pinch Marlise. I just wasn't expecting it to get so far out of hand. The FBI should have given us cover to escape, and that didn't happen."

"The FBI," Cal snorted. "That must stand for Ferociously Bad Intel."

Both Roman and Mina bit their lips to hide their grins, but he saw them and let one lift his lips. He was tired and angry, but he always enjoyed a good dig at the FBI.

"What do we know?"

"We know The Miss is in play and wants Marlise," Mina said, stating the obvious. "We don't know where she is or how to find her."

"What's the chatter from the trial?"

"It's on an indefinite hiatus while the judge determines their next steps," Mina answered. "The prosecution is arguing they can't go ahead with the case if they can't get their witnesses there safely. The defense is arguing to dismiss the witnesses and continue the trial."

Cal grunted with laughter. "Sure, just continue the trial without their biggest players. Of course, the defense would want that, but we can't allow it to happen. Do we need to remand you and Marlise into FBI custody?"

"Absolutely not," Roman said, standing to his full height and blocking his wife from view. "Mina will not step foot into that circus until we have The Miss under lock and key."

"We may not have a choice if the FBI demands it," Mina said, leaning around her husband. "But I'd like to avoid it because they're zero for two in my opinion."

Cal pointed at her. "Marlise and I both wondered if someone on the inside tipped off The Miss."

"I want to yell that's impossible, but I can't," Roman said, rubbing his hands down his face. "Anything is possible when it comes to these people. The government claims they found no evidence of anyone else involved with The Madame from the field office, but that doesn't mean there isn't someone."

"I agree," Mina said, standing and stretching her leg. "It could be someone who works as a janitor or support staff. Like if Marlise could move around the Red Rye house without being noticed, this person could do the same. We can assume she heard it on the news, but until we know what happened today with our air support, we have to assume someone on the inside is pulling strings."

"Which is why neither you nor Marlise is going into FBI custody. You won't make it a day," Roman said, his tone fierce as he reached for his wife of less than a year. "I lost you once and nearly lost my mind. I won't put you into a situation where I could lose you again."

She slipped her arm around his waist and hugged him while Cal looked on. He noted a bit of jealousy toward his brother but immediately shut it down. He couldn't risk his business or life by getting involved with someone because he was horny.

Was he horny, or was he lonely?

Cal refused to answer that question. His job was to protect everyone on the team at Secure One, not just the person in his bed. Mary's face materialized, and he forced it away. He might want her in his bed, but she never would be.

"I agree," Cal said, his voice a little rougher than he expected. "Our priority is to find this woman and expose her. Once we do that, we can uncover any moles left in the FBI."

"I wish we had a place to start," Mina said, kissing Roman before returning to her computer. She stared at the screen for a moment and then started typing.

"What are you doing?" Cal and Roman asked in unison.

"Making a list of the mayors and city managers in small towns around Red Rye and Santa Macko."

"Why?" Cal asked, walking over to stand by her.

"She's looking for someone with an unusually cushy campaign fund," Roman said, a grin on his lips. "That's my girl."

Mina pointed at him, barely missing a beat on the keyboard. "If The Miss learned her lesson from The

Madame, she would need to clean the money coming in. She'll likely fall back on the same way they did it in Red Rye."

"Fair point," Cal agreed, "but that's like a needle in a haystack."

"Not untrue, but we have to start somewhere," she said, her fingers typing almost independently of her brain.

Mina's skills were why he'd hired her on at Secure One. She'd saved a client several times from being hacked by immediately shutting the hacker down and closing the door they got through. Before the trial, she was going through all of his clients' servers, looking for weaknesses. He wanted her to get back to that job, which meant they had to find The Miss sooner rather than later.

"Boss," Eric called from his booth that held the surveillance equipment for the property. "We've got company."

Cal, Roman and Mina were standing next to Eric within a second, and he pointed at the camera that ran along the fence line.

"Lock it down," Cal told the man, then turned to Mina. "Get Marlise in the bunker." He had barely finished the sentence, and she was out the door. He turned to his brother. "Shall we go meet our guests?"

Roman raised a brow and then nodded, a grim smile on his face as he reached for his gun.

Chapter Four

The bunker was silent other than Mina's grunt as she closed the door and locked it from below. When Cal first told Marlise about the bunker, she expected a doomsday scenario with cots lined up along the wall, dried food at the ready and a cache of weapons. Instead, it was filled with state-of-the-art computer and surveillance equipment, a kitchenette and bunks. Not everyone had access to the bunker either. There was a hatch in Cal's room on one end of the lodge and a hatch in the guest room at the other end of the lodge. There was also an exit from the back of the bunker that came out at the boathouse on the lake, but Cal told her if they ever took that exit, they'd better never plan on coming back.

She bit her lip, worry filling her at the thought of Cal being out there somewhere trying to keep her safe. He was one of those guys who kept his thoughts and emotions close to his vest. He was gruff and bossy, but he always had the well-being of everyone on the compound at the forefront of his mind.

Especially so since she came to work here, at least according to Roman.

"Would you like something to drink?" Mina asked, breaking into her thoughts.

Marlise shook her head no rather than answer.

"It's going to be okay," Mina promised, walking over to hug her. Since she'd gotten a new high-end prosthesis, you could barely tell that she was an amputee, but Marlise still felt guilty. The Miss had been torturing Mina while she was running from the house without thought of saving her friend.

That wasn't entirely true. She'd wanted to help Mina, but she knew if she'd gone up those stairs, she'd never have come back down. It had been wiser to get to her secret stash, or so she'd thought. Karma must have been why she hadn't made it out of the fire unscathed either. When Roman had gotten to the house, he'd found her by the front door nearly dead. He'd saved her, but not before the flames destroyed the skin on the left side of her body. It had been almost two years, but she still dealt with pain and nerve damage from the fire.

Her face was no longer symmetrical, and she couldn't smile or blink her eye well on the left side. Self-conscious, she always kept her hair over the weblike skin and wore long-sleeved shirts to hide the burns on her arm and side. Tonight, her arm was sore and tight where Selina had stitched it. The numbing medication was starting to wear off, and it felt like she'd been shot, even if it had only been plastic

that had pierced her skin. Her nerves were so damaged on that arm that she worried this injury would
only worsen it, but there was nothing she could do
about it now.

"What's going on, Mina?" Marlise asked as she
perched on the edge of a chair. "The lights went out,
and Cal said that only happens if someone tries to
infiltrate the perimeter."

"Someone did, but we were prepared for them
this time. All of our alarms worked and alerted us
to them early. Eric was sitting right at the computer
when they showed up on our cameras. I don't know
what's going on. Cal asked me to bring you down
here, and I took off."

"Should we be worried?"

Mina shook her head with a smile. "Not even a
little bit. We had so much warning that the team was
on it right away. They just want to make sure we're
safe until they send the all clear."

"Do you think it's The Miss?" Marlise asked, her
voice wavering slightly.

Her friend's face didn't give away what she thought,
but her shrug wasn't relaxed. The Miss was the reason Mina was an amputee, and the idea she had found
them didn't sit well with either of them.

"No way to know. It could be anyone. Let's face it.
Cal has made a few enemies himself over the years."

An eye roll slipped out, and Marlise huffed. "Sure,
and it must be a coincidence that his enemies decided
to break into Secure One the same night we were

nearly killed going to The Madame's trial. I might look stupid, Mina, but I'm not."

"I never said you were stupid," she clarified. "I meant that we shouldn't speculate until we hear from Cal or Roman."

Mina started tapping away on a keyboard, and while Marlise had no idea what she was doing, she didn't bother asking. She wouldn't understand anyway. Mina's job was far too technical for Marlise to understand when her skills ended at how to do a basic internet search. She paced the length of the bunker, wishing she knew what was going on and if Cal and Roman were safe.

If The Miss showed up with enough people to overrun Secure One, there was no telling how long Marlise would be alive. Mina was confident Cal had found all the weak points at Secure One, but he'd said that when he was tasked with keeping her safe two years ago too.

"Stop worrying," Mina said firmly. "No one is going to get to you here. Cal won't allow it."

The scar on Marlise's arm burned to remind her what happened the last time The Madame got to her. "That's what they said before you were taken."

Mina held up a finger. "And Cal learned a hard and fast lesson about his vulnerabilities. Since Roman and I started working here, they've analyzed every angle of this property, retraced the steps The Madame's men took to get to me and turned Secure One into a fortress. Cal spared no expense in fortifying the perimeter, buying new equipment and training his men. No one walks onto this property unannounced now. That's why we're down here. Someone tried and set off every alarm in the control room."

Mina turned her attention back to the computer while Marlise started pacing again. Something big was going on above their heads, and she had a feeling she was smack-dab in the middle of it.

THE DAY CAL feared had arrived, and he had to force his mind to be calm. He didn't want to do something to put Marlise at risk again. He was already exhausted from their day on the run, but this turn of events most certainly had to do with Marlise. The then meek woman had sent him into a protective tailspin the moment he met her, and that hadn't changed. He refocused his attention on the shores of the lake rather than the woman hiding in the bunker. Tonight might be his chance to end The Miss's reign of terror.

From where they crouched in the grass, he held up one finger and flicked it to the right side.

"Only one guy?" Roman whispered. "Where are the other three we saw on the fence camera?"

"Maybe they just sent one scout to save time," Cal whispered. He scanned the area again and froze, dragging his head back to the left. "Wait. It might be a girl scout."

"A woman?"

"She just turned sideways, and it looks like it, but I can't be sure. She's one of the targets we saw on the fence camera. Wait." He paused and felt Roman tense next to him. "She just leaned her rifle down on a log and walked away."

"Walked away? It could be a trick," Roman said between clenched teeth. "We need to stop her before she gets much further. No one will get near my wife again."

"There has to be more than one scout, right? This has to be a distraction. Mack and Eric," Cal whispered into his wire, "there's only one scout. It could be a woman."

"Woman?" Mack asked in confusion.

"I can't be sure, but I don't trust this. Work your way back to the front of the lodge and cover it, then await further instructions. Roman and I will handle this girl scout."

"This doesn't feel right," Mack said.

"Agreed," Cal whispered.

"You know if we capture her, we have to turn her over to the FBI," Roman whispered.

Cal bit back the snort that tried to come out. "That depends on who she is and what she wants."

"She's got a gun that could put down a horse, and she's dressed in tactical gear with a vest. I think I know what she wants."

"What do you say we find out?" Cal asked his brother with a cock of his brow. "If she crosses the electric fence, she will need to recover from the voltage before she can speak."

The electric fences were designed to stop someone long enough for his team to secure them without scrambling too many brain cells. That didn't mean it didn't hurt, and Cal took a little joy in someone getting what they deserved when trespassing. He'd even started suggesting the fences to his security clients since they offered a level of protection even guards couldn't. A fence never had to sleep.

Cal and Roman worked their way to the right under the cover of darkness and trees. If The Miss found them, she wouldn't send one woman to Secure One. She'd send a dozen. Something was off. They paused in the woods, and they took in the tiny woman standing on the sand, spinning in a slow circle. She wore all black and had a flak jacket and combat vest, but she'd left the gun fifty yards away as though she'd forgotten it.

Cal glanced at Roman, who was crouched next to him. "It's like she's dazed or confused, not to mention her size. She's smaller than Marlise and Mina."

Roman nodded. "It's like she's a lost kid looking for her parents. The rifle is no longer a threat, but she could have a smaller pistol."

"Agreed, so watch yourself, brother. When she turns around again, we go. All we need to do is secure her arms. Let's try to avoid injuring her. I want to get some answers."

Cal moved the night vision glasses to the top of his head, and they waited inside the tree line for the woman to turn away. When she did, they seized the opportunity.

"Lights, lights, lights!" Cal yelled into his wire as they ran out of the trees.

Awash in light, they watched the woman fall to her knees with her hands up. "I surrender! I surrender!" she yelled.

Roman and Cal glanced at each other, but slowed their approach, watching for any tricks. They both had dead aim on the trembling woman still on her knees. Hell, she looked like a kid from what Cal could see. Her blond hair spilled out from under her black stocking cap, and her petite frame was nearly swallowed up by the tactical vest.

Looks can be deceiving, a voice whispered.

Didn't Cal know that better than anyone? He didn't need a reminder. "What do you want?" he asked, only a few feet away from her now.

"I want to surrender," she whimpered. "I surrender."

"Lay down on your stomach and put your hands behind your back," Roman ordered as he glanced at Cal.

She did as he instructed, even crossing her ankles and lifting them to be secured. Roman nodded at him, so Cal holstered his gun and motioned for Roman to cover him while he zip-tied the woman's hands together. He left her feet unsecured so she could walk.

"I'm going to ask you again. What do you want?" Cal said, walking around in front of the girl. She was young, and her face told of the horrors she'd lived.

He'd seen that haunted look in another woman's eyes before. She was currently hiding out in his bunker.

"I don't want to do this anymore. I need help. Please, help me."

The girl started crying softly, and Cal glanced up at Roman, who gave him the what-the-heck hands. Cal shrugged and grabbed hold of the woman's arm, helping her up. "Consider yourself surrendered. Where are your friends? There were four of you."

"They left," she said through her tears, and Cal lowered a brow at her. "I swear. I'm alone."

"Come on," Roman said, grabbing her other arm. "The fences will get them if she's lying. We need answers from her before the other three arrive with backup."

Cal sighed, but agreed with his brother. "This isn't a trick?" he asked the woman, who shook her head as tears streamed down her face.

"I'm tired, hungry and scared," she whispered. "I just want this to be over."

Cal released her arm, jogged over and grabbed her rifle. He covered their backs on their way to the lodge just in case others were lurking. Why did this woman think she had to surrender? Was she being forced to do something against her will? She was part of the group that had arrived near the fence, but where did her companions go? Even if the other three still wandered the property, they didn't have the firepower or the skills to outgun or outrun his men—none of this made sense.

Her head hung lower and lower until her chin touched her chest, and her feet shuffled along as though they weighed one thousand pounds. It wasn't from dread or a ploy to hold them up. It was pure exhaustion. He had two secret weapons he could deploy to get to the bottom of this.

Mina and Marlise.

Cal's mind went straight to Marlise, the woman he'd rescued with his plane two years ago, who'd worn the same look of fear and exhaustion. Maybe she could be the one to get answers from this woman. If they got lucky, Mina might be able to tag her as one of The Madame's, and they'd be one step closer to bringing The Miss down. Cal had promised Marlise last summer he wouldn't stop until she was behind bars, but that was easier said than done. Regardless of how often Cal put his ear to the ground, it was radio silence.

The woman he'd been protecting for over a year now deserved to be free. She had seen things in life that no one should, but she still got up every day and tried to make a difference at Secure One. Cal wanted Marlise to be free to find happiness. She hadn't known a lot of happy times in her life. Raised in foster care and then put out on the streets at eighteen, she had seen things no one should have to see. By twenty-four, she was running the household of a madwoman hell-bent on destroying other women's lives. By twenty-seven, she was recovering from burns over a quarter of her body and wondering why she was fighting to live.

Cal wanted—no, he needed—to be the one to give her that answer. He was confident the woman before them was the key to unlocking The Miss's secrets. He was less confident that doing that wouldn't result in carnage they wouldn't see coming.

Chapter Five

"Who is she?" Mina asked when she joined them in the control room.

"We're hoping you can tell us," Cal answered.

"You're sure she was alone?"

"From what we can tell," Roman said from where he leaned on a table. "We know she wasn't alone when they tripped the alarms in the woods. When we hauled her in off the lakeshore she told us the other women had left."

"That doesn't make any sense," Mina said, biting her lip for a moment. "Do you think she's a decoy?"

"All I know is, this entire compound is lit up like it's daytime, and guards are at battle stations. If someone approaches, we'll see them coming. We need to talk to this woman and find out who she is and what she wants. She kept saying 'I surrender' until she broke down into tears." Cal lifted his palms up to relay his confusion.

"She also said she was tired, hungry, scared and wanted help," Roman added.

"She didn't put up a fight?" Mina asked with surprise.

Roman walked over to his wife. "No. It was like she wanted to get caught. She even walked away from her gun, which is suspicious, if you ask me."

"Let's see her."

Cal hit a button on the computer, and the two-way mirror activated. A woman sat alone at a table, huddled in a chair with her arms wrapped around her knees. She'd been checked for explosives and bugs and wore nothing but gray sweats, with her blond hair pulled back in a ponytail. She reminded Cal so much of Marlise in the early days—scared and alone.

"That's Charlotte."

"You recognize her?" Roman asked with surprise.

"Yes! She's from the house in Red Rye. She was one of The Miss's drug mules, but was just being introduced to it when everything went down."

"She's higher up in The Miss's organization?" Cal asked.

"I can't say," Mina said with a shake of her head. "I don't know what's gone on over the last two years. Something has because that's not the same woman I knew."

"What do you mean?" Cal asked as Mina stepped up to the mirror.

"She's lost weight. Easily fifty pounds. She looks sickly and terrified."

"Maybe she's hooked on the drugs The Miss was

making her traffic?" Roman asked. "Could be that's how she was being convinced to stay."

"That's possible, but she doesn't appear to be tweaking. She just looks..."

"Tired, sad and scared," Cal finished. "She looks like Marlise did when we first picked her up."

Mina pointed at him. "Exactly."

"We need information from her," Roman said, putting his arm around his wife. "Are you willing to ask the questions? She's not restrained, but I don't think she's a threat."

"She never was," Mina agreed. "She was always just scared and confused in Red Rye. In her current condition, I could take her even without my prosthesis. Something isn't right here," she said on a hum. "Charlotte was only one step above Marlise in how she interacted with the men on dates. She could talk to them with more confidence, but she was scared. The Miss sent her on dates with older men because they demanded less of her."

"She didn't want to be part of the house either?" Cal asked.

"Absolutely not. She was tricked into it just like Marlise. A few days before the fire, she secretly told me she was scared and showed me several hand-shaped bruises on her thighs."

A word dropped from Roman's lips that summed up exactly how everyone felt about what went on in Red Rye, Kansas. "Do you think this is a defection then?"

"Honestly, from what I see right now, yes, but I don't trust The Miss."

"Do you think Charlotte will talk to you?" Cal asked, nervously tapping the floor with his boot. "We need to know why she's here, and we need to know fast."

"I could go in and talk to her, but if I were you, I'd send in Marlise."

"Absolutely not," Cal said immediately. "Marlise is not getting near this woman."

Roman lifted a brow at Cal, but he didn't care. Marlise had gone through enough because of The Miss and was finally putting things right in her head. He wouldn't throw her back into that life when other people could ask the questions.

"I'll go in with her," Mina quickly said, "but Charlotte will see me for what I am. An FBI agent. She'll connect with Marlise as someone who lived through the same things she did."

"She's right," Roman said, his brow still in the air.

"Marlise is just getting back on an even keel almost two years later, and you want to stick her in there and bring it all back? No. I won't allow it."

Mina gently touched his arm until he made eye contact with her. "Don't you think we should let Marlise decide? She's a grown woman and a lot stronger than you give her credit for now. If I go in there alone, I could do more harm than good. Marlise has earned the right to make her own choice about this."

Cal ground his teeth together to keep the scathing rebuttal from escaping. The last thing he wanted to do was expose Marlise to anything that had to do with The Miss, but he also knew Mina might be right. Marlise had a gentle touch with even the toughest of his men. She'd hand them a cookie, and they'd be putty in her hands.

"Fine, but she's never alone with her."

Mina and Roman both nodded in agreement.

"I'll go talk to Marlise. Mina, would you grab some food from the kitchen? If she's going in, I want her armed."

Mina grinned. "Meet back here in ten."

MARLISE HATED BEING cut off from whatever was going on, but she had followed Mina's orders to stay in her room. She trusted that Cal would fill her in soon, but that didn't keep her from pacing the small space while she waited.

Her room was right next door to Cal's. In fact, when she moved to Secure One last summer, he'd installed adjoining room doors, so she had access to the bunker at all times. A smile tipped her lips up when she remembered the argument they'd had about where she'd be living. She had insisted a cabin by the lake would be fine, but Cal had flat-out refused to hear of it. He was adamant that it wasn't safe for her to be anywhere she didn't have instant access to the bunker. If tonight were any indication, maybe he'd been right.

A knock on the door made Marlise jump. "Mary? It's Cal. We need to talk."

Her shoulders relaxed as she walked to the door and checked the peephole to make sure Cal was alone before she opened it. The door was no sooner open than he was in the room and it was closed again.

Cal was…formidable. You wouldn't want to meet him in a dark alley if you operated on the wrong side of the law. He wore full sleeves of beautiful tattoos featuring the Greek gods that she'd spent hours gazing at without him even knowing. She'd memorized their placement, colorings and little nuances of shadows and light. Marlise suspected he had more, but she was far too drawn to him to ask where and if she could see them. She needed to stay ten feet away from Cal at all times.

"What's going on?" she asked, taking a step back to remind herself not to touch him. "And don't lie to me."

"I wouldn't do that, Mary, but there has been a development."

"The Miss."

He tipped his head in agreement. "It appears so. We took a woman into custody, and Mina made an identification."

"You captured The Miss?" Marlise stumbled backward and would have fallen if Cal hadn't grabbed her.

"Are you okay?" he asked, and she nodded robotically, even though the heat of his hand seared her arm.

"I'm f-fine. I wasn't expecting you to say you had The Miss."

"We don't," he said patiently. "Mina identified the woman we took into custody as Charlotte. Do you remember her?"

Marlise nodded again, but couldn't make words leave her mouth. *Why is Charlotte here?*

"There were originally three other women with her, but she was alone by the time we took her into custody."

"Where are the other three?" Marlise asked, her voice low and shaky.

"That's what we need to find out. Mina thinks you're the best person to talk to Charlotte. Were you friends with her in Red Rye?"

The nod she gave him was exact. "If you can call what went on in that house friendly. Charlotte was a lot like me. She didn't like the men, but she couldn't find a way to ingratiate herself to The Miss the way I did. She was just starting as a drug mule when the fire happened."

"How did she feel about that? Did she talk to you about it?"

Marlise wrapped her arms around her waist and swallowed over her dry throat. "She had only been doing it about a month, but she didn't like it. She begged The Miss to book her with the older men. She said they didn't expect her to do as much."

Cal's nod was sharp, but his smile was comforting. "That's exactly what Mina said."

"Was that a test?" Marlise asked with confusion. "I wouldn't lie to you, Cal." She turned her back and walked over to her bed, putting distance between them so she could think. If Charlotte was here alone, it was either a trap or something terrible had happened, which meant she was sick or hurt.

"I wasn't testing you, Mary. I was gathering information. Mina may have been told one thing while you were privy to something else."

Her shoulders rolled inward, and she dropped her chin to her chest. "Is Charlotte hurt?"

"Not that we're aware of. Why?"

"It doesn't make sense that she's here, Cal." She stood to pace the room again. "Why would she think she could just walk in and surrender? It has to be a trap."

"It could be. That's why we need to talk to Charlotte."

Marlise squared her shoulders and nodded. "Take me to her."

Cal stepped up into her space, and she fought against taking a step back. His gaze was intense as he drank her in, but she wouldn't back down. His brown eyes darkened to deep chocolate before he spoke. "You don't have to do this. You're just starting to find level ground, and I don't like reminding you of your time in Red Rye under The Miss's rule."

"I'm reminded every time I look in the mirror, Cal," she said, stiffening her spine to appear taller. "I'm not the fragile flower you think I am. I've gone through a lot in this life. Things I haven't told anyone. Talking to Charlotte will be the least difficult thing I've done in my life."

He took another step before he grasped her shoulders, connecting them in a way she couldn't deny. "I don't think you're a fragile flower. You're stronger than I'll ever be, and I'm twice your size. The last thing I want to do is cause you pain though."

"You need answers, right?" she asked, and he nodded, his jaw pulsing as though he hated to admit it. "Then let's go get them."

MINA HANDED MARLISE a plate with a sandwich, cookies and a glass of milk. "Your job at the house in Red Rye was to take care of the girls. Let's go at it from that angle."

She opened the door, and Marlise walked through, the moment captured in Cal's eye as he stood in the recording booth looking through the two-way mirror. He had a wire on both women, so they could hear loud and clear what was said in the room. Roman stood beside him while Mack stood outside the room the women were in, just in case muscle was needed. Cal didn't think it would be. It was easy to see Charlotte wasn't a threat to anyone except possibly The Miss.

"Charlotte," Marlise said to the woman sitting at the table. "I can't believe it's you!" She set the plate and glass down on the table and pulled her into a hug.

His girl could act. He had to give her that.

No. She's not your girl, Cal. You don't deserve a girl. Your lifestyle doesn't lend itself to having any vulnerability in your life.

"Marlise!" Charlotte exclaimed. "You're safe!"

"Yes," Marlise answered, pushing the food toward the woman before she sat down. "I'm the head chef here now. Mina got me the job." She hooked a thumb at Mina, who had sat down at the table.

"Agent August, you mean?" Charlotte asked quite suspiciously.

"Not anymore," Mina clarified. "I left the FBI after what happened in Red Rye. I want to help people, Charlotte, not hurt them. After The Madame was caught, I spent a year helping the FBI take care of the girls from other houses."

Charlotte looked to Marlise, who nodded. "It's true. She helped many girls just like us get therapy and find jobs."

"She didn't help me."

"We couldn't find you, or she would have," Marlise clarified. "Where have you been for two years?"

Charlotte refused to answer. She picked up the sandwich, took a bite and washed it down with a swallow of milk. It was like she hadn't eaten in days, and she attacked the food without another word while Mina and Marlise stared at each other.

"She's starving," Roman said while the woman moaned as she ate.

"I haven't eaten real food in days," Charlotte whispered when she finished the milk. "I don't even care if that was drugged. It was so good."

Mina leaned forward across the table. "The food wasn't drugged, Charlotte. We would never do that to you. We don't know why you're here, but you must be desperate, so why don't you talk to us?"

"How did you get here tonight, Charlotte?" Marlise gently asked.

"We had a car with a preprogrammed GPS to this location."

"We?"

Charlotte nodded and leaned back in her chair, wrapping her arms around her waist. "There were four of us."

"We noticed that on our cameras," Mina said. "But you were the only one who came in via the lake."

"We were just supposed to scout the property and find a way to attack. As soon as we saw the electric fences, we knew that her plan wouldn't work."

"Her?" Marlise asked.

"The Miss," Charlotte whispered after she swallowed nervously. "She wants you. She said you know too much and can't be allowed to testify at the trial. The Madame's men were supposed to have killed you both two years ago, but they failed."

"Why did she wait so long to come after Marlise?" Mina asked with heavy suspicion.

"I don't know," Charlotte answered, and Cal believed her.

"This girl followed orders, but she wasn't privy to

important information," Cal said, and Roman nodded his agreement. "She's also terrified. You can see it in her demeanor."

"She reminds me of Marlise when we first talked to her after the fire—skittish and on guard."

Cal didn't say that Marlise was still skittish and on guard, but she'd earned the right to be. Her life had been hell, and trusting people would never be easy. She trusted him though. She'd told him as much several times over the last year. At least she trusted him with her safety. She shouldn't trust him with her heart or her body.

He shook his head and focused on the women in the room again. He had no right to her heart or her body. He was a loner. A ghost. Someone with no roots. He had to remember that before he did something to jeopardize both his life and Marlise's.

Chapter Six

It was easy to see that the woman sitting across from her wasn't the same woman Marlise had lived with two years ago. What wasn't easy to see was why. She knew Cal must be getting frustrated in the control booth with their lack of answers, but she couldn't push Charlotte to open up to them until she believed they'd help her. That was life experience speaking. Marlise remembered those first days and weeks after the fire at Red Rye when she was scared and in pain. She hated that Charlotte was feeling the same way now.

"You've been with The Miss this whole time?" Mina asked.

Marlise forced herself not to grimace. She would have approached the question with a gentler tone, but Mina was the one trained in interrogation.

Charlotte was silent for several seconds before she nodded. "I don't want to live that way anymore." Tears fell down her cheeks, and Marlise handed her a tissue. She dabbed at her face and then twisted the tissue in her hand.

"Where are the other girls you were with tonight?"

"Gone. They said trying to access the property by the lake was a waste of time, and it wouldn't work."

"It is, and it wouldn't," Mina said with conviction. "You had already tripped the alarms on every part of the property."

Charlotte lifted her chin, even if it was still trembling. "I wanted to get caught. When no one came out after we tromped around in the woods, I convinced them to let me check out the lake alone. They said it was my funeral and they were leaving. I told them I'd meet up with them at the car."

"Do you know where the car is?" Mina asked, glancing toward the mirror.

"Long gone," Charlotte answered. "I gave them a head start back to the car before leaving the woods along the lake. I wanted to miss our agreed-upon time so they'd know I wasn't coming and take off. They don't care. I'm expendable."

"Weren't you afraid of getting shot?" Marlise asked. "You had to know someone would be waiting for you once you showed yourself."

Charlotte nodded, and a tear ran down her cheek. Marlise's heart squeezed tightly in her chest. She remembered what it was like to live that life and how terrifying it was.

"I knew it was a possibility, but I hoped I'd be okay if I surrendered right away. It was a chance I was willing to take. We're never far from death when used as pawns in other people's games. At least I had the control this time."

Mina and Marlise both nodded, but they glanced at each other. Marlise saw the nervousness in Mina's eyes and was sure it reflected in her own. They didn't know if Charlotte was telling the truth or if she was trying to give the other group time to penetrate the perimeter with more firepower. Marlise had to believe that wasn't the case.

"Why did you think it was safe to come here?" Marlise asked the question burning in everyone's mind.

"You're free of The Madame, right?"

Marlise made a so-so gesture with her hand. "I get paid to work here, and I'm not being forced to stay, but I also can't leave as long as The Miss is out there."

Charlotte's shoulder shrugged in a motion of weighted fatigue. "That's true, but you know you're protected here, and no one makes you do…" She paused and closed her eyes on an inhaled breath. "Things you don't want to do with men, right?"

Mina took the girl's trembling hand, nodding at Marlise to answer. "That's right. I don't have to do anything I don't want to do."

Her eyes came open, and she stared into Marlise's with round, blue, hopeful ones. "Then, the way I saw it, this was a safe place. I know I'll go to jail eventually, but I had to get away from The Miss," she whispered, tears streaming down her face. "She's making us do bad things. Worse things than we already do. She wants us to kill people!"

Charlotte broke down into uncontrollable sobbing, and Mina stood, making the cut motion at her neck before trying to comfort Charlotte. Marlise sat back against the chair and tried to process what the woman had told them, but she didn't know where to start.

"Marlise," Mina said sharply, dragging her attention back to the room. "We need to get her to the med bay."

Mina hadn't finished her sentence before Mack opened the door, rushed in and caught Charlotte just as she passed out. He was running with her down the hallway to the med bay before either of the women could speak.

"Life just got interesting," Mina said, staring at the empty chair at the table.

"Again," Marlise finished.

"THE PLOT THICKENS," Cal said once they gathered together again. Charlotte was in the med bay with Selina, being hydrated with an IV and something to calm her. "I'm not sure what happened in there to have her react that way."

"I am," Marlise said from the corner where she leaned against the wall. She walked over to them and leaned on the table. "I remember the plunge of adrenaline when I realized I was safe here. That's what happened. Charlotte realized she was safe."

"You believed her then?" Cal asked, walking over and standing next to her.

"Does it make me naive if I say yes?" she asked, glancing at him and then Mina.

"No," Mina said. "I feel the same way. I just wish we had gotten more out of her before she collapsed. I have so many questions."

"We all do," Mack said. He'd been standing at attention at the door as though he were a sentry for the people inside. In a way, Mack was, but he was so much more than that. He was a brother in arms, and when he needed a place to recover from the trauma he'd suffered in the military, Cal was able to offer him a place to heal and, eventually, a place to work and find a community again.

"Let's make a list of questions, so when she's able, we can ask them," Roman said, pulling out a chair and sitting at the sprawling table in the conference room. Everyone sat except for Cal, who wrote the questions on a whiteboard as they were asked.

Cal stood at the board and pointed at each question. "Here's what I know. We have two major questions we need answered. The first—is The Miss working alone or at the direction of The Madame? The second—where is The Miss hiding out, and how do we get to her?"

"Followed by, is it only The Miss from Red Rye behind this, or did the few who scattered during the raids link up?" Roman finished.

"How many of the misses were unaccounted for after the raids?" Cal asked Mina.

"There were twelve houses, and four didn't have a miss. At least no one fessed up to it."

"Wouldn't the other women have singled her out?" Cal asked, but Mina shook her head.

"Absolutely not. They were traumatized and scared of their shadows. There's no way they would risk their life by ratting out their miss."

"I agree," Marlise said with a nod. "I wouldn't have if you'd caught her that day."

"But then she could start another house and do this to more women. Wouldn't you do anything within your power to stop that?" Cal asked, his head tipped to the side in confusion.

Marlise crossed her arms over her chest and held his gaze. She wasn't backing down on her statement. "You're a man who doesn't know the first thing about being tricked, used and abused, Cal Newfellow. You can stand up there and be judgy and righteous be-cause you've never been sold like a piece of property and treated like garbage. Until you have been, never suggest anything I do is wrong."

Mina stood and put her arm around Marlise, squeezing her. "It's okay. I don't think he meant to be judgy or righteous."

Cal walked around the table and approached her. "I'm sorry. You're right. I can't make a blanket state-ment like that if I haven't been in the situation. I apologize for being disrespectful. That was never my intention. I was simply trying to suss out the major players here."

Marlise swallowed around the dryness in her throat that being near him always caused. If only he knew how he affected her, but she was glad he didn't. She was glad he didn't know how attracted she was to him. Besides, it was probably nothing more than reverse Stockholm syndrome now that she was here and he was the one protecting her.

A little voice inside her head laughed. *Sure. Keep telling yourself that.*

"I shouldn't have said that. I'm sorry." She broke eye contact and looked away, ashamed that everyone in the room saw her lose her cool.

"No," Roman said from where he sat, and she glanced up at him. "Everyone in this room has a right to their opinion and respect when it comes to anything that directly affects them. You don't have to apologize for standing up for yourself and Charlotte."

"That's what I'm worried about, see," Marlise said, glancing between everyone in the room except Cal. She could feel his gaze on her with an intensity she was afraid to confront. "Charlotte is a new defect from the house, so if someone says the wrong thing or asks the wrong question, she might get scared and clam up because she thinks we're judging her."

Marlise's shoulders slumped, and she lowered herself to a chair, completely ignoring the man standing next to her until he walked around the table again and gave her breathing room. That was the most forceful she'd been about her opinions since she'd arrived here, and now she was worried she would lose her job for crossing the one person who had hired her.

"She's right," Cal said from where he stood by the board, and Marlise snapped her head up in surprise.

"I am?"

Cal, Roman and Mack all chuckled together while Mina reached over and squeezed her hand.

"You are. I forget that I have a privilege here that you, Charlotte and Mina don't have, and that privilege is being male. I have power, strength and the ability to make my own choices. The women with The Miss don't, and I need to remember my place. This is what I think we should do, but I want you and Mina in agreement before we move forward."

"We're listening," Mina assured him, and he leaned over on the table, his size an unscalable wall against the outside world in Marlise's mind.

"I want one or the other of you with Charlotte tonight. Mack will pull guard duty when you're there, alternating with Eric." Marlise saw Mack nod out of the corner of his eye. "Once Charlotte is strong enough to answer these two big questions, I want Mary—" Cal paused and cleared his throat. "Sorry, Marlise to ask them conversationally. No Mina, Selina or Mack in the room. We will record the conversation and listen to it when you're done. Do you think she will be at ease enough then to discuss the finer points of the organization? At least so we have a starting point?"

Marlise glanced at Mina, who nodded and shrugged

one shoulder. "All I can do is try, Cal. I'll try my hardest because there are more girls like Charlotte with
The Miss. If what she said is true, and The Miss is
teaching them how to kill, we need to find her and
stop this train before it goes off the rails."

"Everyone in this room agrees on that," Roman
said. "The sooner, the better too. Mina, let's head to
the control room to look at the video footage from
the fence cam. Maybe you'll recognize one of the
other three women in the shot. Marlise can take the
first shift with Charlotte."

"Sounds good. Then I will dig into the files of the
women we rescued from the four houses with the
missing misses. If I find any who have disappeared
again after we helped them, that's another lead we
can follow if necessary."

With the plan agreed upon, everyone stood and
filed out to assume their positions. Before Marlise
could leave, Cal gently grasped her arm and held her
in place. "I'm truly sorry, Mary. It was never my intention to insult or upset you."

"I know, Cal," she whispered with her gaze pinned
to the floor. "It's fine. Consider it forgotten."

He tipped her chin up and forced her to meet his
gaze. "It's not fine, and it's not forgotten. It was a
lesson I learned and won't forget. You might think I
believe that brute force and barked orders get things
done around here, but that's not true. I listen to what
my team has to say and consider everyone's opinion

on the situation before going forward. That's what keeps everyone alive."

"And I'm a member of the team by default, right? I'm here because I need protection from the bad guys still after me, but as soon as you catch them, you'll cut me loose?"

"Wrong. You're a member of this team because you earned your place here. We might be closer than ever to the bad guys who are out to get you, but catching them doesn't mean you're off the team. Catching them gives you the chance to make your own decisions about your future. You're part of this team for as long as you want to be. I think we work well together, and you give the group insight into issues around jobs that we wouldn't have had without you here. Don't underestimate your contributions to this team, Mary. Understood?"

Marlise nodded rather than spoke. She was afraid her voice would hold all the emotions welling inside her chest. She felt pride that she was an integral part of a team that needed her insight as much as she needed theirs. She knew what she had to do as she walked down to the med bay to check on Charlotte. Once she had more answers, she would put her fear aside and talk to Cal. It wasn't fair to put the fight for her independence squarely on his shoulders. She would have to dig deep, trust the man who was keeping her safe and prove that she was a team player once and for all.

Chapter Seven

"How is she?" Marlise asked Mina when she walked into the med bay the following day. She'd gone to bed about 2:00 a.m. and then got up at 6:00 a.m. to make breakfast for everyone before her next shift with Charlotte. Cal was insistent she stay out of the kitchen, but he didn't understand that cooking helped her relax when things were stressful. Besides, she'd suffered worse injuries while working in Red Rye and never broke stride, so a small cut on her arm wouldn't slow her down.

"She's been sleeping most of the night. She just woke up and had some juice. She was much calmer, so we let her rest until you arrived," Mina explained, standing outside the door to the med bay.

"I brought her breakfast," Marlise said, holding up the tray. "I will let her eat and then ask the big questions. Time is short."

"Agreed," Mina said with a head nod. "Selina needed a break, so I told her you and Mack had the space covered. She's going to grab a shower and some food. That will give you the opening you need to ask your questions."

"I can do this," Marlise said, taking a deep breath. "We have to stop The Miss before she gets girls to kill for her. I don't think they'd be doing it willingly."

"Me either," Mina answered with her lips pursed. "The idea that The Miss is teaching young, innocent women to be assassins for her gain is terrifying and enraging. If the FBI doesn't stop her, we will."

Marlise glanced over her shoulder at Mack before leaning into Mina's ear. "Will we get in trouble if we don't hand Charlotte over to the authorities?"

"Turning Charlotte over to the authorities would only put her at risk, and other than trespassing, they'd have nothing to charge her with right now. She defected and essentially claimed asylum from The Miss. Besides, sex trafficked women aren't held accountable for anything they do against their will that breaks the law."

"Okay," Marlise said with a nod. "If she asked, I wanted to reassure her, and I know she'll ask."

"Good luck, and let Mack know if you need anything."

Mina waved and walked down the hallway while Marlise entered the med bay and smiled at Charlotte. "Good morning. I brought you some breakfast. I thought you might be hungry."

"Good morning, Marlise. I'm glad to see you. I was worried when I woke up and Mina was here."

"She's a friend, Charlotte," Marlise promised,

sliding the tray across the table so she could eat. "Mina doesn't work for the FBI anymore."

"That's what she said. She told me that her boss was The Madame's husband. I would never have expected an FBI agent to be married to a woman like The Madame."

"Money will corrupt people fast and ugly, Charlotte," Marlise said, pulling the chair up to sit by her friend. "We saw it over and over at the house in Red Rye. I bet you've seen it more since."

"Like The Miss," Charlotte said between bites of toast and eggs.

"She was angling to be the closest confidante of The Madame's. We saw that in Red Rye."

"Now she's decided to be the woman."

"You mean she's not working for The Madame still?" Marlise asked, hoping Cal was recording the way he promised. She hadn't expected Charlotte to start spilling the tea within seconds of sitting down, but she didn't want to stop her. At the very least, she noticed Mack move closer to the door, so he must be listening.

"How could she? The Madame is in prison."

Marlise shrugged, hoping she looked relaxed. "There are plenty of people running outside operations from behind bars. I wondered if there were plans for The Miss to continue if The Madame was caught."

"From what The Miss said, The Madame never expected to get caught. She was too confident that no one would ever tag her, so she never put any backup plans in place. Anyway, that's what I gathered from The Miss over the last two years."

"And she's not working with any of the other misses right now?"

Charlotte waved her hands in front of her chest. "Not that I'm aware of, but I didn't know the ones from the other houses. We got a lot of new girls joining the ranks though, so I can't say for sure. They didn't catch all the misses?"

"No," Marlise admitted on a breath. "There were four houses where they couldn't prove who was running them."

"And no girl would snitch her out if she valued her life."

Marlise pointed at her and hoped Cal was recording. He needed to hear that she wasn't the only one who believed that. "Exactly. It's entirely possible the misses were taken in with the other girls and then processed back out as survivors. There's no way to know for sure."

"I can tell you that no one else is as high up as our Miss. She's on the top rung and keeping everyone else at the bottom. You only get the information needed for each specific job. I usually overhear things because part of my job is cleaning and laundry duties, so I'm around her trailer more than anyone else. If we aren't doing chores, or out working a job, we're expected to be training."

"Training?"

Charlotte nodded, but dropped the toast back to the tray and pushed it away. "Working out, running, working on our combat training or practicing at the range."

"You were serious when you said she's teaching you to kill?"

"Dead serious," Charlotte said, "no pun intended. If you refuse, that's how you end up."

"Did all the other girls from Red Rye run with The Miss that night?" Marlise asked. She had the answer to one question for Cal, and now she needed to get the second one.

Her nod was enough of an answer.

Trying to gauge the size of the current operation, Marlise asked, "So, ten of you left Red Rye, including The Miss and the two guards?"

"Yes." Charlotte nodded. "But more have been added since then."

"Were you warned about the fire?"

"From what I could understand by eavesdropping on The Miss in the van, she was the one to tell The Madame that Mina was an agent. The Madame wanted Mina tortured to find out what she knew, and then killed to ensure she couldn't spill any secrets."

"But they already knew Mina was an agent. Mina's boss put her there."

Charlotte held up her hands again. "True, but The Miss didn't know that. She was livid that she'd been lied to."

"I don't have any solid memories of the timeline from that night because of the fire. What happened?"

"The Miss sent us to the airport to wait for her and the guards. By the time she joined us, everything had changed. She had changed. Suddenly, her need to please The Madame was gone, and she just barked orders and expected you to comply. She told us we were going by car so The Madame couldn't find us."

"But why? It was another year before The Madame was caught."

"She didn't know any of that though. She also didn't know The Madame put Mina in the house. She knew that an FBI agent had been living with us for a year, and that put everything she'd worked for at risk. If you want my opinion, I think she saw it as a chance to break away from The Madame and do what she'd always wanted to do."

"Run the show?" Marlise asked, and Charlotte nodded once.

"What happened after you left the airport in Red Rye? Where did you go?"

"A van showed up and we rode in it, blindfolded, for days. Breaks were always in the woods, and there were never any signs to tell us where we were. When we got to where we were going, it was hot. That's all I know."

"Hot?"

"Hot, dusty, doesn't rain much, and there are lots of cactus around the mobile homes. The new home base is in the middle of nowhere."

"You live in mobile homes?"

Charlotte's shrug was jerky. "They might be old

camping trailers? I'm not sure. They're silver on the outside."

"How many trailers are there, and does The Miss have her own?" Marlise asked, leaning in as she waited for the answer. She was getting the information Cal needed, and she didn't want to give up now. She had to get as much from Charlotte as possible before the girl got too tired.

"The Miss has a big trailer in the middle," she explained and then motioned to show how the other trailers surrounded it like sunrays.

"What happens if a girl doesn't want to stay?"

Charlotte's head shook, and her lip trembled. "Not a good idea. Not a good idea."

Before Marlise could say anything more, she broke down into racking sobs again, and Marlise took her hand to comfort her, knowing Selina would swoop in and give her something to calm her.

Mack walked in and took Charlotte's other hand with both of his, his thumbs rubbing over the back of her hand in a pattern that seemed to calm her friend. He motioned for her to go, which meant Cal wanted her.

She stood, gave the now hiccupping woman one last look and steeled herself for what was to come.

"WHAT STATES HAVE cactus besides Arizona and California?" Cal asked the team gathered around the control room and computers.

"New Mexico, California, Arizona, Texas, Nevada and Utah," Mina reeled off.

"That's a lot of acreage," Roman said.

"But we narrowed it down to six states," Cal added, his mind spinning as he tried to sort through the information Charlotte had shared. "Mina, you said that the women who went on the drug dates flew to large events. Do you remember what cities? Was there one they went to the most?"

"I don't know."

"I thought you scheduled the dates," Cal said, frustration forcing his hand into his hair, still cut in the military high and tight style.

"I did the regular dates, but the travel dates were different. I scheduled the girl out of the house on the calendar, but The Miss dealt with the rest. I called the pilot and let him know to check for a flight plan for what date, but I wasn't privy to any other information."

Marlise walked in the door, and Cal motioned her over. "Great job, Mary," he whispered, putting his arm around her and squeezing her. "That was flawless questioning."

"I wasn't questioning her," Marlise said, shrugging under his hand. "I just let her talk. Maybe once she rests, she can tell us more. I don't think she knows where they're based though. The vibe I got from her is The Miss doesn't want them to know."

"Charlotte said they were blindfolded the entire drive to the new camp. The Miss must be paranoid,"

Mina said with a head shake. "Paranoid people are dangerous when they feel trapped."

"Our next question when she's rested again is, are they always blindfolded when they leave the camp?" Cal said. "Mina, did you recognize any of the other women with Charlotte at the fence?"

"No," Mina answered. "The other three were not from Red Rye, at least the best I could tell from the grainy images."

Cal turned and took Marlise's shoulders. "Do you have a gut feeling about where they might be based now?"

He noticed Marlise glance around the room before she shook her head. "Could be anywhere. I'm from Arizona, and there are a lot of cacti there." She shrugged, but Cal could see she was filled with fear.

Cal released her and turned to the rest of the room. "I want to know how The Miss is funding this."

Mina let out a loud *ha* from her chair by the computer. "The Miss controlled the money in Red Rye. I know she was skimming. She got on the boss's good side and then ate up every detail of the operation. I was more afraid of The Miss than I was The Madame," she said with a shoulder shrug. "We never saw The Madame, but The Miss was ruthless."

"And since The Madame was never there, it would have been easy to skim money without anyone suspecting?" Cal asked.

"She's right," Marlise agreed. "The few dates I went on, I was supposed to get a certain amount of money, but sometimes I got a lot more. I gave it to The Miss and then got my cut, which wasn't much. She easily could have kept anything extra before she logged it for The Madame."

"Is it a stretch to say that she could have been running her own enterprise by piggybacking on The Madame's business?" Cal asked.

"When it comes to sex trafficking and drugs, anything is possible," Mina said with a sigh. "There was so much money coming into Red Rye, not to mention drugs, it wouldn't be hard for her to build up a parachute fairly quickly without The Madame ever knowing."

"I need to ask Charlotte how The Miss pays them," Marlise said, adding it to her list on a notepad.

"Or doesn't pay them," Roman said. "Charlotte indicated it wasn't a good idea for a girl to say no. Maybe she's just holding them hostage and forcing them to work."

"That or she's promising them great returns on the back end once their operation is up and running," Mina added. "After living with her for a year, I could see her pulling that off with those women. Maybe she's dangling part ownership in the adventure."

"Possible," Marlise agreed. "She was always spouting girl power when she wanted us to get on board with an idea."

Mina started to giggle until they were full-on laughing to the point they couldn't stop. Cal helped

Marlise to a chair, waiting while she wiped her cheeks with her shoulders.

"I'm sorry," she said with contriteness. "It probably doesn't seem like a laughing matter to you, but you'd understand if you'd lived there. The Miss was evil, and we all knew it, but she pretended to like us, hoping we'd do anything for her. It worked on some of the girls, and they were the ones who got the bigger jobs out of state, but it didn't work on Mina or me."

Mina cleared her throat and shot Cal a look of understanding. "She's right. The Miss was wicked, but for the women who bought into her girl squad nonsense, they were rewarded. Charlotte was one of them."

"Apparently not any longer," Cal said with a shake of his head.

"I think Charlotte acted like she was, but only as a way to protect herself," Marlise said. "If she only wanted older men, she had to move up the ladder by helping The Miss."

"I wonder how many other women have tried to defect and what happened to them," Roman said.

"I'll ask her."

Cal heard the tremble in her words and noticed how her pen shook on her pad. "You don't have to ask her, Marlise," he said, resting his hand on her shoulder for comfort. "Mina can ask her."

"I said I would ask her." Her tone was fierce and defiant in a way he'd never heard before. His little mouse was becoming a lion.

Cal lifted his hand and held it up. "Whatever you're comfortable doing. In the meantime, everyone should get some rest. Until Marlise can get Charlotte to answer a few more questions, we're looking for a needle in a haystack. Hopefully, she'll feel up to a longer questioning session in a few hours."

Cal waited while everyone filed out of the room, but he held Marlise back. Once everyone was gone, he turned to her. "I don't want this to upset you, Mary. If it becomes too much, say the word, and I'll have Mina take over."

He noticed her stiffen, and she took a step closer to him before speaking. "Once again, I'd like to remind you that I'm not a wilting flower, Cal Newfellow. If I ever want my life to be my own again, I have to step up and do the hard stuff too. I know you want to shelter me from having to relive my life when I was held captive, but it might be the only way to be free of it."

He gently grasped her wrist. "But you've come so far since that day you ran onto my plane, and I never want to see you in that kind of shape again. You have to promise me that you'll ask for help if you need it."

She nodded, but Cal couldn't help feeling that she was hiding something. When she picked up her pad and left the room, he stared after her, but his mind was stuck on that scene on the plane the first time he saw her. Their eyes had met, and hers were filled with bottomless terror that he'd felt in the pit of his stomach. He knew that kind of terror, and seeing someone like her experiencing it raised a shield of protectiveness inside him. He wanted to give her room to grow and breathe now that she was out of that situation, but her time with The Madame came back to haunt them every time he tried. She could work for Secure One with no expiration date, but Marlise deserved the chance to experience freedom.

Real freedom. Not protection disguised as freedom. Sure, Marlise knew she could leave Secure One at any time, but she wouldn't survive a week unless The Madame was behind bars and The Miss was caught.

Chapter Eight

Marlise paced her room, but stopped by the adjoining door each time, only to turn away before she knocked. She didn't know what to do. Maybe she should wait to talk to Cal in hopes Charlotte could answer their questions. If Charlotte could tell them where The Miss was, she wouldn't have to upset Cal. If she told him what she'd been hiding and he got upset, he might cut her loose from the lodge, and she wouldn't live through the night.

Another trip around the room had her convinced he wouldn't do that, but she wasn't convinced he would ever talk to her again once he found out the truth. Maybe that was okay. Then she wouldn't have to fight this constant attraction she felt for him. She couldn't explain it, but every time he took her shoulders and stared into her eyes, it was like he was trying to fight the same battle.

Exhausted, she plopped down on her bed and sighed. She had to tell Cal. Maybe it wouldn't matter, but she'd never know if she didn't come clean with him. Marlise pushed herself up, walked to the door and raised her fist. After a short pep talk, she knocked on the adjoining door. He said they should get some rest, so she hoped he had taken his own advice and was in his room. Since she'd come to stay here, everyone said he was different. He was happier and didn't work everyone past exhaustion. She chalked it up to his brother moving here when she did, which meant Cal was happier having family close again, but Mina just rolled her eyes at that response.

When Cal didn't answer the door right away, she lowered her arm, ready to give up for the day, but the swish of the door opening ran a shiver up her spine. His whispered "Mary" in a sleepy voice ratcheted her heart rate up a few notches.

"I'm sorry I woke yo—" She'd spun around to see Cal standing before her wearing nothing but a pair of basketball shorts. Marlise begged her mind to work, but it wouldn't form a sentence. Her brain was too busy snapping images of his tatted chest. She could never have imagined what he was hiding under his tight T-shirts. His chest sported an image of Zeus and Leto, side by side. Zeus was gazing at Leto with admiration, while all around them, storm clouds gathered and lightning bolts rained down.

On an inhaled breath, she took a step closer. One of those lightning bolts followed a jagged scar down his chest. Her finger traced the bumpy skin, and his muscles rippled under her touch. "Your hand wasn't your only injury from the war."

Cal's hand had been injured in a car bomb, and that had ended his military career. They'd saved his hand, but he'd lost two fingers at the middle joint. He had a special prosthesis he wore on his hand that filled in for the missing digits. She didn't even notice it anymore, but this injury was new, and the jagged scar that ended in a round one told her it had involved a bullet.

"A long time ago, Mary," he whispered, capturing her hand and lowering it, but he didn't let go. "Did you need something?"

"What happened, Cal?"

"Why do you care?" he asked, his head tipped in confusion.

"We're all scarred," she said with a shrug. "I wish I could turn my scars into something beautiful like yours."

"You are beautiful, Mary," he whispered, his gaze sweeping the length of her without hesitating for even a moment on her scarred skin. "You don't need ink to make it so."

"How can this be beautiful?" she asked, flicking her hand at her scarred face and arm.

"It's beautiful because you are, and the scars are a beautiful reminder that you survived and thrived despite what someone else inflicted on you. Don't ever, ever tell yourself you're anything but beautiful."

If only that were possible, Marlise thought. He might say she was beautiful, but he didn't have to look at her every day. At least not in a romantic way, but then a man like Cal Newfellow would never consider her a romantic companion. She doubted any man would. Her scars went far deeper than her skin, and sometimes those scars were harder to hide. Working for Cal had taught her to trust him, but once out in the real world, she'd have to protect herself from men who wanted to use and abuse her. She'd had enough of that growing up.

"Where did you just go, Mary?" Cal asked, and she snapped her gaze back to his.

"I—I was just thinking about dangerous men."

"I'm not dangerous, Mary."

"Oh, but you are, Cal. Physically, emotionally and vocationally, you are the most dangerous man in my life. You have the power to put me back into The Miss's line of fire."

Marlise wrung her hands and turned her back to him, walking to the other side of the room. There was no way she could tell him the truth about Red Rye. He would get angry and send her away, but the image of Charlotte sobbing and alone drifted through her mind. It wasn't unlike the memory she had of herself in the same place a couple years ago. She had to do this for the other girls who were still suffering.

The door clicked closed, and a sigh escaped her lips. Had he left? She turned to see him lounging against the wall, his broad and beautiful chest making her forget why they were there. He needed to put more clothes on if she was ever going to tell him the truth. Cal didn't look to be going anywhere though.

He had one bare foot crossed over the other as he met her gaze.

"Is that why you're afraid to tell me about whatever is bugging you? You know I don't threaten anyone's job as punishment."

"But you might when you find out the truth," she whispered. "I like you, Cal, and I like working here, but I have to help the other girls Charlotte left behind."

She squared her shoulders and inhaled a deep breath as he pushed off the door and strode over to her. Even barefoot, his size was formidable and overwhelming. She wanted to sink back into the bed, but she wouldn't. She had to stand up for herself and all the other girls who couldn't right now.

"I like you too, Mary. You wouldn't have the run of this place if I didn't. Tell me what you think is so bad that I'd kick you out."

She closed her eyes and let the memories of that night wash over her. The voices, screams and thuds filled her head. The smoke clogged her throat, and the wall of flames throbbed at her from all sides. "The night of the fire," she said, her voice choked as she inhaled again, the scent of acrid smoke filling her head. "I was trying to save the girls, Cal." A shiver ran through her, and he took her elbow to help her sit.

"How were you trying to save them? They found you by the front door. Were you running back in instead of out?"

"I had to get out. The smoke and the flames, Cal, they were everywhere."

"It must have been disorienting to be inside that kind of fire. Were you trying to get to Mina?"

"No," she whispered. "I was trying to get out!"

"Relax, Mary. I'm trying to figure out how you would save the women."

His warm touch jerked her mind back from the fire, and she focused on him. She was sure he could see the terror in her eyes, but she couldn't stop now. She had to convince him to help her.

"In Red Rye, I did what I wanted without anyone taking notice. I was expendable."

"No." His voice was firm, but there was a steel edge to it. "You are not and never were expendable, Mary."

"To them, I was, Cal. I knew it. Mina knew it. All the girls knew it. I think that's why they talked to me."

"Talked to you?" he asked as he dropped to one knee in front of her.

"More like confided in me," she explained, rubbing the scarred skin on her hand. "They told me things about their dates, and…" Her voice dropped to a whisper as she leaned into his ear. "I recorded it."

Cal's eyes widened at her admittance. "You recorded the conversations? On the computer?"

"No!" she exclaimed. "I'm not dumb, Cal!"

He rubbed her arms up and down to calm her, the metal of his prosthesis cold against her skin. There was something uniquely Cal about it though. "I didn't say you were. If not on a computer, then where?"

"When I first started doing all the grocery shopping and errands, The Miss always sent one of her guards with me to 'help.'"

"But it was to make sure you didn't run?" he asked, and she nodded.

"Eventually, they knew I wasn't going to run because I had no money to do it."

"You weren't getting paid to take care of the house?"

"No. I got to live there and eat. The Miss said that's all she would allow since I wasn't bringing in any money."

"If I ever find this woman…"

Marlise took his hand and offered him a sly grin. "I got her in the end though, Cal. It was easy to siphon money off the cash she'd give me for groceries. I bought a smartphone one day but never activated it. I just used it to hold pictures and recordings. Then I rented a post office box to keep it safe. That's where I was going the night of the fire."

"The post office?"

After a nod and rough swallow, she admitted something she never thought she'd tell another soul. "All the girls told me things about their trips, the men and The Miss. When one phone was full, I bought another."

"You don't have to whisper, Mary. No one here is out to hurt you."

"I don't want you to be upset," she said, jumping up and walking to the other side of the room. "I should have told you sooner, but I was scared and didn't think it mattered."

"What changed that makes you think it matters now?" he asked, rising to his full height of six feet three inches. He was taller than her by a foot. She should have been scared of him, but all she wanted was to be wrapped in his arms. She didn't trust most men after what happened in her life, but she trusted Cal.

She trusted Cal.

That thought stopped her in her tracks. She was twenty-eight years old, and for the first time in her life, she trusted a man.

"I trust you, Cal," she blurted out. He didn't say anything. He just rested his hands on her shoulders and squeezed them. It was like he knew how big of an admittance that was for her. "I trust you, and that's why I'm telling you about the phones. The lawyer on television said there's no such thing as a perfect witness." She flipped around to face him. "Maybe there isn't, but I could be as close to perfect as they come since my past is gone. If I can get the phones, I could testify against The Miss and The Madame!"

"The recordings would help the case, but the lawyers will say they were gathered illegally and therefore not admissible in court."

Marlise paced away from him and then back again, worry filling her that maybe he was right. "I wondered the same thing, but I searched the internet when I lived at the group home, and it said as long as one person in the conversation gives consent, then it's a legal recording that can be played in court."

Cal's lips pursed, and he dipped his head in question. "I can ask Mina or Roman. They'd know, but I'm not sure the recordings would add anything to the pending case against The Madame. The risk to reward is too high. I'm sorry, Mary."

"No, just listen, Cal!" she exclaimed, running to him and planting her hands on Zeus and Leto. "The recordings can answer some of the questions that no one else can."

His hands came around her wrists and held them, his brown eyes almost black in the dim light of her room. "Such as?"

"The cities they most often went to on dates, for starters. If you can just get me to Red Rye, I promise they're worth the time."

"Absolutely not," Cal said, his voice dark and heavy. He pushed her hands away from his chest before he set his jaw. "You'll never step foot back in that town. I'll discuss it with Mina and Roman, and if they think it's worth the risk, I'll send my men. End of story."

"That's impossible, Cal. I have to go."

"No!"

Initially, she stepped back, scared by his fierceness, until she remembered he wouldn't hurt her. He'd already shown that a million times over. She advanced on him instead, and they stood chest to chest.

"Yes. I don't have the key anymore since the house burned down. The only way to get into that box is with my face."

A curse word fell from Cal's lips, and she cocked

a brow, waiting for him to say something else. When he didn't, she played her final trump card.

"Those phones also hold real recordings of The Miss as well as a photo of her."

He leaned forward to hear her better. "Did you just say you have her photo?" Marlise nodded as she swallowed around the lump of fear that was trying to keep her secrets inside. "Why didn't you mention this sooner, Mary?"

The tone of his voice told her he was angry, and she shrank back against the bed for a moment. Then she remembered she had the right to defend herself and her choices just like he did. She stood, ready for battle.

"What good would it have done, Cal? They caught The Madame, and we had no idea where The Miss was or if she was even in business anymore."

"If I had known you had a photo, I could have found her!"

"How?" Marlise exclaimed, her arms going up in the air. "We're more of a ghost than you are, Cal!"

"Why did you take her picture if you knew it was useless?" This time, he asked the question without anger, but rather in confusion.

"I had no idea that we didn't exist in any database when I took it. Once the FBI told me that, the picture of The Miss became useless, at least in my mind. Now, I'm not so sure."

"What do you mean?"

"Well, maybe, if we figure out where she is, the

image will help us find her. I don't know, okay?" she asked, frustrated. "Something is telling me to get the phones. That's what I was trying to do the night of the fire, but I never made it out of the house!"

He turned away from her, his hand in his hair, and she noticed his shoulders rise and fall once. "I can't risk taking you back there, Mary. It's too dangerous!"

"Cal, I can handle myself. Besides, we know The Miss is nowhere near Red Rye."

"Haven't you learned anything?" He hissed the question more than he asked it. "Now that Charlotte is here, The Miss also knows you're here!"

"All the more reason to leave." Her raised brow did nothing to goad him, so she stepped into his space again and rested her hand on his arm. She wanted to put her hands all over his hard chest, but she knew there was only one way that could end, and it wouldn't be in her favor. "The Miss has been gone from Red Rye for two years. There's no way she has anyone local on the payroll."

"You can't be sure of that," he insisted. "I can promise you she's got someone on her payroll there. You going there can't happen."

"It has to happen, Cal. I only paid for three years on the post office box, and my time is almost up. There's no other way to get into the box either. You can't break into a post office and not get caught."

"I'm a ghost, Mary. I can be in and out of a place before anyone is the wiser."

"Not in Red Rye," she said, standing her ground

with crossed arms. "It's a hub. Someone is always there sorting mail and loading trucks."

She tried not to take joy in his grimace, but a tiny part of her enjoyed playing that card.

"Stay put. I need to talk to my people." He strode to the door and yanked it open.

"Fine, but I'm not telling you the box number unless I'm along for the ride!"

The door slammed behind him, telling her exactly what he thought of the gauntlet she'd thrown down.

CAL'S THOUGHTS WERE as dark and dangerous as the lake that spread out before him. He was still reeling from the bombshell Marlise had dropped on him. She'd had ample opportunity to mention the hidden information, but she hadn't. He paced the dock, wishing the lights weren't on so he could hide in the darkness. Instead, his lakeshore was lit up with security lights to warn anyone they wouldn't be taken by surprise. No one took Secure One by surprise anymore.

"You better have a beer in your hand," he called out to his brother as he approached from the lodge.

"Do I look stupid?" Roman asked when he joined him on the dock and handed him a bottle.

Cal looked him up and down as he pulled the cap off the beer. "You want me to answer that?"

Roman shoved him in the shoulder with laughter before bringing the bottle to his lips. "Everything status quo out here?"

"As far as I can tell," Cal said. "All the alarms are

silent, and there's been no movement. I'm inclined to believe Charlotte when she said the other three women left."

Roman nodded, but didn't speak as he stared out over the lake. "You know they're going to attack by air, right?"

"Yep," he agreed, acid swirling in his gut. "It's their only option, but I'm not convinced they have the ability to come in by air. She's sending scared women in to do recon. My confidence is low that she could get a plan together to attack."

"Facts. We still need to assume she can and be prepared though."

"I would like you and Mina to move into the guest room in the lodge. She's still hot, and you know The Miss would take her as fast as she'd take Marlise."

"Something we both agree on," Roman said. "We'll sleep there, but we're spending most of our time in the control room. If you want my opinion, you should go to Red Rye."

Cal grunted rather than answered, and Roman laughed, but his head shook. Whatever he was thinking, Cal didn't want to hear it.

"I think you have a screw loose. Red Rye is dead to us."

Roman's shrug said he didn't believe him, which annoyed Cal. "I know how hard it is to put someone you care about in danger to further a case, but from what Marlise told us while you were out here brooding, the information in the post office box might be worth the risk."

"How?" Cal asked, his arms going up in the air as beer flew across the dock. "Okay, so we know what The Miss looks like, so what? Marlise, Mina and Charlotte do too. That doesn't help us when she's untraceable."

"We could run her voice through our programs and see if we get a hit."

"I don't think she's doing television or radio interviews, Roman." Cal sat, and exhaustion hung like a cloak across his shoulders.

"Maybe not," Roman said, sitting next to him, "but that doesn't mean she didn't in her past life. The recordings might give us information about where to find the woman."

"It's unlikely that any of the women knew her bug out plan."

Roman pointed at him as he finished his beer and set it on the dock by his feet. "That's true, but have you considered human nature in this situation?"

Cal stared at him in confusion. He wasn't processing things as fast as he should, and he knew it, but all he could see was a scared Marlise sneaking a phone into the house, likely at great risk to herself, to try and stop what was happening under its roof. Roman grasped his shoulder in a show of brotherly support, almost like he knew Cal needed it. He did, but he would never admit weakness to his brother or anyone else on this property. He was supposed to be steady as a rock and block the blows no matter how hard or fast they came. And he did, except for the blow he took an hour ago. That one hit him out of left field and nearly knocked him out.

"What are you talking about, Roman? I've had two hours of sleep in the last two days. I'm not going to solve riddles."

"It wasn't a riddle," his brother said with a laugh. "It was a genuine question. You say that the women wouldn't know her bug out plan, and that's true, but they knew her, and humans are nothing if not predictable. When we feel threatened, we fall back on the people and places we know best. It's possible that with the information Charlotte can give us, along with those recordings, we might narrow down where The Miss is hiding out."

Cal tipped his head in agreement but stared out over the lake instead of answering. He was stuck between a rock and a hard place. "Risking Marlise's life for 'might' isn't reassuring."

"Might is more than we have right now, Cal. If we want our lives back, we have no choice but to take any chance we have to find The Miss, even if it's the slightest chance."

Cal stood again and set his hands on his hips. "Marlise is refusing to cooperate."

"No, Marlise is trying to take her life back. She's learning to stand up for herself for the first time ever."

"She had to pick me to be the one to stand up to?"

Roman stepped up to him and stuck his finger

in his chest. "Yes, and it's time you stop acting like she's putting you out because of it. She picked you for a reason."

"I'm convenient."

"No," Roman said with a shake of his head. "You're safe. It's taken her two years to learn to trust a man, but your tirade is setting her right back where she was when we brought her here."

"What does that mean?" Cal asked with his jaw clenched. When Marlise arrived at Secure One, she was timid, scared and afraid to do anything that might upset him.

"She's inside the lodge asking Charlotte questions, trying to get more information. I overheard her tell Mina she would do anything to find The Miss so your life could go back to normal. She thinks you feel responsible for her because she's damaged." Cal opened his mouth, but Roman held up a finger. "Those were her exact words. She wants to be part of Secure One and not just as a support person who cooks and cleans for the team."

"Everyone is part of the team at Secure One," Cal said. "No one is any better than anyone else here, and you know it."

"You're missing the point, Cal. Marlise needs to be part of finding the woman who tried to kill her, not hide while other people do it."

"She needs to take her power back."

"Yes!" Roman exclaimed with laughter. "Finally. She has never had any power in this life, but now she finally does. Those recordings only exist because she took a huge risk to make them."

"And now she's the only one with the power to retrieve them."

Roman pointed at him. "I've known Marlise for years, and I'll tell you this, she's firm on her decision to be the only one who goes to Red Rye. Accept it, or don't, that's your choice, but you will damage her confidence by refusing to talk to her. Just think about it."

Roman turned and walked away, leaving Cal to stare after him while his words echoed in his ears. Marlise's power had been taken away at birth, first by her birth parents and then by her foster parents. That dictated the path for the rest of her life. Then she came to Secure One, and he gave her back the power to decide what she did, how she did it and when she did it. He gave her back the power to take care of herself by teaching her self-defense and how to use a gun. He gave her power by asking her to talk to Charlotte and ask the critical questions.

Cal swore as he jogged toward the lodge. Roman was right. He'd been the one to teach her how to harness her power, and he couldn't be the one to take it away. He had to get her to Red Rye, no matter what it cost him.

Chapter Nine

Marlise sat next to Charlotte and held her hand. She was still in the med bay so Selina could keep an eye on her, but she was determined to get more information about The Miss's operation for Cal. If she could, maybe he'd see she was a valuable member of the team and consider taking her to get the phones she'd hidden. The look on Cal's face when she told him about the post office box crossed her mind, and she grimaced. Chances were good he might never speak to her again, much less take her back to Red Rye.

"Are you feeling better?" Marlise asked the woman who reminded her so much of herself just a few years ago. Charlotte was depressed, angry and terrified, but Marlise could see the relief in her as well. She wasn't here as a pawn in a game. She'd found a way out and took it.

"I'm sorry that I lost it earlier. The memories, sometimes they swamp me, and I can't force the emotions down."

"You don't have to apologize," Marlise promised.

"I remember living there. Working for The Madame has lifelong effects, but it does get better. I'm proof of that."

"I know," Charlotte agreed with a wan smile. "I always looked up to you, Marlise. You knew how to work the room, so to say, and keep yourself safe. I told myself if I ever got a chance to run, I would be as brave as you were."

"I wasn't brave," Marlise said with a shake of her head. "I was trapped in the house and almost died. I got lucky and only survived because Roman found me. A few more minutes in that house, and I wouldn't be sitting here right now."

Charlotte shrugged as she toyed with the mug in front of her. "Maybe, but you're working here now and trying to shut her down. I want to be part of that."

"Good," Marlise said, squeezing her hand. "I have a few more questions."

"I'll try, but I know so little." Charlotte shook her head and sucked in a deep breath.

"Sometimes we know more than we think we do," Marlise reminded her. "For instance, can you tell me what cities The Miss sent you to for dates when in Red Rye?"

Her mouth twisted to the side, and she glanced up at the ceiling as though she had to think about it. "I had only been on three of them before the fire, and two were in Kansas City. The third one was probably in Texas, though I wasn't told where. I was in a hotel the whole time. Maybe Dallas? I wasn't privy to any documents with an address."

"I wondered about that since you weren't doing it for long before the fire. What about the other girls? Emelia and Bethany, where were they sent?"

"I don't know. We weren't allowed to talk about it, and we didn't. We were too afraid The Miss would overhear and call us out."

Marlise nodded, but she was thinking about the phones again in Red Rye. She wondered why the girls talked to her without fear. Maybe it wasn't that they were afraid of The Miss, but they were afraid one of the other girls would try to home in on their clients. Then again, maybe they were afraid someone would narc to The Miss about them to get a better standing with her. Marlise couldn't remember all of the cities and what girls went where. Not without listening to the recordings, at least. She struggled to remember a lot of things about her life in Red Rye before the fire. "One question the team had was, how is The Miss paying for all of this? Does she pay the girls?"

"She was confiscating bundles of money in Red Rye when we returned from our dates. She kept them in the safe at the house. I think she also trafficked drugs that The Madame didn't know about."

"She was siphoning off The Madame to set up her own business."

"Absolutely. The Miss believed she was a better leader than The Madame. It was only a matter of time before she tried to part ways and do her own thing. The fire at Red Rye accelerated her plan, but she had the money to get what she needed quickly. As for paying us, she doesn't. If she paid us, we'd have money and might try to run. Our payment is room and board. The Miss is incredibly paranoid. She doesn't let us off the property without a blindfold and a guard. She even has some male guards now. When girls return from dates—" she put the word in quotation marks "—they turn over the money to her immediately."

"If you have to be blindfolded, how did you get to Secure One? How did you even know I was here?"

"We get to take the blindfolds off once the plane is in the air. We can't see out the windows anyway. Once we landed, a car was waiting, and we followed the preprogrammed GPS."

"You're saying that she doesn't want you to know where home base is, so if you're captured, you can't talk."

Charlotte pointed at her with a nod.

"Does she send a guard? How else can she assure that you don't defect?"

The other woman was quiet while she stared at her lap. Whatever the answer to that question was, it took a toll on her.

"There was a guard with us. If anyone tried to run, they'd be—" she glanced up at Mack before she dropped her gaze again to her lap "—shot." The whispered word ran a shiver up Marlise's spine.

"You said it was a bad idea for a girl to say no. Is that what happens if they do?" Her nod was immediate, but her hand came to her mouth to cover it. Marlise wasn't sure if she was going to be sick or was trying not to sob.

"Emelia and Bethany tried to say no, and we haven't seen them since."

Marlise lifted a brow in surprise. "Emelia and Bethany were her top girls in Red Rye."

"They were, and they didn't like how they were treated once we got to the new place. They decided they wanted more of the pie and challenged The Miss. If you ask me, she made them an example for the rest of us."

"If you challenge her, you're buried."

Marlise worried about what would happen when the other three girls returned to home base without Charlotte. Chances were good they'd be buried too.

"We didn't know why we were sent here until I heard on the radio in the car that the trial for The Madame had been postponed because someone tried to kill the lead witness. I might not have a college degree, but I'm smart enough to know you were one of the lead witnesses. Once I heard that, I knew The Miss had failed to get rid of you and had to make a new plan."

"I wonder how she knew I was at Secure One."

"She talked nonstop about the plane you took off on a few years ago, and she finally figured out who it belonged to."

"What were you supposed to do when you got here?"

"The guard had to take pictures and draw maps of the property with entry points for the team that would follow us."

"There are no entry points," Marlise said with a shake of her head. "Secure One is a fortress now."

"Which we figured out quickly. That was why I had to convince the other girls to let me try to infiltrate via the lakeshore. The guard was new, and she was as overwhelmed as we were. She said I could, but they'd leave without me if I didn't return to the car by a set time. She reminded me that meant I could never find my way back to The Miss, but The Miss would find me and kill me if I defected."

With a cocked brow, Marlise asked, "How would she find you?"

Charlotte leaned forward and whispered into Marlise's ear. "My tracker."

Marlise's eyes widened, and she leaned forward so Mack couldn't hear her. "You have a tracker?"

She nodded, and Marlise could read the terror in her eyes. "I cut it out and buried it in the sand." Her whispered confession was tearful and told Marlise of the level of paranoia The Miss had reached since leaving Red Rye. "Once the battery is dead, she'll think I am too."

She held up a finger to Charlotte and walked over to Mack. "Do they make trackers small enough to implant in humans?"

"No, not that I'm aware of," Mack said, his gaze flicking to Charlotte for a moment. "Why?"

"Charlotte said The Miss had a tracker in her. She cut it out and left it on the beach."

Mack's brows went up in tandem. "They make small ones for purses, but still over an inch thick. I suppose you could implant it, but it would be painful. The battery isn't going to last longer than a couple of days."

Marlise walked back to Charlotte. "When did she put in the tracker?"

"Right before we left. She put it under the skin and sewed it up. It was so painful, and we had to try to walk through the woods with it in our legs. She said they'd keep us honest because she could track our movements."

"Is that the wound they found in your thigh when they searched you?" Charlotte nodded, and Marlise sighed.

"I was glad I got rid of it before Cal captured me since they searched for a tracker."

"The Miss will either think you're dead or a hostage now."

"Or that I defected. Regardless of what The Miss thinks, I doubt she will bother with me. She wants to stop you from testifying. Nothing else matters."

"I need to talk to Mary." Cal's voice was loud from the door where Mack stood. Mack whispered something, and then Cal's voice boomed through the hallway. "I don't have time to wait on this, Mack!"

Marlise stood and squeezed Charlotte's hand. "I'll be back. Rest now, and let Selina know if you need anything for pain."

Charlotte nodded with a sad smile. "Thanks, Marlise. Be careful. She's hell-bent on stopping you from testifying any way she can. She just has to find you first."

"I've got one of the best teams looking out for me. I'll be fine."

Marlise turned and walked to the door to deal with her team leader. His attitude with Mack told her he was back in work mode. She had some things to tell him, and she hoped the information Charlotte gave her would tip the scales in her favor and get them back to Red Rye.

"ROMAN SAYS MISSION ACCOMPLISHED. Be careful and follow the plan." Marlise's voice filled the quiet car.

"Tell them ten-four and to keep us in their sights." She nodded and typed his response out to Roman.

At least that was one problem solved. Roman and Mina had found Charlotte's tracker on the beach, driven it out to a lake in the middle of nowhere several hours from Secure One and buried it on the lakeshore. Once The Miss triangulated on the location and figured out it was a lake, she would hopefully believe that Charlotte was dead and no longer a threat. Hopefully. There was no guarantee, but it was the best way to buy time if nothing else.

After a long and complicated planning meeting

and a night of sleep, they waited for dark to descend and then headed south to Red Rye, hoping the phones Marlise had stashed could break the case wide-open. Cal wasn't convinced, but he trusted her instincts. He hadn't heard the recordings, so he couldn't say they wouldn't be helpful until he did.

He glanced over at the woman in the passenger seat. Their plan was tricky. They'd left Secure One in a dummy van and switched cars two hours later. They'd drive their current vehicle into Red Rye as soon as the post office opened, and Marlise would get the phones from the box. Once they had them, they'd transfer cars again and drive west several hours to a hotel. If they didn't pick up a tail from Red Rye, they'd switch cars and drive back to Secure One during the night.

"I wish we could have taken the helicopter." Marlise sighed. "This is tense."

Cal squeezed her shoulder for a moment before putting his hand back on the wheel. "I know, but taking any mode of transportation that could be traced back to Secure One was too risky. The Miss tagged my plane, which means she knows my chopper too."

Cal didn't say how angry he was that The Miss had found Marlise because of him. Once again, he'd failed to offer the protection his entire business was based around. Instead, he'd led bad people to good people not once but twice. Secure One. What a joke. He was the least secure one in the area, and The Madame and The Miss were the ones to teach him that both times.

"And you don't think a van with a fake technology repair logo will trick someone watching?"

"You'd be surprised how easy it is to overlook the obvious. I run a company that depends on technology. Besides, I don't believe The Miss is monitoring Secure One. She doesn't have the manpower."

"More like woman power," Marlise corrected him.

She was right. If The Miss was running this operation with scared women and no one else, then going to Red Rye was worth the risk. Charlotte did say that there were male guards now, but she didn't know how many. If The Miss had enough, she might send them to Minnesota to attack Secure One. Better to find her before they showed up.

He didn't like that they had no backup, but Roman was right. The more cars in play, the greater risk of showing up on someone's radar. It was up to him to keep Marlise safe, and he'd die to make sure she didn't. He shook his head to clear his thoughts. Did he just think that? He'd never thought that about a woman before—not even when Mina had been kidnapped.

Mina was Roman's. Marlise is yours.

No. That was not an option. He had led The Miss to their door. He should have taken more time to develop a better plan, but they didn't have time on their side two years ago. The Madame had forced their hand. And this time, The Miss was forcing it. His jaw pulsed with the internal anger he had toward himself for even thinking he could be with someone again. Being with someone was dangerous, and an excellent way to get your heart broken or someone killed. He had learned that the hard way. While he was on this side of the grave, he would never take that risk again.

Marlise held up the small device in her hand. It was bigger than a cell phone but smaller than an iPad and allowed them to communicate with Secure One on a dedicated line. The information stayed on the screen for only three minutes before it disappeared. It was a solid way to get information back and forth when a team member was in the field without risking it falling into the wrong hands.

"Mina finished her deep dive into the Red Rye postmaster. From what she can see, he's squeaky clean. There were no large deposits made in his accounts, and she couldn't find any gambling debts or communication with anyone she couldn't validate. He has several car loans, credit card balances and a mortgage. She doesn't think he's on any payroll other than the US government's. At least not that she can find."

Cal pointed at her. "That's the important caveat. He could be on the payroll but paid in cash. We'll have to trust that Mina's information is correct, but we need to get in and out fast just in case. Since Red Rye is a hub, it means there will be a lot of employees, and we can't check them all."

"That's true," she agreed, "but the sorting will be mostly done by the time we arrive. We'll only have to deal with the postmaster. I know it's a risk, Cal, but Mina has done the legwork to minimize it as much as possible."

Cal set his jaw and kept the van hurtling down the highway. The sun was coming up, and they'd have to stop soon and use the facilities. He glanced at the clock. It was almost 6:00 a.m. They had an hour left to drive and then an hour to surveil the post office before it opened to the public. He refused to get his hopes up for an uncomplicated mission. Nothing ever went according to plan when The Miss or The Madame was involved. He had to stay two steps ahead of them.

"We have to find this woman and stop her."

Marlise's hand clamped around his giant forearm, and he swallowed down the sensation of solidarity it gave him. He could not fall for this woman. Once they found The Miss, Marlise had to be free to live her life for herself. She couldn't be tied to him emotionally or financially. She deserved to make her own choices independent of him once this psychopath was found and stopped.

"I know you think this is a bad idea, but thank you for taking the chance on me. I won't let you down."

The air left his chest in a whoosh. "Mary, you could never let me down."

"I'd be more convinced if you hadn't stormed out of my room when I told you about the phones."

"I'm sorry about that," he said, running a hand down his face. "The information took me by surprise. It had been years since you left Red Rye, and you never mentioned it."

"I didn't think they mattered," she said, and he could hear the pleading in her voice. "I wasn't withholding them on purpose. They were just a dead end in my mind until Charlotte arrived and told us The Miss had built a new empire."

"Then suddenly those old phones became important."

"At least I hope so, because I know how big of a risk we're taking, Cal."

"Nothing ventured, nothing gained."

A head shake accompanied her snort of laughter. "That is not a motto Cal Newfellow lives by, but nice try."

"You think you know a lot about me."

"You aren't that hard to figure out, Cal. Something happened in the military that you don't talk about now. I respect that. There are things I don't talk about either. Whatever happened is the reason you started Secure One. You want to protect people from the bad guys and go to any lengths to ensure it. You consider everyone at Secure One family rather than employees."

"In the army, every member of your team is a brother. I built my business the same way."

"Why Secure One then? That's incredibly singular."

He didn't answer as he neared the rest area where they'd stop and prepare to make their only move on the board. He pulled into the empty parking lot, chosen because it was nothing more than a small building on the side of the road with plenty of trees to hide their vehicle. They would stay hidden until it was time to finish their drive back into hell.

Once he'd put the car into Park, he turned to her. "Secure one was the last thing I said to the only woman I've ever loved. It meant the area was secure, and it was safe to move. It wasn't secure, and she paid the price. I named my business Secure One so I'd never make that mistake again."

"Falling in love or not securing an area?" she asked, her gaze intent upon him.

"Both."

Without a backward glance, he climbed from the car to prepare for the next mission.

Chapter Ten

Secure one was the last thing I said to the only woman I've ever loved.

The words hadn't left Marlise's mind since Cal had uttered them an hour ago. Since then, he'd done nothing but bark orders at her like she was a soldier on his team. She tried not to take offense to it. He had opened up to her, and she knew how difficult that was for him. She understood it on a personal level most people wouldn't. Whatever happened the day his girlfriend died wasn't all on his shoulders though. When it came to the military, it was never up to one person to secure an area. That was why they had teams. Regardless, Cal was the kind of guy who would bear the burden of any failure so the rest of his team didn't have to. While she understood it, she hated it for him. No one should live that way.

"I killed a man once," she admitted. Did she say that aloud? She threw a hand over her mouth and hoped he didn't hear her.

His hands froze on the straps of his vest. He was

standing in front of her and, in another breath, pushed her back against the car. "Excuse me?"

"I'm sorry. I shouldn't have said that." A tear ran down her cheek, brought about by the admittance and the guilt. "I didn't mean to say that out loud."

Her whispered confession softened him, and he pulled her into a hug. "Something tells me you didn't mean to kill him."

"He was assaulting me," she said in a choked whisper. "If I didn't get him off me, I would die. All I had within reach was a shiv. I accidentally hit his carotid, and he bled out."

"I'm sorry, Mary. I wouldn't wish that kind of experience on anyone."

"You're not alone, Cal. There are a lot of experiences I don't talk about either. You were in the military and probably saw many horrible things, but they don't define you. You're a good person who takes care of your family without hesitation. Whatever happened to your friend was a series of unfortunate events but not your fault. There's a chain of command in the military for a reason."

"You don't know any such thing, Mary. You've never been in war."

"That's not true," she said, pushing him away. "A war is a war, whether it's fought on the street or on foreign soil. You do things in war you would never do in peacetime. No one understands that better than me, Cal," she said, poking herself in the chest. "Don't tell me I've never fought for my life or for something I believed in because you don't know that!" This time, her finger went into his chest, and he closed his fist around it, the metal and rubber fingers clacking as they closed.

"I'm sorry. You know that wasn't what I meant. I simply meant that if you haven't been in the military, you don't understand the intricacies of the missions. I dropped the ball."

"Did you though? Have you taken the time to consider that maybe someone else dropped the ball, and the game was over long before you got on the field? You'll never find peace until you consider that as a possibility, Cal. You're too damn young to sit around brooding for the rest of your life because of one mistake."

"That mistake cost a woman her life!" he ground out.

"But was it your mistake?" she quietly asked. "Really think about it. I've known you for two years, and you're meticulous when you run a mission. You're not like that because of what happened to her. That's your personality and who you are as a person. Have you ever considered that what happened that day wasn't your fault?"

"Absolutely not," he said, his gaze pinned on hers. "I was the team leader, so the mission failure was on me. My intel was bad, but I should have approached things differently. I should have held the team back until I knew for sure. I should have done something more than I did."

"You were given bad information, followed orders, and the mission failed. That's tragic, but that doesn't make it your fault."

Cal slid his hand up her cheek as they stood in the early air of a cool October morning. "Hannah's death will always be on my hands, Mary."

She grasped his wrist and stopped his hand from touching her scarred cheek. "Do you think Hannah would feel that way if she were here? I wasn't in the military, but there isn't a veteran who won't tell you they knew the risks when they signed up. What would Hannah think if she knew your life revolved around her death? Would that make her happy? Would she take comfort or joy in knowing you punish yourself every day for her death?"

Cal's gaze was so intense she was afraid she would combust under it, but what she saw in his eyes scared her the most. He truly believed he had killed the woman he loved, and she would never convince him otherwise. He needed to stop beating himself up for something that went beyond the scope of his job that day.

Slowly, his hand slipped from her face, and he took a step back without saying anything. Cal Newfellow was a crypt, and he couldn't make it clearer that she was not the keeper.

He pulled the car door open and motioned her in. "Are you ready for the resurgence at Red Rye?"

Was she ready? As she lowered herself to the car seat, the answer was easy. No, but she didn't have the luxury of time. If she wanted her life back, she would have to do the hard work, which started back where it all began.

Red Rye, Kansas. Population: four thousand.

WHEN SHE NOTICED her reflection in the post office door, she was glad her coat hid her bulletproof vest. At least she had that going for her. Her fingers played with her blond hair before she took a breath and pulled the door open. Being back in Red Rye hit her in a way she hadn't expected. She'd expected the anxiety to hit hard and brutal. Admittedly, she was anxious to get the phones and get out of town, but that was the only anxiety filling her belly. She was pleasantly numb to any other emotion as she walked into the lobby of the place she had once considered a fortress for her secrets. Once she left here, they wouldn't be secrets for long.

Cal had her back, but now that she was inside, she was on her own in retrieving the phones. They'd been watching the post office for an hour, and nothing seemed amiss, according to Cal, but then The Miss was never obvious. Subtle is your middle name when you're running an illegal prostitution ring smack-dab in the middle of a small town.

With a glance behind her, she made eye contact with Cal. He was loitering outside the door, pretend-ing to smoke a cigarette. His head was on a swivel though, as he "took in the town's charm."

After a deep breath, she approached the counter,

grateful Roland was still the postmaster. He was always so kind to her when she lived here.

"Marlise!" he exclaimed the moment he laid eyes on her. "Well, I never thought I'd see you again! But here you are."

"Hi, Roland," she answered, though her voice wavered. She cleared her throat before she spoke again. "I wanted to pick up my mail before my box expired. Unfortunately, I no longer have the key. You know, after the fire and everything."

"Oh, sure, sure," he said, nodding as though he didn't want to bring up the way the town had been tainted by The Madame either. "I'm happy to get it for you."

She held a bag out to him. "You can use this. Thank you."

The postmaster took the bag with a smile and walked back behind the bank of post office boxes. There would be no mail, only the cell phones. She prayed they'd still charge so they could access the information. Cal told her to act casual, as though it were any other day, and she was simply picking up her mail. She didn't know how hard that would be until she stood there exposed. She forced herself to remain calm as she waited, but he needed to hurry.

There was a bounty out on her head, and if she didn't find a way to stop The Miss, she wouldn't have one. The thought sent a shiver down her spine. The Miss would love nothing more than to have her head, but Marlise had worked too hard and suffered too much to fall back into that woman's grasp.

"Not much in there considering how long you were gone," the postmaster said, jarring Marlise from her thoughts. She jumped but covered it by reaching for the bag.

"I'm sure not. I changed my address immediately when I moved. Thanks again for getting this for me," she said, holding up the bag. "You can let the box go now. I won't be back."

"I'm sorry to see you go, Marlise, but I understand. What happened to you here in Red Rye was terrible. Don't be a stranger if you ever find yourself this way again."

Marlise thanked him and waved before she headed for the door. Not a chance she'd step foot in Red Rye again. This was her past. Her future was out there to find once The Miss was captured. Her gaze locked with Cal's, and she wished for a moment that he were her future. He was the kind of man you trusted without question because there was no doubt in your mind that he'd keep you safe.

Remembering their discussion, she didn't make eye contact on her way past him. She noticed him drop the cigarette and grind it out with his foot before catching up to her, his hands in the pockets of his coat that hid his bulletproof vest. He'd told her to pretend they were a couple on the outs, so she yanked the door open to the car and tossed the bag inside. On a huff, she slid into the passenger seat.

"Did you get them?"

"Yes. Let's get out of here." She donned a pair of sunglasses and crossed her arms over her chest, staring out the window as though she were mad at the man next to her.

The car rumbled as they headed away from the town that had broken her body, mind and spirit. The car was silent and tense until they reached the next county, but when they made it without a tail, she breathed a small sigh of relief. They were still in the race and, with the phones, a few steps closer to the finish line.

"I'm proud of you," he said, glancing at her for a moment.

"For what?" She bent over and tugged a brunette wig over her hair. It wouldn't fool anyone who knew her, but it would fool everyone else.

"You walked into that post office with your head held high and not a nerve in sight. You did what had to be done in a place you wanted to forget. Not everyone can do that."

"Oh, there were nerves," she said with a chuckle. "A whole lot of them."

"You wouldn't have known it, and that's why I'm so proud of you. You've come a long way since Red Rye, baby."

Baby? He didn't mean that as a term of endearment, right? She shook her head at the thought that he meant it exactly like that.

"We've come a long way," she corrected him, offering him a rare smile of genuine happiness. "But we have a few more miles before we can say we crossed the finish line."

His lips pursed, and he nodded. "I know. It doesn't look like we picked up a tail out of Red Rye, which is good. We're still switching out cars before we drive to the hotel. Don't give up. We've got this."

She glanced down at his hand on her shoulder and was suddenly afraid that he got her in a way that went deeper than she might like. She might escape The Miss without further damage to her body, but she'd absolutely leave Secure One with a broken heart.

Chapter Eleven

The walk through the dark streets of Salina, Kansas, had rejuvenated Cal after the long drive from Red Rye. He'd specifically asked for a late and contact-free check-in. They were almost safe for the night, and for that, he was grateful. Once he got them into their room, he'd let Marlise rest while he reached out to Roman at Secure One. He wanted an update on chatter about the trial or The Miss, so he could make a plan to return home. He'd rather not be in the wind with the hottest witness in the country, but he may not have a choice if Secure One was no longer secure.

His disobedient eyes glanced at the woman next to him. She was beautiful as a brunette, but he still preferred her blonde. It was as though she lost her innocence without the blond hair. He was so incredibly proud of her though. They'd been running non-stop for days, but she kept up with him and never complained. He'd been terrified for her when she walked into the post office this morning. Not just about The Miss either. He was worried that being back in Red Rye would trigger memories she couldn't fight through to finish the job. He should have known better. Marlise was tougher than both Roman and him combined.

Cal had been overwhelmed with a feeling that he'd kept tamped down for years, and he'd been breathless for a moment until he pushed it back. He would not fall for another woman, and he certainly wouldn't fall for a woman who was just as headstrong, stubborn and brave as Hannah had been. He forced them both from his mind to concentrate on their next steps. Hotel. Shower. Clean clothes. Food. Recordings. He was anxious to hear and see the woman at the heart of all this chaos.

"Are we almost there?" Marlise muttered next to him.

"Almost," he promised with a smile and tossed his chin at the lights ahead. "A shower and comfy bed are just up ahead. You deserve it." Rather than drive to the hotel, he'd left the rental an hour's walk away at a depot and they'd come in on foot. It was safer that way. If they had to run, they weren't tied to the city grid the way they had been in Minneapolis. On foot, they could go where cars couldn't, and Cal knew if they had to escape, that would be the only way.

"Do you think we're in the clear?" she nervously asked, her gaze flicking around the darkened street as they crossed to their hotel for the night.

"No. I think we're in a lull. The Miss hasn't found

us yet, but she will, and when she does, she will hit us with everything she has. Before that happens, we need to access those recordings, find her and hit her when she's not expecting it."

Marlise was quiet the rest of the way to the hotel room. Because of his late check-in request, the hotel had texted him the room number and code for the side and room door. He wanted to bypass contact with the desk clerk. That mattered to Cal for both their safety and the safety of the innocent people they might come in contact with over the next several days. He punched in the code and pulled the door open with a quick glance around the area, but they were alone. He'd insisted on the room closest to an exit as an escape route as well as to avoid being seen by anyone. Marlise's brunette wig was long, and it hung down over her face to hide her burns. It was harder for him to be unmemorable. His size alone stood out, but there wasn't much he could do about it other than get inside the room as quickly as possible.

"Almost there." Cal pressed in the code for the room, and the light turned green.

He held the door for Marlise, and she slipped through, the heat of her skin brushing against his to remind him of a woman's touch. To remind him of the sensation of holding a woman he cared about in an intimate way. It had been too long since he'd experienced the touch of a woman, but Marlise would not be his next.

You don't mix business with pleasure, Cal.

That little voice gave a hearty guffaw as he secured the door. He ignored it. It could laugh all it wanted, but it would not get the last laugh.

Marlise had stopped in the middle of the room to stare at the king-size bed. "There's only one bed."

Cal was as surprised as she was, but he couldn't let it show. "I asked for a room closest to an exit. I didn't think to ask how many beds." He took her backpack from her shoulder and the hat and wig from her head and set them aside. After he'd straightened her hair, he motioned at the bed. "It's no big deal. One of us can sleep while the other listens to the recordings. Okay?"

"Sure, yeah," she agreed while she nodded. "It's no big deal."

As she gathered her things to shower, he had no doubt in his mind it was a big deal to her. It was a big deal to him too, but he'd never let on, not after their discussion about Hannah earlier. It was a firm reminder that he had better stay in his lane when it came to Marlise, and his lane was not the carpool lane.

WHEN MARLISE FINISHED in the shower, Cal had a pizza and a cold Coke waiting. After they'd eaten, she had to face the phones. She was terrified of them charging and equally terrified of them not charging. If they didn't charge, they were back to square one in the investigation. If they did charge, she'd have to face the woman who'd tried to kill her. She wasn't sure where she'd find the strength to do it.

She glanced at Cal, who was setting up the equipment they would need to listen to the recordings and consult with Secure One. He was her strength. He always stood by her, whether in silent solidarity or to hold her up. He helped her face the trauma from her past life, and she walked away stronger each time.

She yearned to do it by herself though. To rely on herself when the going got tough. Her mind traveled back to Secure One, where Mina sat at a computer while wearing a piece of carbon fiber and steel on what was left of her leg. The Miss had done that to her, and Mina still needed Roman's help when the going got tough. Maybe it was okay that she depended on Cal for moral support?

Don't get used to it, that voice reminded her.

There would be a day when Cal was gone, and she'd have to stand up for herself. She knew it was coming, but for now, for tonight, she'd let him help her through this new wrinkle from her past. After their discussion at the car this morning, she understood him better. He was just as scared as she was. Scared of losing someone again. He kept everyone at arm's length because if he didn't get close to anyone, they wouldn't end up like Hannah. Marlise doubted that he was to blame for her death. A link broke on the chain long before Cal took over the mission, but he was the kind of guy who wouldn't see it. The mission failed, and the woman he loved was dead. That was his fault. It broke her heart to think he lived with that every day.

Wars were ugly. They left carnage and death behind. There was no way to predict what the enemy would do. You just had to be prepared to react when they attacked. Unfortunately for Hannah, she was a casualty of a war she didn't start. The man Marlise had killed was a casualty of a war he chose to start. Someone was always going to lose. Mary had lost a lot in life and so had Marlise, but as Marlise, she saw hope for her future.

"I don't want to go by Mary," she blurted out before slapping her hand over her mouth.

Cal set the tablet he'd been messing with down and walked over to her on the bed. He knelt in front of her. "You've been thinking about it?"

She nodded and swallowed to quell her dry throat. "Mary was someone who suffered a lot in the war on the streets. She did a lot of things Marlise isn't proud of, and that's saying a lot considering who Marlise is."

"And you're speaking about yourself in the third person now." He gave her a wink to tell her he was teasing, but it lifted her lips into a smile. "You do what's right for you. Whether you go by Mary, Marlise or a new name entirely, your past experiences and the people you knew will always be part of you. A name change won't wipe your memories away, even if it wipes away their past from society. Does that make sense?"

"You're right," she admitted, staring down at her hands. "Every experience I've had as far back as I can remember has made me the person I am today. All I know is, I went from Mary to Marlise and, despite being trapped in the sex trade, took a step up in life. Once I figured out how to play The Miss to gain immunity, the stability of Red Rye helped me find even ground for the first time ever. I had plans to put The Miss away, and I worked toward that goal every day. In hindsight, I realize my mistake. I didn't predict how brutal and evil she truly was."

"You couldn't have predicted the fire," he said, taking her hand. "That was set by an agent of the FBI."

"I know, but do you understand what I'm trying to say, Cal?" Her tone was imploring, and he took her other hand with a nod. His thumb rubbed across the scarred tissue of her hand, and she wondered if he even realized that he did it.

"I do understand, and I know whether you go by Mary, Marlise or any other name, you're courageous enough to do anything. You'll put The Miss away for good, so she stops hurting others. If you're ready, we can start to unravel her web of lies so you can have your freedom back."

"What about you?" Marlise asked, her gaze pinned on his handsome face. He was sporting a heavy five o'clock shadow that he was using to his advantage as a disguise.

"What about me?"

"When will you get your freedom back?"

"Never." The word was a rasped whisper, and Marlise shook her head.

"You can't lecture me about being brave enough to take my freedom back if you're unwilling to do the same thing."

He didn't speak or even move. He just knelt there with his gaze so intent it made her insides tremble. This morning when he'd stared at her with the same look in his eyes, she swore he was going to kiss her. There was an internal battle going on behind those eyes. If she had to guess, his steely resolve would win, and he'd put distance between them again. It was his way of beating back the enemy. She wasn't the enemy, even if he saw her as one. The enemy was the voice that told him he didn't deserve to be with anyone again. It told him no one could heal his heart, so it was better not to try. She doubted he ever would. He was too busy taking care of everyone else to worry about his own—

Marlise's thoughts went off the rails when Cal reared up and planted his lips on hers. He grasped the back of her head and kissed her with the hunger and ferocity of a man who had been alone for too long. In her, Cal had found a connection that was undeniably frayed but still holding up to the demand asked of it. Now, he was trying to shore up the connection. Reweave the frayed fibers into a connection he could trust when the time came.

She tipped her head to get closer, to dig deeper. Marlise had dreamed of kissing this man since the first summer she'd lived at Secure One, but he'd hung a do-not-disturb sign long ago. The sign was gone tonight, and his lips were soft as he teased hers. There was the promise of more as his tongue traced the slit of her lips in an unspoken request for entrance. He wanted to be the first to claim the part of her that no man had yet entered. Marlise had been with many men, but she never let them kiss her. That was the only thing she could control back then. She'd wanted to save something for the man who might someday love her despite what all the other men had done to her. Was Cal that man? She doubted it, but her lips parted anyway, giving him the first right to taste her.

When his tongue slipped inside, his heat came with it, and she worried she'd burn up under his lips and hands. It wasn't a bad way to go. His right thumb ran across the scarred flesh of her face as though he were healing it with each caress. Maybe he was. It was easy for Marlise to think he could. When she'd seen the damage to her face and arm for the first time, she'd mourned the last hope that one day someone would love her.

"Cal," she whispered when he broke the kiss for air.

"I'm sorry," he rasped, running his hand down his face. "I shouldn't have done that."

He tried to turn away, but she grasped his chin and held tight. "Don't run away from me, Cal. I'm not the enemy."

"You're right. I'm my own worst enemy. I'm the reason The Miss found you, and I don't have the right to kiss you!"

"Cal," she said, grasping his shirt so he couldn't turn away. "What are you talking about?"

"My plane led her right to Secure One." Cal stuck a finger in his chest. "If she hadn't tagged my plane, you'd still be safe!"

Marlise shook her head while she tried to understand what he was saying. "No," she said without breaking eye contact. "You and your plane saved my life, Cal. I'd be dead if you hadn't come for me when you did. You had no choice but to use the plane."

"I could have gotten you out in an ambulance," he insisted, his gaze focused somewhere over her shoulder.

"Oh, you mean like the one Mack was driving when The Madame attacked? We could never outrun them in an ambulance." His grimace told her he knew it too. "The plane was the only option you had, even if it wasn't a good one."

"I made my business and home vulnerable to these people, and now we're paying the price. I will not lose you the way I lost Hannah."

"So what if she knows where you live? She doesn't have the manpower to attack it, or she wouldn't have tried to pinch me at the trial. Stop looking for any excuse to put distance between us, Cal. You played the hand you were dealt."

"And that hand put us right back in danger."

"Why are you so hung up on the idea that The Miss tagged your plane? It doesn't matter other than knowing we can't use it right now. We knew if The

Miss came back into the mix, this would always be the result—us stopping her."

"I've let everyone down since you and Mina entered our lives two years ago. I didn't have enough time to plan efficiently, which led to too many missteps."

"In the end, you saved the day, Cal. We will again this time too."

He gently took her face in his hands and offered a tender caress of his thumb across her temple. "Maybe that's true, but I liked that kiss way too much for it to be good for either of us."

"I liked it too, Cal. It was my first kiss, and I'm glad I waited for you."

His head tipped slowly in confusion, and he blinked once. "You've never been kissed before?"

She pinned her gaze to the carpet and shook her head. "No, I never allowed it. I wanted to save something for a man who might someday love me despite everything else I've been through."

"Marlise," he whispered, pulling her head down to his until their foreheads touched. "Not despite everything but because of everything you've been through."

"What did you see in me that day on the plane, Cal? I was a shell of a woman who was battered, broken and burned. You risked your life and the lives of your team for someone with little hope for a future."

"I didn't see the shell of a woman who was battered, broken and burned. I saw the woman you would become with a little care, love and respect from people who wanted nothing from you. People who wanted to help you heal from your physical scars and help you live with the emotional ones. That day on the plane, when we locked eyes, I saw the woman who ran through the woods for hours without complaint, all while bleeding. I saw the woman who would help put away a woman hell-bent on mistreating women like herself. I saw the woman sitting before me right now."

"You're just saying that to be nice," she whispered, wishing she could take his lips again and make him forget about everything around them.

"I don't say things just to be nice, Marlise. You know that. If I didn't trust my instincts, you wouldn't be here right now. You'd still be at Secure One if I didn't believe that you had the courage and guts to walk back into Red Rye and revisit your past."

"I even surprised myself," she said with a smile. "But I'm terrified of what will happen when the phones come on, and I have to see the face of the woman who tried to kill me."

"Use that fear," he said, moving his jaw forward and kissing her lips once before speaking again. "Put her image front and center in your mind and keep her there. Remember all the things she did to you and is still doing to other women. Use that fear and anger to help me find her and put her away for good."

"You believe I can, don't you?"

"I always have. I just need you to believe it too."

Marlise stared into his eyes, noticing they were the deepest, darkest brown they'd ever been since she'd been part of Cal's world. Was she the woman he believed her to be?

"You're right," she whispered, her breath held tight in her chest. "I've already done so many things I thought were impossible two years ago. If I could do those things, I can do this. I can help you find her and save the other girls."

"That's my girl," he whispered, his lips dangerously close to hers. "Are you ready to do that now? The phones should be ready to start up."

"I'm ready," she promised, taking his warm face in her tiny hands. She wasn't ready. She didn't want to break the connection they'd found here tonight, but she knew what her reality was, and it wasn't having Cal Newfellow once this case was closed.

"Before we do, I have to ask you something."

"Anything," she promised.

"Would it be okay if I kissed you again? When my lips are on yours, I forget all the responsibilities I face and the heartbreak I've suffered."

"No," she whispered and noticed the light dim in his eyes. "This time, I would like to kiss you because you do the same for me."

There were no more words then, just the sensation of floating in a different plane of existence while Cal teased her lips and showed her, rather than told her, how beautiful she was to him. When the kiss ended, they were both breathing heavily, and they took a moment to catch their breath.

"I know we have a lot to unpack with those kisses," she said, tucking her hair behind her ears. "But they gave me the strength and the courage to face The Miss again, and I don't want that feeling to disappear yet."

He let his hand slip across her face on his way to the desk. "Whatever makes this the easiest for you," he said, unplugging a phone and holding down the power button. She heard the *whoosh* when it came on, and she sat up straighter, strapping on her armor to prepare for battle. "I'll show you this, and then we'll call Roman and Mina and track this woman down. Are you with me?"

She took the phone from his hand and opened the gallery, taking a deep breath before letting her gaze flick to his. "This one's for Emelia and Bethany," she said right before hitting the hidden folder and accessing it with the password. A face filled the screen that usually only filled her nightmares. Not anymore. The Miss was real again. "You're going down," she whispered, right before she turned the phone for Cal to see.

Chapter Twelve

While Marlise processed the image on the screen, Cal took a step back and ran his hand through his hair. He was still reeling from the kisses they'd shared. He tried to conjure up an image of Hannah to clear his head, but he couldn't. His mind wouldn't show him anything but the woman he'd just kissed breathless. It had been thirteen years since he'd been remotely interested in a woman beyond a one-night stand, and then along came this little slip of a thing who ripped the carpet out from under him.

You have a job to do.

He did, and letting Marlise cloud his mind and steal his focus wouldn't get the job done. Resolving not to kiss her again was impossible, but he could flip into his mercenary mode and stay on a singular path. Find The Miss.

That little voice in his head laughed.

That worried him. He had to put Mary out of his mind, or she might end up in his heart. That was an excellent way to get them both killed.

"That's her," she said, rotating the phone for him to see. Staring back at him was a woman who could be anyone's sister, cousin or girlfriend.

"She looks so…"

"Normal?" Marlise asked, and he nodded.

"Look at her eyes."

Cal brought the phone to his face and concentrated on the woman. "They're hollow."

"As is her soul," Marlise agreed. "She won't stop until someone makes her."

"Then let's make her," he said, handing her the phone back and turning on the tablet he had set up to connect them to Secure One. He dropped his boss mask down over his face to hide the man who'd had his lips on a beautiful woman just moments ago.

"Secure two, Romeo," a voice said over the tablet.

"Secure one, Charlie."

The screen came on and Mina and Roman were squashed together to get into the camera. "So good to see you both!" Mina exclaimed. "Are you safe?"

"For now," Cal answered, motioning Marlise over to sit by him at the desk. "We had dinner and then fired up the phones."

"Did you find the image?" Roman asked.

"Yes," Marlise whispered after she sat. "Mina, I want to spare you from seeing her again, but you should confirm her identity."

Cal noticed Mina's lips purse as Roman put his arm around her. "You don't need to spare me, Marlise. I'm in it to win it with you. Show me."

Marlise turned the phone, and Mina's eyes closed for a moment, and she swallowed before she spoke. "That's her. That's The Miss. She looks so innocent, as though she could be an accountant or a teacher. But she's diabolical."

Roman leaned in closer to get a good look at the picture. "I saw her once from a distance in Red Rye. I didn't know it was her until after the fact. On closer inspection of that image, I wonder if she's a different nationality?"

"I always thought she was Latina," Mina answered.

"She did speak a lot of Spanish on the phone," Marlise pointed out.

Cal lifted a brow. "What did she say?"

"I don't know. I don't speak Spanish."

"I do," Roman and Mina said in unison.

"I never heard her speak Spanish," Mina added, "but I couldn't snoop the way Marlise could."

"She has no soul," Cal told his brother. "We have to find this woman before more women die."

"How's Charlotte?" Marlise quietly asked.

"She's okay," Mina said. "I'm checking on her often, but Selina is with her at all times. Mack and Eric are trading off guarding the med bay. I think she'd be more comfortable in a room though. She doesn't need the med bay anymore."

"Put her in my room," Marlise said immediately, but Cal shook his head.

"No, that's not a good idea. Keep Charlotte in the med bay until we get back, but put a better bed in there if you need to. Have one of the guys do it. I want eyes on her at all times."

"Cal, she's not working for The Miss," Marlise insisted.

"Maybe not, but I'm not risking it. I want her with someone at all times."

"Understood," Mina said.

It was Roman who spoke next. "Have you listened to the recordings?"

"Not yet," Cal answered, glancing at Marlise. "We just got in, showered and had dinner."

"Get me a recording of her voice and that image as soon as possible," Roman said. "I'll start voice and face recognition with them, but I doubt that will reveal much."

"I'll do that," Cal said. "Then we'll listen to the recordings and make lists of names, cities and any women she might mention. We need to find her quickly, so we have to be efficient."

"Agreed," Roman said with a head nod. "As soon as you have something, send it. We'll run it down while you keep listening."

"I may have gotten her on the recordings speaking Spanish," Marlise said. Cal turned and noticed it was as though she were talking to herself.

Cal's glance at the camera showed Roman and Mina were just as surprised as he was. "But you don't know who she was talking to?"

"No, but I remember a couple of times the phone was running when I was cleaning because her door was cracked. It always frustrated me when she spoke Spanish because I didn't know what she said."

"If you come across any Spanish recordings," Mina said, "send it over immediately, and we'll translate it."

"It may not matter," Marlise said, her shoulders heavy from fatigue and frustration.

Cal put his arm around her to give her a comforting squeeze. "Maybe not, but all we need is a name that we can trace, and her web starts to fall apart."

"That's our plan of action then," Roman said. "And you need to stay put until we have more to go on. I don't want you driving back here until we know you don't need to chase down a lead closer to Kansas."

"Understood," Cal said. "We'll listen to the recordings and then get some rest while you're reviewing anything we find. My hands are tied here, so I'm counting on you, brother."

"We're a team—remote or in person. We'll get the job done."

Roman and Mina signed off, and Cal turned to Marlise. "Ready?"

"As I'll ever be," she said, but he could tell she was lying.

"Why don't you rest while I start listening? You're ready to collapse."

Her shoulders squared before she spoke, and he bit back a smile. She wasn't going to rest. "I passed exhaustion about six hours ago. I won't lose sight of why we're here. I can rest when we've sent the information to Roman."

"But…"

Her brow lowered, and it stopped him in his tracks. "No buts. Here's the thing, Cal. You can listen *to* the recordings, but you don't know what you're listening *for*. I do."

"Fair point," he had to agree.

"There are only a few hours of recordings, so let's just get at it. The sooner we finish, the faster we find The Miss, get her into custody and free all the girls she's torturing."

He tapped the desk with a grin and pulled the phones and two notepads over to them. He pushed one at her and handed her a pen. "Ready?" On her nod, he opened the first phone, and they settled in. They needed to find one needle in the haystack, and once they did, he'd make The Miss wish she'd forgotten Marlise existed.

MARLISE WOKE SLOWLY, her gaze sweeping an unfamiliar wall. Where was she? It took her a few minutes to remember she was in a hotel with Cal. Their late night filtered through her sleepiness and she remembered they'd stayed up until 3:00 a.m. listening to the recordings. Cal was still messaging Roman when she went to bed, but she couldn't keep her eyes open a moment longer. She was just going to close her eyes for a few minutes, but now the sun was up. She couldn't help but wonder what Roman and Cal had found after she went to bed.

She tugged the blanket up to her chin, but met resistance halfway there. When her brain sorted out the incoming messages, she glanced over her shoulder. A man, giant really, had his nose buried in her hair as he slept. He had his arms wrapped around her, and when she tried to squirm out of them, he pulled her in closer.

"Just a little bit longer," he whispered, his warm breath raising goose bumps on her neck. "If we get up, we have to face bad guys again."

"You mean bad gals?" Marlise asked with a chuckle.

"Them too. I need a few more minutes to hold you and remember the good in the world."

Marlise leaned back and gave him the time he needed. She understood how he felt. No one wanted The Miss found and neutralized more than she did. More than Charlotte did. More than all the girls still under her thumb did. It was up to them to do it. They were the only ones with the means and skills to find her and make her pay. In fairness, she had no skills. Cal had skills. Marlise had knowledge, but knowledge could be a powerful thing.

She rolled over to face the man behind her. They were both dressed, and she noticed his gun on the nightstand next to him. "What happened to sleeping in shifts?"

"I couldn't wake you," he mumbled, but his eyes finally came open and blinked a few times. "I didn't think you'd mind as long as I stayed on top of the covers."

"I wouldn't have minded if you were under the covers. You're like a furnace, and I'm always cold."

"Is that your way of saying you trust me?" he asked, tracing his finger down the scarred flesh on her cheek. She didn't know why she allowed him to do it, but she'd probably make him stop if she ever figured it out.

"I guess it is," she agreed with a soft smile. "The last person I trusted nearly got killed though, Cal. Being around me isn't good for your health."

"No," he said, resting his finger against her lips. "Mina nearly got killed because of The Madame, not you."

"The common denominator then and now is still me, Cal."

"Again, no," he insisted. "The common denominator is evilness and greed. You talk about wars. Well, we're fighting one against evil and greed right now. We're in this together, and it will stay that way. Got it?"

Marlise had no choice but to agree. She knew he'd come up with rebuttals for any argument she made. Her battered heart had to admit that she liked being in this together with him. "Got it. Did you and Roman discover anything after I went to bed?"

"That's a negative. Roman's running her voice through voice recognition and putting her picture into the facial recognition program, but I doubt that will get us any hits since we know she was scrubbed.

Mina and Roman are translating the Spanish conversations this morning and will get back to us."

"Listening to those recordings again was difficult," she admitted. She couldn't admit it last night, but the intimacy of this moment made it easier for her to be vulnerable. "I let myself forget some of the terrible things that went on there. When I heard Bethany and Emelia, my heart broke."

"Hey," he said, wiping away a tear from her cheek. "It's okay to feel that way. What you went through in Red Rye was traumatic, and facing it again is like digging it all up after you just buried it."

"Yes," she breathed out. "So much. I knew we had to, but I didn't want to battle it again."

"But you did. That's what makes you a warrior. You faced a demon from your past, and by doing that, she no longer holds any power over you. I could only hope to be that strong one day."

"You are that strong, Cal. One day should be now. Stop living your life like you're already dead. You're not. You're the backbone of a team that relies on you and looks up to you. You're their leader. Be that leader, Cal. Lead by example."

"I wish I had the belief in myself that you have in me, Mary. I mean, Marlise. I'm sorry."

She rested her finger on his lips. "I don't mind it when you call me Mary. I just don't want everyone to."

"But you said you didn't like that girl."

Her words from last night came back to her, and she realized she'd confused him. She had to explain it in a way that made sense to him. "If I ask everyone to call me Mary, I worry I might become that girl again."

"But you don't mind if I use it?"

"You use it softly. When you call me Mary, there's a layer of understanding there. It's solidarity between warriors. It's an understanding between two souls who have suffered through the same atrocities in battle. You say the name with reverence, and that makes me feel…" She paused and met his gaze, unsure what the right words were. "Cared about as a human being. When you call me Mary, I feel like I deserve to be cared about, and I'm not a lost cause."

"Oh, sweet Mary," he whispered, his eyes revealing his emotions better than his words. "You deserve so much more than caring. You deserve love, happiness and joy in this life. You are not and never were a lost cause, baby."

Before she could say another word, his lips were on hers. It wasn't a hurried kiss of passion, but a tender kiss of caring. Even his gentle kisses raised her blood pressure and made her heart tap faster in her chest. He'd called her baby again. Whether it was consciously or unconsciously, she didn't know, but she would store it away in her heart for when he was no longer part of her life. And there would be a day when he let her go. Especially if he couldn't find a way to let go of the past.

Chapter Thirteen

He ran his fingers through her hair, his lips still on hers in a kiss that went from tender to passionate with one flick of his tongue. Cal leaned over, pinning her head to the pillow as a moan left his throat to fill her mouth. She fought to control the kiss just as a device across the room started buzzing, and Cal groaned. "That will be Roman."

"You'd better get it."

Cal climbed from the bed, and the loss of his heat was palpable. Feeling so bereft quickly scared her more than facing down The Miss.

Cal finally hit the button to end the buzzing.

"Secure two, Whiskey." It was Mina's voice this time.

"Secure one, Charlie."

The team all had code names from the alphabet that matched the first letter of their name. Roman was Romeo, and Mina was Whiskey since her real name was Wilhelmina. They opened any communication with their code phrase, so if the person on the other end was compromised, they didn't put the entire team at risk.

"Did I wake you?" Mina asked when the camera flipped on.

"Just woke up," Cal said, and Marlise noticed him subconsciously straighten his T-shirt. Everyone looked to him when they needed guidance and reassurance, and the way he switched into work mode in the blink of an eye meant he knew it too. He just needed to own it.

"I may have found something," Mina said without further preamble.

Marlise was off the bed and standing behind Cal immediately. "Did we get a hit on her picture?"

"No. We got a hit on the conversation you recorded in Spanish."

"Which one?"

"The long one that you risked your life to record. It was just before the fire. Your subconscious must have told you it was important. I translated the whole thing, but I'll give you the highlights."

Cal grabbed a pen and paper and waited for Mina to speak.

"She kept referring to the other person on the phone as *papá*, which means *dad* in Spanish."

"That's weird," Marlise said, joining them at the desk. "She always told us she was just like us and didn't have any family. That was her whole shtick about girl power."

Mina pointed at the camera. "That's why it caught

my attention so quickly. At first, I thought she was talking to a client. Sometimes they wanted to be called daddy."

Marlise and Mina simultaneously gagged and shuddered at the memory of those men.

"But that's not the case?" Cal asked, somehow knowing they both needed to be redirected.

"I don't think so." She picked up a piece of paper to read. "Everything is ready. I'm prepared to do what needs to be done to get out of this hellhole." Mina paused and then said, "That was loosely translated."

Cal and Marlise smirked at each other while Mina continued.

"My best girls are ready for the challenge. It's time to expose the agent. No, Dad, I'll take care of her myself. You don't need to come here. Stay far away from Red Rye, or this deal goes bad. You have taught me well, and I will not fail. This is our last contact until we reach the desert."

"The desert," Cal repeated, and Mina nodded.

"That was all she said about location, though Charlotte already confirmed they were living in a desert somewhere."

"A state that meets the border?" Cal asked.

"Honestly, it could be any of those, but we have a place to start. That narrows it down to Arizona, New Mexico and Texas. All about the same driving distance that Charlotte mentioned."

"Three states are a smaller hole to hunt than six,

but we need more," Cal said, tapping his finger on the desk.

Marlise stood up and started to pace. "The other conversation she had in Spanish didn't reveal anything?"

"No, but she was talking to the same person. That one was quick, but she said they'd hit the jackpot, and she had to move if they wanted to collect."

Marlise paused on her way past the screen. "Jackpot is a street name for fentanyl."

Mina tipped her head for a moment. "You're right. The conversation was so innocuous and rushed that I didn't link that when I listened. She was excited and talking fast, which made it harder for me to translate. I sent you the transcripts of both conversations. Read them over, and I'll do the same again. Call me when you're done."

The screen went dark, and Cal opened his encrypted phone and handed it to her. "You read it and tell me if you can pick out anything. You lived with her. I didn't."

The short conversation wasn't as innocuous as Mina thought it was. "She also mentions Cactus, a street name for peyote, Red Rock meaning methadone, and Beans meaning ecstasy. If she's referring to drugs, they're moving the hard stuff around."

"More likely her women were moving it."

"And when you move those kinds of drugs around, women disappear."

"Anything else?" Cal asked. Marlise knew he was

trying to keep her focus on The Miss and not the missing girls. Those girls didn't deserve what happened to them any more than she did, and Marlise would be the one to vindicate them.

"Well, we know her dad, whether he is her real father or someone else, was funding her time at Red Rye, and set her up in the new town, wherever that may be. They were using the women as drug mules in Red Rye, possibly with or without the knowledge of The Madame, and she piggybacked on The Madame's operation to build her own."

"But we still don't know where she is."

"Where's that list of cities we made last night?" she asked, handing him the phone and grabbing the pad he held out. She read off the cities to him. "Oklahoma City, Dallas, Fort Worth, Albuquerque and Phoenix were the cities where they did the most business. That matches up with the three states that sit on Mexico's border. If her 'dad' is south of the border, it would make sense she's in one of those states. I would pick someplace around Albuquerque."

"Tell me why," he said, ready to write on his notepad.

"It's the most centrally located to the other four cities. If The Miss is somewhere in New Mexico, her reach to the other cities is like a satellite," she explained, holding her arms out. "East or west, and she reaches one of the cities she used to send the Red Rye girls for dates. She probably kept those clients when The Madame went down because The Madame didn't know they were drug dealers. She was only seeing the escort side of the business."

"Possible," Cal agreed. "I'll call Mina back."

Once Mina and Roman were on the line, Marlise explained what she'd read and her thoughts on where The Miss could be.

"That's excellent linear thinking, Marlise," Roman said, bringing a smile to her face. "It's a place to start."

"Did Charlotte say anything more since we left?" Cal asked, clearly frustrated by their lack of progress.

"She's trying, Cal, but The Miss has them so isolated that she doesn't know much. Even when she flies them out, they're blindfolded until they're on the plane, and the plane has no windows. They fly into small airports, but it doesn't matter if the women know what city they're in by then because they're already away from home base."

"I'm going to be real with you, Mina. We may not be able to locate her. Secure One is good, but without a starting point, no one will find her. We may have no choice but to draw her out, capture her and then find the women."

Roman and Mina glanced at each other before they nodded. "That's what we were thinking too. Drawings of cacti don't help us find a madwoman."

"What?" Marlise asked, leaning on the desk to stare intently at the two people on the screen. "Drawings of cacti?"

"Yeah," Mina said, leaning out of the camera angle for a moment. "Charlotte is trying to help by drawing pictures of what she was able to see around home base." Mina held up a pad of paper with a pencil drawing. "It's like pods that stem off the main house."

Marlise studied the image Charlotte had drawn. It was surprisingly intricate and was easy to picture sitting in the middle of the desert somewhere. The middle house was a large camping trailer, and sitting at angles like sunrays were smaller ones.

"She told us that each of the smaller pods," Mina said, pointing at Charlotte's rounded campers she had colored silver, "house two women."

Marlise counted quickly. "There are fourteen pods."

"Which gives us a good idea of how many women are working for her," Roman said. "But that still doesn't matter if we can't figure out where this pod group sits."

"Wait, what's that?" Marlise asked, pointing at a drawing at the back of the image.

"One of the cacti she drew," Mina said. "I have a better image. Hang on." She shuffled through some papers and then held up another drawing. "Charlotte is an amazing artist," Mina said. "She helped us with several things we needed laid out here, Cal."

Marlise registered Cal's nod, but her focus was on the paper that held images of several different but intricate cacti. "That one!" she exclaimed, pointing at the paper on the screen.

Mina turned it around. "What one?"

"The big one. It's a saguaro cactus."

"A what now?" Cal asked, turning to her.

"A saguaro cactus. The kind you see in old movies that look like trees. They're tall and have arms that come up like branches," Marlise explained excitedly.

"We're on the same page," Cal said calmly and with great patience. "Why does that one stand out in your mind?"

"They only grow in one place in the country! The Sonoran Desert."

"How do you know this?" Roman asked, leaning into the camera.

"I'm from Arizona, Roman! It's one of the first facts you learn about your home state. If you see a movie with a saguaro cactus, you know it was filmed in the Sonoran Desert. Charlotte said it's scorching where they are, and the Sonoran Desert is the hottest one in both Mexico and the United States."

"You're saying that The Miss is hiding somewhere in Arizona?"

"Not just somewhere, Roman. The Sonoran Desert is less than two hours from the Mexican border."

"You don't think she crossed the border and is in Mexico?"

Marlise shook her head almost immediately. "Not with the girls. She'd have to have passports if she tried to enter legally or a safe route to travel by foot across the border, and those don't exist. If she had gone by herself, I would say it's possible, but not if she has that many girls. She stayed on this side of the border to run drugs. Not a question in my mind.

Mina, would you pull up an image of a saguaro cactus and run it down to Charlotte? Ask her if that's the one she intended in the drawing. We'll wait."

Mina nodded and took off, leaving Roman to stare into the camera. "I'm impressed, Marlise." His tone said he was genuine. "That was some great deducting skills. All we saw in those drawings was too much ground to cover."

"This is still a lot of ground to cover. The Sonoran Desert extends into California and down into Baja, but I know The Miss. She never took a girl any further west than Phoenix. She's in Arizona."

"How big is the desert in Arizona, mileage-wise?" Cal asked. "Do you know?"

"It extends above Phoenix to the north, the border on the west and about Tucson to the east," she said without hesitation. "It's still a lot of ground to cover, but I would concentrate on the area near the southern border. If she's running drugs and they're coming from someone in Mexico, she would want to be close. Hell, she might even cross the border legally with a passport and bring the drugs back herself."

Roman raised a brow. "I have some friends south of the border. I'll get the image to them and see what they know. It's risky on her part to use a passport, but we still have to check on the off chance she did."

Mina came back into the room and plopped down in the chair. She must have sprinted to get to the med bay and back that quickly. "Charlotte said yes. Those are the cacti she saw around their camp."

"I cannot believe that a woman with no law enforcement training managed to home in on a woman hell-bent on being a ghost with nothing more than a picture of a cactus. Mary, I'm in awe," Cal said, wearing a grin. He wasn't kidding around. She'd impressed him, and her heart soared.

With her head held high and her shoulders back, she smiled too. She suspected the feeling she had inside her chest was pride. "I want this to end so you can all be free again. Until we find her, we can't even rid ourselves of The Madame."

"What is the news on the trial?" Cal asked Roman, who was still on the screen.

"The trial is on hold. The defense is working hard to convince the judge they need to move forward, but so far, they've failed. The judge put everything on hold for two weeks. She has sequestered the jury but allows family visits in the hotel while supervised. At the end of the two weeks, I suspect the trial will go on, with or without Marlise."

"We have ten days left of those two weeks?" Cal asked, and Mina nodded. "Then we'd better get a plan in place and execute it before we run out of time. We've been here too long and need to get out of this town before bad characters stop by and hurt innocent people. I'm giving Mary point on this one. Are you guys in agreement?"

"Me?" Marlise asked in shock. "Why are you giving me point?"

"Isn't it obvious? Thus far, you've been the one to

find all the little crumbs The Miss didn't know she dropped. You know her and her habits. I'm putting my bets on you being the one to locate her and bring her down."

"I am too," Mina said with a wink.

Chapter Fourteen

The plane was in descent, and Cal was on high alert. They'd made it out of Kansas on a commercial flight to Phoenix, but that didn't mean they'd make it out of the Phoenix airport without picking up a tail. If The Miss was in Arizona, as Mary suspected, they would have to watch their backs until they secured her location.

"Are you sure this is safe?" she asked from the seat next to him. "I'm worried about Mina and Roman."

"They'll be fine," he assured her, holding her hand on his lap. "The Miss hasn't tried attacking Secure One since she sent her team in to scout it."

"That part is weird," she agreed with a head nod. "Why wouldn't she strike if she knew I was there?"

"Because she doesn't know you're there," he said immediately. "She doesn't know that we went back there after the failed attack at the courthouse. Since her women couldn't confirm you were at Secure One, attacking would be wasted resources without confirmation you're there. We also have to consider that she doesn't have a team big enough to attack a compound far from her camp."

"I wondered about that too," she whispered. "I figured she'd have a team watching Secure One at the very least. That's why I'm worried about Roman and Mina."

"That was a chance we had to take. We're running out of time, and driving to Phoenix was time we didn't have to give. We'll meet up with them at the hotel and make a plan in person. We need the backup they afford us, and we all work well together."

Her nervousness was making his belly skitter. Risking his brother's life wasn't high on his list of favorite things to do, but if Roman and Mina weren't with them, they didn't stand a chance against The Miss. His brother was smart, and his wife was brilliant, so Cal was confident they'd make it to Phoenix safely and without extra company. Then again, if Roman brought company with him unexpectedly, it could work to their advantage. They needed to find the woman, and following the fox back to her hole was an easy way to hunt. He wasn't going to tell Marlise that. She didn't need to worry more than she already was.

"I hate to even say this, but would it be such a bad thing if The Miss was watching Secure One? We will have to make contact with her somehow. If she followed us here, that would make it easier."

How does she always know what I'm thinking?

"Let's worry about getting out of the airport to

start with, okay?" he whispered as the wheels touched the tarmac. "Remember, head down, follow my lead and don't let go of me at any time."

He stood and gathered their backpacks from the overhead compartment, then helped her up to stand in line. He'd have to stop and pick up his checked luggage, which contained nothing but his firearms and electronics, but he couldn't risk leaving them behind. He might need both sooner rather than later if The Miss was waiting for them.

The trip through the airport was quick, and when he tossed the backpacks into their rental and climbed in, he refused to breathe a sigh of relief. They weren't out of the woods by any means. Anything could happen once they got on the road.

"Buckle up," he said, securing his own seat belt and ensuring hers was set up for her height. "The hotel is only ten minutes away, but anything can happen in ten minutes." He handed her his firearm. "You're on guard duty. Shoot first and ask questions later."

She glanced down at the gun and then to his face. "I've got your back, Cal."

He nodded once and started the car, but he couldn't keep the smile off his lips when he backed out of the lot and hit the highway. They had a date with destiny, and in his opinion, the sooner, the better, before he did something with this woman he couldn't take back.

MARLISE PACED THE hotel room floor, wishing it was bigger than a cardboard box. That wasn't fair; the room was decent sized, but Cal's presence made it feel smaller than it was. She was also trying to keep her focus off the one bed in the middle of the room. Once again, he'd gotten a room with a giant king-size bed covered in pillows and a plush comforter. It would be a great place if they were in the room for pleasure rather than business. Then again, Marlise wasn't sure Cal even knew what pleasure was anymore. He'd shut himself off from the world for so long that his life revolved around business and nothing else. Maybe she could change that one day, but today was not that day.

They'd gotten word that Roman and Mina had arrived in Phoenix and were on their way to the hotel. Cal was setting up a communications center with Secure One while they waited, but Marlise couldn't sit still. Phoenix was her hometown, and it brought back memories of Mary's life. The faces, names and pain the people in her past caused. The faceless people who had taken advantage of her, first as a child and then as a desperate young adult.

Hands grasped her shoulders, and she jumped at the intrusion to her memories. "Stop for a minute. Remember, there is no one left here who can hurt you. Once Roman and Mina get here, you have three layers of protection from anyone outside of these walls who want to hurt you."

She rested her head back against his strong shoulder and sighed. "How did you know that's what I was thinking?"

"Human nature. Phoenix is your hometown, and the memories will rise to the surface. Don't get sucked under by them. You're above all of that now. You fought against those old biases and now you're here to finish the job. You're here to win the gold against the people in your past who hurt you."

"That doesn't make me any better than them then," Marlise said with a shake of her head.

He turned her to face him and held her close. "That's where you're wrong. You will finish the job by standing on the moral high ground they couldn't find if it were right before them."

"Good prevailing over evil?" she asked, and his head tipped in slight agreement.

"If you want to put it that way, sure. You're in the right, they're in the wrong, and that's all there is to it. We're one step closer to bringing this woman in and handing her over to stand trial with her old boss. I look forward to your day in court because you will annihilate their defense and show the world who they are."

"You sure have a lot of faith in me, Cal," she said with a shake of her head. "I hope I can live up to it."

"I have faith in what I know, and I know you. I've known you were the one who would put an end to this since the day you ran onto my plane with a broken arm, broken nose and fierce determination in your eyes when there should have been nothing but pain. We will follow your lead because you know her world. That will be the advantage she didn't account for when it came to this game of cat and mouse."

"I sure hope so," Marlise said, swallowing around the nervousness caught in her throat. She wanted to be the woman he saw in her, even though it scared her to death to be that woman. Facing The Miss again in any arena was terrifying, but doing it when she wasn't in shackles was downright deadly.

"I know so," he said, kissing her nose as he gazed down at her. "Deep breath in, and remember, your friends have your back."

"Are you a friend, Cal?" she asked, their foreheads still connected. "Sometimes, I don't know if you're a friend or someone who puts up with me."

Before she blinked, his lips took hers on a ride of passion and desire that involved more tongue than the last time. She was breathing heavy and was desperate for air but didn't want the kiss to end. His lips still on hers, he answered the question. "If I were putting up with you, would I kiss you like that?"

"No?" she asked against his lips, and he nipped at hers, making her squeak. She knew what he wanted, and she gave it to him. "No, you wouldn't."

"Damn right," Cal hissed before he attacked her lips again and showed her just how passionate he would be if he let himself go.

Chapter Fifteen

The knock on the door dragged a groan from Cal's lips as he ended the kiss. His breath sounded heavy as he stood in front of her, still gazing into her eyes. What she saw there was lust, fear and an emotion she couldn't name.

"That will be Roman," he said as he grabbed his gun and stood to the side of the door to check the peephole.

"Secure two, Romeo."

Marlise heard Roman's muffled voice just as Cal lowered the gun and opened the door. The moment Mina was inside the room, she had Marlise in her arms in a fierce hug.

"I'm so happy to see you again. I've been worried sick."

"No need," she promised her friend. "Cal always takes excellent care of me."

Mina smiled and turned to face the brothers, who had walked into the room after securing the door. "He does, but we both know The Miss is ruthless and will stop at nothing to shut you up. I'll be worried until the day she's behind bars."

"Or dead," Marlise said with a shrug of her shoulder. "Prison is good but dead is better. Is that a terrible thing to say?"

"From your position, absolutely not," Roman said. "If I needed more proof of how evil she truly is, Charlotte is example C. That poor girl. The Miss put a tracker meant for a car inside her with no regard for the damage or infection it could cause."

"Not to mention she's forcing them to be assassins and run drugs," Cal added.

"Then let's shut her down," Mina said. "Charlotte wanted to come, but Mack wouldn't allow it."

"Mack wouldn't allow it?" Cal asked on an eyebrow lift. "Why?"

Roman lifted his right back at him. "On the defense that she wasn't strong enough to run if need be. Selina agreed. She has an infection in her leg from the tracker. Selina is running IV antibiotics, and said it will clear, but she has to stay off it."

"Mack is keeping everything on track at Secure One, then? Do I need to reach out?"

Roman let out a bark of laughter, then crossed his arms over his chest while he grinned at his brother. "He's multitasking. It'll do him some good to concentrate on more than work for once."

"All of that said, or not said," Mina grunted on an eye roll, "Charlotte is ready to help with whatever she can from Secure One. She sketched the positions of the spotters on The Miss's compound with some realism worthy of a gallery show."

"Charlotte was an artist living on the streets before joining the Red Rye house," Marlise said. "She would tag buildings whenever she wanted three squares and a bed. When The Madame came calling, she told me that she signed on the dotted line to get her record wiped. Supposedly, they'd hired her to do graphic design for their new start-up company. She had no inkling that they were starting up an escort service."

"I'm sure none of the women The Madame trafficked thought that would be the case. You certainly didn't," Cal said, his voice softer than usual when he addressed her.

She worried that Mina and Roman picked up on it, but there was nothing she could do if they had. Cal was right. None of the girls knew they were selling their souls down the road for a chance at stability. The only one who knew that was The Miss, and it turned out she had ulterior motives.

"Marlise, where did The Madame troll for women when you lived here?" Roman asked, picking up a tablet off the bed. "Were there specific places she'd send scouts to hunt for women?"

A chill ran through Marlise at the memory of that time. Cal put his hands on her upper arms and kept them there. It was a reminder that he was there to take care of her, and he wouldn't let her get hurt again.

"The train station, bus station and YMCA. They

also rotated through the public parks with restrooms and shaded areas. Girls hung out at the parks where they had access to water and toilets. They're too smart to pick up girls from shelters, but they do troll the campgrounds. That's where they found me." A shiver went through her when she remembered that first interaction with a scout. If only she hadn't gone with her that day.

"That's still a lot of ground to cover," Cal said, squeezing her shoulders to offer comfort.

That was when she remembered if she hadn't gone with the scout that day, she wouldn't have these people in her life. Wishing for a redo in the past always changed the future. Even after suffering so much pain and trauma, she wanted this future with these people in it. She could only hope that was the case after The Miss was caught.

"I need to talk to Charlotte," Marlise said, grabbing Mina's hand. "Can we call her?"

"Tell us why first," Mina said calmly while her gaze flicked to Cal's.

"Tell us what you're thinking, Mary. We'll listen," Cal promised.

Marlise glanced between them all for a moment. "Well, it's important we know if she's sourcing girls from the bigger cities. If she is, that tells us her camp is somewhere closer to the center of the state than the border," Marlise pointed out. "But my gut tells me she's further south of Phoenix."

"How far is it from Phoenix to south of the border?" Roman asked, pecking around on his tablet, but Marlise could answer him faster than Google.

"It's two and a half hours, which doesn't sound like that long, but if you get a nervous girl in the car, two and a half hours is a long time for her to change her mind. The Madame always kept the commute down to an hour. She also had the scouts talk up all the pampering the girls would get when they arrived."

"How does that apply to calling Charlotte?" Cal asked, and Marlise turned to him, grasping the front of his shirt.

"She lived with those girls for at least a year, Cal. Chances are, she knows where they're from, at least the new girls The Miss brought in."

"She has a point," Roman said, but she waited for Cal to agree.

When he gave the nod, she did an internal fist pump. While Roman got Charlotte on the phone, she forced herself to stay calm. If her theory was correct, they were in the wrong place and had to move farther south if they had a hope of finding this woman before the trial resumed. It might be a shot in the dark, but you missed all the shots you didn't take, and honestly, they had no other shots.

"Marlise has a question for you, Charlotte," Roman said, snapping Marlise back to the conversation.

"I'm happy to answer it if I can," Charlotte said, and Roman motioned for Marlise to ask her question.

"Charlotte, did you get to talk to the new women that The Miss brought to camp?"

"Sure, just like in Red Rye, we lived together, and the new girls were scared and wanted to talk."

"Did any of them tell you where they were picked up?"

The other end of the line was silent, and Marlise was about to ask Roman if the call had dropped when Charlotte spoke. "I should have thought of that before Roman and Mina left," she said. They all heard the disappointment in her voice that she hadn't.

"Don't feel bad," Marlise said immediately to calm her. "You haven't felt the best since you got to Secure One, and I just thought of it myself. I'm hoping to plot a few of them on a map to give us a better idea of where to start the search."

"Give me five minutes? I need to think when I'm not on the spot."

"That's fine," Roman said. "Have Mack call us back or text us the information."

They ended the call and stared at each other with frustration until Cal spoke. "What if The Miss didn't get the women from Arizona?"

Marlise started to pace, but she shook her head while she did it. "I'm sure she did, at least in the beginning. She was setting up shop and didn't have the time or the scouts to extend her tentacles too far. I wouldn't be surprised if the first few girls she got were snatch-and-run homeless girls off the street."

"You're saying The Miss had to build her army fast?" Cal asked.

"Exactly," Mina agreed. "If she were running

drugs through Red Rye, she wouldn't want those clients to defect to a different supplier. We know she was prepared to leave, which means her home base was likely ready, but she still needed women to get it running."

"When Charlotte gets back to us, I want to plot the cities on a map. We'll find the center of all of them and start looking for The Miss's girls there."

"Needle in a haystack though," Cal said with frustration. "When the sun comes up tomorrow, we only have nine days until the trial resumes without us."

"If you'd rather, we can—" Marlise's sentence was cut off when the phone rang.

"I remembered six girls," Charlotte said, "but I don't know if these towns are in Arizona, California or Mexico."

"I think we can rule out Mexico," Marlise said immediately. "You didn't need passports to move around the country, right?"

"No," Charlotte agreed. "That's a good point. Then if we're talking about that desert you mentioned, these towns have to be in Arizona or California."

"I'm ready," Cal said, holding a sheet of paper to write them down.

Charlotte listed off three names, and Marlise stopped her. "Wait, Three Points and Sahuarita are near the San Xavier Indian Reservation. Were any of them Indigenous women?"

"That was the vibe I got," Charlotte said. "Do you know where these towns are?"

"The first three are south or west of Tucson. What are the other three?"

Charlotte listed them off, and Marlise bit her lip as she leaned over Cal's shoulder. "Those towns are all within driving distance of Tucson." If The Miss was taking girls from just one town or specific area, that meant she didn't have time to be picky about who she was taking.

"Thanks, Charlotte," Marlise said before Roman hung up with her.

"The Miss must be desperate if she's taking women all from one area," Mina said, mirroring Marlise's thoughts. "That could put her on police radar."

"Unlikely," Marlise said, sitting on the end of the bed. "She's still only going to source homeless girls. They're already lost girls, so no one will miss them unless they have a close friend on the street."

"True," Mina agreed, glancing at the two men. "It looks like we need to get to Tucson."

"That's less than two hours by car," Marlise said before anyone could ask.

"Once we're down there, do you know where to start looking?" Roman asked, his gaze holding Cal's.

The breath that Marlise blew out was long and frustrated. "That's the problem. There is so much area to consider there. You've got Catalina State Park, Santa Catalina Natural Area, the Catalina Foothills, Saguaro National Park and Tucson Mountain Park. Those are just the ones around Tucson. There are many other wilderness areas along that route going west."

"You're saying we have found the haystack, but it's big, and the needle is still small," Cal deduced.

"We only have nine days," Roman said. "We don't have time to search all those places on the off chance The Miss has sent a scout out."

Her three friends continued to toss around ideas on finding the needle, while Marlise considered something even more important—finding the eye of the needle. They had nine days, and that wasn't much time when the scouts spend at least a week grooming a girl before they take her back to meet The Miss. Maybe when she first arrived, The Miss wasn't grooming the girls out of time constraints, but by now, she'd surely be back to her usual tactics. She wasn't dumb, and she knew that taking too many girls from one area was bad for business. That made a person too memorable to the other girls on the street. The last thing The Miss wanted was for her scouts to be followed back to the base.

"I doubt she's even taking girls from Tucson anymore," Marlise said as a hush fell over the room. "She may not even be recruiting right now."

Mina pointed at her. "She's right. She could be sitting fine with women, other than losing Charlotte. With what happened at the trial, she could be laying low and waiting for that to pass."

"We're going to have to draw her out, and there's only one way to do that," Marlise said, sitting up straighter. "We let her know I'm in town."

"Absolutely not!" Cal bellowed before the words

were barely out of her mouth. "You aren't trained for that, and we don't have the backup!"

Mina grasped his arm to quiet him. "She's right, Cal. If we don't draw The Miss out, we'll still be trying to find her when the trial resumes."

"We'll drive around the whole damn desert looking for her pods before we risk Marlise's life again!"

"We don't have time, Cal!" Marlise exclaimed with frustration as she leapt to her feet. "Some of the roads west of Tucson are nothing but dirt and lead deep into the desert! We don't have time to find the needle. We have to find the eye, and then we have to thread it. If we don't, she will always haunt us. I'm tired of this cat and mouse game, and every minute we stand here safely, another girl could be dying. I have enough on my conscience. I don't need more deaths weighing heavy there."

"It's too dangerous," Cal ground out, his insistence loud and clear, but Marlise noticed an underlying layer of fear.

She walked to him and braced her hands on his chest, but he stepped back, putting that wall back up between them. "You can tag me. You'll know where I am at all times."

"Tagging you doesn't help if The Miss dispatches you on sight."

"She won't," Mina said. "She won't do that in public. She'd have to deal with a body if she did it anywhere other than home base, and Marlise is too well-known because of the trial. The authorities would know immediately that The Miss did it and she was in the area."

"She'd still be dead, Mina," he hissed. "I'm not taking that chance with her life."

"I'll go with her and be her backup."

"Forget it!" Roman exclaimed from the end of the bed, where he was sorting out information coming in from Secure One. "The FBI is already going to have a cow that I took their star witnesses out of town to find a madwoman. Imagine if they get kidnapped! No, this is a bad idea for both of you."

Mina's eye roll at her husband was powerful, and Marlise had to bite back a smile. "The FBI isn't going to say a thing if we catch The Miss for them, which is something they've been unable to do. Besides, they don't own us anymore."

"Even if I wanted to, which I don't," Cal emphasized, "there's no way to tag you without The Miss finding it when you get to her. The first thing she'll do is search you."

"I'll already be there, and you'll have the location," Marlise said logically. "After that, it doesn't matter."

"It matters if she kills you when she finds it."

"You could tag me instead," Mina said, tapping her prosthesis. "She can't take this."

Roman took Mina's face in his hands. "This is not your war to fight, Mina."

"But it is, Roman," she whispered, not backing

down. "The Miss took two years of my life and my leg from me. This is as much my fight as it is Marlise's."

"It's a moot point. The Miss isn't dumb. There's no way she would grab either of you. She'd know it was a trick," Cal said to shut the conversation down.

Marlise's excitement drained away, and she plopped onto the bed. Cal was right. They'd spent the last two years evading The Miss. There was no way she'd believe it wasn't a trap. There was no way she'd believe they'd just throw themselves out there and wait to get snatched. If they were going to get to The Miss, they would have to be subtle. They needed to be found without being obvious about it.

"I know what we have to do." Marlise stood and pointed at Mina. "We need to head to Tucson today, but I'll need you to make a stop. If I give you a list, can you obtain what's needed?"

"Of course," Mina replied. "What's your plan?"

"We know we can't go in dressed as ourselves, so we hit the streets as girls looking for a better life. We visit some parks, knock on some doors and make it known we want out of the street life. Disguised, no one will know who we are, which buys us time."

"No," Cal said, but Marlise spun on him and stuck her finger in his chest.

"Do not tell me no. You gave me point on this in Kansas, and you can't have it both ways, Cal New-fellow! You can't say you want to find The Miss but tie our hands at every turn!" Roman was biting his lip when she turned to face them. "Right?"

Roman shrugged. "I have to side with her on this one, little brother. You did give her point, and you said you trusted her instincts. We're running out of time, and her idea is valid and credible if we put safeguards in place before they go out."

"I'm going with you," Mina said, grabbing Marlise's hand. "We were a team in Red Rye, and we're an even better team now. We have each other's back, right?"

"Right, but Mina, you don't have to," Marlise said, her gaze flicking to Roman, but he didn't look as upset as Cal did. "I'd understand if you'd rather be part of the team monitoring my movements."

"I do have to," she said emphatically. "I want a piece of this woman as much as you do, and I will not let you go out there alone. You've been alone all your life, but not anymore. Secure One has you now, and you've proven yourself to all of us. Even Cal, despite his growling and teeth gnashing."

"Mina," he warned, his jaw pulsing. "Do not push me."

Mina strode up to him and looked him up and down. "Or what? Are you going to fire me? Fine, fire me. I'm still going out tomorrow on the streets of Tucson with Marlise to find this woman. You can get on board or stand in the corner and pout while we make a plan, but we're running out of time. We have no other option."

They stared each other down for long seconds before Cal's shoulders sank, and he shook his head.

"I know you're right, but I don't like it. I don't like it at all."

"Neither do I," Marlise said, stepping close to him so he could feel her heat and know she was there for him. "But I trust you, Roman, Mack and the team at Secure One. I trust that Mina will have my back and keep me safe. For someone who doesn't trust easily, that's saying a lot. You've all proven to me with actions rather than words that you're not letting anything happen to me. You only need to prove it one more time. The most important time."

Cal's brown eyes were wide and held the truth that he hadn't said. He was scared. He was scared for her but also of losing her. His nod relaxed her shoulders, and she gave him one back. The action was of respect for her and her choices, which filled her with pride.

"I will agree to this, but we don't leave for Tucson until morning. We need the rest of today to make a plan and get everyone at Secure One on it."

"Agreed," Mina and Roman said together.

"I can accept that," Marlise said. "It's only ninety minutes to Tucson, so we can still be on the streets by ten."

"If we agree, then let's get to work. I want to find this woman and bring her in so we can get on with our lives without her hanging over our heads."

As Cal, Roman and Mina set up a battle station in their hotel suite, Marlise couldn't help but wonder if the life he planned to get on with would include her, or if he wanted to find The Miss as a way to end his commitment to her. The determination she saw in his eyes told her he was committed to keeping her safe, but the fear she saw in them told her he was just as scared as she was about her role at Secure One once this was over. She suspected they were scared for different reasons, and Marlise hoped that if she came out of this mission in one piece, so did her heart.

Chapter Sixteen

The sun had gone down on them as they'd plotted and planned this mission to the last "what if," but Cal still wasn't comfortable sending Marlise into the field. She knew the streets, but they were always fluid, and she'd been gone for too many years. Roman wasn't any happier about sending Mina with her, but it was better than sending Marlise alone. They could watch each other's backs, and there were better tagging options for Mina than Marlise. They'd tag her prosthesis with a tracker in hopes if they did find The Miss, they wouldn't know she was an amputee. As long as she kept the prosthesis hidden, they could track them.

Roman wasn't going to get any sleep tonight either, and Cal took a bit of comfort in knowing he wasn't alone in his distaste for this mission. Neither of them dealt well with not being part of it. They'd rather be out there clearing the field than sitting on their hands in a car waiting for something to happen. They didn't have a choice this time. Their presence would be noticeable and only hamper the women as they worked the streets. He had to trust Mina and her skills as an FBI agent. He also had to trust Marlise and her skills as someone who'd once lived on the streets. The only part he liked about the plan was disguising them beyond recognition. If they didn't know it was her, the scouts would be more likely to take her to home base as a willing participant rather than a hostage. The women just had to get them onto the property, and Secure One would do the rest.

Mina had gone out and bought the supplies, and in six hours, they'd don their disguises and leave for Tucson. A vast pit opened in Cal's gut, and he grunted, wishing this hell were over and they were back at Secure One. Did he regret bringing Mina and Marlise to Secure One? No, not for one second. This case had cost him time, money and sleep, but he'd gained so much more than he'd lost. He had his brother working with him now, a sister who was also an excellent hacker, and a woman who could be more than an employee and friend if this were a different time and place.

She already is.

He grunted at that voice again. Thinking that way was going to get one of them killed. That voice hadn't listened to him since Marlise stepped foot on his plane two years ago. He fought against it, but it never relented, and it was always loud in his head when the room was quiet. Marlise had gone to bed an hour ago and left him to brood in the corner. He'd sleep there in the club chair, his feet up on the luggage rack, instead of climbing into that giant bed with her. Holding her as she slept would be a terrible idea just hours before he'd have to let her out of his protective grasp. They needed to close this case so he could get Marlise out of his mind and his lodge.

"Tell me what happened," Marlise whispered.

The room was dark, and Cal sighed, glad she couldn't see his facial expression at the request. "I can't, Mary."

"You mean you won't," she replied with disappointment.

"No, I can't. The mission was classified. I can't tell you what happened."

"You can tell me what happened without specifics, Cal. I only need to know what happened to you and Hannah."

"What happened to the meek woman who never said a word when she first came to Secure One?"

"You taught her to stop letting people walk all over her."

Cal snorted, and while he didn't mean for it to be, it was tinged with amusement. "I have to admit that even when you're in my face about something, I still like my feisty Mary to my meek one."

My? Stop. Get that out of your head right now, pal.

"Then stop putting up a wall between us like you don't care."

Cal stood from where he sat near the window and walked to the bed. He lowered himself to the edge of it. "I do care, Mary, and that's why I put the wall up. Doing anything else could get you killed."

"I'm not Hannah, Cal, and it's time you stop treating me that way."

"I'm treating you the same way I would any other witness I had to protect."

"Good sell, but I'm not buying. Tell me what happened."

Why was he even considering her request? He hadn't told anyone what happened since the debriefing the week after the mission. He'd been in a hospital bed, a bullet wound in his chest, but his heart shattered to smithereens.

"We were young and in love. Hannah was, um—" Cal glanced at the ceiling "—on the same team. I'm not purposely being vague, but I have to be careful what I say."

Marlise took his right hand and started to massage his palm below his missing fingers. He wanted to draw his hand away and force her to stop, but her touch calmed the burning nerves. He knew she lived with the same kind of pain and wondered if she knew he suffered too. He tried to hide his discomfort from his team, and the prosthesis helped by protecting the sensitive digits, but he spent a lot of time pretending he was fine when he wasn't.

"I understand. Keep going," she said, her fingers massaging away the pain.

"She was specially trained as an interpreter as well. It was her job to go in and get the information we needed. It was my job to protect her while she did it. The big boss said to move in, but I wasn't comfortable with the lack of recon. When you're working with the government, you're never in control, and they told me the people we were looking for weren't active in our area. My limited recon said the same. We were both wrong. Hannah paid the price. That's the story."

Marlise sat up in bed and turned his hand over, rubbing her thumbs across the scars that crisscrossed it. "What happened, Cal?"

"I just told you!" he exclaimed, sending his hand into his hair on a deep breath.

"What you did was tell me something I already knew. You didn't do your job, and Hannah died. But what happened?"

"It doesn't matter, Mary!" he exploded, standing and walking to the end of the bed. His harsh tone didn't even make her flinch, and that worried him. If she was digging in, he had a problem.

"It does matter, Cal. Hannah mattered to you. You loved her, but you didn't get her killed."

"Yes, I did! I didn't see the rebel hiding in an abandoned building with a rifle! She was a duck in a carnival pond, and I stood there selling tickets!"

"Did Hannah know the risks when she went on the mission?"

"Of course, she did. She was part of the team and had the same training I did, except she was also a linguist."

"I'm not trying to be coldhearted here, but if she was trained and part of the team, she accepted that she might not walk out alive. You did the same thing. If I had to guess, you took a bullet that day too."

"You're wrong."

"I saw the scar, Cal. I may not be highly educated, but I lived on the streets, and I've seen things there. That scar on your chest? The doctors opened you up to get a bullet out of you. A bullet you more than likely took for her. Don't tell me you failed Hannah when you gave everything you had, including nearly giving your own life."

"Is it an option to get the meek Mary back?" Cal asked as he walked to the bed and sat on its edge again. "I'm not sure I like being challenged by this one."

She smiled, but she didn't back down, and that ratcheted up his heart rate until he felt a trickle of sweat down his back. If she didn't stop, he would do something they'd both regret, like take her as his own in this bed.

"Sorry, that woman is long gone. The Mary in front of you tonight has decided to accept the experiences that shaped her and made her the woman she is. You need to accept that what happened to Hannah all those years ago shaped who you are personally, professionally and emotionally. Stop locking up your emotions to avoid being vulnerable. We're all vulnerable, Cal. We all have an innate need to connect with another soul that feeds our own. Yes, you loved Hannah, but she's been gone for thirteen years. When will you start finding connections again that feed your soul?"

She slipped her tiny hand under his T-shirt and ran her finger down his scar. The sensation sent a shiver through him, and he grasped her hand to stop her caress. "That scar is why I don't make connections anymore, Mary."

"Is that why you covered the scar with a tattoo? To avoid being reminded of the one connection that was broken?"

"I covered the scar so I wasn't faced with my failure in the mirror every day. Is that what you wanted to hear? They cut me open to take the armor-piercing bullet from the muscle near my heart. A few millimeters were the difference between life and death for me. They may as well have cut my heart out the day they cut the bullet out. I haven't used it since, and I have no intention of letting that organ rule my head ever again."

Her laughter filled the silent room, and that damn organ inside his chest reacted to the sound with a thump against his chest wall.

"You're ridiculous. As though every decision you've made in the last two years hasn't been led by your heart."

"Don't call me ridiculous," he spat. "And you're wrong. I make decisions based on what's best for my business and nothing else."

"You helped Roman find Mina and then sheltered

them at Secure One. You risked your life and the
lives of your men to get me out of St. Paul and then
nursed me back to health while chasing down a madwoman. You flew your chopper to Minneapolis in
the dark of night because your brother's soulmate
was in danger, and you didn't even hesitate. You
brought me back to Secure One and gave me a job
when Mina batted her eyelashes at you. If you think
that anyone believes you don't have a heart, you're
dead wrong, Cal Newfellow. It's time you accept
that organ has led you plenty the last few years, and
it hasn't steered you wrong."

"The potential is there for it to steer me wrong to
the point someone dies, Mary. I can't allow that to
happen again."

"You can't stop it from happening again, Cal.
Don't you see that?" she asked, her hands holding
her temples in frustration. "There are people out
there who act in ways beyond your control! You can
mitigate the risk as much as possible, but you can't
predict what someone else will do. Why can't you
accept that?"

"Because if I accept that, I'm going to do something I regret! I'll lose someone I care about to something beyond my control again!" His exclamation
came from across the room where he'd darted when
confronted with the truth he always knew but refused to acknowledge.

She was standing in front of him now with her
hand on his chest. "Let's be clear here," she whis-

pered, her gaze holding all the truth she knew about this world. "That statement is coming from fear and not truth. You're afraid you'll lose someone else you care about to something beyond your control. You don't *know* that you will. That's the difference. Unfortunately, that's how life works, Cal. Tomorrow is never guaranteed. Telling yourself you don't care when you do isn't going to make it any easier when that person is gone. You've got to care about people and love them while they're here, or all you'll be left with is regrets."

His silence was the gulf between them, even as she stood inches away with her beautiful, youthful, innocent heart laid bare. The moonlight slipped through the curtains and rested across her face to illuminate the scarred flesh.

She grabbed his wrist when he slipped his hand up the webbed skin of her cheek. "Stop." He could tell she'd wanted it to be forceful, but all he heard was sadness. "Don't touch me there."

"Because?" His voice *was* forceful. He wanted an answer and demanded she give it.

"It's my Mr. Hyde side," she whispered. "I look like a monster, Cal. That's why I wear my hair over it. That way, no one is confronted with the truth of how The Miss abused me. Most especially you. I've been used and abused over and over again in this life, and I wear this skin as a badge of shame. I don't know why you want to touch me at all."

Cal's heart broke, each word splintering off pieces

of it until it lay shattered at his feet. His poor girl had suffered through so much at the hands of these people. The burns may be healed but those scars—the scars that were slashed into her memory—would remain open, weeping wounds until someone loved her enough to heal them.

"Sweet Mary," he whispered, trailing his hand up the left side of her face to her temple, where his thumb rubbed the skin to soothe her eye. "Your burns don't detract from your beauty. They add to it."

Her eye roll was strong in her right eye. "Nice try, Cal. I don't even have a real eyelid on the left. There's nothing beautiful about it."

"I'm sorry you feel that way, love," he said, gentleness in his tone. "Because I think it shows your strength and resiliency to live through an event meant to take you away from this world. It shows your determination to go on with life when you had every reason to call it a day. Your future after that fire was bleak at best, but you didn't care what the future held as long as you were part of it. You want to be here, and you have no qualms about risking your heart or your life to keep someone you love safe."

"I trust you, Cal," she whispered. "I trust you to take care of me and protect me. That's why I can take risks to help those I love. You're the first man I've ever trusted because my heart said you were safe. My heart is connected to yours. Whether you like it or not. Whether it's convenient or not, I can't decide for you. All I know is, when you're near me, I feel safe, even when bullets are flying. If I didn't trust you to keep me safe when we faced The Miss again, I wouldn't have left Secure One to testify. I wouldn't have followed you back to a place that tried to take my life and walked into it with my head held high. I would have been too scared, but you were with me and kept me safe."

I trust you, Cal.

Those four words were a jolt to his head and heart that he couldn't deny. He couldn't deny that everything this tiny scrap of a woman said made more sense than anything he'd told himself over the last thirteen years. Through her eyes, he could see that he'd built his life around getting a redo on that day in a land far away when he'd failed someone he was tasked to protect. Every time he kept a client safe or a mission went the right way, it was another piece of metal he added to his armor when he should have been removing it.

"You're so much braver than I am, Mary," he whispered, his forehead touching hers now. "Your heart leads you to the truth every time."

"It does, Cal," she whispered, her gaze flicking up to his. "You can be that brave too if you start listening to your heart instead of your head."

"My head protects me, Mary. It protects me from all of…this."

"This? Do you mean connecting with someone who wants you to be happy? This? As in having any emotion other than anger in your life? This? Like having to admit that losing Hannah was horrible and the hardest thing you've ever lived through? It wasn't your fault, and you did live through it, so why aren't you living?"

Cal didn't let her finish. His lips were on hers before the next word left them. She wrapped her arms around his neck and fell into him. His strong arm around her waist lifted her off the ground, and her soft mewling mixed with his tight moan as he carried her to the bed. Cal braced a knee on the mattress and lowered her to rest against the soft comforter as he followed her sweet lips down.

This is a bad idea. You'll love her and lose her just like the last time.

"No," she said against his lips, "this is not a bad idea."

How could she know that was his exact thought at that moment?

"I see you, Cal," she whispered. "You wear your self-doubt like armor, but it's invisible to me. The man you hide away is the only one I can see. The good, the bad and the ugly. Just the same as you with me."

"Be that as it may," he ground out, his need pressing against her in a way that betrayed his words, "that doesn't make this the right choice."

"That makes this the *only* choice," she whispered right before she trailed her hand down his taut belly to his hardness yearning for her touch.

The moan left his lips before he could stop it. He

didn't want to stop it. He didn't want to stop feeling this way. Her tiny, sweet hand had slipped inside his jeans and wrapped itself around him. He throbbed against the heat of her hand and the idea that she offered exoneration from his past. He hadn't allowed himself to believe that was even a possibility since that day when he took a bullet for the woman he loved, and it still wasn't enough.

"It was enough," she whispered, her warmth spreading through him as she held him. "You are enough, Cal. It's time to share our pain until it's diluted and insignificant to who we are together."

His lips attacked hers again and stemmed the flow of truth from them. The truth was, he had already lost the battle of not caring about another woman the moment she ran onto his plane. Tonight, as she stripped him bare of his clothes and his demons, he knew it. He knew it when she gripped him in her tiny hand and let her heat soak into him. He knew it when he kissed his way from her lips to her breasts and then to her center. She was everything he'd tried to forget existed. Sweetness. Honesty. Pureness unsullied by his poison. He wasn't poison though. Not to Mary. To Mary, he was salvation.

"I don't have any protection," he moaned against her belly when his senses returned for a moment.

He gazed into her eyes and saw the truth. She was his protection. Her tiny presence in his life had been what could shield him from the ugly all along.

"Let me protect you this time, Cal," she murmured.

He sank into her, accepting her as the final puzzle piece to his unhealed heart. His lips were on hers when he spoke. "Mary," he whispered on a moan of pleasure. "You make me whole. You are home."

She tipped her hips up and let him slide deeper to rest against her center. "I'm more than home, Cal. I'm redemption."

Chapter Seventeen

Cal didn't recognize Marlise when Mina had finished with her makeup. Her facial scars had been covered, and she wore a disheveled wig along with clothes that hung on her slight frame. An old, threadbare flannel shirt covered the burn scars on her arm, and fingerless gloves kept the scars hidden on her hand. The weather in Arizona had cooled now that it was fall, so pants and a long-sleeved shirt wouldn't raise suspicion on the street.

Mina had done much of the same to hide her identity. A pair of men's cargo pants made her prosthesis disappear inside the material and would raise no suspicion. She had traded out her everyday leg for her running blade inside a tennis shoe, just in case they needed to abort the mission and run. Mina ran around the compound every morning and was confident she could escape any situation. He was confident she could too. Regardless of how things went down a few years ago, she was still a trained FBI agent, and she kept her skills sharp. Marlise, on the other hand, didn't have the skills or instinct that Mina did. He hoped she would default to Mina if she told her to run.

He groaned and rubbed his chest with his palm. He'd had heartburn since he woke up yesterday. Marlise's lips on his skin were the only thing that soothed it, but it was back in full force when she stopped. The women had spent the day yesterday pounding the pavement and trying to get noticed, but no one approached them. Once the sun went down, they walked back to a rent-by-the-hour motel. Cal and Roman did the same thing. Cal refused to allow them to sleep on the streets, but he also knew they couldn't all be seen together. He had traded off watching their room with Roman last night. This morning they'd given them a head start and followed in the van. They were down to eight days to find The Miss, and Cal had doubts this would work.

"How'd you sleep?" Roman asked from the seat next to him in the van. They were waiting in a park at the moment. They'd move around throughout the day, so they didn't attract suspicion, but they had to stay close to where the women were.

"Didn't get much sleep. Don't tell me you did knowing you had to send Mina back out to the wolves today."

"Mina has been my partner for years. Yes, she's my wife now, but I still trust her skills as an agent. She's going to take care of Marlise. No offense, but you're jumpier than a cat on a hot tin roof, and that's not the Cal Newfellow I know. What gives?"

"You realize that when someone says 'no offense,' it's obvious that whatever they're going to say is offensive, right?"

Roman's whistle was long and low as he shook his head at his brother. "Wow, your deflection game is strong this morning. What are you trying to hide?"

Cal refused to participate in his nonsense. He'd do his job and focus on keeping Marlise and Mina safe from a madwoman. The last thing he would do was tell his brother he'd slept with their witness. He would remember that night for the rest of his life. The power that little thing held over him was unyielding, and he didn't know what he was going to do about it. How was he going to let her go when this was over? He had to though. She deserved a chance to go out and live her life, but watching her walk out of his was going to gut him.

He kept his gaze trained on the empty grass in front of him, hoping for a glimpse of the woman he'd made love to three times the night before last. No. It wasn't making love. That was dangerous thinking. Seeing it as anything other than a one-night stand was a fast way to lose objectivity when it came to this case. He checked his earpiece, listening to Mina and Marlise talking with other women. They'd been asking questions about where to get a hot meal and a shower, but none of the other women were forthcoming.

"Come on, Mary," Mina said. "We'll go find the YMCA."

Cal and Roman knew that was her cue that they were moving. Within seconds their GPS device popped up with a route to the nearest YMCA. Mack was back at Secure One, blazing a path to save them time. Cal started the vehicle and followed the GPS to an abandoned house near the Y. He parked on the street, knowing the women would eventually walk past the van and they could get a glimpse of them.

"Have you told Marlise about Hannah?" Roman asked as he leaned against the door of the van.

"Why on earth would I tell her about Hannah?" Cal growled the question more than he spoke it. The last thing he wanted to do was engage in a conversation with his brother about his dead girlfriend. Roman had been there that day, and he knew too much.

"Fair is fair." Cal glanced at him with an eyebrow down, not understanding what he meant. His brother shrugged. "If she's going to compete with a ghost, you should at least have the decency to tell her."

"She's not competing against anyone, Roman."

His snicker made Cal want to punch him in the nose. He wasn't a violent man, but Roman never eased up on him about Hannah. It had been this way for years. Every time they saw each other, Roman was bugging him about letting Hannah go and forgiving himself for what had happened. Cal didn't know how. Every job he did, every person he saved, was a way to find redemption from the one time he had failed.

"Marlise is more astute than you give her credit for, Cal," Roman said, shaking his head. "If you think she doesn't have your number, you're dumber than you look."

"Roman?"

"Yeah, Cal?"

"Shut up."

"Not this time," Roman said with a shake of his head. Cal was worried their ongoing pact of telling each other to shut up when they didn't want to talk had ended. "Everyone on this team can see how you've looked at Marlise since we picked her up in St. Paul. When will you be honest with her? The moment before she walks out the doors of Secure One, or never?"

"She knows about Hannah," Cal said between clenched teeth. His gaze was pinned to the rearview mirror as he waited for them to approach. It took several minutes to realize Roman was silent. He had his mouth open when he glanced at him, staring out the windshield. "Don't be so dramatic."

"You have to forgive me for being dumbfounded. I never expected you to tell her."

"I tried to use Hannah as an excuse—"

"And our little Marlise called you on your crap, right?"

Cal's shrug said everything. It brought a grin to Roman's face. "They're approaching."

Roman turned his head to watch the side mirror while Cal kept his attention on the rearview mirror. He wanted to catch a glimpse of Marlise to make sure she was okay.

"It's unbelievable how brave she is to go back into this life," Cal said as the women walked by the van without taking notice. He knew they had, but they didn't let on.

"There's one thing I've learned about women, Cal, and it's simple. As men, we always underestimate them. We underestimate their strength, stamina, grit and how their moral compass guides them. After finding Mina a year after her injury, still trying to solve the case, I was never more aware of how much strength it took her to keep fighting when she had every right to give up. Marlise has all that strength and then some. At least she does now that you've taken care of her, built up her health and acknowledged her contributions to the company. You allowed her to lead, a job she's never had before, and that's why she's out there right now. She wants to contribute to solving this case and freeing herself from her past."

"We're on the same page there," Cal said as he watched them walk toward the doors of the YMCA. "I want her to be free of The Miss."

"But you're afraid that means she will walk away from you."

"From Secure One? Absolutely. She's an asset to our team, Roman."

His brother's snort was loud inside the van. "Sure, you're afraid you'll lose her as a team member of Secure One. I almost buy that, Cal. If you think we can't see something has changed between you two, you underestimate my skills as a special agent of the FBI."

"Leave it alone, Roman. We have one focus, and that's keeping our girls safe."

The goofy smile his brother wore on his face told Cal that he already suspected what had happened between him and Marlise, but he wasn't going to confirm it. His time with Marlise was too special to sully by acting like it meant nothing to him. He hadn't had time to process it all, but he knew it meant something to both of them. Cal regretted his decision not to be honest with her, and he hoped he could be before it was too late.

"Don't ask about showers here," Marlise said to Mina as they approached the doors. Roman glanced at Cal with a questioning look, and he shrugged. "If they say they're available, they'll expect us to use them. A shower is going to blow my cover."

"Good point," Mina agreed. "I should have thought of that."

Cal couldn't help it. He was grinning like the Cheshire cat. "That's my girl."

Roman punched him playfully, but all playfulness disappeared when another woman approached them. Cal flipped the record button on and shifted the audio from their ears to the computer. They both held their breath and hoped they weren't going to blow their cover this early in the game by having to rescue them before they found The Miss.

"Yo," MARLISE SAID to the girl as she approached. "Is the Y open?"

The girl looked her up and down and then did the same with Mina. "Sure ain't."

"Damn," Mina huffed. "I guess there's no point in staying then, Mary. Let's hit it."

Both women turned back the way they came when the other girl spoke. "What ya looking for there?"

Marlise turned back slowly and took a moment to assess the woman in front of them. She wasn't a street girl. Her good hygiene and clean clothing made her stick out like a sore thumb in a place like the YMCA. She was a scout. She was also Latina. Marlise reminded herself she could be a scout for any sex trafficking ring and forced herself to remain calm. She slid her eyes to Mina, who had a brow raised in the air. She was going to leave it to her to feel out.

"We're tired of the street, you know? Looking for a place to get a meal and sleep for the night where we don't need to keep one eye open."

"I could find work again if I could get a shower and some clean clothes," Mina added. "We both could. She cooks, and I clean. We were hoping to find a hotel that was hiring."

"I might know a place," the girl said. Marlise noticed she was trying too hard to be casual. She was excited and nervous, two emotions Marlise knew well.

"You saving it for yourself?" Mina asked. "Respect, if you are. We're all out here scrapping."

"No, but I know the owners, and I don't recommend just anyone to them. I gotta trust them, you know."

Marlise held up her hands in the don't shoot position. "Understood, sister. No harm, no foul. We'll be on our way."

"Wait! I could take you over there, and you could maybe show them your skills?" the girl asked before they could turn away. "They might even give you a room for the night as payment."

"How far is the place?" Mina asked. "We've already walked five miles today."

"It's about forty-five minutes from here, but my car is just up the block. I'm Jen, by the way."

"I'm Mary, and she's Amy," Marlise said, hooking a thumb at Mina as she eyed Jen with suspicion. "What are you doing here if the hotel is forty-five minutes away?" She took a step back and widened her eyes, hoping she looked nervous and agitated. Mina did the same thing, and the girl took a step forward but waved her hands innocently in front of her.

"I was supposed to meet some other girl here who was looking for a job, but she's a no-show. I already told the owners I'd found them some help, and now I hate to go back and tell them otherwise. I saw you two coming and thought you'd be interested. If you're not, that's fine, but I gotta get on my way."

Mina held up her finger and pulled Marlise aside. She put on a show of bending her head to whisper as though they had to weigh their options. Their only option was to find out if this girl was one of The Miss's scouts. "Do we go with her?" Mina whispered near Marlise's ear. "No way to know if she's with The Miss or someone else."

Marlise held her gaze and raised her voice to a stage whisper so the other girl could hear. "We have to take any chance that gets us off the street, Amy. I'll do anything to sleep in a real bed again. Imagine not having to worry about men following us or sleeping in shifts. I know you want it just as much."

With a feigned eye roll, Mina finally nodded once. "I do, but we gotta be careful, you know. And we stick together. No matter what."

"No matter what," Marlise agreed, doing some goofy handshake thing they'd come up with as a way to tell Cal and Roman that they should follow at a distance. The guys could hear them, but Marlise didn't want to take any chances that the mic wasn't working. They needed the backup where they were going. She could feel it in her bones.

Chapter Eighteen

"I don't like them getting into a car," Roman said as he buckled his belt and waited for Cal to put the van into Drive.

"Me either, but we have to trust Mina. All we can do is follow them and be ready for any situation that comes at us. Sex trafficking is so common on the streets that you could walk into a ring on any corner. There's no way to know if this scout is one of The Miss's."

Once the women were out of sight, Cal shifted into gear and idled with his foot on the brake. The computer was up, and they were still recording their conversation as they walked up the road. Thus far, the conversation had remained innocuous about living on the streets and the problem with finding a job when you didn't have a permanent address. Mina and Marlise were spreading it on like peanut butter, and he hoped it wasn't too thick. If this girl was from a different ring, they didn't want their cover blown in town.

"The chances are slim this woman has anything to do with The Miss," Roman said as they waited.

"Maybe not, but we have to take any chance we get. We don't have time to be picky. I hate to sound ominous, but the hair on the back of my neck went up when the girl approached."

Roman's response was simple. "Mine too. I guess we'll know soon enough."

"This is a nice BMW," Mina said.

"Come on, my girl," Roman whispered, his pen against the paper as he waited.

"I've always wanted to ride in a Gran Coupe. The lines are sleek, and the silver paint makes it look like a bullet. I bet it's as fast as one too."

"How do you know so much about my car?" the scout asked suspiciously. Cal glanced at Roman with a grimace, but Roman held up his finger.

"My old man. He got this, like, car magazine, every month. He'd go on about the cars in it during dinner and how he would have one someday. He was a mechanic, so he loved cars, but also booze. The two don't mix, and he wrapped his not-so-fancy Chevy around a tree."

Roman did a fist pump and snickered as he eyed Cal.

"Tragic," the woman said with zero empathy in her voice.

"Not really. Daddy was mean when he drank, and he always drank. The only thing I miss about him was the little bit of support he gave me."

They counted three doors closing, and then the engine purred to life. There was a crinkling of bags, and then the woman spoke. "Here are some snacks. Help yourself while we drive so you aren't hungry when we get to the hotel."

"Thanks!" Marlise said, pouring on the gratitude so thick even Cal smiled. "We haven't eaten in a couple of days."

Cal and Roman listened to the crinkling of wrappers and their fake moaning as they ate whatever snacks the woman had given them. Roman had to hope none of it was laced.

"What do you do for a living?" Mina asked after five minutes.

Cal glanced at the GPS that showed they were headed west toward the California and Arizona border. "Contact Mack and ask him to check for any issues going west on 86."

"Too easy. This is too easy," Roman said with a shake of his head, but he flipped open the phone to call Mack.

"I'm starting to feel the same way," Cal agreed as he stayed out of the car's line of sight but followed the GPS tracker Mina had in her leg. "Maybe not though. The women were out yesterday. Word could have gotten around that they were looking for a job."

"Or one of The Miss's guards was a scout and recognized Marlise."

Roman said the words Cal was trying not to think. Cal didn't respond. He was already thinking ten steps ahead of where they were. If their ride ended at The Miss's camp, it would be up to the women to get that information to them. Once they knew the location, Mack would let the local authorities know in the closest town while Cal and Roman found a way onto the property to protect Marlise and Mina. His experience with The Miss told him it would never be that easy. She was paranoid and wouldn't risk bringing Marlise into the camp without knowing she wasn't being tailed.

Roman hung up the phone and pointed at the GPS. "He's putting in all the roads that branch off 86 up on the screen. I'll focus on the GPS tracker while you focus on making sure we don't get noticed."

Cal set his lips and eased off the gas pedal. He didn't want to spook this woman before they got where they were going. The element of surprise would be challenging to maintain, but if he didn't, he might never see Marlise alive again.

THEY'D BEEN DRIVING nearly an hour when Jen turned off the highway. "We're kind of far out in the sticks for a hotel," Mina said, making a show of looking out the windows on the side and the back. "Who stays way out here?"

"You'd be surprised how many men are looking to play cowboy in the desert. My friend's hotel is always booked."

A shiver ran through Marlise. She knew what kind of hotel Jen meant and wanted nothing to do with it.

Not after spending the night with Cal. Was that only two days ago? It felt like an eternity since he'd held her in his arms. She was determined to do anything to get back to him. She regretted not telling him her true feelings for him before they parted ways. If she didn't make it out of this, he'd never know how much he meant to her.

Her mind went to the way he'd made love to her that night, and she wondered if that was true. Maybe they'd used their bodies instead of their lips, but she'd told him how she felt. He would only have to think about how she loved him that night to know she would love him forever. She shook her head. He'd already lost one woman he'd cared about in this life. Marlise refused to do the same thing to him. She'd worked too hard to show him that life and love were worth taking a chance on again. It was time to put the fear aside and do anything she had to in order to get out of this alive.

"How many rooms are in the hotel?" Mina asked as they bounced over ruts and holes in the dirt road.

"It's a unique property. You'll see once we get there. The owner is very devoted to giving her guests the best desert experience possible. The hotel is in pods, and there is plenty of privacy for the guests."

Marlise glanced over when Mina tapped her knee against hers. Mina nodded. She believed they were headed to the right place. Mina crossed her fingers together, and Marlise understood. They had to stick together and not get separated. Anything else was a death sentence. Marlise's heart pounded with pent-up anxiety when Jen steered the BMW down a driveway and stopped at a gate. Two women dressed in black fatigues stepped out, and Jen put her window down.

Marlise glanced at Mina, who wore total disregard on her face. She turned away and looked out the window as though she didn't have a care in the world. Marlise realized why. The guards were the same two who'd helped The Miss in Red Rye. They were in the right place. The time had come to face the woman who had tried to do everything in her power to break them. She'd failed, and this time, Marlise would finish the job. She bent down as though she had dropped something on the floor and whispered the two words that would set her future in motion. "Red Rye."

CAL ALMOST MISSED the two words that came across the computer speakers. *Red Rye.* He glanced at Roman from where they sat along the side of the road.

"Did you hear that too?"

"Red Rye," he confirmed, and Cal's heart picked up its pace.

"It's go time, brother," Roman said, strapping on his bulletproof vest and then his tactical pack. They needed as much firepower as they could carry. If things went south before help arrived, they'd have to shoot their way in, and out, to get Marlise and Mina.

After alerting Mack, they slid from the van and took off on foot. The sagebrush offered them surprisingly good coverage as they worked their way past the road Jen had turned down, and they followed the GPS on their small tablet that took them along the west side of the property. They'd find cover and then wait for the trackers on the women to stop moving before they approached. They could still hear what was going on through their earpieces. For now. There was no guarantee that the link would remain once they brought Mina and Marlise onto the compound. The recording devices were hidden in a button on their clothing and undetectable to a wand, but that connection would be broken if they made them change clothes.

Cal slowed his breathing as they ate up the distance between them and the women they loved. The word tripped him up, and he went down to his hands and knees, a soft *oof* enough to turn Roman back to him. While he should be on the alert for an attack, he was worried about being in love. It was an inconvenient fact that he would have to face eventually. Now was not the time. Losing focus before they captured The Miss was a death sentence for all of them.

Roman pulled up inside a hoodoo that offered shade and cover from the sun beating down on their backs. "You okay?" Roman asked when Cal reached him.

"Tripped on some underbrush," Cal answered, taking a drink of water from his bottle. He noticed Roman smirking, but he refused to comment on it. "How far out are we?"

"Hard to tell. Two klicks or less from the western side of where they stopped. I've been listening, but it's been quiet, other than the sound of soft murmuring. I think Jen is talking to the guards about her new arrivals." Roman stopped and held up his finger as Mina's voice broke through their earpieces.

"Wow, that's a cool hotel!" she exclaimed.

Roman raised a brow at Cal. Obviously, they'd cleared security and made it onto the compound.

"It reminds me of a satellite or the sun," Marlise said enthusiastically. "I bet the kitchen is a fun place to work."

"Forget the kitchen," Mina said. "Imagine how cute those little pods are on the inside. I can't wait to start working."

Cal rolled his eyes, but he couldn't stop the smile from taking over his lips. It was no laughing matter, but he couldn't help it. "Spreading it on a little thick, aren't they," he said to Roman.

"Fastest way to The Miss is with a brown nose, and both women know that."

"They better slow down until we figure out a way to save them," Cal grunted while checking his equipment. "There are only two of us and an unknown count surrounding them. We don't stand a chance if we have to go in before the authorities get here."

"We need to move as close to the property as possible in case we have to go in. My wife will not be injured by this woman again."

Cal squeezed his brother's shoulder. "I'm hoping

they can buy us some time. If they're going to prove themselves to the boss, they'll have to work for a few hours, right?"

"We can hope," Roman said as their earpieces came to life again.

"This will be your pod while you're here," Jen said after the car doors slammed shut. "There are clothes on the beds, and you're welcome to shower and clean up. Once you've had a few minutes to rest, I'll take you to meet the owner."

"Already?" Marlise asked with fake nervousness. Then again, Cal wondered if it was fake. "Don't you want us to work a little bit to prove ourselves?"

"That's up to The Miss. She prefers to hand out the assignments each day. If we're short-staffed, it's my job to find new helpers."

A trickle of sweat ran down Cal's spine at the mention of her boss. They had found her. His brother's face had turned white. Cal understood the feeling, which told him more about how he felt about Mary than anything. "This cannot be a repeat of thirteen years ago," he spat. "I'm not going to watch another woman die, Roman."

He took off for the property, but Roman grabbed his pack and pulled him back.

"You can't run in there half-cocked, Cal!" Roman hissed into his ear. "We're surrounded by rocks. She could have snipers at the ready. You already know she was training them to kill. Use your head. We're of no use to Mina and Marlise if we're dead."

Cal took a calming breath and nodded, settling back against the wall as he listened to Marlise and Mina question Jen about The Miss. "Tread lightly, Marlise," he hummed, not wanting them to blow this operation before they had people in place to round up The Miss.

Roman leaned in when the mics went quiet. Marlise and Mina were in the pod now, and he had to hope they assumed it was wired for sound. "Let's head north. We're one klick south from where they stopped moving, according to the GPS."

One klick, Cal thought. A little more than half a mile separated them, but it felt like there was an ocean between them. Rather than speak, he nodded at Roman and headed north with his brother tight on his heels.

Chapter Nineteen

Marlise looked around the pod, surprised that it was clean and cool. There was a small efficiency kitchen in the middle and a bathroom, but the beds made a shiver run up her spine. There were two, one on each end of the pod, complete with a door that closed them off from the rest of the world. The bed behind the door was much bigger than necessary for one person, and the mountain of pillows, not to mention the mirrors on the ceiling, told the rest of the story.

Mina pulled her into the bathroom, turned on the shower and leaned into her ear. "I didn't see any obvious cameras, but that doesn't mean there aren't any. I would guess this place is bugged for sound." Marlise nodded, fear filling her now that they had found the woman who had already tried to kill them too many times. There was no way to know if help was coming or if Cal and Roman would find them in time.

They'd made sure to put on a show about how cool the pod was while Jen was with them. The more time they bought, the higher chance the guys would get to them before The Miss did. Before she left, Jen had told them to shower and dress in the new clothes left on the beds. Marlise had already noticed that the black T-shirt and pants were what Charlotte had described when explaining The Miss's new business plan. That was your welcome home outfit. Once The Miss decided where you'd be the most useful, you were given new clothes and a new identity. Marlise knew their disguises might fool the woman for a few moments, but their voices had probably already given them away. If not yet, they would once they stood in front of the woman.

"We're in trouble, aren't we?" Marlise asked, her voice wavering from fear.

"Stay calm," Mina ordered, leveling a brow at her. "Once we change, your tracker will be gone, but mine will remain. Roman and Cal will still be able to find us."

"That doesn't help us if we're already dead," she hissed, swallowing down her regret about agreeing to this mission. It was her idea, but now that she knew she was back in The Miss's grasp, the fear had taken over her courage.

"You have to keep your cool," Mina scolded. "Trust in Cal. He's not going to let you die in here. He loves you. You know that, right?"

"No, Mina, it's not like that," she insisted, even though she knew it was exactly like that. At least for her.

Mina put her finger to Marlise's lips. "It's been

like that since the day he met you. He will find a way to get us out. Besides, you know Roman isn't going to let The Miss have her way with me again."

That brought a smile to Marlise's lips, and she nodded once. "What's the plan then?"

"We stall as long as we can, and once it's dark, we get the hell out of here and hide."

"This entire property has to be under surveillance, Mina."

"Maybe, but the one thing I noticed on the way in is they run on generators. There's no power way out here. Chances are, there's minimal lighting once it's dark. All we have to do is avoid the guards and hole up until the authorities arrive."

Marlise finally nodded, but she knew there was no way they were getting out of this pod tonight unless it was by invitation from The Miss.

ROMAN TOOK A knee and pointed ahead through the underbrush. "There are those tree cacti that Charlotte said lined the property."

Cal dropped down behind him and did a three-sixty search of the area around them. "They're big but not big enough to hide us from view. We need cover to reach out to Mack and find out how long until the authorities arrive."

"If they're arriving," Roman said. "We're practically on the border here, and I didn't see too many towns along the highway with a police force big enough to make a dent in this place."

Cal had thought the same thing on the way down, but Tucson wasn't that far away, and all they had to do was hold out long enough for the big guns to arrive. A skittering of rocks raised the hair on the back of his neck. Roman heard it too. He noticed him unsnap his holster, but Cal hoped they didn't have to resort to guns. The sound from a gunshot would travel for miles in a place like this, which would alert The Miss. She could kill Marlise and Mina before they were close enough to save them.

"No guns unless necessary," Cal whispered, and Roman nodded his understanding. "The sound was on our left. Could be wildlife."

Roman's sarcastic snort told him what he thought of that. The sun was setting, and they had to make a decision. They needed cover. Before Cal could move, there was a soft grunt, a thud and two more grunts before silence filled the desert again. Then came a sound that had never filled him with as much relief as it did today.

"Secure two, Mike," a voice said from their left.

Cal and Roman turned and scurried to a rock outcropping several yards to the west. When they reached it, Mack stood guard with a rifle while Eric tied up three women who were out cold.

"Mack, what the hell are you guys doing here?" Cal asked, trying to make sense of what he saw.

"Maybe you could show a little gratitude for us saving your unsuspecting butts from these three. They had you in their sights," Eric said, finishing with the zip ties. He stuffed gags in their mouths and dragged them behind some shrubs.

"I didn't like the idea of you two down here alone. Once you told me the women were going in, we headed down. The rest of the team is covering the clients while Selina keeps an eye on Charlotte. We have news," Mack said, crouching down. "We finally got The Miss's identity off that picture Marlise took."

"How?" Cal asked in surprise.

"Roman's people came through. Her name is Sofia Guerrero. Her father is Alejandro Guerrero."

"*The* Alejandro Guerrero? He's been suspected of running drugs and guns for years."

"One and the same," Mack agreed. "Turns out, he wanted to branch out and encouraged his daughter to continue his legacy across the border. Her mother was American, so she can come and go as she pleases."

"Is Alejandro involved in this compound?" Roman asked, his head motioning at the property east of them.

"That's less clear. No doubt he is, but we'd have to follow the paperwork."

"We'll leave that up to the authorities. Our only objective is to get our girls back safely. They're in a pod and waiting to be taken to The Miss. How far out are the authorities?"

"On their way from Tucson, but they're at least an hour out. They've been keeping an eye on the property, suspecting it was running drugs, but couldn't prove it. It didn't take much convincing to get them down here on a reported kidnapping."

"Do you have any idea how many armed guards are inside?"

"All we know is two at the gate. They're guards from Red Rye, according to Marlise."

"How do you want to handle this?"

"I want the innocents alive. I don't care if The Miss lives or dies, but I'd like there to be evidence left to prove she was behind the fire and the attacks on Marlise and Mina."

"Avoid setting anything on fire," Mack said with a grin. "Got it."

"My wife is in there," Roman said. "We need to get them out before the authorities arrive. I had hoped to get a confession out of The Miss, but confirmation that she's here is enough for me. We get the women out and let the police round up the rest of them."

All men nodded in agreement. "Eric and I will create a diversion at the front gate. What pod are Marlise and Mina in?" Roman showed Mack the tracker that had remained still for the last hour other than walking about the pod. "That's beneficial. They're on the west side of the satellite. We've already taken out those guards," Mack said, motioning at the women in the bushes. "This might be our only window to get them out before the cops arrive and the element of surprise is gone."

"We need ten minutes to get there, get them out and then to relative safety," Roman said, judging the distance to the pod on the map. "If things go bad, shoot your way out of it and get clear of the compound. We'll meet up at the large rock wall three klicks west."

"At which point we will discuss disobeying direct orders," Cal huffed.

Mack rolled his eyes. "Whatever. You're glad we're here. Give us five to get in place, and then we rock and roll."

His men took off, and Cal took a deep breath. He was glad they had come, but he would be happier when he had them out of that pod and The Miss in custody.

"I'm running point," Roman said in a way that told Cal not to argue. "You've got my flank."

"Every time, brother," he whispered, and then they headed for the cactus and two people who meant everything to them.

THE SUN HAD SET, making Marlise nervous as they waited for someone to get them. They'd been there for hours now, but Jen hadn't returned to the pod. Maybe they were going to wait until morning. Let them sweat it out for the night or see if they'd try to escape. They had already tried the door, and it was unlocked. They weren't trusting. They were self-assured. Girls who left a bad situation on the streets were going to be blinded by the comforts the pods had to offer.

"Hey!" a voice yelled, and Mina instantly stood up

from the chair by the table. There was more yelling and commotion, but it was a long way from their pod.

"The front gate?" Marlise asked, and Mina shrugged, her widening eyes reminding Marlise not to blow it.

"Who knows," Mina said with ease. Marlise could tell she wasn't at ease though. She was standing by the door of the pod listening to the yelling. "Who cares?"

There was a knock on the door, and Mina cut her gaze to Marlise, who rushed to her side before she opened the door. What she saw nearly brought her to tears.

"Secure two, Romeo," Roman whispered and motioned with his head to follow.

He didn't have to tell them twice. Marlise realized the commotion at the front gate was a diversion, and she prayed it wasn't Cal. She nearly fell to her knees when she saw him in a squat with his gun aimed into the darkness while he waited for them.

"Mack and Eric," Roman whispered as they ran toward Cal. "Authorities on their way."

That was all the information they would get as they were sandwiched between Cal in the front and Roman in the back. Cal hadn't so much as acknowledged her when he turned to motion for them to follow. She had to admit it hurt, but she understood he had a job to do. If he was going to get them out of this alive, he had to focus on nothing but the mission. The last time he split his focus, he lost Hannah. She tripped and nearly fell at the comparison. Roman righted her, but she could hardly breathe. They had to get out of this alive. Cal couldn't take losing another person he cared about in this life.

A shot rang out, and all four of them came to a halt as Cal held up a fist. The darkness was working against them now, and they couldn't see anything.

"Well, well, I've seen two ghosts as I live and breathe," a voice said from behind them. They turned in tandem just as a bright beam of light blinded them. When their eyes adjusted, The Miss stood before them flanked by two guards bearing guns. "Don't worry, my girls have already taken care of your men at the front gate. I'd love to chat, but first, I'll have to insist you lower your weapons and toss them over."

Roman held up his hands before he followed her orders, skittering the small pistol across the sand where the guard picked it up.

"You too," The Miss said to Cal. From the corner of her eye, Marlise watched him toss the gun behind him into the dark. "Did you think you could just waltz in here and take my girls after they'd just arrived? All the work I put into finding our perfect little witness, and it turns out, I should have just been patient."

"You can't kill us all," Mina said. "They'll never stop hunting you if they find us dead."

"Who said they were going to find you?" she asked. "You always were a little too by the book, Agent August, or is it Agent Jacobs now? I heard the happy news. Congratulations."

Marlise had a strong desire to punch this woman, but she bit her tongue to keep from aggravating her.

"We know who you are, Sofia," Cal said from behind her. "Is Daddy helping you keep the women hooked on heroin, so they'll stay and run drugs for you?"

"I don't need to hook them on drugs to get them to stay, right, girls?" she asked her guards, who nodded robotically.

Marlise knew drugs, and they were definitely on them.

"Is that why you had to put a tracker in them when you sent them out?" Roman asked. "Just in case they forgot their way back?"

"I would be a fool not to know where my assets are at all times."

"Sad that your team was so unsuccessful at Secure One."

"Were they though?" she asked in a voice that skittered fear down Marlise's spine. "From where I'm standing, I've been quite successful in procuring not one witness but two witnesses for the prosecution. Not that I care what happens to The Madame. She was a stepping stone to bigger and better things for me and my daddy. You four are the last thorn in my side, and then I can finally be free of her."

"The police know," Cal said. "They're on their way here."

"Doubtful," she replied with a reptilian smile.

"The police around here look the other way since my daddy funds their departments and their habits."

Marlise noticed the yelling at the front gate had ceased, and her heart sank. If what The Miss had said was true, then this was it for them. She would go to her grave without the chance to tell Cal she loved him. Part of her wanted to turn around and tell him, just take a moment before The Miss took her life, but fear froze her in place. Not of The Miss or of dying, but of the look on his face when he realized he would watch her die right before his demise.

"Girls, you know what to do." The Miss waved her hand at them. "Take out the trash." She turned just as a shot rang out.

"Cal!" she yelled, jumping to the side.

"Get down, Mary!" he screamed, and she dove to the ground, but not before she saw The Miss stumble backward, her body jerking left and then right. Cal threw himself over her as more shots rang out, and then there was silence for a moment before she heard the most welcome sound of her short life.

"Secure one, Charlie."

"Secure two, Romeo."

"Secure three, Whiskey."

"Secure four, Mike! You'll stay down if you're smart!" Mack yelled, probably at one of the guards. What was Mack doing here?

"Mary," Cal whispered, his voice filled with the pain and terror of the last five minutes.

"I'm okay," she promised, sitting up when he gave

her a hand, but he kept her face turned away from The Miss. "Are you okay?" She frantically patted him down, checking for bullet holes and blood.

He grabbed her hands and held them. "I'm okay, and I love you. I should have told you that two nights ago, but I convinced myself if I didn't say the words, I could pretend that wasn't the emotion in my chest every time I looked at you. I shouldn't have denied it though. My heart convinced me of that when I thought I was about to lose the woman I loved in the same horrible way as the last time."

"You didn't. I'm here, Cal. I'm here."

He pulled her into him and held her so tightly she couldn't breathe, so she sank into his warmth.

"I love you too, Cal. I have since the first day I was at Secure One, and you ordered everyone away and sat with me, helping me stay calm through the pain and terror no one else understood. That was when I knew you'd always be my only one, even if you sent me away."

"I'm not going anywhere, Mary, and neither are you. I'm always going to be here when you need me."

"Will you be here when I wake up?" she asked, the dots in front of her eyes making it hard to form words.

He held her out by her shoulders. "Wake up? What do you mean, baby?"

She gazed into his terrified eyes and smiled, running a finger down his cheek before it fell to her lap. "I couldn't let them take you from me, Cal."

"Roman!" Cal screamed as he rested her back on his lap and frantically searched for an injury. He found it and pressed his hand to her shoulder, the pain sparking a cry from her lips. "Roman! I need medical!"

Her vision dimmed, but she grabbed him and pulled him to her lips, kissing him until her body went slack and the darkness surrounded her.

Epilogue

"It's over," Marlise said, resting back against the head-rest of the SUV. "After all this time, she's finally out of our lives."

"I think she'll always be part of our lives. She brought me you, and I'll always be grateful for that," Cal whispered as he steered the car toward Secure One.

"To The Madame?" Marlise asked with surprise.

"To the universe. To whatever path you took to get here," Cal said with a shrug.

After three long months, the sentencing day for The Madame had finally arrived. They'd made the trip from Secure One to the Minneapolis courthouse to witness it with their own eyes. Cynthia Moore, aka The Madame, had been sentenced to twenty years in prison with no early release. She would be spending her time in Waseca while her husband, former special agent David Moore, spent his twenty years in Leavenworth just outside of Kansas City.

"Conjugal visits don't look promising," Cal said, trying not to laugh.

Marlise snorted at the thought and shook her head. "No, but they both got what they deserved, or they will once they're locked in with the general population."

The mastermind and her flunky would be in their seventies when they got out. If they didn't die behind bars, that is. Chances were good they wouldn't make it long once the other inmates learned who they were. They were initially facing life in prison, which would have been better in Marlise's opinion. Then The Miss died, and her secrets were revealed, so the prosecution offered them a plea deal to avoid another stay on the trial while they sorted through who was responsible for what in the sex trafficking ring. With The Miss dead, they were sure to find evidence, real or fake, proving The Madame had been the one to order girls to be killed for refusing to perform. If they could prove it, Cynthia was looking at life without parole, and she knew it, so pleading to twenty years in prison was an easy decision. It also meant Marlise and Mina didn't have to testify, which was a big relief.

The FBI never found the bodies of Emelia, Bethany or any of the other girls who had disappeared from The Miss's grasp. Where they were, no one knew, but Marlise suspected they were buried in the desert somewhere, or had been sold across the ocean to a land far away. Her heart ached at the thought of either situation. She wanted them found. The FBI assured her they were still looking, but they all knew the truth. The FBI wasn't going to waste resources on lost girls. The thought dampened her joy about the day a tad.

Cal turned the car down the driveway to Secure One as she pondered how it had only been a few hours since they'd left, but her whole life had changed again. Roman and Mina had headed back immediately after the sentencing while she and Cal had done some business in town that was long overdue. She finally had a legal name—Marlise Strong. She thought it was a bit too on the nose, but Cal said it was the perfect fit. She also had a social security card and a legal identification card. After nearly dying at the hands of The Miss twice, she was finally living.

Marlise had followed all the steps she needed to take to have a future. Each new accomplishment was a way to take back what everyone had taken away from her over the years. Her identity. Her passions. Her belief in herself. One man had a hand in giving her back all of those things, and today, he'd held her hand with a giant grin on his face when they'd presented her with a little card that promised a better life.

"I've given it a lot of thought. I'll do the interview for the book, but I'm not interested in the television or the public speaking events. I want people to learn about sex trafficking and the signs to watch for, but I prefer to be behind the scenes," Marlise said when the lights of Secure One came into view. She'd been offered so many opportunities to be an advocate for young women, and she wanted to help, but she didn't want to leave Secure One to do it.

Cal smiled, then shoulder bumped her after he'd parked the SUV below the lodge.

"What are you smiling about?"

"I'm just glad you aren't going to disappear from Secure One and my life to chase the Hollywood dream."

Marlise turned his chin to face her and kissed his lips. "I don't have a Hollywood dream, Cal. My dream is right here in this car," she whispered. "I love you."

"I love you too, Marlise Strong."

He climbed out of the car while she rubbed her right shoulder. It was sore after their long day, but it would be okay after she rested for the night. After surgery to remove the bullet from a guard's gun, she'd spent months doing physical therapy to strengthen it again. She hadn't considered that Cal was wearing a bulletproof vest and she wasn't. When she jumped in front of that bullet, it was a gut reaction to the threat against the man she loved. He'd saved her from The Miss, and it was her turn to do the same at that moment.

When he'd declared his love for her, he wasn't kidding, and he'd proven it every day for the last three months. He'd made sure she got the best care and therapy available and refused to let her do anything but rest and heal.

Cal helped her down from the car and linked his hand to hers. "How do you feel?"

"Free," she whispered.

"I only need that word to understand the emotion. It was the same emotion I felt in the fall when I let the past go and focused on my future."

"I feel like we should celebrate," she said as they walked into the lodge and toward the large dining room. It was where Marlise had found comfort those first few months she was at Secure One. Cal had put her in charge of cooking meals for his staff. That gave her a purpose and something to focus on besides her pain and trauma. There was something gratifying about seeing her friends enjoy something she made for their pleasure. Little by little, it had helped her regain her self-confidence and self-esteem.

"Funny you should say that," Cal said, motioning her into the dining room.

It was dark, so Marlise snapped the lights on, and everyone from Secure One jumped out and yelled, "Happy birthday!"

She turned to Cal with laughter on her lips when she leaned into him. "What's going on?"

"It's your birthday," Mina said from where she stood by Roman, a party hat on her head and a party blower in her mouth.

"Mina, my birthday is in January. You know that."

Cal kissed her cheek and gave her a wink. "We all know that, but when your ID came off the printer with today's date, I decided there was no better day to pick as your new birthday. Today we will celebrate the first birthday of Marlise Strong."

Marlise wiped away a tear as she accepted hugs from her friends and coworkers in the room. It was the final hug from Charlotte that pushed the tears over her lashes. Her friend was living through the same hell she had years ago, and she understood how hard it was to try and assimilate back into society when you were scared of everything. When they'd returned to Secure One after her surgery, Charlotte was still recovering from the infection in her leg, and Cal insisted she stay until she was healed. That would give her time to decide where she wanted to go and what she wanted to do. He'd suggested that she help in the kitchen since Marlise couldn't do a lot with one arm in a sling.

For the last three months, they'd worked together, but lately Marlise was spending more time in the control room learning the business of private security. She hoped that Charlotte would decide to stay and use Secure One as a safe place to heal and find herself.

"Did you make all this food?" Marlise asked after the hug.

"I did! It was fun, and Mack helped."

Marlise resisted the urge to glance at Cal. Mack spent a lot of time helping Charlotte, but no one said a word about it. She supposed Cal felt like it would be the pot and the kettle if he said anything to his friend about his devotion to the tiny, broken girl in the kitchen.

"Thank you. I know how much work it is. I appreciate you, Charlotte. When you're ready, say the word, and I'll help you find a new future."

Charlotte nodded and then motioned at the table. "We should eat before the food gets cold."

No one argued with her. They all took heaping plates of food back to the large tables to eat, chat, laugh and celebrate the end of a long case.

Cal stood up and walked to the middle of the room. "Mary," he said, motioning for her to join him. Abandoning her birthday cake, she walked toward him with a smile. He handed her a small package and motioned for her to open it. "I decided today was the perfect day for this."

Marlise opened the box and found a security badge every team member wore while working. "Secure One, Marlise Strong, client coordinator." She gazed up at him for an explanation. "Cal, what is this?"

"It's your new job. If you want it," he nervously added. "You've more than earned the right to that position. We all know you can do the job. Right, everyone?"

The room erupted in clapping and hooting as she lifted it from the box. "That means I'd have to give up the kitchen manager job."

"I think we've got that covered," Cal said with a wink at Charlotte, who smiled shyly.

"Then I'm ready," she agreed as everyone started clapping for her again. "Why does it say Bravo at the bottom?"

"Secure two, Romeo," Roman yelled.

"Secure three, Mike," Mack yelled.

"Secure one, Charlie," Cal whispered, and the meaning struck her.

"Secure four, Bravo," she called out with tears in her eyes. She hugged the badge to her chest. "Why Bravo? My name starts with *M*."

"Because I'm Charlie, and I'll follow you anywhere."

She threw her arms around him. "Thank you."

"No," he whispered. "Thank you for being mine. You are mine, right?"

"Always," she promised, accepting his kiss. "You never have to question my love for you or my dedication to the place that saved me."

"Then I have one more question to ask on your birthday, Marlise Strong." He pulled away from her and reached in his pocket, pulling out a ring that made her breath catch in her chest.

"Cal…"

"My sweet Mary," he said as he lowered himself to one knee and held up the ring. "I am so incredibly proud of you, do you know that?" he asked, and she nodded, her chin trembling with emotion. "You have come so far since we first met two years ago, and every day I stand in awe of your strength to make a difference in this world. To do good and spread love, even when you suffered at the hands of evil and hatred. I'm twice your size, but I know you're twice as strong. I know you just got that last name, and I'll respect it if you want to keep it, but today,

I hope you're willing to add mine to it as well. Will you marry me, Mary? Will you make your life here with me on this land and continue to make a difference in the fight against evil? Will you love me forever and give me the honor of being your husband?"

Marlise dropped to her knees and nodded, her eyes glistening with tears as he slipped the ring on her finger. "Nothing would make me happier than loving you forever, Cal Newfellow."

He captured her lips as their friends clapped and hooted. Someone turned the radio up, and everyone danced around them as they knelt with their lips and hearts connected. Cal helped her up, and Mina grabbed her in a hug, squeezing the daylights out of her in excitement.

"You deserve this," Mina whispered. "Enjoy every second of it. He loves you so much."

"Thanks, Mina," she said, just as the man in question pulled her back into his arms.

"Dance with me," he said, spinning her out and back into him, where he enveloped her with the length of his body to dance to a slow song on the radio.

"Breaking news alert," a voice said, as an alarm cut off the song. "The body of a young woman was pulled from the Red River today…"

Marlise pulled back and lifted a brow at her new fiancé. In return, Cal lifted one right back.

* * * * *

Don't miss the stories in this mini series!

SECURE ONE

The Perfect Witness
KATIE METTNER
February 2024

The Red River Slayer
KATIE METTNER
March 2024

MILLS & BOON

INTRIGUE

Seek thrills. Solve crimes. Justice served.

Available Next Month

Big Sky Deception B.J. Daniels
Whispering Winds Widows Debra Webb

....

K-9 Shield Nichole Severn
The Red River Slayer Katie Mettner

....

Crash Landing Janice Kay Johnson
Cold Murder In Kolton Lake R. Barri Flowers

Larger Print

NEW RELEASE!

Rancher's Snowed-In Reunion

The Carsons Of Lone Rock
Book 4

**She turned their break-up into her breakout song.
And now they're snowed in…**

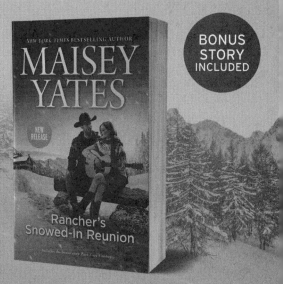

BONUS STORY INCLUDED

Don't miss this snowed-in second-chance romance
between closed-off bull rider Flint Carson and Tansey
Sands, the rodeo queen turned country music darling.

In-store and online March 2024.